SHIELD OF LIES

JERRY AUTIERI

1

Frankia, September 892 C.E.

The Frankish warrior dashed for the tree line, legs pumping over the knee-high grass, eyes white with terror and a scarlet stripe of blood peeling from beneath his conical helmet. Bloodless fingers gripped his sword as its red blade waved like a branch in the wind. Four gray-fletched arrows sprouted from the teardrop-shaped shield strapped to his other arm, and one shook loose as he fled. Flushed cheeks bulged with his panting, and he dared a glance over his shoulder.

Throst had anticipated the moment of inattention and sprang from behind one of the thin poplar trees speckled before the waiting forest. His round shield collided with the fleeing warrior's face. He screamed and slammed backward into the grass. Without hesitation, Throst's blade hewed down and opened the Frank's belly in a spray of gore. A drop of hot, salty blood flecked into Throst's smiling mouth as he admired his work. This had been his fourth kill of the battle, a total to rival any veteran.

The moment died. Two more fleeing Franks converged on him, and these red-faced bastards were roaring their anger at Throst. He understood the Frankish curses hurled at him, though the lead man spit out more of a snarl. "Northman horse-fucker!"

Training carried Throst out of the arc of the strike aimed at his head, his reaction honed to a killing edge from constant drill. The brutish Frank slid past him with a cry as Throst raised his shield for the follow-up attack of the second warrior. The blow shuddered through his shield, numbing his arm, but Throst laughed. He was already striking down, one dexterous jab that pierced the naked calf of the second man. He grunted as he crumpled, and Throst yanked his sword free with a lace of blood following it.

The first attacker howled as he whirled, but the edge of Throst's shield was already spinning back into his face. Fear and anger ruled the Frank, making his movements clumsy and predictable. His nose bridge cracked under the rim of the shield, blinding and knocking him back. Throst spun and buried his sword into the Frank's side, who caved to his knees with eyes wide and mouth hanging open. He expelled a wet gasp as Throst followed him down, careful not to bend or break his sword as the enemy's corpse clasped it like a jealous lover. After the Frank collapsed to his face in the grass, he braced the corpse and dragged free the sword.

Fearing more attacks, he ranged around with his red-dewed weapon but met no threat. The retreating Franks had scattered, their shapes mere bluish outlines of men dashing for the cover of trees with Northmen lumbering after them. Then he spotted the undulating motion in the grass and remembered the second Frank.

He was crawling away, dragging his ruined leg behind. He had abandoned his sword, having snapped it when he fell. Throst shook his head and stopped the Frank by stamping on the ravaged calf. It slipped like a gutted fish beneath his foot, and the Frank shrieked in agony. Throst stepped harder, enjoying the power, then kicked the man onto his back. The Frank was not much older than himself, maybe nineteen or twenty winters. His teary eyes entreated Throst, and his words were no longer so bold.

"Mercy, I beg mercy. My father will pay you ransom. Please."

Throst stabbed him in the guts like a needle through sailcloth.

The Frank curled up on the blade with a low growl of agony. He would die, but slowly and in terrible suffering. Throst twisted his sword, worrying the hole wider and filling the Frank's cupped hands with dark blood as he tried to stem the flow. With a cruel yank, he tore out the blade, then knelt beside the moaning Frank. He used the enemy's surcoat to wipe his sword clean, watching the Frank gargle and spit blood as his life drained into the grass.

"Well done. Three at once. Guess you really were training all this time."

The voice was rich with phlegm and the incoherency of ale. Throst's father staggered out of his hiding place behind a tree. His mail shirt and sword were battle-ready but not battle-worn. Drunk as he was, he walked steadily to Throst's side with an approving smile.

"Course, no one's gonna believe you did it alone. So that's why I'm here."

His father began plunging his sword into the corpses Throst had made, kneeling so the blood would splash over him. He paused to vomit, more from his drink rather than the grizzly work. Throst looked away to the main battle lines.

Ulfrik Ormsson's green standard flew high at the tidemark of bodies. The Frankish warlord, Clovis, had been defeated, and while Throst and his father had hid at the outskirts of the battle, they would share in its glory. Throst regretted he did not have a chance to test himself in the shieldwall. Ulfrik did not know his name, but he would if he had witnessed Throst's mastery of sword and shield.

Farther down the action, he saw women and children stripping dead Franks of their valuables before the men returned to claim their share. Some were Franks and others Northmen, but all were despairing and poor camp-followers. He stared at the women as his father finished disguising his cowardice with enemy blood. Throst's own woman was among them, and he saw her hefting an armload of weapons and other valuables.

"What's that?" his father asked as he came to his side. He followed Throst's stare, then placed an arm on his shoulder. "Your girl? Ain't

3

never going to bring her home to your Ma? She wants you to marry better than a camp-follower."

"She's not a camp-follower." Throst shoved his father's freshly blooded hand from his shoulder. "She's here because I told her to follow."

"Does whatever you tell her? Now that's a good girl. Not like your Ma. Gotta hit her a few times before she listens."

As they watched, a group of Ulfrik's men were walking fast toward the scavengers. In a blink, Throst's woman disappeared from sight, drawing a surprised laugh from his father.

"There's a useful trick. Where'd the lass go?"

"She's like a fox in tall grass," Throst said, a touch of pride in his voice.

His father remained quiet as they observed Ulfrik's men dragging the women from their gathered treasures. The silence grew strong, and Throst turned to his father. His brow wrinkled in thought. Throst tapped his arm to rouse him, but he did not take his eyes from the field.

"You should have your girl come to Ravndal and serve Jarl Ulfrik. A talent like hers shouldn't be wasted on picking junk from a battle-field. She'd do anything you tell her to do?"

"She'd fall on a sword if I asked."

His father grunted with satisfaction. "That's a good girl. Keep her that way. Keep her close to the jarl and to you, but tell no one. We'll learn things, useful things."

Throst smiled at the idea. The Frank he had left to bleed had still not passed into death. He let out a low groan, and Throst stepped beside him. The pasty white face met his, and thick blood flowed over the Frank's lips. He mouthed a plea for death.

Turning away, he left the Frank suffering in the bloody muck.

2

Frankia, November 892 C.E.

It was a day made for death. A day schemed by the gods and Fates, and none of the people gathered at the hanging tree heard the gods' laughter. None saw the black thread pulled into the weave of their lives.

Ulfrik positioned his eldest son, Gunnar, at his right and mounted the lichen spattered rock that the gods had long ago set beside the hanging tree. The rock served as a natural platform from which to address the bloodthirsty throng. Over the contorted faces of warriors, old women, and children, he gazed at the black shape of Ravndal perched atop a hill taller than any other in the valley. The demands for justice echoed across the fields to Ravndal's stockade walls. The gods had made this place for hanging, and Ulfrik had strung plenty from the hoary elm during his years. Nothing had ever come from a hanging but justice and a swinging corpse left for ravens and wolves. His judgment was swift and final.

An old woman, stooped and toothless, eyes creased from years laboring under the sun, raised a gnarled fist and shouted for blood. Others swarmed forward with her, a maniacal chorus fevered with killing lust. Ulfrik nodded and warned them back with raised hands. He glanced down at Gunnar, who remained with arms folded and face impassive. He then scanned the ring of spearmen keeping the crowd at bay, found Einar staring at him expectantly, and gave the order to him.

"Bring forward the accused that he may face justice for his crimes."

The crowd ejected a ragged man held between two of Ulfrik's armored hirdmen. Coarse hair sprouted from the tears in his shirt, which was spattered with rust colored stains. The man's family followed behind: a son barely in full beard and a pinch-faced wife towing a girl so nondescript Ulfrik mistook her for a child's doll. Their clothing matched the sky for its sodden dreariness. The accused man was shoved onto his knees before the rock. His head sagged, displaying pink skin beneath a thin net of hair. The entire clan was grimy, shiftless rabble hardly worth the time spent on this show of power.

"As Jarl of Ravndal," Ulfrik intoned, his commanding voice bringing quiet to the gathered crowd, "I have summoned the community to pass sentence on this man. Where is his accuser?"

A second group emerged from the crowd: a young woman and her two daughters huddled together as if in a storm at sea. All three combined were hardly the size of one healthy woman. The man at Ulfrik's feet tried to stand when she approached, but his guards shoved him down. The mother's face was swollen and the muddy tracks of tears showed on her cheeks. She pointed at the man on the ground. "I am Sigrid Thorkelsdottir and I accuse Gudmund of murdering my husband, Agnar Erlandson."

Cries for justice renewed and consumed the rest of Sigrid's testimony. Ulfrik acted as though he heard, though the facts of Gudmund's night of drunken madness were common knowledge. He was caught staggering down the boards of the main road with a bloodied knife. His clothes were stained with Agnar's blood. Ulfrik raised his arms for quiet, continuing once he received it.

"Here is my judgment in the murder of Agnar. No fewer than six men have sworn witness to Gudmund's crime. None have stood in Gudmund's defense."

"Not so, Lord Ulfrik!" The son threw himself against the hirdmen baring him with a spear. "My father was at home that night. I swear it. He shared a drink with me, then went to bed."

"It's true, Lord," Gudmund added, his face bright. "I had too much to drink and I don't remember nothing. Someone's trying to blame me, is all. She did it, killed her own husband and took advantage of me while I was drunk. That's the truth of it."

The spearmen shoved back against the enraged crowd. Rotten cabbages and onions catapulted from the crowd to fall among Gudmund and his family. Ulfrik glanced at Gunnar, whose calm seemed shaken by the raw aggression of the crowd.

"I demand order," he roared. "Silence!"

Ulfrik's war-voice struck men with awe on the field of battle, and used on his own people it cowed them into submission. He glowered at the crowd, finally settling upon Gudmund with a sneer.

"You will deny it to the end? Your hands are still flaked with Agnar's dried blood. You were seen entering his home, heard swearing to kill him for whatever insults you had imagined, and then captured not more than twenty paces from his front door. And your bloody footprints tracked back to his body. Gudmund, your guilt is witnessed by six sworn men. There is no more to be said."

"No one saw him do it!" The son reached his arms over the hirdmen restraining him.

"I saw him," Sigrid screamed. "I was in the bed when he attacked. He slashed my leg."

"She's only a woman," the son countered. "It's not right that she give witness."

"What is not right, Throst," Ulfrik growled, finally recollecting the name of Gudmund's son, "is the death of a husband and father for an argument that no one remembers the reason for starting. You've had your say; now I command your silence."

Throst stepped back, a snarl on his lips. He fixed his eyes on Ulfrik, and to his shock the boy mouthed a curse at him before rejoining his cowering sister and mother. Ulfrik stared him down, but Gudmund awaited judgment and so turned to him.

"You are guilty of murder. For this you must die and Agnar's blood price will be paid from your family's belongings. Do you have anything to say?"

Gudmund shook his head. "Allow me to go to Valhalla, Lord. Strike off my head and kill me as a warrior."

The request drew grumbles from the crowd. Even Gunnar dared a glance at Ulfrik for his reaction. He expected nothing less from this man who had served him more like a rat in larder than a warrior in a shieldwall.

"You will die on the hanging tree and are condemned to Nifleheim. Your body will hang until it rots, as a warning to all who carry evil in their hearts. You are a shiftless murderer, Gudmund. Your family is banished from my lands, and I declare them outlaws once they've crossed beyond my borders. This is my judgment."

"No," cried Throst. "You will pay for this!"

The jubilation of the crowd swept over the threat, but Ulfrik marked it with a glare. He jumped off the rock without another thought for Throst and ordered Gudmund taken to the tree and his family held pending collection of the blood price. Einar, Ulfrik's capable second, oversaw the process of securing the rope and directing the men. The gathered crowd flung garbage at Gudmund, just as often hitting a hirdman.

A husky voice over his shoulder whispered in his ear.

"Should've killed the whole family, lad, at least the son for making that threat." Snorri appeared at his side, steadying himself on Ulfrik's shoulder. His leg had been speared in a battle with the Franks and, combined with his age, left him unsteady.

"Sending them over the border to the Franks is the same. Besides, they've done nothing to deserve hanging. I'm glad enough to be rid of them."

At last Gudmund stood beneath the noose with hands bound behind his back. The hirdman in the tree signaled the rope was secure, and two others raised him off the ground and looped the noose over his head.

"Avenge me, Throst! I got a dog's death!"

Einar checked Ulfrik for confirmation, which he provided with a slow nod. The men released Gudmund and stepped back.

The crowd thrilled as Gudmund's weight snapped the noose tight around his neck. He thrashed and kicked, his eyes bulging as the rope strangled him. His body twirled and his head hung to the side. The tree limb sagged and creaked with the weight. More garbage struck him, each hit eliciting a collective jeer. Blood spluttered from his nose, splashing down his beard.

Ulfrik watched, betraying nothing of his thoughts. In days past he merely had to dispense justice and be done. He would have pulled hard on Gudmund's legs to snap his neck and end his suffering. Today his followers would consider such action an insult and a sign of weakness. So he watched and hid his revulsion behind a blank expression. He glanced away to be certain Gunnar did not flinch or show any sign of emotion.

At last Gudmund's struggles slowed to reflexive kicks. His tongue swelled and fell from his mouth, and in final humiliation his crotch bloomed with dark wetness as his bladder loosened in death.

A keening wail went up from the back of the crowd. Ulfrik saw Gudmund's wife and family had been allowed to watch, and the wife had broken down at the moment of his death. Ulfrik's snarl enticed the guards responsible for the family to drag them away before anything else might happen.

"It is done," Ulfrik said, then he addressed the crowd. "Murder is the worst crime a man can commit. All of you look on Gudmund's corpse and be reminded that my justice is sure and swift. By law our land is made and by lawlessness it is undone. I uphold the law fairly for every one of you. In turn, I expect your obedience to the laws of common good. Now return to your lives and let no one touch Gudmund's body while it hangs from this tree."

The crowd milled and groused but eventually broke up under the firm guidance of Ulfrik's warriors. Clusters of townsfolk drifted toward Ravndal, while smaller groups headed into the surrounding farmland. Ulfrik rubbed his face and sighed, and when he dropped his hands, cool air bathed his face. Gunnar stood before him, skeptically watching Gudmund's corpse hanging still and silent from the black tree.

"He wanted to die a warrior? When did he ever fight for us?" Gunnar turned to his father, eyebrow cocked.

"Never, he hid from battle," Snorri answered for Ulfrik. "However he came among us, it's a good day now that he is gone. And what about you, Young Lord? When will you carry a sword to battle for us?"

Young Lord was Snorri's pet name for Gunnar, with Young Master for Hakon. For Ulfrik's third son, Aren, he had no name and ignored his existence whenever possible. Now both Gunnar and Snorri smiled at Ulfrik, expecting his answer.

"In time, but not yet. The Franks are canny foes, dangerous bastards all."

"Any other man shoving a spear in your face isn't dangerous?" Snorri quipped as he began to limp down the hill. "You were his age when we stood together in a shieldwall. Your father didn't coddle you."

Gunnar's smile broadened, and in that moment he was the perfect image of his mother's bright charm and colossal will. His eyes shined with mischief from beneath his black hair. Ulfrik chuckled and shook his head. Whiskers now darkened Gunnar's jaw and his voice had grown deeper in his chest, yet Ulfrik saw not a man but only his first and favorite child. The Franks were starving for battle. He would not feed them the blood of his firstborn.

Einar collected the remaining hirdmen and fell in with the group as they all returned to the walls. He stopped them with a thick, outstretched arm. "Riders, flying Hrolf's colors."

Five men on horseback cantered uphill from the direction of Ravndal. One held Hrolf the Strider's red and yellow dragon banner. Heat flared in Ulfrik's belly, for Hrolf rarely sent riders to him and only for dire news. He let the men approach, and the lead rider expertly dismounted and walked the remaining distance. He was dressed for war in mail and helmet, gray cloak dragging across the grass as he knelt before Ulfrik.

"My Lord Ulfrik Ormsson, I come with word from Jarl Hrolf." The young man was unfamiliar to Ulfrik, but he raised a battle scared face to his that proved his mettle. "It is an urgent summons."

"Stand," Ulfrik said, waving the man to his feet. "Five riders to deliver Hrolf's summons? Have the Franks outflanked our lines?"

Snapping to his feet, the rider shook his head. "They probe and prod, as you well know this far into the border. Hrolf's orders are simple and direct: travel to his hall at once. Take only what you need for a few days, for you will return home soon."

Sharing a puzzled look with Snorri, he folded his arms. "What is the reason for the summons?"

"Jarl Hrolf tells us only so much. We are to escort you once you've prepared."

Ulfrik agreed to leave after he fed them and rested their horses. They returned to Ravndal in worried silence, fearing what awaited them at Hrolf's hall.

3

U lfrik had turned over his horse to boys who would feed and rub down the tired animals. He stretched and massaged his lower back as the boys gathered up all the horses at the edge of Hrolf's settlement. Their arrival had drawn the usual groups of curious children and idle gossips, and he recognized familiar faces among them. Their escorts led them toward the mead hall that overlooked the dozens of A-frame homes and oblong barracks. While Ulfrik's escorts would not reveal the reason for Hrolf's summons, they at least ensured him there was no immediate military threat.

"The size of his hall awes me every time I see it," Einar said as he fell in beside Ulfrik. He had come along as his second, taking the advisory role his father Snorri had severed. Though he was young, Ulfrik valued his insight as well as his physical stature.

"A man too tall to ride a horse needs a big hall to stretch his legs in," Ulfrik said, and Einar and their escorts chuckled.

Outside the massive doors, guards hailed their escorts, arms were clasped and polite words spoken. No one had to ask Ulfrik or Einar to remove their weapons, for it was rude for any but the jarl and his guards to carry weapons into the hall. They began to unbuckle their baldrics and pull out their long knives and offer them to the guards for safekeeping. Ulfrik gave over his sword and sax, the short-bladed sword for close quarters fighting, a dagger, and then removed two throwing axes from his belt. The guard raised his brow at the assortment of weapons.

"You come ready for battle," the guard said as he cradled the weapons in his arms.

"Without mail, I am naked," Ulfrik said. "So I carry that much with me to feel less shameful."

The guard smiled and handed each weapon to a younger man, who stopped to review the hand axes with a quizzical eye.

"You've never seen a throwing ax?" Ulfrik asked. The boy shook his head and blushed. His older companion moaned and batted his head.

"Of course you've seen them, you fool. Few carry them anymore, that's all." The older man continued to heap Ulfrik's weapons on his junior.

"Jarl Ulfrik is a master of the throwing ax," Einar said. The younger man looked admiringly at Ulfrik.

"You flatter me. But those axes have saved my hide more than once. They're easier to carry than spears, and as useful for weighing down a foeman's shield as they are for splitting his head at thirty paces."

"Well, you've got to be able to hit a man's head while he's running at you." The older guard's voice carried a note of skepticism that flared Ulfrik's pride.

"It's easily done with practice. Here, hand me one and I will give a demonstration."

"Hrolf won't like you flinging axes at the heads of his men," Einar said, his joke breaking up some of the tension. Yet Ulfrik was already striding around the corner of the hall, searching for a good target.

"Take your helmet and put it against that tree stump. I will put my back to it, turn and throw the ax so it lands touching its left side. Would you agree that is an equal challenge to hitting a charging warrior?"

The guards glanced at each other and nodded. Ulfrik suppressed his smile, paced off the distance and waited for Einar to raise his hand when it was safe to throw. When he did, Ulfrik whirled on the balls of his feet, found his mark, and let the ax fly. It chopped into the stump, exactly to the left of the helmet. The gathered men shouted in surprise and applauded. Ulfrik accepted with a slight bow, frowned at Einar who rolled his eyes at the trick throw, and then retrieved his ax. He tossed it to the young guard.

"Keep it and practice. It may save your life one day."

"Mighty Jarl Ulfrik," Einar said. "Your skill is exceeded by your generosity and then your pride."

More laughter ensued, and all returned to the front of the hall. The older guard opened the doors. "Hrolf will be inside. Always a pleasure to see you, Jarl Ulfrik."

A moment of blindness masked the source of the savory aromas filling the hall as he transitioned to the dimness. The smoke hole was open to allow light to spill in, but it failed to brighten the gigantic hall. He paused as his eyes adjusted, then looked down the rows of empty tables and benches pushed to the sides of the hall. It created an avenue of pounded earth, littered with bones from the last meal and fresh straw to conceal it. Across the glowing hearth where slave women tended black iron pots of simmering broth, the high table was lit with lamplight. Jewels glittered on hands and gold armbands flashed as the mighty men at the table leaned forward to see their guests.

Ulfrik and Einar strode down the hall, between the simple but solid support posts that disappeared high into the smoky darkness, and went to their knees before the high table.

"Get off your knees, friends, please. How fortunate I am to have bondsmen and friends as good as you." Hrolf the Strider stood in welcome. He wore fine clothes beneath a wool cloak lined with fox fur, jewels and gold adorning every finger. His face was wide with a welcoming smile, bright against the darkness of his coarse beard. Eyes of pale blue contrasted starkly with his dark shape, but they were full of sincerity. The men standing beside him and behind him were dwarfed by his massive height. Even Einar, a giant himself, came no higher than Hrolf's severe eyebrows.

"You look well, Jarl Hrolf," Ulfrik said as he stood. "It is my pleasure to be invited to your magnificent home."

Formalities completed, Hrolf gestured he and Einar should sit at the table. Young girls fluttered around him, setting fresh plates of cheeses and dried river eels along with filled mugs of ale. Other servants pulled away empty dishes with subtle dexterity, their dance unobtrusive and efficient. All waited for Hrolf to seat himself on the bench before taking their places. To his right, Gunther One-Eye and his son Mord both smiled in greeting. They had recently fought together against the Franks, and so their bond was close and fresh.

The years spent in Frankia had been generous to Hrolf the Strider. He had carved out a haven for his people and settled the lands north of the Seine and west of Paris, not far from Rouen where the Franks had come to an agreeable peace with him. As he sat at the table, drinking from a pottery mug, a gold ring with a fat green stone flashed as if to confirm his wealth was no mean sum. The success at Paris had enriched him along with a steady flow from his bondsmen and his own raiding both in Frankia and beyond. He had even moved his family from the Orkney Islands.

A long afternoon of pleasant and idle talk ensued. News was traded, the health and welfare of various important people were asked for, and the pretense of a casual visit was upheld. Ulfrik had nearly missed Hrolf's artful shifting of the conversation to the true matter at hand.

"I suppose you've heard news of the famine by now? Haven't felt the pinch yet?"

"No, I've not heard," Ulfrik said, glancing at an equally surprised Einar. "Nor have I felt it. Even at the border, we feast like Ragnarok is upon us."

Hrolf chuckled and waved his hand as if dismissing a foul air. "It's all just rumors, of course. But my ears hear things from great distances. The Eastern Franks are starving, and parts of King Odo's Western Frankia are supposed to have failed crops. They say their god is punishing them for not driving out the Northmen and dividing their empire."

Laughter erupted and Hrolf expelled bits of fish and a spray of spit as he did. Ulfrik joined in, adding his own thoughts. "Their god is strange. Does he not ask them to turn their faces so we may strike them, but punishes them for not fighting back? How can any man know what to do? No wonder they need priests to tell them."

"That is true," Hrolf said, raising his finger as if to enumerate his points. "But whatever the reason, parts of Frankia have been cast into famine. That has been bad for many of our brothers. Some of them are leaving, going to England for the winter."

Hrolf used brother to indicate other Northmen not under his command, a euphemism for hated enemies to either conquer or destroy. Ulfrik began to smile at their misfortune, but then he noted Hrolf's own smile diminished. A quick glance at Gunther, and his one good eye now had a sober, warning cast to it. Mord seated next to him had also lost his smile.

"I take it there is a panic among our own, then?"

Hrolf slapped the table and leaned back biting his lip. "And yet here we sit, eating and drinking away our afternoon. Our gods have not abandoned us. None of my people suffer, and yet there is this panic. Why? Have I ever given anyone cause to doubt my support? Had I feared famine, you must know I would have considered all of you."

"Doubtless, Jarl Hrolf." Ulfrik shifted his gaze among the men seated at the high table, and none dared speak further. The long quiet held as Hrolf stewed, finally abating when he leaned back to the table.

"I know you are a good and loyal man. So I beg you not to be insulted for what I will ask next."

Ulfrik's stomach burned at the possibilities he imagined, but calmed his expression and inclined his head. "I will gladly do all within my power."

Hrolf studied him a moment, as if appraising his sincerity, then he leaned with both arms on the table. "I have gathered the other jarls to me, and they will attend a feast tonight. Some of them are wavering. Indeed, I hear some have sent their families to England already, before the channel becomes too dangerous to cross. I want them to renew their oaths to me. I want you to do the same. Do it first, and do it boldly. Fewer men have a more dangerous position than you. You hold the border with the Franks, and keep them from rampaging inland. How much shame would a man bear to not follow your oath?"

A sigh of relief escaped Ulfrik, and Gunther chuckled. Hrolf, however, stared intently while awaiting an answer.

"I would never hesitate to swear before all men. I would rather starve than dishonor myself."

Hrolf's smile returned and he relaxed again, reaching for his mug which he raised. Ulfrik and the others rushed to join him, warm and frothy ale spilling over his hand as he raised it high. "You have ever been my boldest and most reliable jarl. I toast your choice and thank you for it."

They drank, and Ulfrik watched Hrolf over the top of his own mug. He guzzled with the carelessness of an old warrior rather than the king of the Northmen that he had become. His praise should have eased Ulfrik's worries, but instead it only made him wonder what had happened to make Hrolf worry for his authority over his men.

4

Hrolf's hall smelled of sweat and beer, scores of strong men in furs packed together guzzling from drinking horns and boasting of conquest and victory. Ulfrik shimmied between Hrolf's bondsmen, smiling at familiar faces and glancing past strangers. The heat from the hearth and the press of bodies intensified the odors and beaded sweat at Ulfrik's brow. Flipping the cloak off his shoulder provided a wisp of relief. The doors were opened for the evening air, but nothing flowed far enough inside to help. He turned back to ensure Einar followed. As tall as he was, he still disappeared into the crowd as they wormed to the front of the hall where Hrolf sat at the high table.

Gold bands winked from beneath every sleeve and silver rings and braces brightened nearly every hand, a testimony to the success and generosity of Hrolf the Strider. Ulfrik had been careful to display the many bands he wore on each arm, denoting his status and fame, yet in the crush of men the display bought him no extra deference. More grandiose than all the others, however, was Hrolf himself. At his high table, in a chair constructed for his giant size, he lounged with young Frankish slave girls in attendance. Gold and silver sparkled from every place an adornment could be placed on his body.

He raised a silver-rimmed drinking horn to his mouth and let the beer flow out the sides as he drank. Gunther One-Eye and his son, Mord, sat to his right as a bulwark against the flatters who leaned into him.

"Every jarl in the circle of the world serves Jarl Hrolf?" Einar asked from behind, his words a shout above the raucous laughter.

"He has summoned every man with a fishing boat and rusty sword, it seems," Ulfrik said as he glided between the crowded seats. Gunther One-Eye was gesturing him to join them at the high table. Ulfrik had spent the first half of the evening trading news with his peers from all over Frankia, and some from beyond. Hrolf had established footholds in England as well, and a crew of men had arrived from the island coincidentally in time for the great feast.

Once he joined the high table, a mug was thrust into his hand by a red-faced drunk who babbled nonsense before collapsing into laughter. Mord shoved him aside to clear a place for both Ulfrik and Einar. "Sit with us, where you belong," he said. "Have you learned anything useful from all the gossip?"

"Only that it is as useless as it ever was. No one is drunk enough to yet speak of things they should not." Mord and Einar threw their heads back in laughter and they settled in for a few moments of conversation before Hrolf stood and raised his arms for silence. He was so tall, he did not need to stand on a bench and his presence so powerful he did not need to shout for silence. In moments he had complete attention. He glanced at Ulfrik, then addressed his people.

"Friends, it is my joy to feast you tonight and to make you drunk on my ale." Roars of approval interrupted him. "But before the night grows too deep and the ale works its magic, I have gathered you all for a purpose which you should know, for I have spoken to you individually over these days."

He scanned the crowd and Ulfrik noted many smiles suddenly dropped or eyes flicked away.

"Whatever fears you have of this famine, know that it has not touched us in the least. By gathering you together, it has been my hope that you have all learned as much from your neighbors. All across my lands, we are well fed. The good people of Rouen are happy and trade with us as avidly as ever. Our winter here will be pleasant and nothing should give you cause for flight. Ah, so some of you now look as if this is the first you've heard of that notion. Know that Hrolf the Strider is famous not only for his long legs, but for his big ears as well." Hrolf pulled both his ears forward to display, drawing laughter from the crowd. "Panic is like fire, and it is best put out before it grows beyond control. One bondsman has fled me already, taking thirty spearmen and their families away to England. For what? A rumor? You will know him by the name of Krakki Small-Eyes, and if he should return, know he is an oath-breaker. Make his death bloody and public and I will reward you for it."

The hall had grown still enough that the wind could be heard blowing across the open doors. Once Hrolf had let it sink in, he continued.

"I don't need to remind you that King Odo and his Franks are only a week's march away from here. If we begin to flee, we will invite pursuit. All of you possess more than you ever did before. I know where you came from, and I know where you will go if you remain with me. Each one of you is a part of a shieldwall against the Franks. If the man at your side falls, one must step into his place or our lands will crumble just as the shieldwall does when men cannot stand in lockstep with his sword brothers. Tonight I want to hear your oaths, that you will do what you have sworn and put aside needless fear. We must hold while our misguided brothers in Brittany or Eastern Frankia turn heel. We will remain to sweep up all of this land."

Heads bobbed in agreement and each man looked to his neighbor for encouragement. Ulfrik admired Hrolf's eloquence and his ease of command, and was something he strove to imitate. Hrolf was true nobility, his father being the Jarl of More and one of the most powerful jarls in Norway. He turned to Ulfrik and gestured for him to stand.

"Here is a man you must all know. He has fought beside me for years, brought me victory, and saved my life no less than twice. Ulfrik Ormsson, Jarl of Ravndal, keeps the Franks from your farms. He watches the borders and fights the Franks for nothing more than my thanks and the promise of a future where today's border becomes tomorrow's inland kingdom. If anyone had cause to leave me now, it would be him. Yet he defends us and risks much because he knows he stands at the front of our shieldwall. Don't let me tell you, though. Hear it from him. Ulfrik, only a month ago you fought a major battle against the Frankish Duke Clovis. Tell us of that battle."

Not expecting to recount his war stories, Ulfrik turned a shocked face to the crowd. Most looked on with eager smiles, ready to hear tales of bravery, while others clearly hid jealously behind thin smirks. They cajoled him, and Einar patted his back with some encouragement. At last, he shook his head and told the tale.

"It was luck that carried the day, and my men were eager for a fight." A few voices called his false modesty, and Ulfrik smiled. "I might have laid a good trap for him, too."

"Now that's what we want to hear about," Hrolf said, slapping the table. "How did you draw him out?"

"Just burned enough of his farms and kept pushing into his territory. I let him think he had cut us off, but I had fresh men in reserve. Truth was we were at the end of our tether and he did have us in a bad place. But we kicked him in the teeth."

His memory drifted back to that desperate moment when it seemed he had overextended his reach and cursed his overzealous attempt to bring a final battle to Clovis. He had been warned against seeking glory at the risk of so many lives, but in the end had hacked off a good bit of fame from the Frankish hide.

"They had cavalry but I promise you that Clovis does not know how to use them. He's always seeking to bring a surprise charge, and that day was no different. The arrow storm drove him back, and we clashed with his warriors so the horses were useless to him. It was a good day for killing."

"But Clovis lived," called a voice from the crowd. Ulfrik nodded.

"He did, but not before I left him something to remember me by. He had taken his eldest son to battle, put him in the front rank by the standard. Wearing those pretty things the Franks like." Laughter followed Ulfrik's jab at the bright-colored surcoats the Franks wore. "I found the lad and beat him to the ground. I'd have had his head, but the fool boy got his arm in the way. He lost his sword hand instead. The Franks broke before I could finish the work, and we had to let them go. We were extended as it was."

A dozen voices asked for more details, and Ulfrik answered at length. He did his best to keep his words modest, but the praise and the excitement of recounting a victory before all the great men of Hrolf's lands defeated him. At the end, he was more than ready to swear his oath before Hrolf. He was ready to swear anything. So when the moment came, and Hrolf guided him out of his moment of glory, Ulfrik boldly went to his knee before Hrolf and nearly shouted his oath.

"I do swear to you and before all these good men that I will defend Ravndal and hold its lands unto my last breath, that I shall bring war to the Franks and not cease until Paris is rubble under my feet."

Hrolf raised him up with a genuine smile, and Ulfrik was heady with pride. He faced the cheering men, many who lined up to be the next to restate oaths before their brothers. Ulfrik had tightened his bond to Hrolf and made the chains that bound him to his small parcel of Frankia all the stronger.

5

The wooden stockade walls ringing Ulfrik's fortified town loomed dark and jagged atop its rocky hill. Ulfrik allowed his horse to pick its way through the rocks, goading it on when it balked or hesitated. He had little familiarity with horses since leaving Norway in his youth, and his awkwardness showed in his poor handling. Einar, riding beside him, went ahead to encourage Ulfrik's horse to follow.

"I can smell good food from here," Einar called back. "How can there be a famine in the land?"

"With your appetite, famine should always be a threat to us," Ulfrik said. Einar leaned back in laughter and they continued up the hill.

Strong winds set their cloaks flying and cold drops of wetness striking Ulfrik's face promised rain. Trees in the valley had dropped most of their leaves, and now the winds stripped the vestiges from the branches. Both he and Einar drew their cowls tighter against the cold. As they approached the top, Ulfrik began to search the gates for a guard and found none. They approached the western gate, which faced the interior of Ulfrik's lands and suffered the least threat from Clovis and other Franks. Still, the lax vigilance set his jaw grinding.

Einar also sat straighter atop his horse, seeking someone to challenge them.

They both traveled with nothing more ostentatious than silver cloak pins, and hid signs of status and wealth. Hrolf's escorts only returned them halfway, and even a short distance traveling in a small group left them vulnerable. The land knew no shortage of vagrants and outlaws, which further irked Ulfrik as no one had hailed them even as they closed to bow range. At last someone appeared on the wall, a head of hair flying in the wind that gazed down at them.

"Are you going to challenge us?" Ulfrik called up to the man, straining to identify him against the glare of the sky.

"You speak Norse, so be welcomed," the man said. "Still state your names for me all the same."

Einar inhaled to shout, but Ulfrik grabbed his shoulder as he drew behind him. He shared a sly smile then squinted up at the walls. Another shadow of a man joined the other, though both merely leaned on the walls.

"I am Thor Thorkelson and this is Steinn the Slow," Ulfrik said, drawing the names from imagination. Einar glared as he heard his pseudonym. "Anyway, rain's coming and we'd like to get into a warm hall where we can eat and maybe grab hold of one of your serving girls. You have good serving girls here?"

The heads conferred with each other and the first man answered. "Welcome to Ravndal. The gate is open, but there's a gate tax."

"It's open but there's a gate tax," Ulfrik growled under his breath to Einar. "These fools really didn't expect us today, eh?"

Einar did not reply, his face already red and eyes bulging. Ulfrik feared he would have to save the two men from death at Einar's hands. They dismounted and Einar pushed the gate open. Both stepped through and awaited the guards descending the wall to collect their fee. As they did, Ulfrik and Einar pulled back their cowls.

Both were surprisingly seasoned men, one whom Ulfrik recognized from the siege of Paris six years ago. That man's face had gone white and taut with fear, though the other man ambled toward them with a vague smile. Einar slammed his heavy fist into the man's face, crumpling him to the ground in one blow. The other fell to his knees and bowed his head, realizing his failure.

"You'd let anyone walk in through an open gate?" Einar roared at the man on the ground. "Do you know Thor Thorkelson and Steinn the Slow? You ignorant whoreson! Maybe the Franks will march an army under your nose."

Einar punctuated his words with bone-jarring kicks. Einar was a good man, loyal and fastidious in every duty given him. However, he expected the same from others and his patience was thinner than a decade-old sailcloth. The transgression he and Ulfrik had experienced would likely tear at his mind until he satisfied the doubt that all was perfect again. For his part, Ulfrik could not brook the dangerous laxity of these men, but he understood warriors hated few things more than gate duty.

"Don't kill him," Ulfrik said.

"And why not? He was prepared to let Thor and Steinn enter our town and kill someone else for whatever bribe he planned to ask."

"Fair point." Ulfrik folded his arms and addressed the man kneeling. "You, Hildr Ragnarson, I know you. Explain yourself before Einar decides to kick your teeth through your tongue."

"There's no excuse, Lord Ulfrik." He bowed lower. "No Frank has ever passed this way, and there were only two of you. I was prepared to sound the alarm, Lord."

"And prepared to take a bribe to allow us to pass. We are at war with Clovis, or have you forgotten?"

"Einar, stop kicking that man. He can't make amends if he is dead."

Hildr peeked to the side and snapped away. His companion lay in the dirt groaning and bleeding, Einar hovering over him with eyes still bulging and face flushed. He finally backed down, grabbing his horse and leading him away. Ulfrik finished with his guards.

"Bar this gate," he said to Hildr. "Let no man pass. I will summon you to face justice, Hildr. I'll consider your long service to me, but if you flee then it will go badly for you. Your companion has already received his punishment."

He left them both kneeling beside the gate. Several other guards watched impassively, a few chuckling. Townsfolk routinely made a spectacle out of such events, but this had been so swift no crowd had gathered. Ulfrik did not look back, but guided his horse toward the stables and anticipated seeing his hearth and his family.

6

Runa sat with her three sons gathered to her side at the high table overlooking the spacious hall. Women pumped bellows at the hearth, wiping their brows as the fire snapped higher with each pump. Light from the open smoke hole painted the room with silver daylight of the diffuse sky above, shining on cleared tables and benches where moments before men sat in idle conversation. These same men now lined the walls behind the tables and stood straight and still.

"Father beat a guard to death for sleeping at his post," Hakon whispered to his brothers.

"It was Einar, you fool," Gunnar corrected. Hakon jabbed his older brother's ribs in answer.

"Hush, the two of you," Runa said. "Neither of them would have done such a thing. Now sit up straight for when your father enters the hall."

Gunnar ignored Hakon, who insisted on one more jab before settling beneath Runa's glare. Aren remained still under her right arm and took no interest in his brothers' bickering. Despite being only six years old, he bore himself with the weight and seriousness of a grown man. It frightened most people, Ulfrik included, but Runa never saw anything more than a child needing attention that his older brothers so often stole from him.

Snorri stood, rubbing his thigh where a Frankish spear had ended his days as a warrior. Runa loved the old man like a father, as did Ulfrik, and welcomed the time he spent in the hall with her boys. He now vacated the high seat where he had ruled for Ulfrik in his absence. Despite the infirmity his wound conferred, Runa knew he could still crack heads into obedience if needed and as such held the men's respect as well as Ulfrik's.

The moment before Ulfrik's entrance the room grew quiet. The servants and slaves scurried away to dark corners to hide until summoned again. A smile trembled on Runa's lips, anticipating his return. No matter how many years had passed, or how many younger men her wealth and status attracted, Ulfrik brought her joy no one else could ever match. He was the hero of the saga they created together. If the intensity of their love had vanished along with their youth, the solid core of their bond had only grown stronger.

The doors opened and white light spilled over the forms of two men, one a head taller than the other. Ulfrik and Einar swept into the hall, and Runa rose with her children. Gunnar puffed out his chest, resting a hand upon the hilt of the sword he alone wore in the hall as the jarl's eldest son. Runa grinned as Hakon imitated his brother, though his hand found only a leather belt for a hitch. Aren clung tighter to her skirt as if to disappear.

"A week gone, but how these boys have grown!" Ulfrik strode the length of the hall, weaving through columns and around benches, skirting the blazing hearth. He nodded to his men as he passed, each standing straighter as he acknowledged them. "Snorri, how have you made them taller?"

"Soaked them in water and hung them by their toes all night." Snorri ruffled Hakon's hair as he answered, drawing a stifled giggle from him.

Ulfrik had not lost his youthful stride, even as gray crept into his temples and at the root of his beard. Only a slight softening of his face betrayed his age, along with scars old and new earned from his numerous battles. His smile widened as he seized her forward into his arms. "It is good to be home. All has been well?"

She peeled back from him, a flush warming her face. She relished his attention, but at their age and status such displays seemed out of place. "As peaceful as any six days have ever been. You brought all the excitement with you."

"Did you beat a man to death for sleeping on the walls?" Hakon pushed forward, tugging the hem of his father's cloak. Ulfrik laughed and picked his son off the floor with one arm.

"Rumors travel like flies in this town. I found lazy guards at the west gate, and Einar punished a man for his laziness. But no one died."

Ulfrik deposited Hakon to his feet. Though barely eight years old, he stood taller than other boys his age, and well over Ulfrik's waist. He was the very image of his father, from his pale eyes and blond hair to his wiry strength and purposeful stride. Runa did not doubt he favored the boy for his similarity to himself, though Hakon's bright personality made him likable to anyone. He fixed Hakon's shirt, twisted and untucked from his belt. "Now what you have been up to? You've listened to your mother and Snorri? Been a good lad?"

Hakon nodded earnestly. Snorri coughed. "Good in what way? The young master here has been under everyone's feet these days."

Gunnar presented himself next. Runa watched the curious exchange. Gunnar considered himself a man, as did Runa, but Ulfrik struggled to accept it. This had strained their interactions, though in no serious manner. The two regarded each other, Gunnar standing back while Ulfrik awaited an embrace. When it did not come, he raised a brow.

"Have I ruined your day returning so soon?" Gunnar answered with a chuckle and then embraced his father. Ulfrik gave Runa a perplexed smile as he hugged his son.

"Gunnar has a girlfriend. I saw them holding hands." Hakon proclaimed his news with waving hands, as if words alone would not get attention. Gunnar hissed at his brother, while Ulfrik laughed. Runa had heard the rumors, and saw the lovesickness in her son's actions, but never openly dealt with it. The days of freedom in romance would soon end with an arranged marriage to strengthen ties with Hrolf. So she did not begrudge him his time.

"A girl, is it?" Ulfrik slapped Gunnar's back. "Keep it to holding hands. I've no plan for bastard grandchildren."

"Ulfrik!" Runa snapped. "Don't embarrass him in the hall. Now, you've not greeted your youngest."

She guided Aren before her, resting her hands on his small shoulders. Ulfrik mimicked Aren's shy pout, then smiled. He knelt to his eye level, and with one hand that seemed gigantic beside Aren's small frame tugged him a few steps closer.

"And how is my young warrior?" he asked, his voice lowering. "Have you been good?"

Aren shrugged as if to discount his own statement. "Yes, Father."

He stood out from his brothers in appearance and temperament. Aren's hair was straight and coppery, so thin it seemed painted to his head. His face was wide and square. None of those features were common to either of his parents, but much like a man Runa once knew too well. Aren was Konal's child, a man she had rescued and ultimately slept with six years ago. The timing of Aren's birth left his parentage open to interpretation, but as he grew, no one who knew Runa's history could doubt Aren's true father. Ulfrik never questioned her. The one time she tried to raise the possibility with him, he had placed his hand over her mouth and shushed her. He told her that blood did not always make a son or a father, and that he'd welcome as many sons as she could give him. She had never thought her love could deepen for Ulfrik until that day.

Now the two stared gravely at each other. Finally Ulfrik patted Aren's head and stood, "Good boy. Mind your mother."

With welcomes complete, and Einar quietly finishing with his own wife and two daughters who had waited for him at the far end of the high table, Runa now dared return to matters at hand. "What did Hrolf want? I've heard that famine is driving men from the land. Was that it?"

"Of course it was. How have you heard?"

Runa rolled her eyes and shrugged. "Unlike you, I listen to what tidings men bring to the hall. They are not all lies and tricks of the Franks. Besides, we've felt the pinch ourselves this summer."

"We have?" Ulfrik unpinned his cloak and threw it across the table, then sat which then signaled the others to relax and return to their duties. "I've eaten well all summer."

"You are the jarl, and would be the last person to starve." Ulfrik straightened to protest, but she held out a hand as she sat on the bench beside him. "But I don't mean that we've suffered, just that we've not replenished as fast as years past. So back to Hrolf. Is he ordering men to stay put?"

"He had us renew our oaths to serve him and needed me to persuade others to do the same. But before I left, he mentioned he might take a tour of England himself. Just to see if there are opportunities there." Ulfrik brushed imaginary dirt from his knee, as if the news were as unimportant as dust.

"So he binds you to fight for his lands while he leaves." Runa twisted on the bench to face him directly. "That is cruel."

"He is free to do as he pleases. Besides, he has not decided on making the journey. In any case, he knows how important I am to holding his lands, and he needed to be sure of it. There was gold in it as well as glory. Got an armband for my success against Clovis."

Ulfrik cleared his throat and held his arm up. His face was as bright as a young boy's and eager for her praise. She often felt he acted like her fourth son rather than her husband. "It gleams brighter than all the others," she said with a wry smile. "Though I'm not sure it was worth the risk you took to earn it."

"There is no life without glory, and there is no glory without risk."

"Foolish words," she scolded playfully and he laughed. Yet in her heart, she meant them. Ulfrik courted glory, more than ever before. Back in Nye Grenner, he was prideful, if naive. Since coming to Frankia and serving Hrolf, he had grown into an appetite for glory and station. Victory alone was no longer enough, but had to be achieved in a way that earned the envy of men. His battle plans, to

Runa's limited understanding, had become more convoluted and dangerous, all in the name of "being worthy of a song."

"Yet you don't count gold a foolish reward," he said to her, drawing her back from her thoughts. She decided not to foul his good mood with worries. The battle had long finished, and Ulfrik had assured her Clovis had been dealt a hard blow from which he could not recover before winter.

"True, now get yourself ready for the evening meal, and my own reward for you later tonight."

7

"He claims to have served you, Lord Ulfrik. He leads seven men in full war gear, who are waiting outside the southern gate. He gave his name as Konal Ketilsson, and said you'd let him inside."

Everyone at the high table spoke at once, and the messenger below them stepped back in surprise. Ulfrik snapped his head to Runa, who sat straighter at the name and pursed her lips. Her eyes narrowed and her head shook with studied caution.

"Konal has returned?" Gunnar stood, his face bright with excitement. "This is great news. Father, of course you'll let him in."

The messenger turned an expectant eye on Ulfrik, as did all the others within the darkening hall. Twilight had arrived and the moon would soon rule the night. Already men were gathering their families in fire-lit halls, drawn to savory cooking pots simmering with an evening meal. The arrival of visitors at such a late hour was uncommon, and many faces showed open worry.

Ulfrik's gaze skimmed past Gunnar, meeting Runa again. She had not shifted from her expressive silence. In the knit of her brows and the throbbing vein showing in the gentle curve of her neck, he witnessed all her fear. Konal had owed Runa a life debt, which he counted as repaid, but Ulfrik also secreted a fortune in gems that had once belonged to Konal. He had stayed on in Frankia with his twin brother Kell, hoping to find their lost gems. They believed Anscharic possessed them, but as Bishop of Paris he was as unattainable as an evening star. Konal and his brother eventually departed for Ireland, and Anscharic died four years ago. No one had expected to see Konal or Kell again.

"We must tell them something, Lord," the messenger said.

"Father, you can't doubt Konal?" Gunnar frowned at Ulfrik. "He saved my life once. Why would you doubt him?"

Ulfrik smiled, patting Gunnar's shoulder. Runa blinked hard and turned aside. *If only you knew, son*, he thought, *there's more reason to doubt him than to trust him*. Then he saw Aren, sitting quietly next to his mother, face placid and eyes darting from person to person like a master assessing his charges.

"Allow them inside as long as they surrender their weapons. Lead them directly to me." The messenger bowed to the command and made to leave before Ulfrik halted him. "Konal is a friend, and as long as he behaves as one you will treat him with courtesy."

The hall fluttered with the news of a new arrival. Many of the hirdmen recalled Konal, more for being a twin than being an outstanding warrior. Gunnar's excitement spread to Hakon, who was too young to remember Konal but jumped in glee nonetheless. From the far end of the high table, Einar shrugged at him and returned to his wife, Bera, and their daughters. A spasm of envy overcame Ulfrik, wishing he could share Einar's carefree indifference. Instead, he smiled falsely and called for a servant to fill his mug. When Snorri finally hobbled down from his seat with Einar, he whispered in Ulfrik's ear.

"You can't fool me; you're worried about him. Why allow him in?"

"Why deny him?" Ulfrik countered, constantly scanning the servants and hirdmen circulating through the hall, nodding to those whose glances searched him for reassurance. "He has never done me any wrong."

He did not want to look at Aren, but he did. Runa was stroking his

34

hair and hunched to speak to his tender ears. She blocked his view, and so he turned back to Snorri. His scarred and craggy face looked hard into his own, and Ulfrik knew how well his old friend read his thoughts. "What do you think of my son?"

He held Snorri's stare, until he shook his head and turned away. A fierce anger erupted and he latched hard onto Snorri's arm. "I asked a question and want your answer. For six years you've held something in your heart you won't tell me."

"And here is the place to tell you, where a hundred ears lean in while pretending to be busy? Have some sense, lad."

Releasing him, Ulfrik scowled and turned aside in sullen quiet. He studied the table in front him, wrapping himself in his thoughts. Snorri doubted Aren's parentage, he was certain, but he had more to say. Aren was a strange child who was unsmiling and distant to all except his mother. Still, Ulfrik had attended his birth and raised him as his own.

He roused from his black mood as people flitted about the edges of his vision. Gunnar spoke incessantly about all he could recall of Konal. Runa offered platitudes, but from her tone Ulfrik knew she wished to speak of anything else. He sat up straight in time for the hall doors to open again, now a dark square lit only by two men carrying brands overhead. Yellow points gleamed from the forms of armored men between them, and the hall's chattering hum died as the group entered.

Hearth smoke laid a white haze through the spacious hall, sapping colors from the air, but still the lead man's bright yellow hair was unmistakably Konal's. Ulfrik's hirdmen had not dressed in mail, but stood with painted shields and spears to form a corridor through which Konal and his men would pass. Behind them, curious children peered through gaps or stout women raised on their toes to glimpse the new arrivals. The two torchbearers doused their brands at the door, and showed the men inside.

Konal led his small band, a russet-colored cloak covered him and he left his cowl drawn so that once he entered the fire-brightened hall shadows swallowed his face. His seven followers wore mail over their clothes, thought they bore no weapons, and followed Konal with their eyes lowered. Their armor jangled as they passed deeper into the hall, where Konal finally stopped before Ulfrik.

"Konal Ketilsson," Ulfrik proclaimed, standing in greeting. Runa slowly rose with him, as did Gunnar. "You have journeyed far to bring gladness to my hall. Be welcomed."

The hirdmen flowed behind the visitors, essentially trapping Konal and his men. Ulfrik could have waved them down, but he still did not know Konal's mind.

"My men and I come with peace in our hearts, Lord Ulfrik." He bowed, keeping his cowl up so that his bright hair spilled out as he leaned forward. "We humbly ask for your hospitality."

"Of course you shall have it." Ulfrik now waved his hirdmen back, and they slowly dropped their shields and faded back from the visitors. "You and your men will sit with me as honored guests. Come, share a meal with us."

"Do you remember me?" Gunnar stood forward, his eager face split with a smile. Ulfrik pressed a hand to his chest and shot him a frown. Despite his excitement, he had to demonstrate reserve as a leader. Gunnar tucked his head down and fell back, chastened.

Still, Konal only replied with a slow nod of his hooded head.

Ulfrik ordered his servants to begin serving the evening meal, and families and hirdmen shuffled amongst each other to find places at the tables. Talk began anew in the hall, yet most remained fixed upon the visitors, who had not moved. Runa and Ulfrik exchanged puzzled glances at Konal's inaction.

As he and the others took their seats, Ulfrik asked Konal to join him again. "What has brought you so far from home?"

Konal's head subtly turned to the man closest to him, a warrior with grizzled hair tied into a long braid. Their pause drew stares and the hall again grew silent.

"We have all come far to offer our oaths to the one man worthy of us." All of the men, Konal at their lead, bent to one knee and bowed their heads. "Let our lives be sworn to you and our swords fight for your banner."

Runa's gasp echoed Ulfrik's surprise, his own hand rising to his chest. Even Einar, who had thus far leaned back in indifference now raised his brow and sat straighter. Ulfrik's first instinct told him to deny the request, yet Konal had admirably served his wife and children in the past. The absence of his twin brother, Kell, made him wonder at Konal's motives.

"You do me a great honor," Ulfrik said, finding his words as the men remained kneeling before him. "We certainly have much to discuss before I can accept your offer. Come sit with us. You must have a story to share."

Konal and his men held their position for a moment, then Konal rose. As he did, he pulled the cowl from his head and again Ulfrik heard Runa gasp. The left side of Konal's face and all of his neck were terribly scarred. Ulfrik recognized it as burn scarring, Konal's skin ruined as if a flaming finger had stirred through his face turning it to white and red whorls of tortured meat. His beard no longer grew where flames had torn his neck.

"The story is both long and painful," he said. "And I will tell it in full, if you will hear it."

8

────────

Space at the high table was cleared and Konal sat opposite Ulfrik with his men shoulder to shoulder beside him. The meal was a soup of barley and leeks with chunks of mutton. Runa had sent Hakon and Aren to eat with others of their age at the far end of the table, while Snorri and Einar leaned in to hear the story. The steaming bowls sat beneath them, untouched as Konal related his tale. Ulfrik broke off a stiff piece of rye bread, dipped it into his soup, then chewed as he listened to Konal. He studied the man across from him, unflinching from the wounds etched into his flesh. After a life of war, he had seen far more hideous disfigurement. Instead he sought holes in the story, or signs that Konal intended something other than offering his oath.

He had described his life after returning to Ireland, and forsaking the recovery on their treasure. The details were inconsequential until he began to describe the familiar rivalries that develop between powerful jarls. He found himself grimly nodding to Konal's descriptions of the battles and betrayals he and his brother fought against family rivals.

"My father had grown too old to lead his hirdmen, and it fell to Kell and me. Our other brother had died in battle two months before our return, which my father believed was a sign from the gods. We had fared badly, and for all my father's ferocity, we could not hold the land. We'd been pushed back. Finally, we were trapped in our hall one night, all of us. My wife and daughters, Kell and his family, all of us. They arrived in the night, eliminated the guards, and burned us all inside. Me and the others sitting here tonight are the only survivors. All of us carry the scars of that night, though the gods have chosen to write my failing upon my face."

"It's no failure to survive a hall burning," Ulfrik said. "Few do."

Konal held his gaze a moment, as if weighing the comment as an insult. He filled the pause with a sip from his bowl, then continued. "I went back for Kell, into the fires of Muspelheim, but it was for nothing. I felt his death," Konal placed his hand on his heart, and Ulfrik noted the red scars circling his fingers. "I should've died with him, but my men pulled me out. Scattered before our enemy's spears, running like rabbits to the woods. We'd lost everything but one ship, and I took it with whomever else I could find to join me."

"And you came here?" Runa asked, her hand clutched upon her chest, echoing Konal.

"No, that was over a year ago. We hid in Ireland, nursed our wounds and let the scars form. The pain, I can tell you, never goes. One of our brothers threw himself overboard holding a rock, such was his agony." Several of his companions bowed their heads at the words. "After wasting months finding no place to welcome us, I decided to seek you out, Lord Ulfrik. I own only what I carry upon my back and a small, leaking ship. We've wearied of scurrying into dark holes like vermin every time a bigger ship appears on the horizon. None of us have family any longer, no more ties to Ireland. I thought of my time in your service, and realized this is the closest I have to family. In that, I am luckier than the men following me."

He shifted his gaze to Runa, then to Gunnar, finally fixing on the bowl before him. Ulfrik leaned back, refusing to look to either his son or his wife, though feeling their eyes on him. Instead he looked to both Snorri and Einar, who both sat with arms crossed and offered only a brief shrug.

"Your story is tragic, but all too familiar. Only a coward cannot face his enemies on the battlefield." Ulfrik offered the words both as sympathy and a test, since he had used a hall burning once in the events that led to his possessing Konal's treasure. If Konal recalled this detail, he made no sign but merely grunted and slurped his soup.

They passed the meal with lighter conversation, mostly led by Gunnar's memories of training with Konal back in Nye Grenner. Konal smiled and chuckled, but his preoccupation was obvious. Both Snorri and Einar asked pointed questions about Konal's fighting ability, which he offered to demonstrate at any time. "The burns have not taken the fight out of me. In fact, I feed on the pain in battle and let the rage carry me."

After the meal finished, benches and tables were pushed to the walls and families and hirdmen sought their places for sleep while some left for other beds. Konal patiently awaited Ulfrik's decision and his followers matched his decorum. They neither ate nor drank more than enough to sate their appetites, and remained seated placidly on their bench. As the groups broke up, Ulfrik sent Aren and Hakon to bed and in a brief moment of privacy had words with Runa.

"I don't like this," she whispered as she carried a sleeping Aren over her shoulder. "He is a good person, but what if he knows about ..."

"And those are safely hidden where no one will find them except for us." Ulfrik placed his hand on her shoulder. He did worry that Konal suspected Ulfrik had his fortune in gems and somehow planned to obtain them. "He will not find them."

"It's not finding them I worry for; it's what he might do seeking them. Send him to another jarl. It's just too complicated with him here." As soon as she spoke the words, her eyes widened in surprised and a flush drew to her cheeks. Aren snored on her shoulder, and both were reminded that Konal was likely the boy's father. However, neither had ever given voice to the thought.

"I will speak with him and make my decision." He kissed Runa's head and sent her toward their private rooms. He returned to Konal, who waited expectantly, then asked him to walk with him outside the hall.

The night was chill and moon-bright. Points of orange flame showed where men stood at posts around the ringed stockade walls. A few dark shapes flitted between buildings as they strolled. At last Ulfrik stopped Konal as they entered the central square of the fortress.

"Your arrival is both fortuitous and burdensome. A famine has apparently taken hold about us, and more men to feed is no easy thing in the best of times. However, you are not so many that we will be undone. Your numbers will fill the losses that we cannot avoid. Men die in peace and war."

"How true," Konal agreed. Ulfrik held Konal's gaze steadfast and searched him for hints of defiance. Instead he saw the same shrewd, appraising look on Konal's face that he remembered from years before when they had first met. He had come outside to get the measure of Konal's intentions, but now his stomach tightened with the realization that the reverse was a truer statement of events. "Let me ask you, Lord Ulfrik, why do you hesitate when more fighting men and another ship come so many miles to follow you?"

"Because you have come so many miles, that is exactly the matter. Between Ireland and Frankia, there must be scores of jarls willing to take on a talented crew of warriors. Why bypass them to find me?"

"As I said, I am a man without family. My brother was the other half of my life, and with him gone I have no rudder. He was the best half of my life, and he showed me what to do and I did it. I don't want to lead, Lord Ulfrik, I want to follow. But I don't want to follow a fool. I did pass scores of them between Ireland and Ravndal."

He looked around, not waiting for Ulfrik's response, inhaling and admiring the fortress. "This was only just built when I left for home. It has prospered and the people here do not worry for food or safety. That is unlike most places in the world. So why is it unusual that I want to rejoin you?"

"There is little safety with Franks attacking the borders." Ulfrik shrugged, finding no good reason to deny Konal. Even if he intended harm, he was better watched up close than at a distance. "Very well, Konal, tomorrow you and your men will swear your oaths to me right in this square. Hundreds will witness and you will be welcomed here. I will find a place for you to live, but for now you may remain in my hall."

Konal folded his hands behind his back, simply nodding with deep satisfaction. Ulfrik smiled, though his hand touched the silver amulet of Thor's hammer hanging from his neck. He had lived too long to not recognize the hands of the gods at work, and he prayed their schemes would be merciful to him.

9

Ulfrik surveyed the faces of the hirdmen arrayed before him. The hall was tight with their numbers, ranks of shadowed men with hard faces and deep scars, snarls full of fury and a smoldering battle-lust. The silence was heavy with the force of their presence, and only the errant flapping of window covers from the shallow breeze made any noise. All but the hird had been cleared from the hall. They had ushered inside the scouts and their news of Clovis's activity. Morning light flashed haphazardly as the hide covers swayed over the windows, distracting Ulfrik as he stood before his men.

Snorri and Einar were to his left and Gunnar had proudly taken his place at Ulfrik's right side. The rest of his trusted men and companions had melded into the crowd, becoming one body that demanded action. Ulfrik had considered his options and knew what he must do.

"You are certain Clovis is not looping around to attack us, but merely cutting through our lands to head northwest?"

One of the two scouts standing at the front nodded, then turned to address his companions. "We followed until Flat Rock Hill, where he should have turned south again if he intended to attack us. Instead he continued straight, where he made camp at the creek."

"He's headed to Ull the Strong's territory," offered one of the crowd, a swarthy man with a heavy black beard and wild eyes. Voices rose in agreement, and again the chatter drowned out any one voice. Finally, Ulfrik shouted for quiet.

"I saw Ull at Hrolf's gathering, and he has suffered from Frankish raids out of the north. It is possible Clovis is working with other Franks to crack Ull. It would give him another border to launch attacks. But he cannot hold Ull's lands and his own, not unless King Odo is willing to send him men and supplies, which I doubt."

"Odo can't get his ass out of Paris these days," Snorri quipped. "Don't mind him in your plans."

Ulfrik shook his head, knowing he had dealt Clovis a blow that should have ended his raiding season. Whatever had drawn him out must have been at the order of a higher power, maybe King Odo himself. The Franks had remained woefully uncoordinated during the break up of their empire, but recent years showed them cooperating more fully. The suddenness of the move gave some credence to that possibility; had he been building for an attack, Ulfrik's lookouts would have noted it, but a sudden order into action would have gone undetected. He had his reservations, but he also had a hall of blood-thirsty fighting men watching him think. Then he thought of Clovis and his horses stretched into a line, their fortress left with only a bare guard, and knew he could not let it go.

"I have decided." Ulfrik paused, playing the moment for his men and ensuring he had their silent attention. "Ull will have to contend with whatever attack is coming to him, and we will have no way to send warning. But we will cut the snake off at the head. His fortress is close enough to strike while he is gone. No matter how he fares with Ull, he'll return to ruins and be finished."

Cheers greeted Ulfrik's decision. Einar shouted out assembly orders to the men, and their war band would be marching within the hour. Ulfrik appreciated Einar's efficiency of command. He took over the details of running organization better than any before him.

Runa's brother, Toki, had taken long years to grow into the role Einar filled fresh out of his youth. He caught Snorri smiling, and the two shared a brief moment of shared pride.

The hirdmen broke up and leapt to their duties, boasts of how they would capture Clovis's banner or dance on his ramparts flowing out with them into the morning light. Ulfrik turned to prepare, and ran into Gunnar standing behind him with his hand on the pommel of his sword. He read his son's thoughts and responded without delay.

"You'll remain here. I'm leaving archers on the walls, and you will lead them."

"I don't want to lead archers; I want to be at the front of the battle with you. I want to carry our banner."

"Gunnar, you'll be hard pressed to keep your head in one piece without the burden of a banner to guard. Do as I say and remain in the hall."

Runa emerged from their rooms, Hakon following closely behind her. Once he saw the scowl on his brother's face, his own lit up with glee. "You've got to stay here with me! See, you're not so big!"

The words hit Ulfrik harder than he expected. Out of dark memories, he recalled the very words from his own younger brother, a man who had poisoned their father and nearly murdered Ulfrik. "Respect your brother!" he shouted, setting both Hakon and Runa back in shock. "He will lead here in my absence and you'll obey him as you would me. Is that clear to you?"

Hakon's bright eyes had widened like a fish and he nodded slowly as he shrank behind Runa's skirt.

"Gunnar, are you clear?"

"When will you take me into battle? This is not fair! A victory is at hand and you'd deny me the chance to be part of it? Some of the hirdmen are only a few years older than me."

When Gunnar grew flustered, he looked so much like Toki that Ulfrik nearly reacted as if it were his wife's brother before him. Ulfrik felt hot stares from Snorri and Runa, and knew Einar studiously ignored the conflict while he ushered the last men from the hall. No matter what anyone thought, Gunnar was his to raise and he judged Clovis an enemy never to be underestimated. Furthermore, Clovis would delight in the chance to maim Gunnar the way Ulfrik had maimed Clovis's son. He could not accept the danger. He loved all his sons, but Gunnar was most dear to him.

"Gunnar, your day will come, but not now. I promise you, as my son, your whole life will be nothing but fighting the moment you take up your sword as a man. Do not be so eager to kill; for all the bragging men make of their battles, it is to hide the fear and disgust of what they have witnessed. One day, you will drive that sword you carry deep into an enemy's guts and you will feel his heartbeat throbbing up your blade before it fades away. His eyes will lock with yours and you will see in him the faces of friends or family, and you will know a mother or a wife will weep for the life you slashed from the world. But you will have to press on, for the slain man's friends will seek vengeance and so you will kill until the end of your days—until that day when your attention wavers and you see the blade flash too late as it punches into your breast and blood fills your mouth. Then you will lock eyes with your enemy and his hatred will be your last sight of this world. So don't be so quick to step on this path. You'll be on it soon enough, and you will never step off."

Ulfrik straightened himself, realizing his heart pounded and his breathing labored. Gunnar held his eyes for a moment, then dropped his gaze to the floor. He nodded to his father and mumbled something before leaving. Ulfrik considered calling him back, but he had already spoken his heart to the boy. Instead, he returned to preparing for the upcoming battle, looking at no one but Runa who nodded appreciatively. He paused by her side, and her cool, smooth hand touched his cheek.

"He is in love with the stories of glory and battle," she said. "Konal's arrival has rekindled all those foolish tales he used to weave when Gunnar was a boy."

"It's not Konal." Ulfrik took Runa's hand and kissed it gently before returning it to her. "He is ready to be a man, but Clovis ..."

"I know. I will leave Gunnar alone for now, but will try to get through to him later when the sting is gone. I expect he'll look to his girl for comfort anyway."

"That's what I have always done." Runa laughed as he turned from her, Hakon still huddling behind her. "Now I'm gone to crush a Frankish lord so that his back is broken for good."

10

By midday, Ulfrik's war band had marched into the woods of black trees now crowned in the red and gold of autumn. No sooner had he stepped onto the brown carpet of leaves and forest debris than he realized he was marching into a trap.

He stopped the loose column of men with an upraised fist. Hands sought weapons and shields raised in anticipation of a foeman's unseen strike. Einar halted, carrying Ulfrik's banner and shouldering his long-hafted ax, and his green eyes were wide behind the shadows of his helmet's noseguard. "Do you see something?"

Ulfrik pulled off his own helmet, an over-mended trophy he had claimed from his brother over a decade ago, and tucked it under his arm. He scratched his scalp with his free hand and grimaced. "I see that I am an overeager fool running into the jaws of a wolf. Our scouts reported Clovis is taking cavalry to attack Ull the Strong. Horses can't run up walls. Why would he need cavalry?"

"To run down Ull's warriors in the field." Several men drew closer to listen as Einar offered his opinion. Konal and his crew joined the small group as the larger army held to silence.

"Why are Ull's men in the field?"

"Because he's retreating."

"Do you know that Ull's retreating? I haven't heard such news."

Ulfrik studied the realization spreading from Einar to other listeners. The forest was silent but for the crackles and creaks of men lingering among the trees, impatient for the order to resume. Konal rubbed his neck and laughed, and others shared concerned glances. Einar's face now darkened with an angry flush.

He dropped his ax head-first into the soft ground. "He's coming after us."

"He lured us out of a place of strength to fight on a battlefield of his choosing. As soon as our scouts departed, he turned back and marched all night to set an ambush along the path to his fortress. His cavalry will burst out of hiding and trample us as we merrily run for his abandoned stronghold. We'll get hit from behind, totally surprised, and he'll hack us to bits. Why did I not see it? I followed what he wanted me to see, rather than what I should've seen for myself."

Ulfrik flung his helmet into the dirt and spun on his heel. He folded an arm across his chest and ran his fingers through his beard as he thought. Those around him dropped their heads and moved back. Hundreds of lives depended upon his decisions, and acting with discipline little better than that of a greenhorn put all of these people in unnecessary jeopardy. His only relief was in recognizing the trap before it was sprung. Pacing in a tight circle as he weighed options, he met no one's eyes. All looked to him for leadership and a safe escape from the trap. Clovis likely had seeded the approach with scouts who would spot a withdrawal and bring Clovis in close pursuit. He twisted a finger into his beard, and stopped as a plan began to assemble in his imagination.

Einar stepped into his vision, holding Ulfrik's helmet in two thick hands. "You've got a plan; I see that look upon you."

Ulfrik accepted the helmet, brushed a clod of mud from the face-plate, and donned it again. "Clovis still thinks we're stupid barbarians because we won't sing songs about his dead god. That's quite an advantage he gives us."

"And he wouldn't expect us to realize we're being baited," Konal

49

said. "So he will expect us to head straight for the prize he's waving before us."

"But we won't do that. We will comb these woods until we kill all his scouts and find where his men are hidden. Then we will attack inside these trees, where his cavalry are useless."

"And so is our shieldwall." Einar raised a brow in challenge, but Ulfrik only laughed.

"The Franks are tired from marching up and down these lands and expect surprise to carry them. They will try to drive us toward their fortress where I don't doubt scores of archers await panicked targets. But we're not giving them any of that. I'll trade the shieldwall for the pleasure of destroying those plans."

"I'll get the best scouts we have ready to go." Einar shared Ulfrik's smile, and hefted his ax onto his shoulder.

"In the meantime, we'll continue to march ahead as Clovis expects. I don't doubt the first of his scouts are nearby and we don't want to raise suspicions. If we do this right, we might still get what we want."

The column resumed the march, most of the men unaware of Ulfrik's plans. He did not doubt his men's ability to adapt to a new plan. The majority had fought with him for years and they all knew Clovis had a weakness for complicated bluffs. Even with so many aware of Clovis's wiles, they had all been misled when offered what they wanted. He would not forget this lesson again.

He had kept progress slow enough to give the scouting teams time while not arousing suspicions of Clovis's hidden watchers. Men began to cluster and bunch, and Ulfrik used it as an excuse to stop and reorder as well as whisper the new plan to his warriors. Soon, scouts returned with fresh blood sprayed on their leathers or fewer arrows in their quivers. They reported no fewer than ten kills along the lightest pathways through the woods. Most anticipated was the location of Clovis and his main force. As expected, they hid at the edge of the woods, with cavalry and their horses a good deal away from the main lane of approach so that the animals would not betray them.

Now Ulfrik began his encirclement. Among his men were Franks who served him, just as other Danes had gone to serve the Franks. These men had proved their loyalty and usefulness too often to count, and Ulfrik had clapped gold armbands on them to ensure they never had cause to leave him. He found two of them now, and sent them on an important task.

"Go ahead of us, to where Clovis's scouts were set, and send word back to Clovis that we are delayed with an argument in our ranks, but are coming as expected."

"What if we are found out?"

"You won't. Be hasty and play your part well. Don't approach their main line, just relay your message to the first man you find. Speak from the shadows. Just as we so readily believed what we wanted to hear, so will Clovis and his men."

Knowing smiles shared all around as the two Franks slipped farther into the brown darkness of the underbrush. Ulfrik now let his scouts lead them to where the cavalry was positioned. The proud animals were patient and quiet, constantly comforted by their riders who stared out of the edge of the woods toward the bright field of amber grass. Two dozen mounted warriors awaited to spring their trap and not one noticed Ulfrik's careful approach.

He drew his men into two lines to hit from different sides. Swords remained sheathed and helmets and mail had been hastily splashed with dirt to prevent an errant glint of the dappled light filtering from the canopy of leaves. Every snapping branch or disturbed bush made Ulfrik seize in fear, yet the Franks waited oblivious. Nearly upon them, he slowly drew his sword and others followed, a gentle sigh of metal echoing through the trees.

A horse began to nod and toss its head and its fear spread to its companions. The Franks stood in confusion, and Ulfrik knew the moment had come. "Kill the horses first. Go!"

Hundreds of screaming warriors burst through the trees at the astonished Franks. Horses screamed as axes and swords bit into their necks and spears drove into their bellies. The lightly armored riders barely had a moment to arm themselves before fending against a dozen strikes. Blood sprayed the ground, men shrieked in death, and war cries shattered the silence. A few horses bolted into the field, one with a spear hanging out of its flank.

Ulfrik did not strike a blow beyond the first hapless Frank he met, chopping him at the shoulder and then through his neck as he flailed on the ground. Confident the isolated cavalry had been defeated the moment he had ordered the charge, Ulfrik turned to his rear lines which now became his main defense. Einar, Konal, and his other best men formed this group, for they would turn to receive Clovis's charge.

"A sad waste of horseflesh," Ulfrik said as he joined Einar. "We'll not be able to carry all that back to Ravndal, and I hate that we just did Clovis a favor." Einar gave him a quizzical smile. "He's got two dozen fewer men to feed and hundreds of pounds of horse meat for the others."

Their laughter was short-lived. With no more need for stealth, the Franks bolted through the trees with curses and war cries driven ahead of them. However, the first clash did not come from the front where Ulfrik expected. Franks sprung up from Ulfrik's right and were among his men before anyone realized.

"Where in Loki's name did they come from?" Einar shouted, not knowing which way to turn. "Are those Clovis's men?"

"Who else?" Ulfrik saw the first flashes of enemies from the front hurtling through the spotted light. "Must be guards for the cavalry that no one saw. No matter now. This is going to be one gods-be-damned fight!"

Einar planted Ulfrik's green banner emblazoned with black elk horns and readied his ax. In moments, Clovis's banner of a white swan in a black square appeared and the first of his men rushed to battle.

Ulfrik braced his shield as screaming enemies launched themselves over fallen logs and low rocks to collide with the loose line he had formed. Throwing spears flew over his head, though the trees, and chaos foiled ranged attacks. The first Frank rushed forward, but Einar stepped in with his long-hafted ax and slammed the man away as easily as hitting a child's ball. Einar's ax was intended for use in the second rank to hook or break shields for front rank attackers to exploit, but he was tall and mighty enough to wield it as his main weapon. He worked in tandem with Ulfrik, for after he struck he appeared overextended and enemies targeted him only to find Ulfrik's sword in their guts. The ploy worked in every battle, for few lived to warn their companions.

More Franks joined and Clovis's banner wavered and dipped as he fought through to where Ulfrik stood defending his own. Weapons hammered on shields and men shrieked in pain and anger as metal found flesh. In moments, the battle became a swarming mass of men hacking and cursing each other. The woods offered horrible footing, increasing the lethality of the combat. Rocks, roots, slippery leaves, and logs tripped men from both sides and falling to the ground in combat meant death followed in moments.

Ulfrik moved little during the battle, tenaciously holding his ground and avoiding the problem of footing. He fought in a tight circle about the banner, sending men reeling with blood trailing from their wounds. The carnage was the worst he had seen since Paris. A Frank who had taken a spear to his face staggered past him with his eye missing and the meat of his cheek torn to reveal his teeth. One of his own men had his sword arm hacked off at mid-arm, but instead of falling he howled in rage and stuck the bloody stump into his enemy's face while bashing him with a shield. Another man rested in the bole of a tree, holding his glistening guts in his hands as he cried. Dismembered corpses littered the ground, piled atop each other like stacks of firewood. All around his banner disorganization and chaos consumed the men, so that any semblance of lines had disappeared.

He watched Clovis's banner drawing nearer, and finally he stood before his own standard and shouted. "Clovis, come meet your death. I am right here if you're man enough to get through to me."

Both he and Clovis understood each other's language well enough. While Ulfrik had forced himself to learn the Frankish language, his mouth could not form the misshapen and twisted sounds. His challenge had its intended result, for Clovis broke through to Ulfrik.

He was not a large man, but strong and fast. He had a narrow and royal head with close-cropped black hair turned gray at the temples. Even in the heat of battle, smeared with mud and gore and wading through ground smelling of blood and urine, he still appeared above the disorder. He was clean shaved, wearing only a thin mustache that framed his disdainful snarl.

"You ignorant fool," he shouted at Ulfrik, drawing his shield to his body and setting his bloodied sword low for a strike. "You are trapped here. Now die!"

With no time for a rejoinder, Ulfrik danced away from Clovis's strike, but lamely hit him on his mailed shoulder as he spun past. All around them, men chopped and stabbed and bled and choked in death. Clovis recovered, drawing up short before Ulfrik's banner. He paused as if considering whether to topple it, and Ulfrik jumped into that moment, slamming into him with his shield and following through with a wicked stab. His blade turned on Clovis's mail, but he heard the crunch as links broke. Clovis screamed as Ulfrik's blade dug into his shoulder blade.

"Now you go to sing songs with your dead god." Ulfrik drew back his sword for the killing thrust. Clovis crawled forward, a pitiful yelp escaping as he clawed through the wreckage of the forest floor.

Then men swarmed him, knocking him aside. His sword fell from his grip and he lay atop his shield as someone wrestled with him. His left arm was pinned, but his right hand was free to search for a weapon. The man atop him was too close to see, but he felt the cold knife blade press into his throat in preparation for the slice. In the same instant, Ulfrik laid his hand on the hilt of his boot dagger.

Freedom. The man lifted from him and Ulfrik reacted as fast as a cat. He ripped out his sax, the short blade warriors hung from belts across their laps, and turned on his opponent. Konal had pulled the attacker from Ulfrik, and now hovered over him with sword ready to plunge into the Frank's throat.

Clovis scrabbled to his feet and raised a horn to sound the retreat. He blew three short notes; Konal rammed his blade into his enemy's throat with a wet crack; and Ulfrik shouted as he charged Clovis. But men were fleeing in both directions. Everyone had broken, the danger and death too thick to withstand. The Franks fled to the open field, running for their distant fortress and Ulfrik's men running back through the paths they had cleared. The fight was done, and Clovis darted off like a deer before woodsmen.

Finding his sword in the dirt, Ulfrik picked it up and looked for Konal, who was calmly rummaging through the fallen's possessions even as men fled all around him. Einar stood beneath the banner, face covered in blood, and looked to Ulfrik for orders.

"Sound the retreat, at least to save pride for the men already running." Ulfrik scanned the scene, bodies and parts of bodies littered this patch of woods, and he saw many of his own lying among them. "We will be hard pressed to call this victory."

11

———

Night fell early on the battered men. They marched in ragged groups towards Ravndal where dark shapes of men gathered on the walls showed against the purple twilight. Heads were bowed in shame and defeat as they trudged across the last stretch of field before the sharp rise of the hill. They were less grand than when they had set out in the morning, helmets lost, shields broken, swords bent, and mail rent. They carried some of the dead they had found in the scramble to escape, though most had been left where they had fallen. The injured either hobbled behind the main group or were carried on the backs of their companions. Ulfrik bore one man on his back, a young warrior named Gert, who had his left thigh hacked to the bone. Gert moaned with every step, and Ulfrik sweated and strained under the weight, but his step quickened as Ravndal drew closer.

The gates opened as they approached, no cheering or bragging men greeted them, only worried faces of kin searching for their loved one in the weary group. Despite their own condition, Ulfrik knew his army had done enough harm to Clovis that he would be silenced for a while. The destruction of his cavalry was a rare victory, though the cost had been heavy. Whatever the true situation, for the men and for those who had died under his leadership, he would declare this a valiant triumph worthy of a song. Gert moaned again, as if reading his thoughts, and Ulfrik spoke over his shoulder. "Hold on, we're at the gates now. You'll get that leg stitched and be dancing on tables before you know it."

People crowded him as he led his men inside. A dozen questions assailed him at once, and he spun around looking for someone to relieve him of Gert so he could address them. Ornolf, a fat man who was nearly as old as Snorri, came forward and took Gert. Ornolf was his best surgeon, skilled at extracting arrows, stitching cuts, and amputating what could not be saved. "Be careful with him," Ulfrik said. Gert was only a few years older than Gunnar and the similarity tugged at him. "You've got a busy day ahead."

As more straggled through the gates, questions turned from Ulfrik to the new arrivals. The mood was solemn but still laughter sprouted up where an uninjured man returned to his kin. More painful to hear were the names of men he already knew to be slain. As the dead were carried in, wives and daughters cried and young sons stood trembling with balled fists.

Runa burst out of a crowd of women straining to find their own. She dragged Aren by his hand like a doll flying behind her. "Where is Gunnar and Hakon?"

"They're with you," Ulfrik said, and Runa froze. Her mouth made half-formed words and Ulfrik's blood turned to ice.

She shook her head slowly, then she punched him on his mail hard enough for her knuckles to come away bloodied. "They've been missing since you set out. Gunnar followed you!"

"With Hakon?" Ulfrik could see Gunnar disobeying him, but not Hakon. "He's only a child; Gunnar wouldn't ..."

"You've got to find them," Runa hissed, her face contorted with anger. "Look at this mess. If they went after you, I don't want to think of it."

"You're getting ahead of yourself." Ulfrik grabbed her by the shoulders and shook her. She calmed as he spoke evenly to her. "We don't know exactly what happened. What has Snorri said?"

"Ask me yourself, lad." Snorri followed on Runa, his lame leg stiff and ungainly. "Gunnar said he would keep watch on the eastern wall for you, and Hakon didn't tell me anything. He took his toy sword, and I assumed he was going to play. We didn't know they were gone until you were spotted coming from the trees."

Ulfrik thought of Gunnar, as headstrong as his mother and as eager for battle as he had been at Gunnar's age. In many ways, he had half expected him to follow, but never with Hakon. Visions of the carnage in the woods replayed in his mind's eye, and he had to push the thoughts aside. He had only one choice.

"You are both certain they are not here? Gunnar didn't go find his girl?" Runa shook her head and Snorri rubbed his face.

"Lad, I've had men tearing up every corner of this place. There's a few good hiding spots, but not that many. They're gone."

Einar, smiling with both his daughters clinging to his legs, joined them. Konal also approached. Ulfrik informed them of Gunnar and Hakon's disappearance. Konal smiled without mirth at the news.

"He begged me to take him along," Konal said. "Claimed that he'd not let you find out."

"What did you tell him?" Runa snapped, nearly lunging at him. "I hope it was sensible."

"Is telling him to obey his father sensible?" Konal's ruined face rippled with his strained smile. "He was saddened, but I told him to wait for his time and to heed his father's words. He left me with a promise he would, but I see desire got the better of him."

Runa began cursing and Ulfrik felt his own anger rise. "I'll go to search the woods. Einar, organize whoever is still able and bring torches."

"I'll go as well," Snorri added. "My eyes are not what they were, but you need help."

Ulfrik did not deny the need for help. After the battle, wolves would descend on the bodies left behind and they would not be averse to attacking two boys in the wood. Runa and Konal volunteered and soon Ulfrik led a half dozen search parties armed with torches back to the woods. Many were as weary as he, having fought and labored with heavy mail armor all day. His shoulders slumped and his back ached with the weight, but his sons were lost in these woods and the urgency to find them drove his feet forward. The dark trees echoed with calls of his boys' names, and nothing but a thick blackness remained when voices fell silent.

By midnight he was staggering and had fallen too many times to count. Runa pushed on with her group, but he had to rest as did many of the others. Exhaustion claimed the searchers one by one, and the search succumbed to it in the cold hours of the morning. Ulfrik insisted Einar take Runa and Snorri back to Ravndal, and he would sleep in the forest to resume the search the next morning.

His stomach growled, arms trembled, and feet throbbed as he slipped into the bole of a tree with only his cloak to protect him from the cold night. He drew his sword and laid it across his legs, and promised himself he would only sleep a few hours. As he drifted into sleep, he imagined he heard both his boys speaking to him, but it was merely the taunt of his imagination and he finally slept knowing his sons were lost in the forest.

12

T hrost's belly grumbled and his arms trembled, but purpose drove him forward. He had eaten nothing better than stale bread in days. He had tried to catch fish or wild game, and realized it was much harder to do than it seemed. The constant whining from his mother and sister had grown from a distraction to a consuming fixation for him. Even one complaint from them drew his ire.

The three of them stumbled along the trail in the woods, rocks and roots battering their feet as they went. Leaves and debris hid depressions and his mother fell on her face at least seven times since setting out that morning. Throst did not wait for her. She was a burden more than anything else, and her only use was in keeping his young sister in conformity with Throst's plans. He heard her curse as she again crunch down into the dry leaves. This time he stopped and turned, dropping a hand to his sword. His mother was on her face, and his sister dragging her up by the arm. Her head cover had long been lost, and her tousled gray hair caught a rim of yellow light falling through the autumn canopy above.

"All right, you two are stopping here. No more following me." Throst glared at his sister, expecting her to release his mother back to the ground, but she continued to pull her up. She staggered to her feet, and brushed down her tattered skirt.

"I'm not born for living in the forests. I was always a village girl. And I'm starving. Will these men have food?" She gave Throst the same pathetic pout she used to give to his father, which aggravated him in the same way.

"Now you belong to no one," Throst said. "Thanks to the great Lord Ulfrik Ormsson, you are a widowed outlaw. So get used to starving."

"I asked about food. You said you could hunt and that's a lie. What am I going to eat?" She folded her arm and lined up with his sister, as if the ten-year-old girl were an enforcer in her employ.

"Listen, Mother," he spit the words like chewed gristle, "I'm the man of this family now that Father is gone. You'll eat after I eat, unless you can get your own food and then you owe me a share."

"I want to eat too," his sister said, sliding closer to their mother as she did.

Throst rubbed his face, trying to force patience he did not feel. "I've got a plan, and I'm going to make it work. After this morning, I will have us a home and men to serve me. But not if you two fools drive me mad first. Just shut up."

His mother drew herself up straight, puffing out her chest and cheeks like she always did when she presumed to have authority over Throst. "How dare you threaten your mother like that!"

Throst's slap sent her reeling back and she tripped over a root, sprawling on the ground. He would have laughed were he not about to risk his life. His sister rushed to their mother's side, but she recoiled when he yelled at her to stay away. He hovered over his mother. "I'll speak to you anyway I like. Father always said you needed a few hits before you understood anything. Remember who will protect you with him gone? Me, I'm all you can depend on, so do what I tell you."

His mother rubbed her face and glowered at him, but she did not move. His sister knelt on the dead leaves with her head down. Throst lingered over them a moment before continuing. "Lord Ulfrik thinks

he has seen the last of me, but I've got plans he can't even understand. When I'm done, he'll regret killing my father and making me
an outlaw. You want to see Lord Ulfrik cry like a baby, don't you?"

His mother nodded and slowly righted herself, a lock of gray hair
hanging over her face.

"I will make him cry until he has only blood for tears, I promise
you this. But before I can do that, before anything else, I've got to
succeed today. To do that, I need you two fucking fools to stay here
and remain out of my way. Can you manage to do that one simple
thing?"

His mother glared at him and his sister picked at the dead leaves
before her. Satisfied he would not have any more interference from
them, he continued to follow the tracks through the woods. His belly
tightened in anticipation, knowing his plan would either glorify his
name or end his life. Death mattered little; with his father gone and
Ulfrik outlawing him, he had no life. No Northmen would associate
with him and no Frank would take in a stranger. Ulfrik had sentenced
him to death, all while pretending to be merciful. Throst was
unwilling to die and more unwilling to suffer humiliation and defeat
before all of Ravndal. Avenging his father was secondary to proving
that Ulfrik had tangled with the wrong man. Throst had been underestimated and that was an advantage he would fully exploit, but first
he had to succeed today.

He came to the end of the path. Sliding behind a tree, he studied
the collection of burned-out homes. One had completely collapsed
into black ash with only a few columns sticking out at the sky. Three
other homes were in stages of collapse, but the main hall had fresh
thatch. Throst drew a deep breath, then strode confidently into the
clearing, one hand on the hilt of his sword and the other tucked into
his belt by the thumb.

"Come out, you fools! Meet your new leader." Throst's shouting
drew instant response from the hall, the doors flying open and eight
men who lived in it spilling outside with drawn weapons. "That's a
proper greeting. Hurry, who leads this sorry group?"

Throst knew the names of the men and their leader. He had been watching them since locating their hideout in this abandoned Frankish hamlet. These eight were either lord-less Northmen or Franks who preyed on both sides of the border, all united under a Frank named Pepin. He purposely avoided Pepin and looked to the other ugly and angry faces arrayed against him, not wanting to indicate he knew anything at all of them.

"Look where the bird shit landed, right outside my door," Pepin said in fluid but accented Norse. He broke from the semicircle of men closing on him. His sword was rusty and dull in the light as he used it to point at Throst. "What's this you squawking about, bird shit?"

"Then you must be the leader of these men? I'm here to offer them a better choice, one who will lead them to more than living in a burned down village."

Laughter erupted, just as Throst expected. He laughed with them, which stopped several of them, notably Pepin who angered at the insolence.

"You're going to the slave markets, is all you're doing. Take him alive; he'll fetch us a good price if he's in one piece."

"I challenge you to single combat, Pepin." Throst drew his sword and leveled it at the stunned Pepin. His jaundiced eyes bulged in shock at hearing a stranger call him by name. "That's right. You have grown famous enough to attract challengers, Pepin. Fight me alone, and if I win I will take your place as leader."

"And when you lose, if your head is still on your shoulders, you're gone to a slave market." Pepin drew his sword, and one of his men who had been alert enough to grab a shield handed it to him.

"A shield? This is not a fair fight." Throst withheld his smile. A fair fight was never in his plan.

"Deal with it, bird shit."

The semicircle pulled back as Pepin leapt forward with a wild shout and his sword high. Throst skittered to the right and avoided the undisciplined blow, his blade licking Pepin's arm as he carried past. His men began to shout and cheer, encouraging Pepin to kill Throst and be done. As Pepin regained his balance, he smiled at his companions and laughed with them, as if he had only toyed and would now become serious. Throst smiled as well, jumping his sword in the palm of his hand.

Both men went into a crouch, Pepin behind his shield with his sword held against its edge. Throst considered grappling Pepin, but his size gave him a slight advantage and might encourage one of the onlookers to strike him. The worried look in Pepin's eye betrayed all the swagger and curses hurled from the others ringing them. They circled each other, and Throst easily led him to the position he wanted. He planted himself in the grass when he aligned the sun to his polished blade. Now he only needed Pepin to launch his attack to pull off his tricks.

"You're afraid to come out from behind your shield? You're worried I'll cut your handsome face? It'll be an improvement."

Pepin growled but did not jump at the taunt. Throst had patience and knew Pepin's friends would cajole him into action. The strike came suddenly, but Throst saw it in Pepin's stance before it launched. Pepin counted on his shield to pin Throst's sword arm, and he would follow through with a slash at his leg. It was what Throst wanted. He had the rare ability of equal skill with either hand.

As Pepin charged, Throst flashed sunlight in his eyes. The charge stumbled but did not stop, giving him the delay to toss his sword into his left hand as Pepin's shield rose up to pin his arm. In that instant, Throst hacked down and chopped the back of Pepin's thigh to the bone. The meat of his leg split and blood gushed. Pepin screamed and careened forward with the momentum of his spoiled attack.

Throst whirled and followed up, stamping on Pepin's sword hand. Blood pumped from the gaping wound and his companions cried out at the sight of it.

"I yield," Pepin shouted and cried, releasing his sword. Throst kicked it away.

"Have I defeated you?"

Pepin nodded, his face twisted with suffering as he turned on his back. "Who are you?"

"None of your concern."

Throst rammed his sword into Pepin's throat, nearly decapitating him in a single blow. The others fell silent at once, and Throst faced them with his gory blade ranging before him. Now was the key moment. Men would either accept him as their leader or another would challenge him.

"Pepin was a weak turd, not worthy of you. That's why I came here. Do you only dream of stealing food from the Franks and picking the crumbs the Northmen leave you? Did Pepin tell you that you were doing better with him than alone? Did he constantly remind you of how good life was without a lord to follow? Yet, what have you got? Look at you. You're living in a hall crumbling on your heads."

"But our bellies are full," one of the men challenged him, and nodded at a few for encouragement.

"Eating is all you want? Listen to me. Eating is good. I am hungry, for food but also for more. I want power and wealth just like all of you. Will you find it hiding here between the Northmen and the Franks?"

"You don't have anything to give us," said another man. "You're full of golden words, but have no real gold to put on my arm."

"You all know Jarl Ulfrik Ormsson. What if I told you we could have his treasures?" Throst smiled and let his offer take hold, the men sharing skeptical glances. "That's how big my plans are, and how much more you can ever get than following Pepin. Who is with me in this?"

The largest man, his head and beard forming a frizzy circle of red hair around his head, went to his knee before Throst. "If your promises are true, I will give you my oath. Ulfrik is no friend of mine, but neither is he so easy to defeat. What can you offer me to prove you are true?"

"Give me six days and you will have proof that I will be able to defeat Ulfrik. Then you can swear loyalty to me."

The men considered his offer and soon all of them agreed to his terms. Throst grinned and imagined the horror Ulfrik would experience once he realized what Throst had done to him.

13

Ulfrik slouched in his chair, his joints throbbing and body burning in a dozen places where cuts and bruises reminded him of his battle of the day before. His feet were studded with blisters, and swaddled in leather boots they felt as if they were on fire. Discomfort only added to his foul mood as he sat in his hall with his two sons kneeling before him. The hall had been cleared of all but family and those who were witnesses to Gunnar's lies. The late morning light splashed from the high windows at the left, a silvery color that emphasized the bruises and cuts on their skin. Hakon sniveled while Gunnar held his silence. Runa sat in her chair at his right, her face a tight mask of hot anger.

"You've both had all morning to think on what you've done," Ulfrik said. "What do you have to say for yourselves?"

Hakon peeked at his older brother for a sign, but Gunnar knelt with his head hung in shame. At the first light of dawn, a group of Ulfrik's hirdmen had found the two of them at the edge of the woods. After reuniting with his boys, neither Ulfrik nor his sons spoke a word the entire trip home. Once inside the hall, Runa had examined their wounds, judged them healthy, and kissed each their heads before consigning them to a corner of the hall.

"So you've nothing to say?" Runa asked, her voice far calmer than Ulfrik knew her mood to be.

"If you call yourself a man, Gunnar, then behave like one." Ulfrik straightened in his chair, his back protesting with a stripe of pain that made him grunt. "You defied me, lied to both Konal and Snorri, and took your brother into danger. What kind of punishment does a man deserve for defying his lord and betraying the trust of his friends?"

Gunnar did not stir and Hakon continued to steal glances at him. Ulfrik gripped the armrest of his chair and pulled himself forward, screaming. "Answer me! I am your father and your jarl! Would such insolence come from another, I'd have him whipped until I could count his ribs. My father would have had no hesitation to do the same for you. So do not tempt me further. What were you thinking?"

Never before had Gunnar received such fury from his father, and the shock of it raised his head and widened his eyes. Runa's hand drifted to Ulfrik's arm and she squeezed it as if to ask would he truly whip his son.

"I wanted to participate in the victory over Clovis," Gunnar said, his eyes darting between his parents.

"So I remember," Ulfrik said. "Let's not cover what we both know. You lied to Snorri and Konal, and defied me. I trusted you with defense of Ravndal."

"You never expected an attack," Gunnar dared as he met Ulfrik's eye. Despite his aching body, he leapt out of his chair.

"Do you dare question my decision? If you are so clear on what I expect, then you should never have spoken those words. You shame yourself. Tell me why you took your brother."

Gunnar again bowed his head but now glanced sidelong at Hakon. "For that I am truly sorry. He wanted to go, and threatened to tell everyone what I had done if I prevented it. I thought I could protect him and still take part in the battle. We followed close behind, and no one paid us any mind. But once in the woods, everything became confused. When the fight started I did not know where to go. The fight was everywhere and there was no one to stand with me. I covered Hakon with my shield and we fled."

Pausing to swallow, Gunnar closed his eyes and remained still. Ulfrik returned to his seat, and Runa glanced worriedly at him. They both waited for their son to resume his story.

"I had to flee because Hakon was too vulnerable and the battle too wild. We ran until the sounds of battle faded, but then became lost. Whatever paths men left behind, I could not tell if they were from our own or the enemy's. After night fell, we slept until I found the edge of the trees and the rest you know. That is the whole truth of it."

"I saw Odin," Hakon said, standing up and forgetting himself. "He was walking between the warriors and he saw me. He had one eye and Hugin and Mugin sat on his shoulders. He smiled at me!"

The revelation froze Ulfrik to his seat. Hakon beamed while Gunnar remained on his knees with his head down. Runa gasped and leaned forward. "Are you certain of what you saw?" she asked. "Few people ever see the gods, and fewer still are recognized by them when they do."

"As soon as he smiled at me, I never feared." Hakon touched his chest with a dirty, scabbed hand. "Odin blessed me with his smile. It's true."

Ulfrik looked over his shoulder to see both Konal and Snorri peering at Hakon as if he were standing before the setting sun. "And what did Gunnar see?" Ulfrik asked.

"I saw nothing. But Hakon did call out for Odin and he was calm after that moment."

Silence filled the room and both Ulfrik and Runa sat back in their chairs. The battle had been fierce and Odin reveled in such carnage; he could easily have been drawn to the ferocity. Perhaps his son had been seen and preserved by the All-Father. Such an amazing event bespoke of a great destiny, and presented everyone with a puzzle. When so many grown warriors had died, why had Odin favored a child? He could not answer the question, and soon roused himself from the same thought in which the other adults were doubtlessly absorbed.

"We will put that matter aside for now," Ulfrik said. "The gods do as they please, and we cannot understand them. For now, there is only the matter of punishment. Hakon, you are young and foolish. Other children are still knocking you out of the shieldwall during practice. Do you believe you could stand with men?"

His moon-bright face darkened and he lowered his head, shaking it. Ulfrik let the silence linger a moment, knowing Hakon was only acting like any other boy his age. The true issue was Gunnar, who now raised his head in anticipation of the punishment.

"You have gravely disappointed me, son. I understand your eagerness, no matter how confused you believe me to be. But I did not jest about my father's whipping. He would not have stopped to ask what was in your head, but just drag you to a post and whip you bloody. Could you bear such punishment?"

Gunnar raised his chin and wore the same defiant look he so often saw on Runa or his Uncle Toki. "I will bear whatever punishment you give. I am a man, Father. I will take it."

Ulfrik stood, and Runa grabbed at his arm with wide eyes. He pulled free and stepped down to where his son watched with shimmering eyes and a trembling lip. "Stand up."

Gunnar stood, and Ulfrik held his gaze steady. His son swallowed and sweat formed on his brow.

"Give me your sword." Ulfrik held his hand out for the weapon. "Until you can behave like a man, you will not carry the weapons of man."

"But ... what of the whipping?"

A vision of Ulfrik's long-dead brother, Grim, and memories of his father's murder passed through his thoughts. "I don't believe everything my father did was right. Besides, this hurts you more than any stripe across your back, doesn't it? You'll remember this longer. Give me the sword. You'll get it back when you prove you honor your words."

Unbuckling the weapon, Gunnar let the sword crash to the earthen floor. Without a word or a glance to anyone, he stormed from the hall. Hakon remained on his knees beneath his father, quivering as if he had been left in a snow storm.

Facing the others, he could not read their reactions. Runa sat holding her hands tightly at her lap, while both Snorri and Konal met his inquiring look with nothing more than flat expressions. He turned from them and followed Gunnar's exit from the hall. Now he understood why his father preferred the whip and decided next time he would follow his example.

14

Runa stopped short when Konal stepped onto the track leading from the main square to the hall. Wooden long-houses flanked both sides, laughter and curses echoed deep inside. The women attending her did not notice and continued several paces before they also paused. They lowered their baskets of wool as they waited for Runa to regain herself. Konal smiled from behind them, his cowl drawn to soften the horror of his scars. His hand held in place against the cool morning wind, and for the first time she noted the red and white scars on the back of his hand. One of the women followed her gaze and soon others turned to face him.

"Go on," Runa said to her girls, placing her basket of wool on the dirt path. "It seems Konal wishes to speak with me."

"And so I do." Konal bowed with a wry smile. Even with half his face distorted with scars, he still projected the same swagger and confidence she remembered of old. "But if this is inconvenient, I will find another time."

The girls, many no older than Gunnar, did not know how to react to Konal who was still a stranger to most. Runa noted how a few stepped back and how others furtively touched their necks as if frightened. It provoked an odd reaction in Runa, and she suddenly felt keenly annoyed with her girls. Konal's scars had not turned him into a troll.

"In fact, this time is perfect. You girls go to the hall, and take my wool with you. I will be along shortly."

"Will you be all right, Lady Runa?" one of the girls asked with wide, brown eyes.

Runa stared at her, and not finding a kind word, restrained herself. At length, the girl gathered Runa's basket and joined the others as they moved down the track. Konal drew to her side as they both watched the girls leave, a few glancing back as if being chased.

"My days of impressing the girls are long done," he said with a sigh. "I rather liked the one with the big brown eyes."

Almost laughing, Runa reset her expression of annoyance. "What could you possibly want in returning here? Don't you remember what I told you when you left the first time?"

She folded her arms and Konal mirrored her, only his smile broadened. "I do, but I doubt you remember or you would not have asked me."

Hot shame flooded into her cheeks and she recalled encouraging him to return to his family to be a father and husband, and not to look back at her. "I meant leaving our relationship in the past. I'm sorry about your family. I have not had a moment to tell you so."

He shook his head. "Family is what I wish to discuss. Do you think it wise to speak here, where a dozen curious people pass us every moment?"

Regarding him levelly, she pointed with her chin at the track. "Walk with me and help me draw water from the well."

"The jarl's wife draws water from the well?"

"There is always work to be done and I can't abide sitting on a chair all day while others treat me as if I am made of straw."

They began to stroll as people hustled through their midmorning routines. A chicken wandered into their path, and fluttered and cried as the two drove it to the side. Neither looked at the other, and Runa felt her pulse quicken knowing full well what Konal intended to ask.

"So you no longer wear a sword and pants? I remember you swearing to bow to no one on that matter."

Runa laughed, a tense and nervous sound that made her wince. "When I ruled in Nye Grenner, I did as I pleased. Everyone knew me and understood why. Here, I have few friends and no understanding. I still practice my swordplay, and that is barely tolerated. I sometimes believe all the Franks need do to destroy this fortress is put all our women in pants. Every person would die of fright and the walls would collapse."

Konal's gusty laughter was warm and familiar, a soft touch of a time fast fading from memory. Despite the horrors of those days when he had dwelt with her, now with all of Fate's designs completed, she remembered them with fondness. Gunnar still had been a boy who clung to his mother and sometimes slept in her bed. Now things were so different.

Laughter fading as Runa grew pensive, Konal clasped his hands behind his back. "You practice still? That is good, but not so useful without a sword at hand in time of need."

"How little you know me. I keep a long knife strapped to my leg, beneath my skirt. I learned to draw it from a false pocket without it catching on the material. Without it, I feel as though I am naked."

Again he laughed, and Runa smiled with satisfaction. Her hand sought the knife handle at her left hip. The skin beneath the sheath had grown rough and thick, but it was a fair trade for protecting herself and her children.

"I pray the gods you won't draw it on me. You are a strange woman, Runa, and that is why I have always liked you."

Even such a banal comment cooled the air between them. She found herself stepping away. They continued farther in silence, until the hall came into sight.

"The well is just behind it," Runa said.

Once at the well, she positioned herself for an easy exit. Konal felt like the man she had once known, but if age had taught her anything it was that people change and not always for the good. Her hand again sought the blade beneath her skirt and Konal's eye was drawn to it.

"You really do carry a weapon under your skirt? I thought it a jest."

Runa stared at him blankly, until he withdrew his cowl and revealed his whole head. Up close, his scars were fiercer and angrier than when softened in shadows. He returned her blank stare, as if allowing her to see him the first time.

"No more idle talk, then. You asked why I returned. Ulfrik asked me the same. Here is my answer. I returned because I have no family left in this world. Kell's death has left me floating, and I need an anchor stone. I need a purpose."

"Justice for your family is not a purpose? Revenge? That is what honor demands, is it not?"

"Honor demands much. Revenge will come in time, but my enemy is strong. Imagine he is like the king of the Western Franks, Odo. He sits in Paris behind impenetrable walls with hundreds at his command. How would a handful of men avenge themselves upon him?"

"Sneak inside and kill him."

"Only to die in the attempt?"

"Won't you join your father and brother in Valhalla?"

"Would that be your hope for Ulfrik? Should he die in an attempt to avenge your death?"

"Is that not what men call glory?"

"So it is. And what if it were your son? Gunnar? Hakon?"

"Enough." Runa turned her head aside as her argument faltered. "You wanted to speak of family?"

Konal stood straighter and Runa turned a stern eye to him, her stomach tightening and her hands cold. She folded her arms across her chest, tucking them underarm to both warm them and conceal their trembling.

"Your son, Aren, has a peculiar look; would you agree?" Konal raised an eyebrow that tugged on the thin flesh of the burned side of his face. Runa did not answer, but folded her arms tighter as she listened. "When I left for home he was a babe, so small and sick that I

74

feared he would not survive. But somehow I knew he lived. He is bigger now, and he reminds me of someone I once knew."

"Stop this, Konal. He is Ulfrik's son."

"Then why should Aren have my father's face? Why should he stand and walk like him? And most of all, why should I know in my heart that the sick child I left behind still lived?" Konal stepped forward as he drove his points, and Runa backed away with her hand falling to her hidden knife. Seeing this, he stopped and wiped his forehead with the back of his arm.

"Forgive my excitement, but I know my own blood when I see it. I have always felt the lives of my kin. Remember how I knew Kell survived the storm that wrecked me on your island? It is a gift of the gods."

Runa's heart beat against her ribs, feeling like it would burst through the root of her neck. Whether she believed in his gift was inconsequential; she believed Aren was Konal's son. She had always carried the burden of that doubt with her, and Ulfrik saw her struggle with it, but never had the words been given voice. Konal stared at her with his chin titled up as if to defy any challenge, though his eyes shimmered with emotion. She spun around to put her back to him.

"You had best control your excitement," she said quietly. "I am none too pleased that you have returned, and further vexed that Ulfrik allowed you to stay."

Runa remained facing the hall. The sight of it made her think of poor Aren, a young child who did not know how to play with others and was liked by so few. Only Ulfrik accepted him, and then only because of Runa. If she ever died, she wondered what would become of Aren. Finally, Konal found his reply.

"He is my son, Runa; the only family left to me in the whole circle of the world."

"And what would you have me do? Ulfrik has chosen to raise him as his own. Did you come this far to insult Ulfrik and claim one of his sons for your own? Or do you have other designs?"

"I only desire to know my son, and be near family."

Runa smiled, but did not laugh. Troubles with Konal ran deeper than Aren's parentage. He had lost a fortune in jewels that Ulfrik now possessed in secret. To this day, only she knew of the treasure and its hiding place. As touching as Konal's story had been, his loss of status and wealth likely hurt him more. Could he have more in his heart than a wish to see his kin, she wondered. Could he be here to dig out treasure he long considered his own?

When Runa did not answer or face him, she heard him sigh then walk off. She closed her eyes and prayed the gods Ulfrik had not let a traitor slip into his own hall.

15

Unable to locate Runa in time to respond to the news, he collected his three sons along with Einar, Snorri, and every hirdman in the hall and lining the track to the southern gate. The wind tangled his cloak against his body as he lined up before the dark log gates. The guards atop the walls and at the bar of the gate watched for his signal, which he gave with an impatient flick of his wrist.

Even Gunnar, still sullen from his rebuke, began to smile as the heavy bars lifted and hirdmen dragged open the gates. His other sons stood beside him, but were far more skeptical of the commotion. Half of Ravndal had gathered behind Ulfrik's group.

"His timing's not bad," Snorri said, standing behind Ulfrik. "But how many more visitors are we taking in?"

"This is family," Ulfrik corrected, his own smile broadening.

Wood stuttered along the pounded earth as the gates swung wide. Framed in the rectangle view of the fields and forests beyond Ravndal stood an orderly column of warriors, spears and shields held at ease. At their fore was a strong man in freshly scoured mail that flashed white in contrast to the dark, curly hair that flowed from beneath his helmet. Once the gates had widened enough, he stepped inside.

Ulfrik strode forward, his arms outstretched. "Toki, you miserable bastard! Welcome!"

They clasped arms then embraced as brothers long-parted. His oldest and dearest friend had been gone six years, sent to rule Nye Grenner in Ulfrik's stead when they had still been struggling to breach Paris. Now the two examined each other as warriors did, looking for new scars or missing parts. Toki appeared as he always had, but for missing a few teeth and a spray of gray in the roots of his black beard. Toki gently slapped Ulfrik's cheek.

"You've had a few near misses, I see, but you've kept both eyes. You look well and strong." Toki pulled back and scanned Ravndal. "And you're as powerful as rumor claims."

"But it is good to see you, brother." Ulfrik hooked his arm around Toki's shoulder and turned him to face the others waiting for him. "And I'm not the only one glad to have you here."

Toki's astonished face took in all the changes time had wrought in his absence. Gunnar struggled to maintain a dignified stance as he clearly wanted to leap into his uncle's arms like he had done as a child. Hakon was only in swaddling when they had last met, and Aren was not known to him.

"Is that over-muscled boy Einar and the snow-haired man leaning on him Snorri? That proud young warrior can't be Gunnar, can it?"

All pretense of dignity fled and suddenly Toki was swamped with his old friends clamoring to greet him. Ulfrik stood in the middle, experiencing a lighthearted happiness he had long forgotten. No matter Toki had brought thirty people with him that would be challenging to feed in winter, for now he let himself go with the joy of the reunion.

"Where is my sister?" Toki asked, his face suddenly grave.

"Runa went to fetch wool or some such chore," Ulfrik explained. "We will certainly find her back at the hall. Be warned; sitting in the hall all day has made her as feisty as a mother hen."

Toki instructed the rest of his column to enter and all shifted aside to allow the group to assemble. Soon the gates closed and the bars dropped back in place. Ulfrik examined the crowd and took heart that most were warriors. A group of women sheltered Halla, Toki's wife, in the center, but she had only come forward to offer an insincere greeting that bordered on insult. Despite being engrossed in talk with Snorri and the others, he caught his wife's shameful display with a sharp bark. Ulfrik played it down, knowing the real conflicts would begin once Runa and Halla met again. Many good reasons kept Ulfrik away from Nye Grenner, but the bad blood between Toki's wife and his own had been chief among them.

They took a leisurely walk to the hall, where Ulfrik gave a history of all that had happened, starting with the recent battle with Clovis and working backward to when Toki had departed. By the time they arrived inside the hall, Toki had a general sketch of events from the last six years.

Runa met them at the door, and Ulfrik feared her reaction upon meeting Halla, who now walked with slaves and servants and two young girls who Ulfrik knew were her daughters from the platinum white hair they shared with her. However, Runa only had eyes for her brother, and the two embraced as if reunited for the first time. She was courteous to Halla, which gave Ulfrik a breath of relief. Inside the women had set aside their baskets of wool and moved their looms to the wall and were flitting about the hearth to prepare a welcome meal.

They passed the afternoon swapping news and stories, and of all the happy voices in the hall none was louder than Ulfrik's. For a moment he forgot the troubles of rulership, the pressures of holding and expanding territory, the thanklessness of enforcing law, and the duties of being a gold-giver to hundreds of men. With Toki at his table again, he returned to a simpler time where wind flowed through his hair and sea spray misted his face as they sought fortune together. Only by evening, when the second meal of the day had been completed and the autumn sun fell behind the horizon, did Ulfrik finally ask the question no one had dared yet to ask.

"Why have you come?" Ulfrik's question drew sharp looks from everyone at the high table. Only Hakon's squabble with his younger brother distracted attention, and Runa hushed the boys as she added her own question.

"And why have you come with so many men?"

"Men are needed for rowing and for security. It's not a light undertaking," Toki answered. Halla, who sat at his left, turned from her children and peered at him with as much interest as the others. "I came because I've heard so much of the prosperity and peace here. I wanted my daughters to know their family."

Ulfrik studied Halla's face reddening as she stared at Toki, and immediately recognized she had been told something else to convince her to make the journey. She made a better showing of her temper than Ulfrik had expected, sitting back on the bench and returning to her plate without a comment. Still, Toki had more to share and he would not do it before everyone.

"Never a better reason," Ulfrik said, extending his hand to the girls. "Two beautiful maidens to brighten my hall, what more could I ask?"

The oldest girl flashed a smile, and he saw the familiar twist in it that had passed from Toki and Runa to her. The younger girl melted behind her sister and blushed. Their reactions drew laughter all around, successfully diffusing the tension. Ulfrik nudged Runa, and she responded with a nod.

"I must check on the servants, but please sit and enjoy the evening." She stood and dragged Hakon away as he whined in protest, whereas Aren followed without interest in anything beyond his mother. In the same moment, Gunnar approached the table. Ulfrik smiled at him, but Gunnar ignored it. Instead he asked to sit with Toki.

"Actually, Toki and I have much to discuss and were going to step outside. Is that your girl trying to hide in the crowd? Have her join you at the high table. She'd like that, I'd bet. Introduce her to Halla. She can be her guide while she settles into Ravndal."

The recognition he offered to Gunnar's girlfriend brightened his son's face. "I'm sure she would like that."

"Excellent idea," Toki said to Halla, who shrugged and stumbled with a weak smile. "Get to know the girl while I speak with Ulfrik. We won't be long."

Once outside, they walked down the black boards of the main road and past the last of the towsnfolk settling into their homes where lamplight glowed orange around the door frames. Soon, those lights would extinguish as the fortress settled into slumber. They strolled a short distance before Ulfrik renewed their talk.

"You have spoken much today, and you've spoken nothing at all. I have not summoned you, and you and your crew do not seem in distress. So answer me truthfully. Why are you here?"

Toki rubbed the back of his neck and sighed. They both stopped walking. Having removed his mail surcoat, he now wore only plain clothes and a gray wool cloak and seemed far less grand than he had in the morning. Somehow he seemed smaller and less sturdy without leathers and mail padding him.

"It's as I said. My daughters do not know their family and it is time they met you."

"I'll let you consider that answer again," Ulfrik said, a wry smile on his face. "I will not judge you, old friend."

"But you should judge me," Toki said and met Ulfrik's eyes. "I have defied your orders to remain in Nye Grenner until your return."

"You think overmuch. Fate's hand is at work, and it is time for our threads to intertwine again." Ulfrik clapped Toki's shoulder and he chuckled. "Do you remember our first meeting?"

"When you broke my nose with your shield? Not something to forget, is it?"

They laughed together and Toki's posture relaxed. "Well, that day I knew Fate drew us together and I was not wrong. Today you arrive at the moment when I've lost a fair portion of men in battle with Clovis. Is that not Fate's design made clear? You were meant to come and that is all. But I want to know what the gods planted in your heart to get you to return to me."

"The song of battle," Toki said without hesitation. "Each night when I close my eyes I hear the clash of shields, the clang of weapons, the battle cries and the screams of the dying. All my life I have lived in the heart of the fight, shield and sword against my enemies and only blood and pain to give or receive. But I haven't feared for my life in six years. Nye Grenner and the islands are at peace with all the ambitious men gone to Valhalla. I've become a farmer, and I can't stand it. I cannot risk dying in my bed. My fate is to stand at your side, with my brothers, and destroy our foes and claim glory that I can carry with me to the feasting hall when I am finally slain."

Ulfrik smiled approvingly, feeling the strength of Toki's words and drawing satisfaction from them. "Noble reasons, every one. You will find no end of enemy here. I've been seven years in this land and the Franks are the most stubborn people I've met, as unbending as their blades. But they are weak and divided. You'll remember Odo from Paris? Now he is their king, but only to the peoples of the west. The Eastern Franks have a different king. If we keep hammering, soon they will have a third in Hrolf. The gods want us to take this land, and by the right of our strength we should possess it. The Franks are not wise enough to recognize this. So, my friend, you will battle droves of foemen and your sword will grow dull in hacking them back from our borders. Welcome to Frankia, and welcome back to my side."

They clasped arms and Ulfrik laughed in delight. "You bring me thirty warriors in my time of need. Fate is kind to me for a change."

"My thirty men are not battle tested," Toki said, lowering his voice. "They've tired of life in Nye Grenner and followed me here, but I would not trust them to hold against hardened warriors."

"Practice will come soon enough," Ulfrik said, then guided Toki by the arm to start back toward the hall before the way grew too dark. "Now I have better news. I have a share of treasure I've held aside for you. There is much I owe you for your service, but I could never send it north nor leave my duties here."

He stopped short of explaining it was the share of the treasure they had sought together in Paris. With Konal's return, secrecy had to be preserved.

"That is well," Toki said with unexpected indifference. "It would have only served to trouble me in Nye Grenner, but now I am glad for it."

"Who did you leave in charge of Nye Grenner? I am not eager to abandon those lands, not after so much blood has soaked that grass to keep it mine."

"Gunnbjorn Red-Hand. He is Frida Styrdottir's son and her family is well respected. He has sworn a public oath to me, and I believe he will serve the people well. He is one of them, unlike me."

"I remember them both. Gunnbjorn will be a fine leader," Ulfrik said. The two walked a short distance before he summoned the courage to ask his next question. "Halla is not pleased to be here. What have you promised to gain her agreement?"

"She is a changed woman," Toki said, choosing to examine the stars above. "There is nothing left in Nye Grenner with her family all dead. I promised there would be many Christians here for her to deepen her understanding of her god."

Ulfrik snorted. "She still clings to her faith in the dead god? She wastes her life on a weak god. The dead god's priests are worse than snakes and we kill them by the score without any notice from him. But when we call out to Thor or Odin, they answer in thunder and war. The new god is failing his people in Frankia; anyone with eyes will see as much."

"Let Halla discover this on her own, and don't share your thoughts." Both men laughed as they closed the final distance to the hall. Ulfrik stopped them on the track.

"Look, Runa has not mentioned your wife in six years. I am hopeful she has left her anger behind, but I cannot be sure. I will find you and your family a place in my fortress, but it might be best to keep you separated for a while. Has Halla put aside her differences?"

Toki remained silently searching the night sky, as if his answer were hidden there. Ulfrik could not help but follow his gaze to the brilliant eyes of the night sparkling overhead. In time, Toki spoke his answer softly.

"My sister, your wife, cut out Halla's mother's tongue. The wound never healed and she suffered two winters before she died in agony. I say keeping Runa and Halla separate is a good idea. For all that Halla speaks of her god's love of forgiveness, she has little place in her heart for it."

16

Throst clung to the shadows of Ravndal's stockade walls awaiting his prey. His heart raced, not from fear but from anticipation. The sun was diving toward the western tree line, and already the cold air of nightfall chased people back to their hearths. Crows lifted from rooftops, protesting the end of day as they winged toward their woodland nests. His hands trembled with excitement and he wrapped his right hand tighter into the sack of rocks that he had cushioned with old rags. He weighed it in his other hand as he pressed against the cold, rough logs of the wall.

Regaining access to Ravndal had been simple. Ulfrik had taken pains to keep an army from sneaking upon his fortress: clearing trees and other hiding places, digging ditches and lining them with wood spikes, not to mention setting his fortress atop the highest hill in the valley. A single man would still find challenge in threading this gauntlet to reach the gates, but not if that man still had friends inside.

Killing his father and tossing Throst and his family across the border let Ulfrik believe he had finished them. Yet, he had not paused to consider friendships and other relatives. He had even appeared bored at the execution of Throst's father, as if impatient to dispense his duties. Throst's father still swung from the hanging tree, and he planned to ensure Ulfrik would regret that day. Whatever people had thought of his father, Throst had friends left behind and some who had owed him life debts. One such man watched the western gate, and had abused his position to extract bribes from the vulnerable. Contacting him had been too simple, and after Einar had beaten him nearly to death, he was all too eager to help.

Tonight he found the gate ajar and no one watching the approaches for a lone traveler. One man can often go where many cannot. His father had told him so, though it was his excuse for sneaking about and robbing others. Throst had grander designs.

He roused from his thoughts as the two boys came into view. Murky light rendered them indistinct, though the fine clothing of one of them was more than enough to confirm for Throst that his young accomplice had succeeded.

"It's just this way," said the accomplice, a brown-haired, lanky boy of seven or eight years. "Hurry up before it gets dark."

The other boy, Throst's prey, hesitated. Throst felt his heart flop at the pause, but the accomplice was talented. "I know it's scary, but you said you weren't afraid of dead things. This body has been dead forever, just bones. Come on and see it."

"I should tell my father first." Hakon's voice was thin and frightened, but at the same time Throst could see him looking into the shadows to see what waited.

"Our parents would only ruin this. Hurry up. Just behind this building. I'll go first." Throst watched the boy skip around the corner, and call back to Hakon. "See, it's safe. You're not afraid, are you?"

"No," Hakon replied in a small voice. He crept forward and the accomplice led him back step by step.

"See, nothing happened."

"But where's the skeleton?"

Throst leapt from the shadow and slammed the bag of rocks over Hakon's head. He crumbled like a brittle twig and gave no sound other than a moan once he hit the ground. Throst bashed him again, not certain how hard he needed to hit a small boy until knocked out. Blood flowed from Hakon's nose, so Throst stopped and crouched to find Hakon's pulse. He pressed the soft neck until he felt a throb beneath his finger.

"That was good work," he told his accomplice. "Help me get him in the sack."

Throst unrolled a large, heavy linen sack and laid out a length of rope. Both he and the boy glanced around as they gagged Hakon and then folded him into the bag.

"You've got my reward?" the accomplice asked. He was a half-Frank named Atli whose father had died and left him with only a dumb sister. Throst had used his contact to arrange for the boy's complicity.

"Yes, here it is," Throst said as he reached into the folds of his robe. Atli extended his hand. Throst seized it and yanked the boy to him. In one deft motion, he snapped Atli's neck, the crack no louder than stepping on a branch in the forest. He followed Atli to the ground as he died, and laid him against the back of the building where shadow now engulfed them. "You'll keep my secret better if you're dead."

With his grizzly work complete, he hefted Hakon over his shoulder and accompanied the shadows of the walls back to the gate. Night had fallen and the risk of tripping and revealing himself demanded he tread carefully. Once a guard in heavy leather armor and a shield glided by with a guttering torch, but he held his breath until the guard rounded a building. At last Throst arrived at the gate and his contact awaited him.

"Olaf," he whispered, "is it safe?"

The man named Olaf leapt at the voice from the shadow, and Throst shook his head in disgust. Such jitters were not only unseemly but would draw attention. His contact nodded, his shape a black mass rimmed only by a faint glow of torches on the walls. His bulky form was filled out with a sword and shield as well as a large sack tossed over his shoulder. He stepped closer, and his face was revealed in the light. Throst had not seen him up close since his beating, but now the swelling and bruises were accented in the shadows. He looked like a walrus without tusks.

"We've only got a short time before the others return. Hurry."

Throst hefted Hakon again, the boy giving a murmur and shifting in the bag, and crept forward while scanning the area. No one was close, everyone gone to their halls as the last light of the day fled. "You are coming with me?"

"Well, I can't stay here," said the man named Olaf, his swollen eyes barely opening with his shock at Throst's question. "Once they know what happened, they'll come looking for me. So is that Ulfrik's kid?"

Throst patted the sack. "It is. I suppose you're right about leaving. I could use another fighting man too. But if you follow me back, you must swear an oath of service."

"Yeah, anything," said Olaf, as he began to back toward the gate. "Whatever it takes to get out from Einar and Ulfrik and hurt them on the way."

"Oh, I'll hurt him," Throst said, smiling. "Now let's get this kid out of here before anyone knows he's gone. They'll be looking for him now, and we've got to flee."

Barely cracking the gate, Olaf slipped out and Throst followed. It was all he could do not to laugh with delight, and once Ravndal was no more than a dark smear crowned with points of torchlight, he did laugh and dreamed of the riches and revenge that lay ahead.

17

The hall was filled to capacity now that Toki and Konal had added their crews to the evening meal. Runa moved among the press of people, hirdmen and craftsmen and others who Ulfrik favored. Their voices joined together into a tumultuous din that Runa found both comforting and bothersome. Loud, friendly talk was a sign of good times, but the demands of overseeing so many tired her. She slid past two red-faced men in the early stages of a shoving match that would result in one of the many quick fights that punctuated each night. Fighting men never knew when to stop fighting, she thought as she passed them for the high table.

Ulfrik sat flanked by Toki and Einar with Snorri and Konal opposite, and the square of men were talking over each other and laughing like boys. Runa's smile faded as she skimmed past Halla, who sat with her two girls at the far end of the table. Over the years she had thought Halla no longer mattered to her, but as soon as Runa reunited with her brother's wife, all the old feelings rushed back. She hated the woman, and it was mutual.

Putting aside the thought, Runa circled around the table to where Aren waited patiently and alone. He studied her as she approached, his icy eyes alive with an intelligence that made him different from all the other children. As she sat next to him, she patted his head and could not resist a glance at Konal, who appeared to be straining not to look at her. "Where are your brothers?"

Aren did not answer, but pointed across the hall to where Gunnar stood at the far end. Over the tousled hair of the men and the covered heads of the women lining the benches, Runa saw her son with a girl. The two stood too close together and Aren noted his mother's reaction with his own observation. "She is not as pretty as other girls that like Gunnar."

"What's her name?" Runa asked, recognizing the face but little else. Then she realized Aren's comment was beyond a child of his age. "And who told you that?"

Aren shrugged and looked away. When Runa turned back to Gunnar, he was already alone and pushing toward the high table. When he arrived, he ignored his father and the other men and slid up to Runa's side without anything more than a mumble.

"Where's Hakon?"

"He's not here?"

"He was with you last, but I see you ended up with someone else. So where's your brother?"

Gunnar's face flushed and he lowered his head. His answer was barely audible over the crowd, and Runa asked him to repeat it. "I said he went to play with another boy. I thought he'd have the sense to come home by dark."

Runa folded her arms. "You mean you shoved him off to someone else so you could have time with your girl. We'll talk about that, but your brother comes first. Who did he play with?"

"Atli Hrappson, I think it was."

"The orphan whose father died last spring? He's a bad seed, that boy. Why would you let Hakon go with him?"

Gunnar did not answer and Runa blushed once she intuited the answer. Her anger flashed hot, but Hakon was gone and probably up to no good. She stood and scanned the hall, but a small boy amid so many would be impossible to find. She drew Snorri's attention and in turn all the other men stopped to regard her. "What's wrong?" Ulfrik asked.

Not wanting to create a disturbance, she stepped out from the bench and went to Ulfrik's side. "Hakon has not returned, and he was with that troublemaker Atli."

The four men glanced at each other, and Ulfrik put his arm around Runa's waist. "Atli is not a troublemaker; he tends the riding horses and raises chickens with his sister. Good work for a boy his age and no other kin to guide him."

"All the same, Hakon is not back and it's dark. We should look for him."

Ulfrik's arm dropped and he gave a sigh that Runa knew was a prelude to protest. She headed it off. "If you will not look for him, then I will."

"All right," Ulfrik said. "I'll go find the boy. What has gotten into these kids?"

"No, if you go looking it will cause a stir." Einar put his hand on Ulfrik's shoulder as he interrupted. "I'll round up a few men to find him. Stay and enjoy your meal."

"I'll go with you," Snorri said, limping up from his bench. "It's not like the boy to do this."

Runa sat beside Ulfrik where Einar had vacated, and he patted her back before returning to his meal. Konal stared at her, and she gave him a wan smile before turning aside. Her concerns had silenced the men's jovial conversation, but she knew they were genuine. She worried for Hakon's vision of Odin. While her son took it as a favorable omen, she knew Odin All-Father to be a capricious and untrustworthy god whose blessing was hard to gain and easy to lose.

"He's probably still stinging from the shame he caused Gunnar," Ulfrik offered, his mouth full. "Snorri'll bring the young master home."

Runa smiled at the pet name, but shook her head at Ulfrik's explanation. It made no sense for Hakon to hide days after the event, especially when he had not done so before. Folding her hands in her lap, she peered over the heads of the dinner guests and through the milky smoke curling above them and watched the door for Hakon.

In time, Einar and Snorri returned. She read their faces and even at this distance she knew they had not found Hakon and were worried. Her hand grabbed Ulfrik's knee beneath the table, digging in her fingers both to grab his attention and control her fear. The two pushed their way to the table, and now all the men of the high table watched their approach. Runa noted Halla's gaze and the faintest of smiles upon her lips. *That pale bitch*, she thought, *takes pleasure in this and yet eats from my table. Toki, why have you remained with her so long?*

"It's true," Einar said as he drew between Ulfrik and Runa. "Hakon is nowhere to be found."

Snorri staggered up later, his limp delaying him. "Lad, there's not a star in the night sky. Can't see nothing without a good number of torches."

"Why do you need to see him?" Runa asked, her voice trembling. "He should answer your calls, right? You don't think he's hiding from us?"

"Maybe he's had an accident and can't answer," Ulfrik said, gently placing his hand atop hers gripping his knee. The warm and rough touch was a mild comfort, but she needed anything offered.

"We can't sit here." Runa pulled her hand free and stood. "We've got to keep looking for him."

"That we will," Ulfrik said softly. Then he stood and drew the dagger at his hip, flipping the blade around so the pommel protruded from his fist. He rapped the table and shouted until the hall silenced and all eyes turned to him. He regarded them as if surveying his warriors before a battle, then sheathed the dagger as he addressed them in his commanding voice.

"My son, Hakon, is missing. No doubt he's up to boy's mischief, but it is unusual he be gone so late. Has anyone seen him today?"

A few answered, providing no more information than Gunnar had already given. Runa stared at her oldest son, whose face had turned ashen as he listened. Her breath grew hot and she wanted to slap Gunnar's face for letting his brother slip away.

"All right, everyone will search until he is found. He may be hiding, or he may be hurt." Ulfrik began pointing to hirdmen. "Form groups and check every corner. You men take brands from the hearth and light the paths. The first one to find him, return here and sound one note on the alarm horn."

Excited patter engulfed the hall, and Runa heard a few men wager on where Hakon was likely to be found. When one named the bottom of the well as a likely spot, an ember dropped into her gut. She grabbed Ulfrik's arm, "I will search with you."

The two left with the crowd into the night, and it was as dark as Snorri had promised. Gunnar accompanied them, and showed the last spot he had seen his brother. Aren toddled along, holding a string tied to Runa's belt. After a while, she felt that string pull tight and whirled on Aren. "What do you want? We are looking for your brother."

"Atli likes horses," he said, his child's voice unnaturally calm. "Let's see Atli and his horses."

She and Ulfrik had been trudging off where Gunnar had pointed them, but the logic of Aren's words highlighted her stupidity. She felt her own face grow hot with embarrassment. Ulfrik, having over-heard, dropped his head and slowly turned to face Runa.

"Corrected by a child," he said, a bemused smile on his face. "We should grab Atli and have done with this. They're probably asleep in the stables. Let's go."

Runa scooped up Aren in her relief, kissing him on his cold, smooth cheek. She followed Ulfrik who stomped off shaking his head and cursing himself. "We're always too ready to believe the worst. The boys probably just tired themselves out and here I'm going to look like a fool for my worry. Gods, I'm supposed to get wiser as I age."

Ulfrik's angry monologue did not bother Runa, now that she knew Hakon would be fine. Gunnar even cheered and raced ahead to the stables. Once there, they only found Atli's sister, who could not speak and had only the wits of a young girl. Instantly Runa's fears rekindled, and in the next moment, standing outside the stables in the chill, animal-rank air, Gunnar's scream shattered her nerves.

"Gods, Atli's dead!"

The small, lifeless body was shoved into the corner behind a nearby building. The head was turned nearly to the back, and the skin looked black under the wavering torchlight Gunnar held over it. Were it not for Atli's wide, blank eyes she would not be able to tell it was a face staring up at her.

Ulfrik dragged the body out, frisking it for other wounds. As he did, Runa covered Aren's eyes and averted her own. She squeezed her son, suppressing an urge to scream or cry. Something horrible had happened, and Hakon was in danger.

"Hakon killed him?" Gunnar asked, leaning over his father's shoulder.

"No, the bruise on Atli's neck is from a hand too large to be Hakon's. Look at it."

Runa did not follow, but closed her eyes and bit her lip. Aren struggled to be let down and free her hand from his face. Then he stilled as three sharp notes of a horn sounded in the distance.

"The western gate," Ulfrik said as if he had spoken words of dark magic.

In moments they were running with others who flocked toward the gate. Once there, Einar stood with his torch held overhead, a brilliant ball of yellow light illuminating the scene. His face was grim.

"The gate was unbarred."

"Atli is dead." Ulfrik's words drew a rush of gasps from the gathered men. "Hakon is in danger. I fear we all are."

18

Ulfrik led his men in combing the surrounding lands for any sign of Hakon, but had found nothing. The longest day in recent memory had passed followed by a second evening of restless gulps of sleep. Runa had joined the search as well, and suffered the same curse of sleeplessness. In the morning, the two regarded each other as haggard ghosts and wordlessly began their morning rituals.

For Ulfrik, nothing could be worse than having his son snatched from the bosom of his fortress. One of his own men, the fool who Einar had beaten, was missing and likely the culprit. The next time Einar wanted to beat a man to death, he would not deter him. All of the hall was a quiet pantomime of what a normal morning would be. People moved through their chores as if in a dream, each person carrying the fear of having been struck by enemies where they expected safety. They hunched over their bowls, eating and gathering strength for another day of searching. No more sounds were heard than bowls clacking on wood tables or benches dragging on the earthen floor.

Runa did not attend her women as usual, but sat with both Aren and Gunnar. She stared ahead, her hand idly touching the knife she hid beneath her skirt. Toki joined her, and with great relief Halla and her daughters sought their places away from her. However, Halla offered Ulfrik what she considered solace as she passed him. "I will pray to Jesus that your son be returned safely."

He nodded thanks, but something in the glitter of her eyes reminded him of the spiteful flare he remembered of her father. No doubt, she prayed to Jesus for other things that likely had little benefit to him and his family. He left her to clutching the wooden cross she boldly hung from her neck and murmuring her prayers or curses in the corner.

The hall doors burst open, and Einar rushed in with Konal trailing. One of the women screamed from the unexpected shock, but Ulfrik was already on his feet.

"Men who claim to have kidnapped Hakon have proclaimed themselves," Einar shouted as he strode through the hall. "They've come close to the gates, but out of bow range. Konal went to speak with them."

Everyone stood and made way for Konal to deliver his news. He scanned all of them, his scarred face bright with sweat. "There are four men, though one is big enough to be counted twice. Their leader claims to have snatched Hakon from under the eaves of your hall and is keeping him hostage in a safe place. He gave me these as proof of his claim."

Konal's gloved hand extended toward Ulfrik, and everyone at the high table strained to see it. The object was a tarnished silver cloak pin that Ulfrik had bestowed on all his children, and a lock of Hakon's fine yellow hair was wound in it. The tie came apart in Ulfrik's hand and the strands of his son's hair tumbled across his palm. He folded his hand over the pin and closed his eyes.

"What is the name of this fool so desirous of a miserable death?"

"He called himself Throst Gudmundarson."

Ulfrik stood straighter, not recognizing the name until he exchanged glances with Snorri who had also joined to see Konal's proof. In that moment, he recognized regret and resentment in his old friend's eyes, and remembered his advice to kill all of Gudmund's family. The son had returned to take revenge for what he deemed his father's unjust death.

"You know this man?" Konal asked as he stepped back. "He is young still, not more than two seasons older than your first son. He demands you meet him to hear terms for Hakon's release."

"Throst is a boy, the get of a murdering father and shiftless mother. He will not live to manhood, I promise you this." Ulfrik handed the pin to Runa, who took it absently.

"Don't do anything rash," she said. "Hakon is in danger."

"I know what to do," he said, far more calmly than he felt. "I will see to it Hakon is released unharmed."

He scanned the faces of his loved ones: Runa, Gunnar, Aren, Snorri, Toki, and Einar all stared back at him with taut, grim expressions. No one doubted he would save Hakon and send Throst's soul screaming into the frigid mist realms of Nifleheim. He did not doubt it himself. From this moment, his will would be bent to nothing more.

"Take me to him," he said with a curled lip. "I'll have Hakon returned by nightfall."

19

Ulfrik closed the distance to where Throst and three men waited for him. They stood at the foot of the hill, ragged figures in ill-maintained mail and tattered hides and furs. Throst stood out, standing at the fore of his henchmen with his hand resting on the pommel of his sword. His clear face was now smudged and dirty, but his malefic pale eyes remained bright. He stood as if he had overrun a great army and now rested his foot upon its warchief's head. In fact, he had his foot atop the stump of a small tree and his three men seemed incapable of overrunning a mug of mead without difficulty. Only one was of any account, a giant man whose frizzy hair and beard circled his head like an explosion of brown fire.

"Where's my son?" he demanded as he drew within spear's length. He unhitched his sword in its sheath and tugged it loose for a quick draw.

Throst did not move, but his eyes ranged farther up the hill. Ulfrik had taken twenty hirdmen, all archers, and spread them in a semicircle. If Throst made one threatening move, he and his henchmen would be riddled with arrows.

"If I don't return by midday, my men have instructions to hang

Hakon until he pisses himself. Control your archers or your boy dies today, Lord Ulfrik." Throst spit the title out of his mouth like gristle.

"You've got men?" Ulfrik snorted and sneered at the three arrayed behind Throst. "Are these dogs examples of your men? You, the giant one, you take orders from this boy? Is it because he sucks your prick?"

The giant man erupted with a stream of curses and drew his sword. Throst's cool demeanor shattered and he scrambled to keep his man from attacking. The other two joined only after he cursed their inaction. The three of them dug their feet into the dirt and slid back against the bluster of the giant man. Ulfrik did not bother to draw his sword, but continued to tease.

"So you have taken the boy for a lover! No wonder you hide in the woods with him. Do you share him with the others?"

The man's unimaginative cursing streamed past Ulfrik. Beyond enjoying a simple teasing, he wanted to understand how much control Throst exerted over his men. Judging from the time it took to calm the giant and the reluctance of the other two to assist, Ulfrik surmised Throst's hold tenuous at best. He kept that thought for possible use against him.

After settling his henchmen, Throst whirled on Ulfrik. "Your wit is a dull as your vigilance. Your son's life is in my hands, or don't you understand?"

Ulfrik stared hard at Throst before answering. "I understand."

"Then listen well and I'll return your son. I'll take sixty pounds of silver in exchange for Hakon's life."

Even Throst's henchmen flinched at the outlandish demand. Ulfrik marshaled his expression but felt the burn of anger from the pit of his gut to the back of his throat.

"You don't even know how much silver that is, do you, boy?" Ulfrik spit on the ground before Throst's feet.

"It's what Odo paid Sigfrid to leave Paris, so it sounds like a good sum to me," Throst said, smiling.

"Odo is king of the Western Franks and has the wealth of Frankia at hand, and he was ransoming his whole city to Sigfrid, not one boy."

"I don't care how much it is, but I've just named the ransom for your son. If you can't pay, I'm certainly not planning to feed your brat all winter." Throst's smile faded and he folded his arms. "So your son's life has a price higher than it's worth to you? I'd not have guessed that from the mighty and just Lord Ulfrik of Ravndal."

"I don't have such riches," Ulfrik said through gritted teeth. In truth he could pay the ransom. However, now that he stood before Throst and saw the foolish boy and his equally stupid friends, he no longer believed Hakon was in serious danger. Throst wanted to extract revenge along with as much ransom as he could obtain. Killing Hakon would gain him nothing and end his life; for Ulfrik would have him cut down the moment he appeared from hiding. So in the end, Throst would accept whatever Ulfrik chose to give him and then flee.

"Such a shame that your son will die today, since you are not as wealthy as everyone believes." Throst shrugged as if he had just lost a friendly debate. "I suppose I'll just go back and strangle the little goat fucker until his eyes pop out. I'll leave his body someplace you can find it, like hanging from a tree or impaled on a spear."

Ulfrik had Throst by the throat before anyone could react. He crushed down on his neck as he pulled him closer. "Still that tongue or I'll string you up beside your father's rotten corpse."

The three men started forward but halted; Ulfrik did not need to see his archers to know their arrows aimed at the three.

"Your boy is dead," Throst managed to gasp as he squirmed help-lessly in Ulfrik's grip. His haughty face now twisted in a deep red mask of desperation.

"Ten pounds of silver for the return of my son; that's more than enough for you and your mangy friends." Ulfrik shook Throst to emphasize his words. "And not one scratch or bruise upon him. If you keep those terms, I'll allow a half day's start to flee before I come for you. If Hakon is harmed or you kill him, you'd do well to hang your-self before I find you."

He cast aside Throst as if discarding a small fish back to its lake. Shaking and choking, Throst glanced at his men who now regarded him with a skeptical eye. Ulfrik smiled, knowing he had saved his son. He had shaken Throst's men, who now would want to get their silver and run rather than follow a fool of boy who would lead them to death.

"You underestimate me," Throst managed to wheeze, his face still red. "You'll soon learn who the real fool is."

"Tomorrow at dawn, I will bring your silver," Ulfrik said, unheeding of the empty threats. "Return my son and treat him well in the meantime. Then be ready to flee, for I will have your skull for a drinking mug not long after you take your silver."

He turned without care for Throst's reply and stalked back up the hill toward the archers. They kept arrows knocked as he strode across the yellow grass. Like his father, Throst could not resist a final word. He shouted from a safe distance, "Your pain is only just beginning. You will learn, Ulfrik, and I will be the one to teach you."

20

At dawn of the following day, Ulfrik arrived at the base of the hill bearing ten pounds of silver in a deerskin sack. Pink light seeped into the clouds, and the frosted grass crunched beneath his feet. Arrayed behind him were thirty hand-picked men, along with his closest family. Even Snorri fought the pain in his leg to witness Hakon's ransom. Ulfrik's breath curled into the air before his face, and he drew his cloak tighter around his neck.

Throst was not present, only a wiry Frank whose dark-circled eyes darted warily among the converging bulk of armed men. He huddled beneath a gray wool cloak too clean and fresh to be his own. His toes poked from holes in his boots and his pants had patches over patches.

Ulfrik's lip curled and his eyes drew to slits. "My son?"

"The place for the exchange has changed," the man said in heavily accented Norse. "I will lead you to it now."

His sword hummed as Ulfrik tore it from its sheath and pressed the point on the unarmed man's chest. "If it's a trap, you die; you know this, of course."

The lanky-haired Frank paled and flinched, but nodded slowly before turning to lead them to the north. Ulfrik kept him close and all thirty men followed with weapons drawn and eyes searching every direction for signs of a trap. Runa walked close behind, carrying Aren who fussed and complained about the cold wind. "Where's he taking us?" she asked as she caught up to him.

"Unless we're going to march half a day, he's not taking us farther than the edge of the woods or more likely one of the wider streams. He probably thinks a stream will delay our capturing him after he releases Hakon."

"Will it?" Runa asked.

He did not answer but began to consider the point of the relocation, which was obviously to shift advantage to Throst. Unless Throst had raised an army in the short time he had been gone, Ulfrik could not understand what threat he presented. As they traveled, Ulfrik tried to extract information from their guide, who refused to say more than he already had.

They turned west into hilly land that had long been cleared and now sprouted stumps and rocks in equal measure and the occasional crooked tree. The ground here was terrible for fighting, and Ulfrik had not considered it until their guide led them into a shallow valley between the hills. A smile came to his face as he guessed Throst's plan.

"So he thinks to use the land against us," he announced to the guide. "I'd already promised him half a day to flee before I pursued him. He doubts my word?"

The Frank stopped and regarded him with the wide eyes of a man who feared the next moment. Others noticed and swords hissed as the hirdmen unsheathed them. "Lord Ulfrik is to hang the sack on the lowest branch of that tree." He pointed to the lone beech tree that crowned a low hill, its sparse golden foliage clinging to its branches in the final days of autumn. "When Throst sees it, he will release your son."

"I don't like this," Snorri muttered beside Ulfrik. "What's this boy's game?"

"He wants to make a target of me for his hidden archers. I'd make a fine target against the morning sun, wouldn't you think?"

Snorri chuckled and Ulfrik raised the sack of silver to their guide. "You will fix it on the branch, and ten archers will have their arrows at your back the long walk up that hill. If you even stumble, I'll have you killed. String up my son's ransom and return directly to me, or I'll also have you killed. Do you understand?"

The Frank's mouth moved but no words formed. Ulfrik shoved the sack into the man's chest, knocking him back. He pressed it against him until the Frank folded it into his arms and started for the tree. Archers stepped to the fore and strung their bows. As soon as he departed, Ulfrik ordered ten men to follow close. "Keep in striking distance of the silver, in case Throst is stupid enough to try to grab the sack and run."

"He carries that sack as if it weighed a hundred pounds," said Toki, who stood with Snorri and Einar.

"It's because he sees his death coming," Ulfrik said, watching the Frank trudge uphill. "Throst sent him to die, either at my hands or his. To what end, we shall see."

They waited silently as the Frank wormed his way up the tree and struggled to balance the silver on the branch. The weight of it made for ungainly work and he nearly fell from the branch, but soon he had it secured and began trotting back down the hill, passing the group of hirdmen positioned beneath the crest of the hill.

A horn sounded from the opposite hill, and Ulfrik turned to see six ragged shapes emerge on the crest. They were black shadows against the sky. The giant among them identified them as Throst's group. Two more men crested the hill and held a struggling boy between them.

Throst's bright voice carried well across the distance. "You have my silver, Ulfrik?"

He pointed with his sword at the tree. Runa drew a sharp breath and grabbed his arm as Hakon struggled between his captors. Throst's laughter carried even across the distance. "I'm going to trust your word on this, Ulfrik. How do I know it's not a bag of rocks?"

"If you didn't have me hang it on a tree you could've seen it first, you fool," Ulfrik shouted back. "Of course I honor my word. Now bring me my son!"

More laughter echoed off the hills and Ulfrik felt his face grow hot. Runa's arm tightened around his as she strained to see Hakon, who continued to struggle. The Frank guide returned as instructed and stared at him for direction, but remained ignored.

"Stand down your men and lower your bows. Back them down hill and I'll send Hakon to you." Hakon's shadowed form grew still and Throst's shadow melded with it as he spoke to him.

Ulfrik waved down his archers and his men sidled down the hill until they were at the base, only then did Throst guide Hakon forward.

"You are an honorable man, Ulfrik. So here's your son." Throst punctuated his shouted words by shoving Hakon forward. His son's small body stumbled and he struggled to get to his feet, as his hands remained bound behind his back. "Remember your promise to give me a lead in eluding you."

The next instant, the rope snapped and the sack of silver plummeted to the ground where the small shadow of a man sprung up to catch it. Ulfrik wanted to order his men to capture Throst's henchman, but Hakon had not cleared Throst's reach.

Now Hakon staggered into the light, and Ulfrik noted a cloth sack was tied over his head. He did not seem to know which way to go to escape Throst. Ulfrik and his men began calling his name, even the Frankish guide began to yell. Hakon faced the noise and began to charge forward.

"That's not my son," Runa said softly. Ulfrik turned to her, saw the frown on her face and her shaking head. "That's not Hakon."

"How can you tell from here?" But Ulfrik watched the boy's awkward gait and constant stumbling and suddenly shared his wife's suspicion. He broke from her grip and ran toward the boy. He did not understand why he had delayed, and cursed himself for letting Throst lull him into inaction.

Tripping and stumbling over rocks and dead branches, he met Hakon in the middle of the shallow valley. He was already shaking his head, hands trembling in frustration and rage when he unbound the sack from the boy's head and tore it away.

A boy of Hakon's age stared through swollen and blackened eyes at him. His mouth was crusted with dried blood and his lips were split. Ulfrik shoved the boy aside, and lurched forward. "After Throst! Move!"

Throst had chosen the ground with care and Ulfrik and his men struggled to mount the hills and once over the crest there was only a short sprint to the forest and eventually the Frankish border. Winded, he paused to study the tracks Throst had left, which peeled down the hill and would doubtlessly lead to the forest and then fade into the underbrush.

Within moments, others concluded the same and slowed their pursuit, gathering on Ulfrik who stood watching the forest. Throst could be tracked, but it would have to be a patient thing and not a rushed pursuit. Deadfalls and traps could await the unwary, and such a plan did not seem beyond Throst's cunning. He had already twice demonstrated the depth of his plotting. At the least, he had likely fled toward his hiding place and so gave Ulfrik a direction for this search.

The boy who had posed as Hakon now clasped to the Frankish guide's side, and the two were herded before Ulfrik. The man's face was streaked with tears as he enfolded the boy in his thin, dirty arms. Ulfrik's gaze darted between them, and he immediately understood the deceit.

"He is your son, not mine."

"Yes, Lord," the man said, his voice quivering with emotion. "He snatched us from our farm. My wife and daughters ..." his voice trailed off and the man looked away as he searched for words.

"Killed?" Ulfrik offered, and the man shook his head. "Can you return to them?"

"Yes, but I don't know where we are. We are Franks from over the border. Look what he did to my son!" The man pressed open the boy's mouth, and Ulfrik saw the black stub of a tongue along with several broken teeth.

"So he can't tell us where Throst hides. And what of you? If you want revenge, tell me where Throst is."

The man babbled about how both had their heads covered and were only snatched a few days ago. "And I never heard another boy's voice the whole time."

"You and your son may recover in our home, and you will be free to return to your family." He dismissed them and met Runa's hard, worried stare. She looked at him as if Hakon had been found dead, and he drew her close and stroked her hair. She remained frozen and stiff, and like her, Ulfrik worried for the life of their son.

21

Gunnar placed his feet on the bench and stripped away his boots. Cool air flowed over the red and hot flesh, and he wiggled his toes enjoying the refreshing cold. Ravndal's hall stood emptied of all but a few men and now in the afternoon only servants remained to tend to their chores. Gunnar sat by the entrance, eschewing the high table where his mother lingered with Uncle Toki's and Einar's daughters, telling them of the fruitless search for Hakon. Each girl held their pale hands either over their mouth or their chest as they listened. Gunnar focused on rubbing his feet, sore and bruised from kicking through rough forest terrain. He did not want to see any more sad faces or hear any more speculation on Hakon's fate. It hurt too much to think upon it.

The sweet scent of fresh wood on the hearth fire reminded him of how Hakon enjoyed stoking the flames and throwing dried twigs into it. Every young boy was fascinated with fire, and his brother was no exception. Gunnar sat back on the bench and sighed. He had vowed not to dwell on his brother's memory every moment, but he found it impossible to prevent. This debacle was his doing, and though no one blamed him, he knew it was so. His father, whenever he could spare a glance for him, accused Gunnar with his eyes. His father's every word, no matter how trivial, held an icy accusation within it. Nothing had to be spoken for Gunnar to clearly hear what should have been said aloud: "Your brother was in your care and you failed in your duty. Now look at what has become of him."

His mother's update with the girls ended in a flurry of waving hands and sighs, and he was certain his cousins glanced his way. Runa left Aren with them and retired to her room, and his brother immediately peeled off to sit alone and stare at Gunnar across the hall. He was the strangest child Gunnar knew. His eyes were intelligent but cold; he too often guessed a man's thoughts; and did not play with anyone. In fact, he did not seem capable of playing but only of hitting and biting, and more recently manipulating. Were he not a jarl's son, Gunnar figured Aren would be mercilessly teased. Knowing some of the children of this hall, Gunnar expected Aren would nevertheless be tested in secret. Yet another duty to protect that fell on Gunnar's shoulders. He returned to massaging his feet, shaking his head at the thought.

"So it is true. You've returned before the others." The bright and soothing voice of his love, Astra, came from over his shoulder.

He whirled on the bench to face her standing in the hall door with a basket of fresh leeks laced over her arm. Her smile was clear and white, her face wide and pale and without a blemish. She filled him with immediate joy merely standing before him.

"It's more like dismissed from my father's presence," he said. "My mother could not take searching any longer, and so Father told me to see her home."

"Now that doesn't sound like a dismissal," Astra countered as she entered the hall, closing the door behind her. The backlight had bleached Gunnar's vision a moment, but now he could see her full beauty. She was every bit the traditional Norse woman despite being half-Frankish. She was tall with wide hips but a tapered waist. She wore a traditional head covering that could not diminish the brightness of her golden hair. She swept into the room and laid her basket aside as she sat upon the bench beside him. What Gunnar appreciated most was the delicacy of her movements, which he found endlessly fascinating and delightful. He could not imagine a more beautiful woman than Astra, and now she sat beside him on the bench.

"There is a fortress full of hirdmen to escort her, but why me? All the men continue the search, but I am sent away. Ah, but there's the problem." Astra raised a brow at the bait Gunnar threw out, and he responded with ready anger in his voice. "My father says I'm not man."

Astra pursed her lips and slid closer to place her warm hand upon his knee. She rubbed it gently, and smiled coyly at him. "Your father is wrong."

Her hand lingered enough to pass beyond simple comfort, and she turned her head away at Gunnar's smile. His reaction was immediate and strong, and his breath grew hot. He reached to touch her hand, but she suddenly recoiled with a giggle. The silvery chime of her voice filled him with an icy tingle of delight. Her eyes sparkled with promise, but despite many close moments, she had not as yet delivered herself to Gunnar. Despite the pain of forbearance, he enjoyed this. Being the jarl's eldest son had brought many girls willing to lay with him in secret, but none of them had held his attention. Only Astra, ever elusive and more beautiful with each day, commanded his desire.

They fell silent and in that moment, Gunnar recognized the shamefulness of his thoughts. His brother was a captive and likely beaten or worse, and he was dreaming of Astra. His heart was full of impulses that shamed him and made him wonder if his father was right about him after all.

"I'm sorry, that was ill-timed," Astra said, apparently recognizing Gunnar's thoughts. She pulled herself straighter on the bench and smoothed her apron. "Tell me of Hakon's plight. Does your father know where Throst is?"

Her voice was earnest, almost intense. Gunnar appreciated the way she shared his worries, another trait lacking in all the other girls he had known. Putting his boots back on, he described all the events leading up to when Throst escaped. She listened with rapt attention, her eyes searching him constantly as if trying to see what he had seen.

"It was a cunning plan to split our attention between the ransom and the boy he posed as Hakon," Gunnar said. "Even my father had to admit he could not decide where to commit the chase, and in truth he wasn't even certain the man who spoke was Throst. The trail they left led to the forest, but once inside it was as if they disappeared. Maybe Throst has a bargain with the elves of the forest, or has some magic to cover his escape."

Astra laughed aloud, but quickly silenced when Gunnar frowned at her. "Sorry, that sounds incredible to me."

"Well, plenty of men believed it possible," Gunnar said, feeling slighted at the laughter. "But I suppose he probably used the streams to travel without leaving a trace. He just disappeared so quickly. We were on his trail as soon as the ruse was revealed. How else could he have done it?"

Astra shrugged. "So what now? Will your father look beneath every stone in Frankia? The world is wide, and Throst can be anywhere. What's his plan?"

"To search until there is no place left to look. The world is wide, but even Throst cannot travel the whole of it in a few days. He must be close, and so will soon be found out."

"But what if he is not?" Astra persisted.

"Then my father will return to Ravndal, but he will not stop searching. This is family, Astra. We will bring Hakon back and take revenge for the evil done to us."

"And how will that happen if Throst can't be found?"

Gunnar drew breath to answer, but suddenly Astra yelped in shock.

Aren had appeared, seemingly from nothing, between them on the opposite side of the table. Astra had not seen his approach and when he stood she startled. Gunnar laughed. "Calm yourself, it is only my brother."

Astra leaned away with her hands on her chest and a hateful scowl on her face, staring at Aren who returned a blank stare of his own. The two faced each other like stray cats in a territorial fight and neither moved nor changed expression. Finally Gunnar waved at his brother. "What are you doing here? We're talking, or can't you see. Go play and leave us alone."

If he had been a cat, Aren would have swished his tail with disdain, but being only a child he still managed to glare a chill and silent warning before climbing off the bench and wandering away. Astra remained in her repulsed state after he left, as if Aren's stare had frozen her. Finally she relented, smoothing out her apron as she returned to normal.

"A strange child, would that he'd been taken too."

The insult rankled Gunnar, the first time he had ever felt anything negative toward Astra. "Don't repeat such evil words. He is different, I'll say, but he is my brother."

For an instant Astra's eyes flashed with what Gunnar thought to be anger. His stomach turned cold at the realization, but she shifted back to a smile so quickly he thought himself mistaken.

"I'm sorry, he surprised me, and his stare is unsettling. You must know that." Gunnar nodded and Astra continued, her smile softening her face. "You should do something to find Throst. Your father squanders your talents by sending you away."

"I don't know what that would be," Gunnar said, shifting so that he leaned on both knees. "I have already angered him enough, and don't dare press him."

Astra again slid closer, leaning in as if whispering a secret. "But you must do it for yourself, yes? If your father returns without your brother, then it means he needs help. Your help. Think on it for now, and I know in time you will know what to do."

She stood and gathered her basket of leeks, brushing Gunnar's cheek with her hand as she did. The warm touch stirred his passion again, but she had already stepped an arm's length away.

"I will think upon it, but I'm sure my father will not return in defeat."

Astra gave a small smile, and joined the other women at the hearth. Gunnar watched her at work, admiring her gentle sway and bend, but soon his gaze slipped past her to Aren. He sat at the high table, alone and solemn as if he were a jarl himself. His expression was stern, and he slowly shook his head at Gunnar before he slipped from his bench and toddled off for his mother's room.

22

———————

"I'd be happier with a fire than silver. Think I've caught my death of a cold in this cave, you know."

Throst's mother stared into the handful of hack silver Throst held out to her. Though she complained, she still picked the largest bits from his hand all the while sniffing and snorting. His sister stood on tiptoes to see over their mother's shoulder, rapping her side while insisting on her share.

"Give it one more day before we light a fire," Throst said, waiting until his mother had taken her part of the ransom. "Or your suffering will have been for nothing if Ulfrik sees the smoke and finds us."

Wan light filtered into the cave mouth, which had to fight hanging roots and moss to illuminate the entrance. Water dripped over the narrow opening, mixing with the mud to fill the cave with a heavy earthen odor, remnants of the morning rain that Throst hoped further confounded Ulfrik's search.

"Cold food and cold mud ain't no good for an old woman," his mother continued, wrapping her drab cloak tighter while shooing her daughter. "All my joints ache and my teeth chatter. You're trying to kill me, so you can keep all the silver yourself. Don't think I can't see your plans, because no one knows you better. I bore you in the coldest winter and nursed you only to be treated like this. Well, you owe me for saving you; your father would've thrown you out with the scraps of his dinner. No forgetting, now."

"No forgetting," Throst repeated as he stashed the remainder of the silver into a leather sack. He palmed a piece for his sister, Tora, and slipped it to her while his mother blew the snot from her nose onto the ground. Tora's face widened in a surprised smile, and Throst placed a finger to his lips gesturing that she should keep it secret. The silver bit disappeared beneath her cloak and her smile vanished as quickly.

"I'm going to die today," his mother stated. Throst had no fear for his mother, and simply patted her shoulder before leaving her to continue complaining to Tora.

He picked his way over the rough cave floor, squeezed between a tight crack, then popped into the main cavern where all his men huddled in darkness. Only a crack in the cave roof allowed the faintest illumination to brush a milky outline over them. The largest man, Dan, stood as he entered while the others huddled miserably on the cold floor.

"Is it safe to move on now?" Dan asked, his gruff voice made fuller with the echo of the cave.

"I want to wait another day before we return home," Throst said as he joined the circle of men. "Let Ulfrik find it empty and so discount it in the future."

"Look, I'm as happy as anyone to get the ransom for Ulfrik's brat, but it's cold and wet and I'm living worse than a rat in this cave." Olaf, who had been eager to leave Ravndal and join him, now led the complaints for Throst's men.

"The caves were an incredible idea, and have saved our lives," Throst countered. "Ulfrik must think we've disappeared from the face of the world."

Several men chuckled, but Olaf's head dipped and he ran his fingers through his hair. No matter what he or the others thought of living in a cave, it was key to the entire plan. No one knew of these small caves but for one of his own men, a local Frank who had braved exploring them in his childhood. It was no small feat, for even now grown men of his gang hesitated to enter, fearing dwarfs or worse living in the darkness. It was unnatural to live beneath the ground, and so it was yet another reason these caves made a perfect place hide from Ulfrik.

"All the same, we can't remain here forever," Dan said.

"Clear out your ears, you oaf. I never said we'd stay here forever. Odin's balls, did you think snatching Ulfrik's son and robbing him of his silver would be a simple thing? You expected to go home like returning from a day of hunting? Ulfrik has twenty men for each of us at his command, so do some thinking on that. We can't hit him in the face and expect nothing to follow."

Throst surveyed the shadowy forms of his men and none met his eyes. Dan, chastened, settled back to the ground and lowered his head. Throst let his words settle on them, then he shifted his sight to the back of the cavern.

"And speaking of the brat, is he still alive?"

"Sure is," answered one of the men. "The shit-licker bit my hand when I took off the gag to give him some water. See if he'll get any more from me."

Muted laughter spread among the men, and Throst smiled as he picked his way to where Hakon lay bound. The small form of the boy was a gray lump in the darkness curled into a crack in the wall. A torn and muddy cloak covered him against the damp. Throst noticed glints of light reflecting at him, Hakon's wide eyes brimming with tears and studying him.

"I'm going to remove your gag, and you'll not scream or bite or I'll crack your head with a rock. Do you understand?"

The small head nodded, and Throst untied the saliva soaked rag that served as his gag. Hakon immediately spit on him, a thin glob landing on his hand.

Throst laughed, "Well, I didn't tell you not to spit. I see I'm going to have to be clearer."

His backhand struck Hakon's cheek with a crack, snapping his head to the side and collapsing him against the cave wall. He did not cry out or scream, but took the blow in silence, which Throst admired. It seemed Ulfrik at least raised one strong boy, not that it mattered now.

"You should know I'm holding back so you won't be too damaged for what I intend. But if you tempt me, little man, I will pop out your eyeballs with my own thumbs. Do you want me to do that?"

Throst smiled and in the darkness he barely discerned Hakon's terrified face staring back at him in silence. Throst bowed his head as if suffering, entwining his fingers behind his neck. "When I ask a question, you answer me. If you don't then I get madder and madder until the jelly of your eyeballs are smeared all over my thumbs. So, do you want me to pop your eyes?"

"No," Hakon said quickly, backing farther into the cleft in the wall. "But Odin protects me, and you won't hurt me."

Throst unfolded his hands and looked up in surprise. A few of the men behind him hissed through their teeth. "Why do you think Odin protects you? Did I hit your head so hard you've gone mad?"

"Odin has seen me and smiled upon me. He has other plans for me."

A few men laughed and others grumbled, but Throst faced Hakon with his mouth open and no words to meet such a ridiculous statement. Hakon sat up straighter, as if he had won a contest. In a way he had, for Throst could only laugh and not answer. The gods were capricious and gave their favor where they pleased. If Odin had shown himself to the boy, it made no sense to Throst's mortal mind. Rather than hear any more, he replaced Hakon's gag.

Returning to the circle of men idling in the darkness, he sat beside Dan. He felt his stomach rumble and gestured that Dan break out the dried fish and bread for a meal. Food had become the highlight of their days, with nothing more to do than hide in the caves and allow enough time to pass before exiting. Now as the dried fish made the rounds, spirits lifted and more animated talk began.

Once all were tearing into their shares, Olaf renewed his complaints. "So, now that you've tricked Ulfrik once, how do you plan to trick him again? We've still got his kid, and you've got plans for him. Suppose you tell us what those are."

"In time," Throst said. "We have to pass this trial first, and then begin the next part of my plan."

Olaf snickered, then tore at his strip of fish with his yellow teeth. "You don't respect us enough to tell us the next part? Who do you think you are, keeping us holed up in a cave with nothing more than a promise of a better future."

"Watch your tongue," Dan growled. "Show respect to your leader."

Warm satisfaction spread in Throst's chest, for Dan had become Throst's enforcer. The death of Pepin had been such a release for the giant man, who apparently had grown to detest his former boss, that he eagerly transferred his allegiance to Throst. Now anyone who rivaled Throst would have to deal with Dan's mighty strength as well.

"It's fine, Dan," Throst said with false magnanimity. "Olaf has a fair point."

He scanned the hard faces in the dim light, each one craggy and scarred from a hard life of fighting. That he commanded their loyalty amazed Throst, and in such a moment as this, with every eye searching him for leadership, he felt as strong as a giant. Though he only had eight men in his gang, it was the seed of greatness. With the right reputation and a solid cache of wealth, he would attract more followers and forge himself a destiny.

"I still have designs on his eldest son, Gunnar, and he is still in reach, even if Ulfrik would believe otherwise."

Heads turned to face each other, but Olaf was the fastest to ask the questions. "Even I believe otherwise. I was your man inside, and if you think the others left behind will risk so much for you, you're a fool. Some may not like Ulfrik's ways, but I don't think they'll like yours better."

"Thinking was not what I wanted from you when I accepted your oath," Throst said, and a few of the quicker-witted men laughed. "Just know that Gunnar's freedom is at my pleasure, and I can pluck him from Ravndal at any time."

The boast drew laughter from all but Dan, who glared at the

others. "He didn't let us down so far, did he? If he says he can nab Gunnar, then he can."

"I can," Throst agreed. "After one more day hiding, we will return to our base. And then, I want to increase the pressure on Ulfrik. Once we have returned, I will contact Clovis who will pay in more than gold to get his hands upon Gunnar." He clapped and laughed at the idea. "Ulfrik will not know which way to turn."

23

Every sinew in Runa's body ached, and her stomach burned with worry. Her mind was a furor of thoughts and images, none of them good. She sat on the edge of her bed, no longer willing to chase sleep like it was a rabbit fleeing down a hole, and held her head in both hands. The change of clothes refreshed her and the cold air on her throbbing feet felt good. The cool and quiet darkness of her private room was soothing. But none of these comforts made any difference to her.

Having returned to Ravndal ostensibly to rest, she considered it defeat. Time had passed in a blur, and combing the lands for signs of Hakon had lasted long enough to spend all her strength. Ulfrik had finally insisted she would better serve them at the hall, in case news should come while they were gone. At the time it made sense to her addled mind, but now she realized he wanted her out of the way and that she needed the break. Needed or not, waiting in the hall for something to happen would never satisfy her. Regret for having returned now filled her heart.

Hakon remained the prisoner of a madman and she would not rest until he was freed. She wished Throst had hanged alongside his father. Snorri had warned them that mercy had a way of twisting back on a man. Of course, no one could have guessed this. She massaged her temples, and tried to stop thinking about something that could not change. Throst lived and now took revenge upon them.

Slipping on her shoes, she stood from the bed and adjusted her skirt. Her long knife was still strapped tight against her thigh, and she snorted in disgust at it. "What good did this do me? My son was still snatched from home, weapon or no."

After roughly combing her hair, she exited to the main hall where a quiet darkness enveloped the empty spaces. With no large meal to prepare, the hall sat emptied of all but the servants who slept within it. Two thin Frankish girls lay on the floor by the gently glowing hearth, the embers pulsing a low heat. Runa felt her stomach match the rhythm and burn of the hearth fire and she placed her hand over her belly. The two girls stood as she entered, but she waved them away. Einar's wife and daughters sat opposite of the low hearth, bundling wool that had been spun earlier in the day.

"Where's Aren and Gunnar?" she asked. Her stomach burned hotter at their absence.

"Aren is asleep under the table," said the oldest girl, Matilda, who pointed to a dark lump bundled into a brown wool cloak.

"And Gunnar went to watch the walls," Einar's wife, Bera, said as she piled her bundle of spun wool into a basket. "Though he should return soon with sunset near."

Runa sat down, as relieved as if she they had dispelled bad news. She rubbed her face, knowing full well she could not worry at every absence of her children but was unable to stop. Bera set aside her work and joined Runa on the bench, taking Runa's hand into her own.

"I'm certain Hakon will be found. I can't imagine your suffering and worry. Matilda is only a few years younger than him, and the thought of one so young ..." Bera's voice trailed off as she blushed at her artless words. Runa could not help a small laugh at Bera's humiliated expression. She was a good woman but naive in her youth. She and Einar made a good pair, for both shared a simple and honest personality and worked hard for what they desired.

"No need to speak of it," Runa said, and squeezed Bera's hand. "I know your intent, and I am glad for it. It will be a happy day when Hakon returns home, and I too believe that day will be soon. The men are searching every corner of the forest and watching the trails. Throst will be caught and my son freed."

"Well then, that is good," Bera said with a smile, and again Runa laughed. It was the first time she had smiled since Hakon had disappeared, and it felt strange on her face. Still, even if short-lived, the smile lifted her mood.

Then the hall doors opened, the orange light of the late hour flooding around the slim figure of a platinum-haired woman. Runa recognized Halla immediately and her heart fell and the burn on her guts redoubled.

She swept inside, head swiveling to take in the hall, and she paused inside the door until she fixed on Runa. She flitted across the room toward her, and Runa stood. Bera also stood, and stepped away as Halla neared, excusing herself with a murmured apology. She passed Halla, who did not spare her a glance, and gathered her basket and daughters to prepare to leave.

"My dear sister, it's true that you've returned," Halla said with a false breathlessness that instantly set Runa's teeth clenching. "Why did you not call for me after you arrived?"

"Why disturb your rest?" Runa said, standing stiffer and feeling her hands tremble. She had avoided Halla since her arrival, and quartering her and Toki in another hall had made it easier, but she knew eventually they would have to interact. She just did not want it to be this moment.

"And how can I rest knowing my nephew is in the grip of a murderous wolf? When I close my eyes, I can only see poor Hakon suffering horrible tortures. No, you should've summoned me immediately."

Runa stared hard at her. Halla's pale eyes and snub nose reminded Runa of her father, and the same wicked glint as her father flashed in them when she described her fears for Hakon. Whatever appeal she held in her youth, age had stolen from her. The frown she always carried had written itself into her flesh, so that even the false smile she now wore appeared mean and angry. Her lustrous hair, once her pride, was now dull and thin. Halla was an evil witch, and Runa had always known this. What her brother saw in her and why he kept her all these years was a mystery and a curse for Runa.

"And so you have come and expressed your worry," Runa said. "Now I am tired and want to rest. Don't let me keep you."

"Never say it. I will be at your side during this horrible time. I will pray to Jesus Christ that Hakon is safely returned home and is spared agonizing torture, or worse yet, death. How trying it must be for you to know your son is being torn apart and you are powerless to act. I must remain with you!"

Runa's glare froze the room, and her vision fogged around Halla's face. She was actually smiling as she dug at Runa with her unconcealed malice. Through the haze, Runa saw Bera and her daughters fleeing the hall and the serving girls fading into the shadowed corners. She felt her eye twitching and her hand tingling to find the hilt of her knife.

"You little witch," Runa hissed. "You take joy in my son's terror?"

Halla's ice-clear eyes went wide with mock consternation. "How could you say that? I am your brother's wife, and the pain of his family is my own as well. I just can't stop seeing poor Hakon with his eyes torn out or his tongue cut from his head, or even worse."

"Silence, bitch!" Runa's hand drew back but stopped as Halla defied her with a honey-sweet smile. "Whatever you think I won't do, think on it again. You are testing me to my limit."

"Oh, so now it's Runa the Bloody once more?" Halla placed her blue-veined hands over her chest. "She solves all her worries with the stroke of her sword. Well, here's something she can't cut to bits and make go away. Her son is lost, no doubt due to her own carelessness, and her sword has no one to strike."

"Your head would be a fine place to strike," Runa hissed and reached down for her blade, but again stopped.

"Try it," she said with a smile. "Here's my head, ripe to be split. But you won't, will you? We are family, after all, and your brother loves me above all others."

"And for what I shall never know. You are worm-shit at the bottom of the world. You are a cockroach to be crushed underfoot. You are a pig-nosed, lying, evil-minded whore!" Runa's shouts echoed through the hall, and she recoiled at her unbridled anger. Her head was hot and unwanted tears puddled in her eyes. Her heart pounded as if she had run up a mountainside.

Halla moved closer, and her voice was low and full of threat. "You believe I wanted to come here? I'd sooner slice open my own belly than live within a thousand leagues of you. But your brother has suffered from the neglect of your arrogant, stupid husband and he could not be happy apart from this awful place. So I am here to please Toki, and he is glad for it. Slander me with whatever filthy names you can imagine, but I am a better woman than you. What do you bring to your husband but your complaints and demands, your temper and your fixation with swords? You weren't even faithful to him, and then you force him to father another man's bastard."

The slap crashed hard into Halla's face and staggered her. Runa's hand stung but the release of anger compensated. "I'll have your tongue for that. Never repeat such trash."

Holding her face, Halla straightened herself and brushed her hair aside. "Like you did when you murdered my mother?"

"Your mother was an oath-breaker who sent men to rape and murder me. Cutting out her tongue was mercy."

"No, you murdered her. That cut was ill done and her wounded tongue never recovered. She suffered for a year before dying from it, all while you rolled in bed with your young lover."

"I warned you," Runa said, raising her hand again, but Halla laughed. It was a horrible, breathless sound more akin to choking than laughter.

"I am not afraid of you any longer," she said. "Jesus Christ has blessed me and I fear nothing while I stand in His light."

"I see no light around you. Now be gone from my hall, and do not return. You can smirk all you want, but I will soon grant your wish to send you far from here. At such a time like this, all you can offer is grief. You are not welcomed here, and will not be permitted to stay."

"Your husband makes those decisions, and he has chosen to have Toki at his side. I think I may yet be here a while. So, as I said, dear sister, I will pray that Hakon does not have his balls sawed off and stuffed into his little mouth while he is abused by the captor you carelessly let into your so-called stronghold. You will need my prayers, since your own efforts as a mother are complete failures."

"Get out," Runa growled and pointed at the doors. Tears streamed down her cheeks and she no longer cared.

Halla inclined her head, her cheek bright red where Runa had slapped it. She glided halfway across the hall, then turned back to offer one last jab. "His face is ruined now, a horrible mess. Do you still want to lie with him, or was his prick destroyed in the fire too?"

Runa shrieked and leapt for Halla, but she sprang like a deer and bounded for the exit, laughing as she escaped. Runa stumbled forward, tears and dirt smearing her face, and bellowed at the doors as they slammed closed.

24

Wet, cold, and out of food, Ulfrik and his hirdmen stood bedraggled and listless in the center of the destroyed Frankish hamlet. The sky was leaden gray, boiling with clouds that promised to renew the rain that had blanketed them during the night and the morning of the search. Groups of hunched, dark men made quick searches of the few buildings that had not collapsed into piles of rotting wood and thatch. Ulfrik stood at the center of the abandoned community, huddled in his cloak and frowning out at the work. Snorri leaned on a sturdy branch he had found to support him, and Ulfrik's peripheral sight caught him rubbing his leg and wincing. The damp weather aggravated his old wound. Even Ulfrik's old injuries hurt almost as bad as when they had been fresh.

Einar, who lead the search with Toki to aid him, emerged from the main hall and carried a bit of cloth with him. He held it up in the bland light as if it were something significant.

"Finally something," Ulfrik grumbled to himself, and started toward Einar. Snorri limped alongside him.

"Scraps and nothing more," Snorri said. "We can't even be sure Throst came this way."

Ulfrik had heard the same complaints from his men when they thought him asleep or out of earshot. He could not deny the truth of it. Throst's trail had long gone cold; in fact, it had disappeared almost immediately upon entering the forest. Toki suggested they had waded along one of several creeks, and it had made sense until no footprint or other sign of passage ever emerged along the length of any creek. Without a definite path to follow, he had nothing more than guesses to serve as his guide. There had been only so many places where Throst could have gone in such short time, but every one of them had yielded nothing. He began to despair, and left men behind to continue the search while he moved out toward ever less likely places. Now they were over the Frankish border, still not too far from Ravndal but farther than Throst should have been able to reach in the few days of searching. He had remembered this place from his early battles to secure these lands, and guessed it could hide Throst. He would soon find out.

"I found this," Einar said as he held out a scrap of green wool cloth. "It was on the floor, beneath a table."

Ulfrik took the cold cloth into his hand, rubbing it between his fingers. Others began to join, and Toki arrived along with Konal. Both of them leaned in, and Toki took the cloth from Ulfrik's grip.

"You think this might be from Hakon?" he asked as he examined the scrap.

"There is nothing about it that would tie it to any man. It is junk," Ulfrik said, looking skyward as a pinprick of cold rain hit his face.

"But it is fresh," Einar added. "And there is sturdy furniture in the buildings and straw on the floor."

"And the midden pits have seen recent use," Konal added.

Ulfrik regarded their hopeful faces, but beyond them the hirdmen slowed in their searches, breaking into small groups that drew their cowls against the cold and sat on the grass. They knew what Ulfrik believed.

"Anyone could be using this place, likely bandits shelter here."

"But they have gone, and nothing says anyone was here for several days, maybe as long as we've been searching for Throst." Einar took the cloth from Toki's hand and held it up. "Look at this; Hakon wore a green cloak."

"Boy, every other man here is wearing a green cloak," Snorri said, drawing gentle laughter from the cluster of onlookers. Einar's face turned red, but he smiled.

"We've come far," Ulfrik said, patting Einar's shoulder. "But at last I have to admit defeat. Someone has been here, but we cannot say who or when. We're now in Frankia, and have been away from Ravndal overlong. The men are tired and hungry, and we've got nothing left to seek. At this point, I feel foolish for having gone this far afield. Without a doubt, Throst is playing me for bigger gains. He wanted sixty pounds of silver, and he will contact me for it."

"How did he elude us?" Toki asked, shaking his head and kicking the soft earth. "We scoured that forest. It's as if he flew from the ground and left no trace."

Shoulders shrugged and heads shook. No one could understand it. Men feared the forest, particularly at night, where they heard the voices of elves and dwarfs mock them in the darkness. Some believed Throst had made a pact with the spirits of the forest to cover his escape. Even Ulfrik, normally at ease in the woodlands, felt a strange sensation of being watched while in those dark woods. Had it not been his own son in danger, he would have long abandoned the search. When it came time to send Gunnar and Runa back, he did not lack for volunteers to escort them.

"Perhaps we might shelter here ourselves," Ulfrik said, again glancing skyward. "If the hearth can be lit, we can dry out and rest before returning home."

"So you're done searching?" Snorri asked, his voice carrying an edge of accusation.

"Done searching with these men, who never expected to be in the field for days. But I will never stop searching. I will have every road and path watched; men will sit on every ridge and hill and look for movement. I will lead patrols. I will not stop, never fear. Sooner or later, Throst will show himself and I will be ready to pounce."

The men grumbled in satisfaction, and Einar dropped the scrap of green cloth and began to organize the men to make camp. Toki and Konal lingered on, and Konal picked up the scrap again.

"Do you see something we overlooked?" Snorri asked.

"No," Konal said, stashing the scrap into his belt. "This Throst is a tricky bastard. We'll have to match him for it, if we're to catch him."

Everyone agreed, and soon they all drifted to different tasks to prepare for their stay in the ruins. Ulfrik remained with Snorri, folding his arms and studying the sky. Throst had won this battle, but Ulfrik swore to himself that he would lose the war.

25

T hrost checked Hakon's bindings a second time, pulling the
rope tighter around the wrists until the boy squirmed with
pain. Then he loosened the rope enough so the hands
would not go dead. He patted Hakon's head. "Put on a smile, boy. I
might trade you off today to a man who lives in a stone castle.
Wouldn't you like that?"

The frown he received in answer reminded Throst so strongly of
Ulfrik that for a moment he could have believed it was him. He
slapped his captive's cheek with an open palm hard enough to get his
attention but not enough to damage. Still, the frown remained.

"You think Odin watches you? If he does, then he is pleased to let
you be my prisoner. Think on that, boy."

The hall was dark and the hearth fire guttered low with a rippling
orange light. The air was fiercely cold and damp, and defeated the
heat of the fire. His few men huddled around it. Dan's hulking girth
blocked the doorway and was a black blot against a gray light as he
watched for signs of approaching riders. Olaf, sitting with his back to
the hearth and braiding his beard, continued to check the doorway
every moment.

"Clovis will come, no worries there," Throst said as he joined the men by the hearth. The heat warmed his nose and cheeks, but his stomach was cold. Despite his words, he wondered if the mighty Clovis would merely send another in his place. It mattered greatly to his prestige that Clovis answer, as he had specifically demanded when he sent his messenger days ago. The men regarded him with flat expressions, neither believing nor denying. Eyes that glittered with reflected fire met his, and he nodded at each man.

He housed his mother and sister in the other functional structure, a smaller home with a hole in its roof but a decent hearth. Their time in the caves had made both sick with a phlegm-thick cough. In some ways, their illness had saved them, for Throst had noted the secret glances some of the men had given his sister. Olaf had been chief among those who stared after her. Fear of sickness kept Olaf and others at bay. After food, Throst decided, women would be a priority for his men, if only to safeguard his family. Perhaps his deal with Clovis could include female slaves as part of the bargain.

Throst half feared Ulfrik's return, but knew it would be unlikely. As he had predicted, Ulfrik had found their base but failed to realize its significance. They were all surprised to find he had camped in the hall, and had even left firewood behind when he departed. He would have to remember to thank him for saving the effort of gathering it.

Dan suddenly exited the hall, and Throst bounded after him with the others rousing from their place at the fire to follow. No one needed an alarm to hear the thunder of hooves beating the ground. Under the milky gray weave of clouds the flat light cast the riders in dead colors, greens, reds, and browns, all sapped of life. Five of them in scoured mail and the conical helmets of the Franks thundered into the center of the hamlet, pulling their horses to a halt. Throst saw his mother and sister peek out their door, and he waved them inside with an irritated snarl. No need for the Franks to know about them.

"We are here for Throst the Shield-Biter," proclaimed one of the riders in a thick, disdainful Frankish accent. "Show yourself."

"I am he." Throst had awarded himself the name Shield-Biter, thinking to add ferocity to his reputation. Men put much stock in such nicknames, and having a strong one was of utmost importance. "And are you Clovis?"

The riders laughed and Throst tried to keep the disappointment out of his expression, though the cold place in his stomach grew more chill. The tree branches behind the men waved in distracting arcs as the wind strengthened. Earth still wet from the rain seeped through his boots as he stood expectantly, but the men merely leaned on the necks of their horses. Throst regarded the animals with healthy respect, for they were thick-muscled and their coats lustrous. Apparently Ulfrik had not slain all of Clovis's horses as rumors told.

"Well, have you ridden this far to see how long we can stand idle in the mud? You've entered my land, and so you must identify yourself to me."

The riders hooted at Throst's claim, which he understood was overly grand and unenforceable. Still, men must hear words often before they believe them.

"You brigands are on Lord Clovis's territory," said the lead rider. "And by rights we should run through the lot of you and be done with it. But lucky for you, my lord was interested in your proposition. He has summoned you to his camp not far from here."

"I had asked Lord Clovis to join me at my hall." Throst relished the look of utter disgust his challenge elicited.

Spears lowered and Dan, who stood beside him, drew his sword. The others stepped back in fear. "You'll do more than bite your shield when I'm done with you, boy. I'll ram the whole thing down your throat before I poke a hole in your guts. Now you've been summoned to my lord's camp. Either come on your own accord, or come beaten and bloodied, but come."

Throst smiled as if being patient with a child. "I understand, and we will follow you to Clovis."

"Only you and Ulfrik's whelp," the lead man did not retract his spear and neither did Dan stand down. The rest of Throst's men hovered between flight and surrender. He would have to do better than this pathetic bunch if he were to one day be a great jarl.

"Very well, but I cannot be distracted with holding the boy

hostage while speaking with your lord. Allow me one man to lead Ulfrik's son to Clovis."

The riders conferred with each other, reverting to Frankish. While Throst hardly spoke the language, he understood it well enough to hear their confusion over Clovis's instructions. Throst needed someone to hold a knife to Hakon's throat, lest Clovis seize him outright. At last he heard the riders agree one more would not be a threat, and the lead rider announced as much to them in Norse.

"Olaf, bring the boy and be ready to cut his throat if Clovis thinks to take him. Dan, keep these men in line and protect the honor of my sister." Dan lowered his sword with a scowl at the riders, and Olaf hesitated as if to protest then went to fetch Hakon. Throst scanned the faces of the remaining six men. "Hold out a while longer, and you will enjoy greater riches. Don't flee now, when greater wealth is just in reach."

Once Olaf emerged with Hakon, arms tied at his lap and a rope fixed about his neck, the riders turned their horses and guided them a short distance to a clearing where several tents had been erected. Clovis's banner of a white swan on a black square flickered and cracked in the wind and the tents billowed with each gust. Clovis had suffered greatly after the arrival of Hrolf the Strider and Ulfrik, but he was still a mighty war leader. That he took caution in dealing with Throst filled him with pride.

"Surrender your weapons to us," the lead rider said, breaking his long silence. "Then go inside. He awaits you in his tent."

The small campsite held about twenty warriors, but only the five had horses. One horse was tethered to a tree near Clovis's tent, which must have been his personal mount. The men in the campsite did nothing more than talk in small groups, leaning on spears or sitting on the ground. As the riders delivered Throst to Clovis's tent, they paused and watched but offered no sign of worry. The guard at the entrance to the tent stopped them as Olaf tried to enter with his knife at Hakon's back.

"It's surety for our captive," Throst explained. "If you seek to grab him, we will make him useless to all."

133

"No weapons," the Frank said, and Throst doubted he had understood anything he had said.

"You have my word that I will not take the boy without paying a fair price." The tent flap opened and the man beyond could only be Clovis. "Give up your weapons and speak with me, Throst Shield-Biter. We've much to discuss."

"As you say." Throst inclined his head and noted how Clovis's dark eyes narrowed on Hakon as the boy passed beneath him. Inside the tent, Clovis set himself on a stool. He wore no armor, but carried a sword at his side. His clothes were rich and clean, his shirt as white as snow and his pants a vibrant green. His clean-shaved face hinted at a heavy beard where whiskers darkened his firm chin.

"And so this is Ulfrik's boy?" He crossed a leg over his knee and leaned forward. "I won't even ask for proof, since I see that swine in the boy's face."

"My father is not swine!" Hakon's sudden protest drew a delighted laugh from Clovis, but Olaf slapped the back of Hakon's head to silence him.

"He has his father's temper as well," Throst added. "As well as his foolishness."

Clovis's expression darkened and he appeared to drift into memory of something offensive, for his lip curled and his nose wrinkled. "So why do you ransom him to me, rather than Ulfrik? He would pay you far more."

"Then you will be surprised to know the great Lord Ulfrik did not place much value upon his son's life. He refused to pay my demands, and so I have come to you instead."

"This one is not his firstborn," Clovis said, sitting back on his stool. He looked up at Throst, one thin eyebrow cocked. "If Ulfrik finds no value in this one, why would I want him? So let's waste no more time with this child. I merely wanted to see him, to be sure you had truly done all you had claimed. I admire how you've managed to snatch his son from his hall."

"Your admiration flatters me, Lord," Throst said with a broad smile. "And I have hopes that we might work together, to benefit both of us."

"Work together?" Both of Clovis's brows rose. "Work together? You are a Northman, and though I speak your horrid language do not mistake that for love your kind. I just want to be able to understand when you people are begging for your lives under my sword. There will be no working together."

The cold returned to Throst's stomach and he felt Olaf's eyes on him from behind. Clovis wore an expression of singular distaste and physically leaned back as if the thought of cooperation was something that might touch him with filthy hands. Yet Throst did not let the show dissuade him, but pressed his point.

"Then at least we can benefit each other. I can provide the son you really desire, and you would be willing to pay for his capture. Of that I am certain."

"And you are right," Clovis replied, again his eyes narrowing at the thought. "Do you know why? Last summer, Ulfrik maimed my eldest son in battle. He humiliated him, battering him to the ground, and rather than do the honorable thing and kill him, he struck off his sword hand at the wrist. Now my son will never lead men in battle, never be a whole man. It's bad enough Ulfrik and his kind have wrested away lands my family has possessed for generations, now he has to take away the future as well. I will deliver the same to him, and so I have sworn. Once I would've been satisfied to kill him and be done, but now I want to destroy his future first, just as he has for me."

The hateful words filled the tent, and a gust of wind rippled the walls. Outside men murmured and some laughed, contrasting with the rage inside the tent. Clovis's eyes burned with anger, and Throst smiled as if in sympathy, but now he knew Clovis could be controlled. His hatred would rule him and make him pliant. Throst only need to manipulate it to get what he desired.

"A more horrible tale I've never heard," Throst said, glancing at Hakon and Olaf. "But I can aid you in seeing justice done. If the small one here is of no interest, then allow me to deliver his eldest to you."

"How will you get inside? I would pay you to show me the way into his fortress. I can make you a rich man, so long as you are true."

"I will make my target come out, for the way inside is now barred to me, at least for a short while." Clovis's eager expression fell flat, but Throst continued. "But that is not important to securing Gunnar. I will have him in your hands within a few weeks, as long as the price is reasonable."

"What is reasonable to you?"

"Sixty pounds of silver."

"You are mad. Ask again, and know it is your last chance. I'm beginning to feel foolish for coming out here to treat with you."

"Then thirty pounds of silver is half as much, but yet I will still deliver Gunnar in two weeks."

Clovis stared at him, and for a moment it was like looking into the eyes of a wolf that stalked from the forest underbrush. His lip curled again, and his words were low and rough. "Fine. If you truly bring his eldest son, it will be worth it to me. Hang on to this boy, for if you can bring me both then I will have all I need against Ulfrik."

"Why not take him now, Lord?"

"Because I don't want the trouble, especially if you can't deliver the eldest son. You can be worried about feeding this one and keeping him alive."

Throst inclined his head again. "As you say. But there is one thing I will need, and that is something to show my men. They must believe there is gain for them, for this plan is not without danger. A small token is all I ask, and know it will go towards taking your revenge upon your hated foe."

Clovis stood, seemingly on the edge of rage, but then he exhaled a long, defeated breath. He fished out a necklace of silver from which a silver cross dangled. He held it before Throst, who raised cupped hands to receive it. "This is proof enough, and more than you should've taken for doing nothing more than make promises. But if this keeps your men's hearts in the fight, so be it."

Throst clasped his hands around the silver cross still warm from hugging Clovis's chest. "This is generous of you, Lord. You will not regret it."

"You will regret it!" Hakon shouted. "My father will kill both of you. You'll never capture Gunnar!"

Olaf slapped Hakon's head again, and when he began to struggle, Olaf dragged him to the ground and gagged him with a cloth.

"I look forward to what you can do for me," Clovis said after the commotion had ceased. "Ulfrik and his kind need to be humbled."

"I couldn't agree more," Throst said, and smiled at Hakon as he lay flattened and heaving on the ground.

26

After a sodden trek home and a bleak walk through Ravndal's mournful roads, Ulfrik clambered into his hall, shoulders slouched, hair matted flat to his forehead, eyes couched in purple-ringed bags, and collapsed into his seat at the far end of the hall. A serving girl delivered a hot draught of apple water sweetened with honey into his waiting hands, and he savored the flavor as well as the steam on his face. Runa and Gunnar returned shortly behind him, with Aren clinging to Runa's skirt, and each took a mug of the hot apple water as they joined Ulfrik at the high table.

"No sign of Throst or Hakon," Runa's question fell as a flat statement of fact as she sat beside him. She had aged a decade in the days since Hakon's kidnapping. She had failed to care for herself, with her hair becoming lank and tangled and her face smudged. She slept in her clothing, giving her the wrinkled appearance of a rag used up and tossed into a corner. Gunnar, pulling a bench for himself, appeared far better than either of them, though he seldom smiled or spoke since the kidnapping. Only Aren remained unchanged, silently observing with his weirdly intelligent eyes. His tiny hands barely fit about his mug as he studied the steam rising from it.

"Throst will show soon enough. He will want more silver for Hakon's release and he can't get it if he remains hidden."

"And you will pay him what he asks?" Runa's question was laced with anger, for she had learned of Ulfrik's previous negotiations.

"Anything he asks I will give." Ulfrik tiredly swept the hall before him with his hand. "I'll give him my hall if he demands it. For it will make no difference. Whatever he takes I will retrieve when I chase that fool down to the miserable death he has earned."

The family sat in silence for long moments, sipping on their drinks and awaiting the servants to cook a proper meal. Snorri and Toki entered and joined Ulfrik at the table. Their flat expressions and slow approach testified to their weariness. The quiet deepened as everyone reflected upon the failure to locate Hakon.

Ulfrik finished his mug and placed it on the floor beside his chair, then leaned forward on his knees. "I have been thinking of how Throst managed this trick. He needed help to get inside. I have a feeling that man might still be here."

He scanned the group and expectant eyes turned to his. Only Aren remained uninterested, a child among adults with nothing to do but keep still. "How valuable would a spy be to him?"

"Lad, that much is obvious," Snorri said. "But do you know for certain the traitor is still among us?"

"I am not certain," Ulfrik said. "But he has evaded a thorough search, and that leads me to wonder if someone is signaling him. How else could he have eluded me?"

"They are but a few men," Toki said. "We've doubled back often enough to tramp over signs of their passing. It's not unbelievable that he has hid from us."

"True, but my heart tells me Throst has a man among us. All of us must be careful of what we say and where it is said. I don't know who this man is, but I will root him out by his beard and have his head on a spear."

"He might not have a beard," Runa said carelessly, staring ahead as if too tired to even meet anyone's eyes.

Ulfrik turned to her, twisting his lips and furrowing his brow. "Do you think the traitor is a boy? Who do you say it is?"

"Halla."

Ulfrik felt his belly flood with fire and he instantly snapped his eyes to Toki, who leaned back with confusion plain on his face. The old feud between the Runa and Halla was bound to erupt, but Ulfrik could think of no worse time than now.

"Wife, that's a heavy accusation to make."

"And a stupid one, at that," Toki added, recovering from his shock. "She has pledged herself to peace and forgiveness. You cannot insult my wife's honor without more proof."

Runa's eyes finally moved and she remained level despite Toki's instant rise in anger. "But I do have proof. While you were all gone, she came to this hall to insult me and vomit out her hatred for my family. She told me she hated life here, that she'd rather cut open her own belly than live here another day."

Toki began shaking his head and rose to his feet. "We discussed this journey at great length. She agreed to come here, to be closer to where her god is."

"You have been deceived," Runa said, her eyes again listlessly falling upon no one. "She hates me and my children, and by some means only the gods know she has helped Throst work his mischief. She gloated in it when she spoke to me."

"You are mad, sister. Throst was gone before we ever arrived here," Toki shouted, and Ulfrik rose to calm him. All the others stood, leaving Runa sitting wearily beneath them.

"Peace, Toki," Ulfrik said, as he patted his shoulder. "Runa's heart is as weary as mine, and her words are ill chosen for it."

"My words are what they are," she said, her voice rising. "I struck her in the face and banished her from my hall. She fled in shame, but not before cursing me and delighting in Hakon's misfortune. Now where is she? Plotting more evil?"

"You struck her?" Ulfrik rounded on Runa, his face pulled into a frown. She shrugged at him and sipped again from her mug. The gesture reminded him of Aren whenever he was asked a question he disdained. His young son was alone among everyone without a frown, simply watching with wide eyes.

"And will you banish me next?" Toki asked, throwing his hands in the air. "We came here expecting a place in your hall as kinsmen, and this insult is what you hand us?"

"You know this is not how I feel," Ulfrik said quietly, ushering Toki away from the group, but Toki tore his arm free.

"I'm beginning to wonder if you would have ever called me from Nye Grenner," Toki said, glaring at Ulfrik. "I think it best I find my family now."

Watching Toki stride from the hall, Ulfrik felt a tremor building in his arms. He whirled on Runa, who sat cool and still with a tired expression of indifference. Snorri examined his feet while Gunnar flushed red in confused embarrassment. The whole scene drew Ulfrik's rage to the surface.

"All of you, out of my sight." No one moved, shocked to suddenly receive his anger. "Go!"

Gunnar snapped to his command and swept from the hall, while Runa rolled her eyes at him before collecting Aren and heading to their room. Snorri, slowed by his age and old wounds, began to hobble past but Ulfrik stopped him with an outstretched hand. As the others faded away, he released Snorri's arm and sighed wearily.

"Lad, those women are going to be at each other's throats until the end of days," Snorri said in his age-ragged voice. "You and Toki must rise above it if you're going to keep peace and friendship."

"Was I wrong to let Toki go?" Ulfrik asked. He rarely doubted himself, but since Hakon's disappearance his confidence had been broken. He no longer knew if he was helping or harming a situation.

"No," Snorri said. "Toki is right to be angry. Let him wrestle with his anger for a bit, and I'll try to talk sense into him if I can. He will understand in time; he always does."

Ulfrik nodded, then rubbed his temples. "This is one more battle I can do without. Right now, someone in my ranks is not true and I must find who he is. I must rescue Hakon, and not be distracted with petty arguments."

"The arguments aren't petty," Snorri corrected. "But they are ill timed. Fight this battle another day, lad, and let's bring the little master home. I'll do my part in finding Hakon. I may no longer be any good on the battlefield, but I can still fight with my wits."

Both men chuckled, and the feel of it refreshed Ulfrik. He allowed Snorri to leave with a whispered thanks, then sat on his chair and brooded upon where Throst's man was hiding.

27

Runa sat beside Ulfrik at the high table, presiding over a subdued feast to thank the hirdmen for their efforts in the search for Hakon. The hall swam with men and servants, and the scents of ale and simmering beef in the cooking pots flowed around them. Oil lamps and brands drove shadows into the corners and gleamed in the wide eyes of the feasting men. She had sat through too many feasts to count, but this one was the strangest of all. Not for any difference in the men—for whenever they gathered around a fire with food and drink then songs and spats would ensue —but for Runa's distinct feeling of betrayal. Somewhere her young boy suffered in cold fear, in conditions she dreaded to imagine. Yet she sat with her face warm and belly full, idling in a smoky room of high spirits.

Despite his wrathful display earlier, Ulfrik spoke in upbeat if subdued tones with Einar and Snorri across the scraps of bone and bread left on their plates. They poured each other ale from a clay jug and chatted of inconsequential matters. Toki and Halla had even attended and her brother's easy smile returned, though something stiffened his posture and she knew he was on edge. She was thankful he had sense enough to sit at the far end of his table and concern himself more with his daughters than anyone else. She would have to apologize to him soon, and ask forgiveness, but her opinion would not change. She did not anticipate the conversation, but owed her brother more than what she had given him.

Others visited the table, to offer support to her and Ulfrik and vow that Hakon would be recovered and Throst brought to justice. Some men seemed genuine while others simply sought favor in Ulfrik's eyes. Runa cared not for their motivations, only that they commit to saving her son. Einar's wife, Bera, watched her like one of her own daughters and Runa smiled when their eyes met. She realized she had not looked the part of a jarl's wife since Hakon was taken, and had overindulged in excuses.

"Do you feel well?" Ulfrik asked her, long after the meal had finished when men leaned on each other and forgot the lyrics of their songs in raucous laughter. "You look pale."

Touching the base of her neck, Runa sat up straighter. "I feel fine. Do I look ill?"

"Maybe, or just tired," Ulfrik said as he placed his warm hand on her shoulder, squeezing it gently. "Why not go sleep? And take Aren, too. He is up late."

"Since when do you have a bedtime for our children?" Runa raised a brow at Ulfrik, who had never minded the details of the children's care. "He is awake and sitting quietly with me. We will retire when we're ready."

Ulfrik's smile faded and both Einar and Snorri found something else to look at. "You should rest, and take Aren with you. He needs his sleep."

His insistence only increased her opposition, and she looked down on Aren who sat wedged to her hip. He shook his head and Runa smiled. "In a while we will sleep, but I prefer to remain here for now. And if you are so concerned with your children, then look to your eldest. Where has Gunnar gone is a better question."

A twisted smile appeared on his face, and he scanned the room. "He's probably trying to make us grandparents."

"Well, that's a poor choice while his brother is held captive. You ought to talk to him about propriety and duty."

"Of course," Ulfrik said in a voice that indicated he would never have the conversation. Snorri spluttered a laugh, but Runa did not think it humorous. She began to crane her neck to find Gunnar herself, but instead she spotted something else that arrested her search.

Amid the laughing and drinking hirdmen sat eight men who were as hard and somber as black rocks in the frozen snow. They sat at the edge of a table, one man astride his bench so he faced Ulfrik, legs sprawled out before him and one hand gripping his mug. He glared with hard and sharp eyes, his ruined face made more horrible for the hate written in the folds of his ravaged skin. The man was Konal.

He dragged himself from the bench, his silent men bowing their heads deeper as he stood. He staggered past others at their drink and blundered up to the high table, where he braced himself on Einar and Snorri.

Ulfrik looked up with a bemused smile. "Konal, you have been quiet tonight. Come sit with us and drink."

"From the smell of him, I'd say he's not going to hold more," Snorri said while fanning his face. Ulfrik and the others laughed, but Runa saw the threat in Konal's eyes.

"It's more than drink that I want from you." His voice was thick and hissing. Runa felt her stomach burn and her heart pound as he punctuated his statement with a deep belch.

"Well, tell me what you want," Ulfrik said, the smile dropping from his face. "I will see what I can do for you."

"You have something that belongs to me, something you stole. I want it back."

Runa's hand felt for the knife strapped to her leg. Had he discovered the treasure that Ulfrik kept hidden for so long? It had once belonged to Konal, though Ulfrik claimed he had lost it and no longer had a claim. In his destitute state, Runa feared he would demand it from them.

A hush overcame the high table and some of the men close to it, though the hall still hummed with happier sounds. Ulfrik's eyes did not flinch from Konal's and he did not reply immediately. The two men faced down each other, until Konal sneered and turned aside to spit on the floor.

"What have I stolen from you, my friend?" Ulfrik's question was deliberate and clear, free of threat but unyielding. "Your drink has surely clouded your memory, for you have nothing I would take."

"Nothing to take? And you call my memory clouded!" Konal pulled himself straight, and to Runa's horror he twisted to her, his fire-ravaged hand stabbing an accusing finger at her.

"I want my son. Aren is my son."

Had she not already been seated Runa would have fallen. As it was, the next moments were nothing but swooning confusion. Silence gripped the hall and Konal's words crashed like swords falling on flagstones. Her vision faded and her head buzzed. She gathered Aren to her as if protecting him from a hailstorm. Had he really done this? Had he named Aren as his own son before Ulfrik and the entire hall? Yes, she had feared such a confrontation, but never expected it to unfold before the whole community. Only blood could follow now.

Ulfrik rose carefully, head bent and watching Konal from beneath his brows. Snorri and Einar stood aside, faces aghast. Runa's vision had shrunk as if she watched through a hole in a black cloth, her hands frozen around Aren.

"You are drunk," Ulfrik said. "Get some air outside. The cold will help clear your thinking."

"I may be drunk, but I've never been clearer." He wavered at the edge of the platform, flexing back as if to fall then pitching forward to balance himself. His finger jabbed again at Aren. "That boy's my son. He's the living image of my father."

The silence hurt Runa's head. Dark and red fury began to coil beneath Ulfrik's skin. Already on edge, he was likely to explode into deadly violence. To Runa's amazement, he still maintained an even voice though it crackled with threat.

"You slander my wife and dishonor me in my own hall. You are my bondsman, Konal Ketilsson, and a valued one at that. But don't think to try me further. Take back your words and I'll allow you to step away with your dignity."

"I did not journey so far to only gaze at my son from afar. All my kin are dead, but my son is alive and here before me. You don't deserve him. He belongs with me."

"You persist," Ulfrik said with a laugh. "Aren is my son and none other. Whatever face you see in him, it is because you wish to see it. One last time, for all the years of good service you rendered before we parted as friends, take back your words."

Konal wavered, then leapt for Runa. "Aren, look at me! Let me see my son!"

His sudden movement ignited the violence Runa had expected. Konal only succeeded in crashing into the table and falling atop it. Ulfrik lunged for him. In the same instant, Einar and Snorri grappled with him, and Konal's men stood to defend their master.

Angry shouts banished the shocked silence. Konal cried out for Aren and his men shouted as other hirdmen seized them before they could join the scrum unfolding at the high table. Benches overturned and plates clattered to the floor as Einar with his giant strength lifted Konal from the table, then he locked Konal's arms behind his back, ending the commotion.

Runa, for all her training and confidence in her fighting skills, had sat dumbfounded throughout. She remained sheltering Aren, who squirmed and demanded to be let go. Smothered beneath her enfolding arms, she refused to release him and crushed him tighter. She watched Konal struggle against Einar's hold, then slump with a low moan.

"You dare raise your hand to my wife, and at a time like this?" Ulfrik stood with both hands on his hips, his face twisted in a snarl.

"What better time? You've already lost one son, and I don't want you to lose mine. He's my only kin left in this world."

Many drew a shocked breath at Konal's audacity. Runa did not immediately understand his insult, but Ulfrik had clearly grasped it.

He shoved the table aside, sending its contents crashing to the floor as he pressed his face to Konal's.

"Your insults and disregard for my family have no place in my hall or my service. Take yourself from my lands and never show yourself again. You and your men, be gone!"

Konal stared hard at him, and seemed to sober. He nodded and turned his head aside to address his men being restrained behind Einar. "Hear that? We are no longer welcomed here, and for what? Speaking the truth is all I've done. I will have my kin at my side, Ulfrik. I've no need of you or this foul place. I curse you and your family for fools."

Another gasp rushed from the crowd and Ulfrik waved him away. Einar snapped Konal around and shouted for hirdmen to lead Konal's other men out. Runa watched Konal go, not resisting and head bowed. As he and his men were dragged into the press of onlookers, Gunnar appeared before him with fresh tears on his cheeks. She feared her son would shame himself with pleading and begging, but instead his quivering mouth bent into a frown and he backhanded Konal across his face with a meaty slap.

Aren broke free and called out for Konal, who did not look back as Einar and the other hirdmen shoved him and his men out of the hall. The remaining hirdmen kept an embarrassed silence, their eyes averted to their feet. Ulfrik stood amid the ruined table, scanning his men and the horrified faces of the young girls who had sat at the high table. Runa avoided Halla, but saw Toki staring at her husband. He seemed caught between wanting to act and fearing to move. Finally, Ulfrik stirred.

"You and the boy, get to our room," he ordered. "I will see to it Konal is ejected this very night."

Runa no longer resisted the idea, but instead welcomed the chance to flee the heavy shame Konal had inflicted upon her and her family.

28

Throst's heart soared with joy. The woods around him may have been sinking into the decay of winter with bare branches waving above cold and muddy earth, but he moved through them with a light step. The morning was bitter cold and his nose and cheeks were raw and red, but his heart was warm with promise. Dan strode alongside him, matching Throst's amiable pace, and the two led five others of his band. They bundled in mud-spattered, gray cloaks of wool and beneath fur-lined hats, and did not match the positive gait of their leader.

At the edge of the clearing, not more than a few hours walking from their base, Throst came to what he had sought. He paused, stopping Dan with an outstretched hand. The others drew in closer, rubbing hands together against the cold. "Are we really going to take on more men to feed? My stomach is hurting enough already," one of the men grumbled.

"Then learn to be a better hunter," Throst quipped without looking back to see who had complained. Dan would undoubtedly silence any more dissent with a withering glare. "These men are sent from the gods, right in time for our need of them."

Throst heard more back talk but paid it no mind. He hid behind a tree and watched the encampment for signs of movement. Four tents of dirty yellow cloth billowed in a clearing. The campfire smoldered, and no one tended it. He could not keep the smile from his face, for inside those tents were eight men fresh from Ulfrik's hall who would share his grudge against that arrogant jarl and double the size of his force. He had lurked at the edge of their encampment and heard their complaints and knew their hearts. They were not bright men, setting a campfire for all to see, but they were well armed and armored. He only needed their fighting strength.

His band did not possess the same fieldcraft skills as he did, and Throst cringed at their undisciplined noises as they stumbled in the woods. He could not trust them to scout, which is why he did it himself. For now, he needed a show of force in case Ulfrik's former men had other ideas. As Throst watched from the edge of the woods, men emerged from their tents. Some wore mail, all had sturdy shields and fine swords. In fact, they appeared wealthy, and Throst suddenly felt poor.

"They look powerful," Dan said, his voice small.

"Don't mind that," Throst said. "They share a common enemy with us, and you know what they say about that."

"What is said about that?"

Throst disregarded Dan's slow wits, and addressed all of his men. "Follow my lead and let me do the talking. You're here to demonstrate our strength and nothing more. These men will join us before we are done, mark my words."

Drawing a deep breath, he straightened himself and stepped from his hiding place. After a few paces, his men fell in behind him. He approached the camp, his arms relaxed at his side and a smile on his face. No one appeared to notice him, and he hailed the group with a wave of his hand.

"Good morning to you, wanderers. May we join your fire on this cold morning?"

The men spun to face him, and swords were freed of their scabbards within moments. The air filled with the song of iron blades that gleamed in the diffuse sunlight, each newly honed tip pointed at him.

One man caught him short, their leader who Throst had heard protesting his fate in the darkness. His face had been badly burned and the red and white flesh appeared loose and melting on a once handsome head.

Throst stopped and raised his hands, and his men did the same. "Peace, we did not mean to startle you."

The leader scowled at him and his blade did not lower. Other men spilled out of the tents, creating a semicircle of stern faces and bright blades. "Yet you did, and you would do well to stand still."

"If we intended an ambush, you would have all been stuck with arrows by now. Please, lower your weapons. You see we have not drawn ours. I want only to share your fire and conversation."

The scar-faced man smiled without humor. "Such fine manners for so ragged a bandit. You bring many men to your conversation, and I can't help but wonder why."

"Look to yourself, then," Throst said. "I see eight blades pointed at my heart. But let's not dwell on what sets us apart. Allow me to approach and my men will stay behind."

The scar-faced leader lowered his blade and the rest followed, though all remained alert for trouble. Throst respected their wariness and reminded himself to refrain from provoking them. When the leader stood to the side to allow him to join his group, Throst moved with exaggerated care. He nodded Dan and the others to step back, which they did all too easily. The cowardice made him wince, and reminded him again why adding these new men to his force was so vital. These were hard-bitten warriors and not homeless criminals.

"Do you have a name?" asked the leader as Throst came to the dying embers of the campfire. A low warmth pulsed around this feet and legs as he stood by it.

"I am called Throst the Shield-Biter, and not long ago I assume you were hunting these woods for me."

He spoke casually and seated himself on a dry log that his hosts had dragged to the fireside when they had established their camp. Carelessly flipping his cloak aside as he sat, he did not look at the others, as if his name meant nothing. Despite his show of indifference, his hands went cold and his heart raced. These men might consider capturing him to earn Ulfrik's forgiveness, but he had heard enough the prior night to believe they would not. Once he settled upon the log, he glanced up at the leader with a bright smile.

All the men had drawn closer, their lips pressed tight and swords tipped up. The leader was a standing stone, a breeze tousling his hair across the good side of his face and leaving only his ravaged side exposed. The two stared at each other, but the leader finally relented with a snort.

"Would that we had this meeting a week ago, maybe my fate would have been much different. So you are Throst? You are smaller than I imagined. From the way Ulfrik cursed your name, I expected a giant." He returned his sword to its sheath then laid it on another log as he sat. The other men relaxed and Throst released breath he had not realized he had held.

"You compliment me, but I am no larger than any other man. But I do know how to inflict hurt, and so I have taught Ulfrik. Now, honor me with your name, friend, for I believe you and I may have common cause against Ulfrik."

The leader coughed a dry laugh and shook his head. "My name is Konal Ketilsson and I lead these men, who have followed me into banishment and disgrace. I do not deserve their love, but never have there been better companions."

A few of the men nodded as if embarrassed, though most others folded their arms and set their legs wide in challenge. Throst grunted agreement at Konal's sentiments. "That kind of loyalty is something Ulfrik does not understand, would you say?"

"That I would. Curse that man to a dog's death. He has my son, held from me just as surely as you hold Hakon from him. Did that help him understand why I must be reunited with my only kin? Of course not! Instead, he shamed and banished me. Years ago I served him, risked my life for him. I once saved his eldest son's life, and do you know that meant nothing to him? One drunken night and a few loose words and now I am a bandit as low as you."

The frown passed from Throst's face in an instant, but the jab rankled him. Two of the men laughed at Konal's derision, and Throst noted who they were. If he ever got control of these men they would learn better respect, but for now he looked to the sky as if checking for rain and hopefully conceal the flush that heated his face.

"So do you have Hakon still, or is he dead?" Konal continued, picking up a stick to stir the embers of the fire.

"He is alive and well, and in fact I have plans for him that will make me and my men quite wealthy."

Konal paused in stirring the fire and shared glances with his men before turning to Throst. "So you're not satisfied with the silver you nabbed the first time. You plan on taking more than that?"

"Far more, and I am certain he will pay me all I ask. He will have no choice. But I speak overmuch, for while you have been a fair host, you are no ally of mine. At least, you are not yet." Throst smiled and leaned closer. "For what I plan, I will need more fighting strength than I currently possess. Finding you camped here, so obviously abandoned like many who have served that arrogant lord of Ravndal, is a great boon. If you were to join with me, I could offer you a part in my plan and the riches that will follow. But best of all, I could reunite you with your son. As I have shown, I have a way to get at his children."

Konal shot to his feet with such suddenness that Throst fell back and reflexively grabbed the hilt of his sword. The other men crouched as if to spring into action. Yet Konal did nothing more than stand with both fists balled until his knuckles turned white. His fierce face glowed with hate and rage and his yellow teeth were bared.

"Aren is my son and none other. If you promise me my boy, then you will have my sword and the swords of my men at your service."

Throst laughed, a nervous thing he detested for its show of weakness, but his heart pounded at the base of his neck. Konal had exploded like a lightning bolt and could have easily killed him in one stroke. Such explosive power had to be managed carefully, and for a brief moment he wondered whether to enlist this man. Yet Konal's rabid hatred and desire would make him pliable, and Throst needed his men.

"Consider your son as good as restored to your side." Throst did not know why Konal believed Ulfrik's child was his own. He did not know Ulfrik's history and knew nothing of Konal other than his usefulness. Perhaps he was mad. He would learn Konal's details soon enough, but for now securing his oath was paramount.

"Then I will give you my word to serve until that day. But Konal Ketilsson will never again be a bondsman to anyone. We will split the riches and I will have my son, then you and I will part ways."

"It is a fair deal," Throst said as he stood. "Once I hear your oath, then I will take you to where Hakon is kept and you will see that I have the power to grant what you most desire."

Konal smiled wickedly, deep lines forming in the thin flesh of his burned face. "I desire justice, and a good measure of revenge."

Both men laughed and Throst again felt his heart race, this time with the thrill of knowing he had concluded one more step on his path to greatness.

29

The thin crescent of the moon did not throw much light and Throst's torch guttered in the night breeze that tore at his face. Winter would be harsh this year, and he vowed to live in a proper hall before it began. On the low hill with the single, thick oak tree, he saw the ball of orange light from a brand. Though certain of being unseen, he still searched over his shoulder for followers. He had made sure no one observed him slipping away, but caution was always necessary. No one could be completely trusted.

The oak had carpeted the base of the hill with dead leaves that rolled in the wind with a sound like rain. He protected his torch from the wind, turning to cup his body around it while the breeze died, then trudged up the hill to meet his contact.

"Throst, my love?" came the sweet voice of the dark shape hidden by the wide oak trunk.

"Astra, it is me," he said, mounting the final steps.

She was a plain-faced girl but with skin perfect and unblemished as polished stone. She wore a heavy gray cloak, hiding her pleasing shape in a lump of shadow, but she threw her arms wide to accept his welcome. Both embraced and were it not for the awkwardness of holding aside their torches they would have done so with more ardor.

Her face swam with flickering shadows thrown by the torch and her eyes gleamed with yellow points as she searched him.

"But it has been too long! When will you let me join you?" She pulled away, and Throst regretted the loss of her warmth and scent. Hiding in caves and ruined halls with sweaty men had heightened his appreciation of a woman's comforts.

"Very soon, my soul, you will live with me in a hall of our own, but for now there is little time to entertain dreams. You have news for me?"

"News of all kinds," she said with an impish smile. "Ulfrik had a falling out with some of his men a few days ago. One of them claimed Ulfrik's youngest was his own, and it led to him and his men being banished."

"And his name is Konal Ketilsson; his face is badly burned." Astra stopped in surprise and he saw the smile grow on her face in the darkness. He told her how he had spied on Konal's camp and then recruited him. "I hoped you could prove his tale, and you have."

"Oh, I witnessed it with my own eyes. Since that day Ulfrik has taken to drink and his wife has become a horrible shrew. They fight every day over his inaction and Ulfrik has taken to sleeping under the table in his hall. His friends don't know what to do, and Gunnar feels cut off from him. It's perfect!"

Throst nodded in deep satisfaction. "A pity he won't suffer like this for long, but I cannot give him too much time to figure out my plans. I have met with Clovis since we last spoke, and as I guessed he did not want Hakon but greatly desires Gunnar. I assume you have captured his attention?"

Astra's voice quaked with barely controlled laughter. "He is hooked like a fish and does whatever I suggest. I swear I could make him fall on his sword if I promised to spread my legs for him."

"But you haven't given him that much?" Throst seized her thin arm without thinking, and Astra drew a sharp breath. Feeling his face warm with shame, he dropped his hand which drew a smile from Astra.

"Of course not, and he's not brave enough to take it for himself.

Ulfrik is raising a gutless puppy. He's already a man, but he's not even allowed to piss without the leave of his father. Gunnar hates him for it, but he can't confront him."

Throst grumbled his pleasure at the news. Angry people were so easy to shape, and Gunnar's lust and frustration would lead him directly into Throst's hands.

"It is odd for a jarl's son not to just take his pleasure with any woman he chooses. He may yet find his guts, so be wary of him." He gave her a warning look and her smile twisted in the strange shadows of the torchlight. Astra was not a virgin when he had found her, and sharing women did not matter unless she belonged to him as Astra did. No one should have what is his until he has finished with it, and he was not done with her.

"Do not worry for that. Gunnar has strange ideas about what is right, and thinks he should not force himself on a woman he loves." She snickered and covered her mouth.

"Gods, I'll be doing Ulfrik a favor to rid him of such weakness. It's that strange mercy Ulfrik cultivates which has ruined his leadership and passed onto his son. Neither of them would kill me when they should have, and now they both will regret that mistake. Life is made by the strong and the weak are sent to ruin."

"And though your enemies live in fortresses and wear gold on their arms, you are stronger," Astra said as she drew closer to him. She laced her free arm around his waist and pressed herself closer, the softness of her body thrilling him.

"Control yourself, woman. I'll not be tempted by you now. Both of us must return before we are missed, and you have a task to fulfill for me. When all is done, we will lay together for days on end."

"Promise?"

Throst gently removed her arm with a nod. "You've my word. Now here is the plan."

157

30

The night was a foul darkness, no moon or stars shining, all hidden behind clouds as thick as gathered hay. The frosty cold was early this year, and Ulfrik worried for the winter ahead and securing his son before it arrived. He vowed that Hakon would be returned to the warmth of his hall before winter clenched the land. Now all he had to check the cold was his cloak and the guttering orange flame of his torch. His hand shielded its light, for in the perfect blackness it would be a beacon to anyone watching. He only hoped one man would see it, as any other could bring him trouble.

At the edge of the woods where he had snared Clovis in a trap not long ago, he waited. He had counted the days and trusted to the gods that his plans succeeded. The deceit he had to visit upon every person he loved was a sharp pain in his heart, and he could not be sure of its worth until this night.

Escaping his own fortress had been difficult, and how his enemy's spy managed it remained unknown. At last he had to confide in one lone man to allow him in and out. To his chagrin he had revealed more to a barely known bondsman than his own wife. As he huddled against the cold, keeping the torch as close as he dared, he thought of how he tormented Runa. She did not deserve to suffer as she did, thinking her husband had given up to ale rather than fight. Yet no one could know his plan, and least of all her. His heart told him somehow the spy worked through her in ways he did not know. Nothing more than a thought, but one he would prove this night.

Once the cold and boredom had sapped Ulfrik's will, a single orange light bobbed between the trees. He revealed his torchlight to it, and the corresponding torch made directly for him. As it grew closer, his free hand gripped his sword hilt and he widened his stance. Then the approaching torchlight halted and a raspy voice hissed from the darkness.

"Lord Ulfrik? Is it you?"

Relaxing, he stood looser and dropped his hand from his sword. He drove his torch into the soft earth, and placed a rock to brace it. "None other. Come, be welcomed."

The torch raised higher to light the final distance as the man approached. At last his bulky shape billowed out of the darkness and the man stepped into the light.

"Welcome, Konal," Ulfrik said with a smile, opening his arms to receive his friend. He fixed his brand next to Ulfrik's then embraced his lord in greeting.

"It is all as you had expected," Konal said as he stepped back, a satisfied smile deepening the folds of his face. "Throst found me and was desperate to take me in."

Ulfrik's heart raced and his arms trembled. A dryness filled his mouth, and he did not understand the fear suddenly overtaking him. His first question was harder to ask than he had imagined. "Is Hakon well?"

"He is surprisingly well," Konal said with a smile. "He is tied and guarded always, but Throst's sister cares for him. I've been not more than three days in his company, but I've not seen him mistreated. Mind you, he has bruises and scabs, and is thin and scared. But his will is strong and he is defiant. Throst had me strike him to show my contempt for you."

"And I trust you did what you must?" Ulfrik winced at his question, strangely hoping Konal passed the test.

"I belted him like a man, and cursed both him and you to unending shame in Nifleheim. No one doubted me, least of all Hakon. But he took it better than a man, and he defied me to do worse and again claimed Odin had his one eye upon him."

Ulfrik's pride swelled at the thought his son's bravery. "Perhaps the All-Father watches him, but I put no faith in Odin for protection. The gods' ways are strange. Yet if it gives him power to fight, then it is good."

"I promised him Odin only watched for him to die," Konal said, his voice smaller.

"You have played your role convincingly, maybe too convincingly. You had some surprising words for me the night we began our ruse."

"Not more than we had planned," Konal said, but Ulfrik detected a waver in his eyes even in the strange shadows thrown from the low torchlight. Still, Konal had taken considerable risk and shamed himself in public to make this a success. Ulfrik trusted him, and whatever he imagined he put aside.

"Runa is quite distraught, with our fight and the gossip swirling about her."

"And what of Aren? I had hoped for him not to see our act."

Ulfrik shrugged and rubbed his chin. "Nothing ever bothers that boy. He has no serious temper."

Konal opened his mouth as if to counter Ulfrik, but then fell quiet. "He is better raised in your hall, Lord Ulfrik. I am poor and cannot offer him the future that you can. You have cared for him since birth, and raised him without question as your own. You are a greater man that I ever will be, for I would not have owned your child. That you will allow me to remain near him when this is done, I am ever grateful."

Ulfrik waved aside Konal's statement. "We chat like we're in the mead hall during a summer night. Reveal all to me and let us make our plans. I mean to have Hakon back and Throst in chains. We've little time to waste tonight."

Ulfrik frowned as Konal described how they had camped in Throst's hideout, and he cursed not following Einar's intuition. Then he told of Throst's alliance with Clovis. Mention of the scheming Frank imparted a deeper chill to Ulfrik's core. Konal further revealed the plan to capture Gunnar and turn both him and Hakon over to Clovis for a minor fortune in silver.

"And I have discovered the traitor; you'll not like who it is. Gunnar has been the unwitting fool for Throst's lover, Astra. She plies Gunnar for information and relays it to Throst, and she will lead your son to his doom."

Closing his eyes, he shook his head at the news. "How I wished it was a pock-faced, coward of a man instead of my son's first love. I never realized Throst had a lover. What a fool I've been."

"I've not met the girl, but Throst got word from her only yesterday. He explained our role in the scheme. Astra will lead Gunnar outside with the promise of a good fuck. I guess your boy hasn't got around to doing it yet, and so the promise of it will be a strong lure. I can't imagine Gunnar being dumb enough to fall for this, but I guess if his prick is leading the way it is possible. Anyway, you can imagine the rest. We overtake him as he's getting ready to mount the bitch then drag him off to Clovis."

Listening with his eyes still closed, Ulfrik imagined each step in the plan. He recalled when he was Gunnar's age and how every glimpse of a calf and every skirt that hugged a woman's curves would drive him wild with lust. Those urges, particularly if restrained, would defeat any caution when the moment came to fulfill them.

"How is she getting in and out of Ravndal?"

"I asked Throst the same question, but he would not answer. His sister was more forthcoming, and apparently a hole under your north wall is just big enough for her to wiggle through."

"Like a damned mutt digging her way out? Such a simple thing, and yet I hadn't thought of it."

"Sometimes it's the easy things we see last," Konal said. "No one else considered it, either."

The two sat in silence, and Ulfrik's mind began to form plans.

Suddenly he realized this was an opportunity and not a disaster. Konal frowned in confusion and Ulfrik began to pace with his hands locked behind his back, uncaring of the cold night air that billowed into his cloak.

"How confident are you of overtaking Throst and his men?" he asked as he paced. "What do you make of Throst?"

Konal tucked his head down and considered the question. "If we act soon, I am confident we can kill them to a man. They only need to sleep and us to remain awake." He drew the edge of his hand across his neck. "Then it's a slaughter. As for Throst, he is smart and knows how to control his men. They fear him, and I've heard he killed their former leader in a duel using his left hand. I've not seen him fight, but I've not survived this long because I under-credit my enemies. What makes him dangerous is his youth. He thinks with a young mind, one that is selfish and vengeful. I cannot say what he will do next, and I expect he might not even know himself."

"What about his relation with Clovis? Does the Frank trust him?"

Konal shrugged. "I cannot say. It seems Clovis gave him silver to seal their bargain. To a Frankish lord, it might not be much, but Throst stores great value in it."

Silence resumed as Ulfrik stopped pacing to consider his options. His instincts railed against his thoughts, but the chance to smash his enemies was too great. "When we first planned to bait Throst with your betrayal, we expected to uncover the traitors then tear them down. I did not expect to find more to exploit."

In the wavering light, Konal's head cocked to this side. "I can free Hakon this night. In fact, we must act before tomorrow or the trap with Gunnar will force my hand."

"Such was our original aim, but now I have new information." Ulfrik bowed his head and rubbed his eyes with the heels of his palm. "It pains me to use my sons, particularly Hakon, but they will be key to smashing Throst and Clovis at the one blow."

He smiled and immediately felt shamed for it, recalling Hakon's smooth face and innocent smile. He continued, straightening himself and focusing on the plan. "Astra is feeding Throst information, but we can control what she knows. Let her give him information valuable to Clovis, so valuable Throst will want to pass it on for a reward."

"You want to bait Clovis into a vulnerable spot?" Konal asked, folding his arms. "But what of Hakon?"

"I give you responsibility for Hakon's rescue, and I will reward you and your men with gold. You will have to coordinate your timing with great care, and if at any point in your judgment Hakon is in danger of being killed or maimed, then you must save him."

"Of that you have my word, and I need no encouragement of riches to do so. I knew him when he was a babe, and have grown fond of him since my return. Your family is as my own, Lord Ulfrik; there is no one else left to me."

"But your men will be motivated by riches, and so they will have them. There is no price too high for the safety of my son. Do what you must to prove your loyalty to Throst: curse me, beat Hakon, swear yourself to Clovis, anything to strengthen the ruse, and after three days from tomorrow you kill them all and bring Hakon home."

"You do not want Throst alive?"

"If possible, but with Clovis involved now, Throst is a bug to be crushed under heel. Deal with him as the moment dictates. I will be grinding Clovis into bonemeal while you are cutting the legs from under Throst."

Both men laughed, and Konal grew serious. "Now how will you use Astra to get Clovis to where you want?"

"You will encourage Throst to contact Clovis after Astra makes her report." He put his arm on Konal's shoulder and drew him closer. "Now let me tell you how it will be done, and you may offer suggestions to improve the idea."

31

Gunnar stared at his father in the early morning light slanting through the open smoke hole above the hearth. The words spoken could not be true, yet his father's sad eyes fixed on him and he nodded with a barely perceptible finality. Gunnar shook his head, felt a sudden quake in his knees and heat in his eyes. Now he was grateful that his father had cleared the hall and forbidden even his mother from entering, for unmanly tears threatened to flow.

He wanted to hate his father, to call him a liar and accuse him of a lame attempt to control him, but he could not. He could see it for himself now. Astra had strung him along and he had been willing to overlook every question: how she suddenly appeared to him after the hanging of Throst's father, the vagueness of her history, her lack of family in Ravndal, her interest in his father's activities. All of this he had glazed in a dewy, foolish infatuation with a woman who seemed to always speak whatever he needed to hear and always hold what he most desired just out of reach. So many other girls had hoped to catch his eye, but Astra had done so effortlessly and he could not understand how.

"It hurts worse than any blade, I know. She was never worthy of you," Ulfrik said, his tired voice warm with understanding. Gunnar looked at him again, seeing a haggard face so unlike the vigorous man he had grown up idolizing. Did he really understand? His father always won every battle and succeeded in every venture. How could he know failure like this?

Faint sounds of Ravndal waking to the new day reached into their awkward silence in the morning-bright hall. Laughter floated through a window, and Gunnar wondered how anyone could laugh at such a time. Enemies within and without worked to ensure ruin for all, and yet men still found laughter. Would he laugh again, he wondered. Did he deserve it, being such a fool?

"I wish there was more time to heal," Ulfrik said, stepping through the shaft of white light and into the darkness with Gunnar. Both stood at the center of the hall, no other person within, not even the servants and slaves, and faced each other. His father placed a cold, rough hand on his shoulder and squeezed. "But your brother's life hangs on our next move, and you must be the one to save him."

He frowned in confusion at his father, who nodded solemnly. "How so? Haven't I been the fool all along, bringing this disaster into our hall?"

"Foolish words," Ulfrik admonished, bowing and shaking his head. Again he squeezed Gunnar's shoulder before letting his arm drop. "This won't be the last time your trust will be betrayed, my son. When it happens, you will curse your blindness and swear to never trust again, but this is wrong. Trust is at the heart of all things. You cannot stand in a shieldwall without trust in the men at your sides. A jarl cannot lead his people if he cannot trust them to obey their oaths. My son, many shields at your side will falter and many oaths will be spoken in ill-faith, but no matter. You are not to blame nor can you always know when trust will be broken. You will bear no shame for it, though stupid men might call you a fool. You will stand aside from those who soil themselves with dishonor, and not even the hem of your cloak will be dirtied for it."

Gunnar nodded and chanced a smile. He loathed how he still felt like a child, even at sixteen years of life, but his father's words soothed him and exonerated the shame he placed on himself. Still, he craved a way to demonstrate he could carry himself as a man and make wise decisions. "You say I will save my brother?"

"You will, but more remains to explain." Ulfrik began to pace, as he always did when excited for something. He revealed the trickery he and Konal had plotted in secret, dreamed up in a single afternoon. A surge of shock, relief, and dismay filled Gunnar as his father described the careful setting of place and time for contacting each other.

"I struck him in the face," Gunnar said. "I wanted to kill him."

"A perfect accent to heighten the ruse," Ulfrik said, then smiled thoughtfully. "He richly deserved it as well."

"So is none of it true?"

"All of it is true, except that Konal and his men were not drunk and he is not banished. His men only knew they were forbidden to drink that night and had to follow him no matter what. He had only revealed the details to them moments before he launched into his act. It was well done."

"So Aren is not your son."

"He is not my blood, but he is my adopted son. Konal's return makes no difference, and he has agreed. Time will reveal how wise that choice is, but I trust Hakon's fate to him today."

Gunnar's elation at no longer needing to hate a man he had admired all his life crumbled when he thought of his mother. She had been shamed and embarrassed, and her desperation heightened daily. "Will you tell mother?"

"In time, but for now only you and I will know the truth. Deceiving your mother is a heart-pain unlike any other I have ever felt. Your Uncle Toki will be brought in, as you will see in a moment, but all others must remain ignorant until the moment the twin blades of my trap cut down both Throst and Clovis."

Ulfrik sat on a bench and leaned back against a table, then began to explain how Gunnar would rescue Hakon. As his father relayed the plan, Gunnar sat attentively on a bench across from him, leaning in to absorb the details of the plan.

The plan was based on continuing the ruse Ulfrik and Konal had begun. Gunnar's role was to feed Astra vital information that would ruin Throst's plans while creating an opportunity for him to redeem himself with Clovis. Ulfrik planned to send Gunnar along with Toki and his men to seek aid from Hrolf the Strider. The supposition being Ulfrik needs more men to comb the land for Throst while still defending against Clovis, and that since Ulfrik cannot leave he would send his oldest son to represent him. Gunnar would leave this day, and deny Astra the chance to lead him to danger.

"Once you tell Astra this news," Ulfrik said, his eyes bright with excitement and leaning forward on the bench, "she will head straight to Throst with it. If he doesn't see the opportunity himself, Konal will encourage him to inform Clovis that you are with a small band of inexperienced men. You are the bait in the trap, Gunnar. He'll come for you, and I will lead a force to hit him from behind while you and Toki double-back to catch him between us."

"This seems risky. Won't Clovis know you have left with your army as well? His scouts are as shrewd as ours."

"Night will mask us from scouts. Once I have seen Astra return, she will be captured and I will lead half of my men under the cover of darkness into the woods. Footing is treacherous, but the woods are not far. By sunrise we will be following behind you and Clovis as well. No one will have observed my warband exiting Ravndal, and Clovis's spies will still see men on the ramparts. They will have nothing to report."

"Then what of Hakon?"

"By this time Konal and his men will have either killed or captured Throst. They are an even match to Throst's men, but Konal and his crew are warriors and not witless bandits. They will prevail and bring Hakon home. In two strokes, both of my enemies will be destroyed. Clovis will either surrender to me or I will kill him in battle. His overeagerness to avenge his son will be his undoing. He cannot think clearly when his mind is addled with vengeance."

Gunnar considered everything his father had said, and realized his role in it had been exaggerated. His father sat back with a look of

167

supreme satisfaction, but Gunnar did not share it. "I am merely a piece of cheese to lure out the rats. Where is there glory in this? What if I were to refuse?"

Ulfrik's smile dropped and he wiped his mouth as if to forestall a curse. "Clovis's cavalry is destroyed, and he won't leave his fortress undefended. He'll take just enough men for the battle and no more. You needn't worry about success."

"I'm not worried about success," Gunnar interrupted, nearly as shocked as his father to find his voice raised against him. "You are using the promise of my life to gain an advantage over your enemy, and you are proud of it? Is this why not even Mother can know this plan?"

They stared at each other for long moments and a tremor developed in Gunnar's legs that made him thankful he was already seated. Neither man wavered, and Gunnar knew now more than ever he had to prove that he could stand up for himself or forever remain in his father's shadow.

"Son, the plan has been set and Hakon depends on this."

"No, this has nothing to do with Hakon. I am not a child, Father, no matter how long you want to deny it. I can think with a grown man's mind. You just said Konal will free Hakon on the third day, and that happens whether or not you've shoved me in front of Clovis. You just called me bait."

"Yes!" Ulfrik snapped with such sudden force that Gunnar flinched. "So it is true. I've been charmed by my own plan, and placed it before you."

His father seemed to age before his eyes, slumping deeper into his seat. His golden cloak pin glinted in the reflected light, winking and glittering in contrast to the dull and dispirited man wearing it. He put his rough and scarred hands over his face and exhaled a long and weary breath.

"I know I have made mistakes," Ulfrik said through the cover of his hand. "Too many to count. Perhaps this could have been the worst one of all. I saw a chance that surely the gods themselves must have set before me, and so I grabbed at it like a child does a toy. Every word you have spoken today is the truth, and is a shame on my judgment. You are my son, not bait for a trap. Not even my father would've have spoken so carelessly, and he was a callous man. I am humbled by your courage, son. You knew I was wrong, and you told me so."

Letting his hands drop from his face, he flashed Gunnar a suffering smile. His eyes were red from lack of sleep and circled in black. Gunnar searched his father for something of the man he had known, but found only a face that resembled him. Nothing of the force that had driven him for so many years remained. Had this ordeal with Hakon drained him so, or was there more on his mind yet unspoken?

"Hakon's safe return is our first task," Gunnar said, moving to the bench beside his father. "Clovis is a different matter."

Ulfrik nodded, and slapped Gunnar's knee. He stood and stretched. "Of course, you are right. Wait here a moment," he said, then went to his chambers at the back of the hall.

Gunnar watched him shamble toward the darkness and waited, his foot tapping nervously. As his father disappeared beyond the door, he mulled Ulfrik's plan and grasped the shrewdness of it. Maybe the gods did plan justice for Throst and Astra, for diverting their plots to gain advantage was as satisfying as it was just. Hakon was not in danger with Konal and his crew to watch over him. Indeed, it was a cunning plan and his part, if not glorious, was key to it all.

His father reappeared, and in his hand he carried a sheathed sword. He held it forward to Gunnar. "I was wrong to take this from you. You are a man today and have been longer than I cared to admit. Take this sword, wear it with honor, battle with it for glory, and die with your hand upon it."

Taking it into both hands, Gunnar stood and held his father's eyes. He smiled and the two embraced. Ulfrik hugged him close and whispered softly, "I am sorry, my son. You deserved better from your father."

"These are trying times," Gunnar said, struggling to find the words as the two stepped back from each other. He weighed his sword in his palm and a smile played on his lips. Raising a brow, he met his father's eye again. "Now we must hurry and inform Toki of your plan. We must act fast if we are to lure out Clovis and send that Frankish bastard to his grave."

Ulfrik's eyes widened in surprise, and then the two of them laughed together.

32

Runa's hair spilled from the hood of her cloak and brushed her face in the morning breeze. With a snort of irritation, she stuffed it back inside and lowered her head so none could see her face within. The chicken pen beside the northern hall, where Toki and his crew lodged, was a ramshackle affair that only contained the chickens if they chose to remain within. The girls who tended these feisty hens were in awe when she suggested they leave the feeding to her. Now she took her time with the feed basket, scattering stale bread, grains, and scraps of other food for the noisy birds. Though she undertook the task for another purpose, the scent of the hens and their frantic scramble took her back to a simpler time when this chore might be one of many to occupy her day. Now there was nothing for her but to sit at a loom or give orders to servants.

And too much time to think.

A hen pecked at her foot, impatient with her lazy pace, and she shooed it away with a squawked protest before casting more feed on the cold earth. She continued to watch the doors of the north hall, noting all the visitors and turning her head at any glance spared for her. More people arrived at this hall than expected, but since Ulfrik had closed his hall for some mysterious purpose, hirdmen and tradesmen alike had drifted to the other barracks for their meals. She considered this morning might not have been the ideal time to spy on Halla, particularly when she was not certain what to expect.

Einar and Bera had taken Aren for her without question, as Aren always seemed more at home with Einar's girls than his own brothers. In truth, she probably could have used Aren's keener eyesight, for at her age people in the distance were becoming smudgy and indistinct figures. In fact, Aren seemed to be the sanest of all her family since Hakon's kidnapping and he was merely a child. She could stand some better counsel than what she had in her husband.

"What am I doing out here?" she muttered to herself as she crumbled the last of the feed from her hand. "You've lost your mind, Runa, that's what you've done."

She flung the basket into the corner fence, several hens jumping in protest, and then collapsed onto a tree stump that served as a stool and a collection point for debris. An old bucket filled with scummy water sat next to it, and the morning light reflected on the surface. Runa saw her reflection in it, obscured by the floating junk, and kicked it so that the ripple erased her image. She did not want to look at what she had become. Folding her arms into the plain wool cloak, she tightened against the chill.

Men in fur hats and heavy cloaks arrived at the north hall, greeted at the doors by friends, some with great warmth and others with hardly more than a nod. Many faces were familiar, others complete strangers. Once she had known all the men and women of her hall and the surrounding farms. They had relied on her, looked to her for leadership and protection. Their relationship had true meaning and real benefits. Now here, in this place called Ravndal, she was nothing more than a symbol to the men and mistress to the women. Strangers were the norm, and these strangers guarded her and her family. Hakon relied on these men, men she hardly knew, for rescue.

Then she remembered what she was doing here and her jaw set with purpose.

While Ulfrik shamed her and himself with drunkenness and

inaction, she had to do something. None of these strangers cared for her son. None of these men, without an order from their jarl, would step away from their cozy hearths and search for Hakon. Her husband had been enfeebled since his confrontation with Konal. This morning he seemed a different man, but how much time had passed without Throst showing as expected and nothing at all being done to find Hakon? No, her purpose here on this chill and bleak morning was to do whatever she could to bring Hakon home.

She knew, beyond any doubt, that Halla had somehow betrayed them all to Throst.

Peering at the log walls of the barracks, she imagined Halla inside, partaking of hospitality while plotting against her betters. Her brother, however dear he was to her, was a fool and always had been a fool in matters of the heart. He could not see Halla for who she truly was. Maybe now with daughters to care for, he chose to not see. No matter. He had dragged her from those cold and foggy islands at the top of the world and spread her poison here. Runa had to stop it.

"You're searching for someone to fight," Ulfrik had told her after she had confronted Toki. "You can't get to Throst and so imagine Halla is your enemy."

Runa rubbed her nose violently as she scowled at the barracks hall. She wanted to believe him, but Halla always seemed to wear a smug expression since the fire. She wanted to leave these lands, and if she could not then she wanted to hurt those she blamed for keeping her here. She knew something more, and Runa would find out.

The thought repeated on her like a bad stew gurgling up from her bowels, increasing in intensity as the cold of the morning wore on. When she thought to give up, she spotted Ulfrik and Gunnar striding purposefully for the barracks. Her heart leapt. What if he caught her at this? As if catching her fear, the hens clucked and one began to chase another in a circle and sent feathers twirling up. She turned her head aside, not wanting to be humiliated. No matter how important she felt her task, squatting in a shit-strewn pen with hens cavorting at her feet would be a shameful and embarrassing thing to explain.

Both Ulfrik and Gunnar huddled together, her husband's excited animation clear in the way his hands swept at invisible landscapes. Gunnar nodded and inserted his own gestures as the two arrived at the hall. They stopped to be greeted with a curt bow and then vanished inside. Runa sat straighter and wondered if she should try to listen, or if directly joining them was a better idea. Unable to decide, she sat back on her stump and waited. Soon, they emerged out the back door with Toki. The three huddled together like boys planning to prank the serving girls. Whatever they discussed, all three seemed excited and Toki continually looked north as if expecting something. She could not hear them from this distance, and feared to move lest she give herself away. Their meeting lasted longer than it would take Runa to cook a dinner, and she began to lose patience. At last Toki and Ulfrik embraced, followed by Gunnar, and they departed.

Runa covered her head again, as Ulfrik and Gunnar cut around the barracks and passed close to the pen. She overheard scattered words, but none of them were coherent. The tenor of their speech was of excitement and anticipation. She noticed Gunnar wore his sword, and seeing it flapping at his waist nearly drew her to her feet. They passed her, both wrapped in their plans, and returned the way they had come.

"Now what?" she muttered to herself. "Something is happening, but not what I came to learn."

Stubbornness alone saw her wait longer, and only a few men left the hall, hirdmen who picked up shields and spears and tightened their furs against the breeze as they drifted off to their duties.

Then the gods rewarded her persistence.

Halla appeared behind the barracks now. She was alone, wrapped in a gray cloak, but her platinum hair was brilliant even in the shade. She paused and then looked about herself. Runa's heart stopped beating when Halla looked directly at her, but her gaze slid past. As if she might melt, Runa steadied herself on the stump and watched carefully.

Halla disappeared from view as she stepped back to the barracks, but then came out again with an empty bucket and ladle. She walked a short distance to the tree and then placed the bucket in the crook of its roots. With a glance over her shoulder, she carefully arranged the ladle to lean against the bucket and then stepped back from it before returning to the barracks.

Craning her neck higher, Runa wanted to investigate the bucket yet was not certain if Halla had gone inside or if she was just out of sight around the corner. This was a strange thing for anyone to do, and falling right on the heels of Ulfrik's visit only heightened the suspicion. She determined Halla had gone inside, and prepared to approach the tree where the bucket lay.

Then a horn sounded, one long note to summon their hirdmen to the main hall. The reaction was almost instant, though the single note indicated only a summons and no danger. Men were flowing out of the barracks and surrounding building and heading toward the hall. Runa would have to join Ulfrik, or her absence would arouse worry. She glanced at the bucket, but already men were exiting from the back of the hall. Toki would surely join them.

She cursed in frustration at the timing, but she retired from the pen, scattering hens as she left. That bucket was a signal to someone, she knew. If she could not learn now, she would learn without any more delay who Halla wanted to signal. For the moment, she had to answer the call of the horn. But as she took the back path to the hall, she smiled. Halla would be revealed for the traitorous witch she was, and she would know where Hakon was being held. It had been a good morning after all.

33

Gunnar constantly touched his sword as if to assure himself it would still be there. Several warriors had congratulated him with a back slap or friendly knock on his head after Ulfrik gathered the hirdmen to announce Gunnar's mission. He burned with pride for it. He was one of them now, even if not yet tested in battle. That would come soon enough, he thought. The day had refused to warm despite the bright sun and his breath curled before him in threadlike wisps as he waited at the center square for Toki to prepare his men. A few of his friends clustered with him and idled in the midmorning cold. They joked about Gunnar presenting himself to Hrolf the Strider on his father's behalf. "You'll have to kneel before him, something you don't know how to do. You should practice with me," one said to the amusement of the others.

Gunnar smiled but his thoughts were far away. His uncle had his own preparations to make for the journey, and so did Gunnar. While Toki was busy arranging supplies for what would normally be a week-long foot journey, Gunnar had to see Astra one last time. He scanned the approaches for her as his friends continued chattering and laughing. She was long overdue by his estimation and should have come for him after the announcement at the hall.

At last he saw her, entering the square from the northern path. Their eyes met, and his stomach burned. She had changed. No longer did she seem a radiant beauty whose every motion was a mystery of womanhood. Her hair no longer shimmered like gold, nor was her face a clear pool of beauty. Now she was a common girl, dressed in plain gray skirts with a smudged overdress. Her smile was a falsehood to conceal her snake's tongue. When she paused in her approach, Gunnar realized his face might have revealed too much of his thoughts. Even as his stomach roiled he schooled his expression and waved to her. Excusing himself from his friends, he met her at the edge of the square.

"I came as soon as I could," she said and stepped closer. Gunnar stiffened and she hesitated, biting off her next words.

"Sorry, I am nervous for this journey," he said. "It could be dangerous."

"I've heard you are leaving with a band of men, and that your father plans to sacrifice three goats to Thor to safeguard your trip. Is that all true?"

"Of course it is." He swept his hand behind him. "I am leaving right after the dedication of the sacrifice."

Astra searched his face and he glimpsed the faint squint of her eyes. How often had she appraised him like a sack of grain at market, he wondered, and yet never saw it for all his foolish infatuation. It galled him to realize she was far less skillful than he had thought, and himself far more gullible.

Her brows knitted in worry and she lowered her voice. "Then do be careful, Gunnar. Who will be traveling with you?"

"My Uncle Toki and his crew are all we can spare. To be honest, they are not the best fighting men. Farmers from the Faerayjar Islands mostly, and not enough have been in true battle. I guess I fit well with them, but I pray the gods we don't meet trouble on the road."

Gunnar imagined Astra smiled for a moment, but her concern only deepened. "Then you must demand better men. The land is never safe, but it's so much worse now with Clovis and Throst about."

"Neither has the guts to fight in the open, even if we were to lay facedown in the grass for them. I'm more concerned for bandits finding us than either of those fools."

A hint of pink tinged Astra's cheeks and her delay was louder than a shout to Gunnar. *Take that taunt back to your lover*, he thought.

"Then I don't suppose you have much to worry about," she said, scanning the people behind Gunnar. "Why are you going overland when a ship would be faster?"

Now Gunnar paused and her eyes met his with a sudden wickedness he never expected. In truth they traveled overland to lure out their enemies, and travel down the Seine would be more efficient for thirty men in need of haste. Did she see through the ruse?

"The ships are all dry docked in their boathouses, and we've no time for portage to the Seine. Besides, carrying a ship overland would be a signal to anyone watching for us. Like I said, we don't want to draw attention. Anyway, Hrolf will send us back in ships along with the men we need."

Astra nodded and the breeze shifted a lock of hair across her face. Only yesterday he would have delighted at the delicate hair playing in the wind, but now he saw only ugly falsehood. Would she have laughed as Throst's men overpowered him and dragged him away, pants down and face bloodied? Would she have taunted him in imprisonment, and watched Clovis chop off his right hand in vengeance? He still could not imagine it, but the truth of her deceit remained.

"Be careful, my love," she said at last. "Come back to me as soon as you are able. I will want to welcome you home with something special."

She smiled and leaned into him, pressing her soft breasts on his arm. He stiffened at the venomous touch, witnessing the temptation his father promised she would offer to lead him into doom. It was all true. All of it.

"It will be a passionate homecoming," he said with a smile that trembled in near collapse. "For now, be well, Astra."

He pulled away and strode past her, heading north to see what delayed Toki and to escape the pain that threatened to overwhelm him.

34

"So it is only you and I left behind," Runa said softly. "And all the others who my husband doesn't trust."

"That bitterness does not fit you," Snorri chided. "The fewer who know the better, and part of the hird must remain in case Clovis sees Ravndal as the better choice."

Runa and Snorri walked the northern track toward the mead hall. Aren held her hand and listened attentively to all she said. Einar's wife, Bera, went ahead with her girls and bore a torch aloft to light the early evening. Glowing lights from open doors winked out as the tradesmen and their families settled for the night. All the men who had just slipped out the gates under Ulfrik's command had drained Ravndal of activity, leaving behind confused families who had only learned of the departure moments before it happened.

"Ulfrik assures me Clovis won't be able to resist catching Gunnar in the open," she said as if the words were bile in her mouth. "This is madness, using our own son as a lure for a trap."

"Not madness, lass. It's daring plans like this that have raised him above others, and your son was willing to do it. It's how he'll learn these tricks for himself. Hold on, my leg. The damned cold makes it stiff."

She and Aren stopped while Snorri worked his thigh. Bera and her daughters continued to amble ahead and the circle of light went with them. Runa glanced at Aren, who stared pensively into the gloom of nightfall. She wondered what his young mind had made of all the recent events. Then there was the brutal farce Ulfrik had exposed to him. "I tried to get the two of you to leave, but you wouldn't go," Ulfrik had explained. Whatever his intention, he had failed and she believed their son hurt for it.

"That's better," Snorri announced. "Let's get to a warm fire. Nothing more to do until someone returns."

Runa smiled but said nothing, and the two walked in companionable silence. Snorri was like a father to her as much as he had been for Ulfrik. He loved her children, though he ignored Aren, and he would serve them with his life. He would never voice it, but she was certain he chaffed at Ulfrik's deceptions and being excluded from the action. She grasped the tactical sense of Ulfrik's plans, and admired how he would beat both Clovis and Throst at their clever games. Yet being fooled into believing he had abandoned hope and surrendered Hakon to fate had injured her. She barely had time to demonstrate how hurt she felt, but she would ensure he knew after his return. However much he would celebrate victory before his men, behind closed doors he would have to work hard to make amends to her.

At the hall, Bera and her daughters were already ordering servants to stoke the hearth and heat up the stew from dinner. The savory scent made Runa's mouth water, and Snorri expressed her thoughts. "Smell that? No need to go hungry just because the men are on the march."

As they ate, small talk filled the time. The evening the men left to war was always the strangest. Their faces were still fresh in mind, their voices still clear in memory, and fear of their deaths a passing thought. Yet the men were gone and their protection as well. Those left behind struggled to preserve normalcy that would be dead by the next morning when the women awoke to a cold spot where their husbands should be.

"Where is Halla living with Toki gone?" Snorri asked. Runa stiffened at the casual mention, knowing well that Snorri was reminding her of a duty to invite Halla into her home while Toki and all his men were away.

"She has not seen fit to approach me since we last spoke. I assume she has the company of other women."

Snorri nodded, not looking at her. All conversation ceased. Bera fussed with her youngest daughter, then she excused herself with an embarrassed smile. Runa let her go, seeing the nervousness at the mention of Halla's name. Once she had gone to the far end of the hall, where they made their home in a small room, Runa continued.

"Well, are you accusing me of being a poor host?" She glared at him, and his eyes widened and shoulders shrugged. "I already tried that and you know what it earned me. Besides, the little witch is plotting something. Don't give me that look. You know it. She has been Loki's right hand from the moment she stepped into my hall."

"I know you've never had any love for her, but for your brother's sake ..."

"My brother asked nothing of me before he left," Runa snapped. "If he wanted me to comfort his wife he'd have told me. He's such a love-struck fool. How old is he by now, and still the woman has him blinded."

"I wouldn't say that. I think the two are actually devoted to each other."

Now Runa's eyes went wide and her mouth bent in a shocked smile. "I expected better judgment from you, Snorri. All your years have imparted no deeper wisdom to you?"

"Not more about my age." He rolled his eyes. "Look, Toki and Halla are happy together. And as for your fears of her betrayal, that's a bit far-fetched even for you. She has been here barely a month, and after the troubles with Throst. How could she cause all these problems? Lass, it's better for you to quit looking for trouble with her."

"Not so. Today she left a sign for someone right after Ulfrik left. I saw it. She put out a bucket and ladle in a certain spot. Who was she trying to signal?"

"Her servants?"

"Don't mock me."

"Lass, you are spying on her? Listen to yourself. That's no way for the jarl's wife to behave. You'd shame yourself like that, just to accuse her of putting out a bucket and ladle?"

"Someone has to watch her." Runa's face grew hot with embarrassment. In the heat of her anger she had revealed too much. With her actions given voice, she heard how foolish they sounded. She had mucked about with chickens and disguised herself with poor clothing for no better reason than to convince herself Halla was at the bottom of her worries. Of course, Throst was the true enemy, but far out of reach.

Tears began to well in her eyes and her lips pressed tight. She was not helping Hakon, nor her husband or anyone else. She was striking out blindly and making life harder on everyone. Halla was still a witch, and her horrible words at their last meeting were unforgivable, but maybe she had nothing to do with the troubles in Ravndal. Maybe she had just hoped for it, to justify her hatred for the woman.

"Don't cry, Mother." Aren's small voice was a surprise and he tugged at her sleeve as she wiped a tear away.

Runa gave a watery laugh, and patted Aren's head. "Don't fret for me. Mother is all right, just realizing that she might have been a fool."

"Not a fool. Only desperate to lay hands on the enemy," Snorri corrected gently. "No one blames you for wanting that. Just get your hands on the right enemy."

Runa laughed and dabbed her last tear, not knowing what to do with her hands or where to look. Such humiliation was unfamiliar territory for her, and her sole respite was that only Snorri had to witness it.

"No, Mother." Aren again tugged at her sleeve. "Halla and Astra are friends, but they don't want to be friends. They're not real friends."

"What do you mean?" Runa shared a worried glance with Snorri.

"It's like Astra and Gunnar. Astra is not his real friend. She is pretending."

Runa's hands grew cold at the simple innocence of Aren's statement. How could he have known when Runa only learned the same from Ulfrik last night? He had roused her from bed, taken her into the hall, and Aren had slept through all of it.

"What do you mean?" she asked, followed with nervous laughter.

"Astra is a bad person. She hates me, and she hates Father too. She doesn't make a real smile to Gunnar, or say real words. Gunnar thinks she is his friend, but when he is not looking Astra has a mean face for him."

Snorri shuddered and turned aside, rubbing his sides as if a cold wind had blown through the hall. Runa also felt the chill, for a child should not be so observant or concerned with nuances of the adult world. Yet, he was always the overlooked presence, and few people understood or expected his acuity. They might carelessly reveal much to his young eyes.

"So what do you mean about Halla and Astra? I didn't know they were friends."

"They pretend they can't see each other, but they always meet by accident." Aren emphasized his last word, and again Runa held her breath at the strange maturity of his speech. "They want to be friends, but can't be because you wouldn't like it."

"No, I wouldn't like it. Why do you think they fear I'd be upset?"

"They are always looking at you."

"Enough of this," Snorri said, louder than was reasonable. "The boy wants to please you, lass. Can't you see that? He doesn't even make sense."

"It makes sense to me. As it is said, birds of a feather most flock together."

"And it is also said, what people wish they soon believe. So it is with you. Now even the words of a child will sway you."

Runa bit her lip and stared hard at Snorri, who returned her stare with equal ferocity. Glancing down at Aren, his expression was calm but resolute. His small hand again yanked on her sleeve, but rather than speak he simply raised his brows. He was too young for the games Snorri suggested he played. Children pleased their parents by working hard for their attention and doing their chores, not by subterfuge. For all his uncanny intelligence, Aren was still a child.

"Al right, Snorri," Runa said with a smile. "Let us see what happens upon Astra's return. Give new instructions to the men you set on watch for her. Tell them to allow Astra to return and see where she goes."

"She's not going to return, not if she believes what she is reporting to Throst. There's no reason to come back here. She will probably be caught when Konal springs his trap."

"Nevertheless, will you do what I ask?"

Snorri stared at her long moments, his tired, drooping eyes searching hers. At last he nodded. "Aye, if it will stop this foolishness, but I can't let it go overlong. I promised Ulfrik to seize her as soon as she returned. If she does not meet with Halla within the day, I will move on her."

"Fair enough," Runa said. "Now, in the meantime, I think Halla should be invited to my home as you hinted."

"There's a bad idea." Snorri ran his hands through his hair and sighed. "If you can't make her guilty through Astra, you intend to pick a fight?"

"I intend to keep my enemy where I can see her. Whatever you think, I believe she's had too much freedom and has used it for ill. I'll take a few men and Bera with me to convince her. First thing tomorrow morning."

Snorri waved his hands as if surrendering. "I miss the shieldwall more every day. At least you know where the blades are coming from."

Runa smiled, not at his quip but at her knowing now that she would have Halla under her thumb. She patted Aren's shoulder and he gave a faint smile tinged with wicked satisfaction.

185

35

Gunnar strained his vision against the thin light of morning and no longer saw what he had glimpsed on the crest of the hill. He pulled at the collar of his mail coat, the cold chain links catching at the skin of his neck, and scanned the crest again. Toki, also dressed in mail, stood beside him, and to their backs thirty men in various leathers and furs leaned on their spears. Some slung their shields onto their arms, anxious for the battle they expected.

"It must have been a bird," Gunnar said, blinking to clear his eyes. "Too soon for Clovis to have acted." They had only been awake an hour and set out at the stain of dawn. This was the first full day of travel and Gunnar wanted to distance himself far enough from Ravndal to embolden Clovis.

"The sooner we mount that hill, the easier I will feel," Toki said. "Low ground is a poor spot for battle. If you have doubts about something beyond that crest, then what should you do?"

Toki had deferred leadership to Gunnar, and even though it was more ceremony than actual trust in his abilities, it gave him enormous pride. The men following him were near strangers, but he still enjoyed being a part of them. Toki guided his decisions, and Gunnar appreciated the help even if it felt strained. Right now, black dots of birds circled beneath clumps of iron gray clouds high above the ridge, and he could not shake the image of a man crouched atop it. The shape had risen from prone and briefly silhouetted against the morning sky. Or had it?

"I'll send Eskil to scout the crest before we mount it." He gestured for the guide Ulfrik had assigned them to come forward, then dispatched him up the hill. Eskil was the only man who knew the way to Hrolf's settlements near Rouen. As he neared the crest, he went to his belly and crawled the final distance to peer over the side. He sat motionless, pushed himself higher after a time, then finally waved his arm to signal the ground was clear.

Gunnar smiled in relief, and Toki chuckled beside him. "Caution is right for our situation," Toki said. "We have plenty to fear and being caught without Ulfrik's support would be a disaster."

They followed the crest line, both to keep watch for danger and to display themselves to Clovis and his allies. They left a clear trail behind them, both for Ulfrik and Clovis to track them. Gunnar slowed their pace, fearful of outstripping his father, but Toki insisted there was nothing to fear. He took heart from his uncle's easy confidence, even if his men appeared as skittish as a herd of foals. Soon the crest led them down to the grasslands that spilled out to the horizon. Eskil advised Rouen was still days away though most of their journey would be through forest paths after they cleared the plain.

"If we gain the forest, then it will be harder for my father to close the trap, and if we stay on the plains he will be spotted before he can." Gunnar looked at Toki for affirmation, and his uncle nodded slowly but offered no advice. He frowned and gazed across the plains in silence, considering the safest action to take. "But we're not really headed to Rouen. So let's head south, as if we plan to follow the Seine. It will bring us closer to Clovis's borders anyway."

Again he searched Toki's face, but found nothing but indifference. Making decisions for thirty men was a lot harder than he had thought, even for something as banal as this. If he chose poorly, men could be killed, but if he led them straight he would risk spoiling the trap. Had his father only told him what do, he would have followed. Frustration yielded to shame as he realized his father had entrusted him to figure out how to make the trap work. If he would be a man, he would have to make choices and live with them.

"We go south," he said more firmly. "Eskil, will my father find more cover there?"

"Much more," Eskil agreed. "And we can show ourselves to the farmers there, who will be sure to send word back to Clovis as soon as we do."

They renewed their trek and Toki offered little conversation as they walked. No one had pushed themselves, but Gunnar's legs were beginning to stiffen. Sensing the others suffered the same, he ordered them to stop and the men gratefully sat themselves in the grass.

"Could you not have at least waited until we gained that hill?" Toki asked. "I hate the low ground."

"That's a hill?" Gunnar looked across at the gentle rise and snorted. "I wouldn't say there's any advantage to holding it."

"But we can't see beyond it, can we? We're blind down here."

Eskil shook his head and volunteered to scout the hill, departing without a word. "You're not letting him rest," Gunnar chided.

"He's young yet. Let that strength be our benefit."

Both laughed and watched Eskil perform his same scouting maneuvers, crawling on is belly to the edge of the crest.

But this time, he did not wave.

He scrabbled back down, then gained his feet and dashed the final distance hunched over as if running through a hailstorm. Toki and Gunnar both stood as he stumbled to them, and others nearby turned to listen. All faces were tight with fear, and Gunnar felt his knees weaken at the sight of Eskil's wide eyes.

"There are dozens of tents pitched in a field beyond that hill, and horses picketed in line. Maybe fifty horses. It's an army, flying Count Odo's flag of blue and white. We're practically on top of them."

"By Odin's one eye!" Gunnar cursed, feeling his guts turn to water. "How did we not see them first?"

Toki bared Gunnar with his arm. His other hand touched his

temple as if he were in pain. "Odo should have his men in Paris, not this far into Hrolf's territories. Unless, of course, he's planning a raid, which must be Odo's intent."

"How did we not see them first?" Gunnar insisted again. He had chosen this path, and led them right into an army they would be pressed to defeat even with his father's aid. If Clovis was headed for him, then he had consigned all of them to death between both Frankish forces. "An army like that should make some noise, right?"

"It matters only that we've seen them now, before they've spotted us," Toki said. He dropped his arm from Gunnar's chest, then gestured for the men to gather. They had already begun, the men closest spreading the dreadful news to those in the rear.

Suddenly Gunnar stood pressed into the center of wide-eyed men who trembled behind their shields. He could not think of what to say, nor what they should do. His mouth was dry and his head began to ache. Fortunately, the men looked to Toki for direction and not him. Being a jarl's son, their dismissal stung his pride. Yet he had expected more from himself at the moment of danger, and came up wanting. The men could not be blamed for seeking confident leadership, which Toki immediately provided.

"We're going to back up the way we came and once away we race for Ulfrik. Depending on what Clovis brings to the fight, we should be fine if we join with Ulfrik's force."

"This whole plan has gone to shit," one of the men said, and other nervous voices agreed.

"Silence," Toki said in a hissing voice. "Not one more word, and no sounds. Turn and put some distance between us and the Franks."

Gunnar echoed Toki's orders, if only as a meditation on success. If they followed that plan, they could get away. Gods, he wanted to fight in the shieldwall, but not with frightened men outnumbered by royal warriors. Once beside his father's veterans, he would have a chance at glory. It was a simple thing to move off unseen. Many were already flooding away, and a few at the far end started to run. See, it was easy, he told himself.

Only beneath his feet was the easy trail they had left for Ulfrik and Clovis.

Toki and he walked at a jog as more of the men began to run. Gunnar refused to look behind, as if to look over his shoulder would bring the Franks.

It failed him nonetheless. A horn blared behind him, pealing like thunder over their heads. A full route began and the men scattered like leaves in a wind. Toki swore, grabbed Gunnar's arm and began running. "Fall back to the woods," he shouted. "We can lose them there. Run!"

Gunnar and Toki ran, but their mail caused them to lag and the others plunged on ahead. The grassy plains no longer seemed flat, and every dip or rise thwarted the fleeing men with stumbles and falls.

Then the thud of hooves and the first Frankish riders zoomed past on both sides.

Their horses pounded the earth, sending clods of dirt into the air. The riders' cruel spears lowered and men howled as the shafts pierced them. Gunnar saw a man lifted from the ground, a broken shaft square in his back and brilliant scarlet flowing over his green jerkin.

"Shieldwall!" Toki shouted, and jerked Gunnar short. "Don't die in shame. Fight!"

Gunnar spun with his uncle, who pulled his shield onto his arm. "Get your shield on," he snapped as he drew his sword.

A dozen of Toki's men gathered to their sides and shields raised as spears pointed at the Franks. The riders plunged to either side, bypassing them for the cowards who fled. Their dying shrieks were wet and short, and the whoops of the Franks gave a voice to evil.

Gunnar drew his sword and touched his shield to the man at his side. His neck throbbed and his vision hazed. No one could help him now. He tightened his grip on the hilt of his weapon, the rough shark-skin wrap biting into his sweaty palm. He stood at the center of the small cluster, sweat rolling from his forehead into his eyes. More Franks bolted past them, but as one strayed too close, Toki licked out with his sword to slash the beast's legs. The animal screamed and both beast and rider crashed behind them.

"Sell your lives well," Toki shouted. "We will meet in Valhalla soon."

Gunnar did not doubt it. As more riders galloped past, giving them a wider berth, a solid block of Franks approached on foot. They were a black mass of sharp spears and conical helmets. Their long, tear-shaped shields were painted blue with a white diagonal stripe, the colors of King Odo of the Western Franks. At the fore of these men came a standard bearer and beside him a regal man in bright mail. Gunnar wondered if it was the king himself.

The block of Franks halted and Gunnar crouched behind his shield, expecting arrows to rain upon them. Nothing happened. He looked to Toki, who just stared at the enemy with his teeth bared. "What will they do?"

Toki shrugged. "Stay close to me if they charge. Each of us is worth ten of them. I know the Franks, and they fight like old women."

From the enveloping scent of blood, Gunnar doubted the Franks were so weak. In the next instant, the horsemen returned. They galloped their mounts in a wide circle. The beating of hooves drummed Gunnar's head and their dizzying pace confused his vision. The men drove their beasts with careless ease, seeming to delight in the blurring speed.

"They're playing with us," said a man to Gunnar's left.

"This will be the last game they play," Toki replied and he rapped the edge of his shield against Gunnar's. It galvanized him.

"We will have too much horseflesh to carry back home," Gunnar added with bravado he did not feel. "It will be a shame to leave so much on the field when we are done."

A few of the men laughed, and Toki glanced at him with a weak smile. Gunnar straightened himself at the approval, and snarled at the circling Franks. As long as he died fighting, he would be rewarded with a place in Valhalla where his uncle and father would surely meet him. Fear had no claim on him now. He need only to trust his sword and fate.

The mounted Franks suddenly broke away, turning back for the rear of their lines as the footmen approached. Gunnar again raised his shield, but the arrows did not come. Toki hissed between his gritted teeth. The spears lined up against the Franks wavered as the men gripping them began to lose courage.

"Steady now," Gunnar said. "We'll take ten of them for every one of us."

The haughty Franks stopped within spear-throwing distance, as if to tempt them to waste their weapons. The leader stepped forward and scanned the line, his eyes settling on both Toki and Gunnar. Their mail coats betrayed their status, and Gunnar suddenly wished for more humble furs rather than mail.

"The young one must be important to stand at the front of his line," Gunnar heard the leader say to another warrior who came to his side. Unlike his parents, Gunnar had learned Frankish nearly as well as his own tongue. Many of his friends were Franks and the language was everywhere. He could hardly remember a time when he didn't speak it, and realized that now he was likely the only one who understood.

"All your companions are dead," the Frankish leader shouted at them. The sun gleamed off his helmet and Gunnar could not see his face, though he imagined a royal face with predatory features held in a false smile. The image was distinct in his mind, even if he could not see the man clearly. "Surrender or we will run you down."

Gunnar glanced at Toki, who had not shifted from his snarl. He realized no one understood the ultimatum, and began to translate. "He wants us to ..."

"Surrender or die," Toki finished for him. "No surprise in that. Now the question is do we fight or lay down our weapons?"

He gave Gunnar a look as if the decision were as simple as choosing the best pin for a cloak. Yet he was asking Gunnar to pick between life or death, and not only for himself but for all the men who had stood with him. What value was there in a life lesson when life was measured by the breath, he thought. Death hovered only a spear's length away, and the horsemen had reformed behind their lord as if to emphasize that one charge would trample them all into pulp. There was no choice. Toki watched him impassively, as if his life mattered not at all.

"There is no glory in wasting our lives," Gunnar said hesitantly and reading Toki's face for a reaction. His uncle held his expression flat, and Gunnar continued without knowing if he displeased him. "My father can pay our ransom, which the Franks must want if they have not finished us yet."

Toki nodded slowly, but said nothing. Several of the other men were less heroic and threw their weapons and shields on the grass the moment Gunnar voiced his thoughts. This drew derisive laughter from the Franks and the leader waved his hand in dismissal.

"Live to see the sunset, a wise choice," the leader said. "You are my prisoners now. Come forward, young one. You speak a real language after all."

Gunnar translated for the others, then tossed his weapons to the ground. The remaining men dropped their spears and shields in silent disgust. Only Toki held his longer than any other, and once all his men had surrendered he placed his sword carefully atop the criss-crossed pile of spears.

The Frankish lord did not look much different from what Gunnar had imagined. His head was rounder and his features softer. His beard was indeed neatly trimmed and his face clean, marred only with a white scar across his nose. Gunnar knew he was not the king, not with that scar, but he still held himself rigid and proud like royalty. When he spoke, he peered down his nose rather than incline his head.

"What is your name? Who do you serve?"

"I'm Gunnar Ulfrikson, and I serve my father who serves Hrolf the Strider, who is master of this land."

The Frank raised a thin brow, and a wicked smile formed on his red lips. "A fine ransom you will make. I'm already repaid for making this damned journey."

"And who are you?"

The leader clucked at Gunnar and frowned. "I am your master;

that is all you need to know. What difference could it make to you, pup?"

"If I don't know your name then when I sing about the day I killed you I will have to call you the Frankish Pig."

The leader burst into laughter. Gunnar had expected a beating, but instead the Frank dismissed him to another who started to bind his arms behind his back.

Toki was shoved forward next to Gunnar, and he gave a wan smile. "I'd forgotten what this was like."

"You've been captured before?" Gunnar had never heard of such things. His father's exploits were always of great victories and never of defeats.

"Not something I've enjoyed, but yes. This one is hard. We only struck one blow before defeat."

Gunnar was about to reply when a Frank slapped his head and yelled for silence. Soon, all of them were bound and being led toward the Frankish camp. A glance over his shoulder revealed shattered bodies splayed out in the grass. Gunnar swallowed hard, faced forward, and dared not look back again.

36

Ulfrik stood at the center of the dead bodies, flocks of birds circling overhead and screaming at him and his men for disturbing their repast. He hardly knew these men, having been only with him for a short time, yet their deaths pressed on his heart. Einar and the others walked quietly among the slain like cloaked phantoms, bending over the fallen to close eyelids or place hands on weapons. The corpses were already cold and hardened in death, and fat black ravens had already pecked and tore the eyes from most of the bodies. Flies buzzed over the thick pools of blood and unlike the birds persisted in their feast.

Gunnar and Toki were not among the dead. He had searched every body, scoured every inch of ground, and found nothing. It was small comfort, realizing the two of them plus a handful of others had become prisoners of whoever had overcome them. The mass of hoof prints indicated Frankish cavalry working with a contingent of footmen. The remains of a camp were over a low crest, meaning they had come from a distance, most likely Paris, though he could not be sure.

"The day is late," Einar said as he joined Ulfrik. He squinted up at the flocks of birds crying in rage. "We've no sign that Clovis took the bait yet. What will you have us do?"

Ulfrik tucked is helmet underarm and scrubbed his face with both hands. "This was not how it was to end. There was never to be another Frankish army out here. These men were not to be run down like animals. My son and brother were not to be taken captive. I was not supposed to have you do anything more than shatter Clovis's army."

He bit off his last sentence, aware that his voice was both rising and breaking. The men with him were veterans of long service, and hardened to the worst the battlefield could offer. They would understand his frustration and anger, but they would never brook indecision or self-pity. A few dark faces glanced at him, then returned to dragging the corpses together. Others searched for stones to build a rough cairn for the slain. No one had asked them to do it. They simply knew these men deserved better than to be fodder for ravens.

"This is fate," Einar said, putting his hand upon Ulfrik's shoulder. "You cannot blame yourself, for what is done is over. You've told me that yourself, do you remember?"

Ulfrik smiled and nodded. "Fate rules the lives of men, how true. But it is cruel and spiteful. Today Hakon will be freed, and Gunnar takes his place. Worse still, I fear I know where these Franks are going with him."

Both men shifted their eyes toward the east, back the way they had come, where Clovis's fort held a salient of Frankish land in Hrolf's domain. The trail leading from camp pointed straight for it.

"Then we must make haste to catch them before they can get to Clovis." Einar touched the silver amulet of Thor's Hammer at his neck and spit on the grass.

"We must travel throughout the night if we're to have any hope," Ulfrik said. "I can't be certain of their numbers, be we might be enough to challenge them. But if Clovis arrives ..."

Both men stood silently, neither wanting to give voice to the thought of being outnumbered and exhausted in a fight. Ulfrik watched two men carry a stiff corpse between them, a shattered spear thrust through the trunk and thick ropes of blood dangling beneath it. He had seen worse, far worse, but the silhouette of death broke something inside him. He heard Gunnar's voice in his head, saw his eyes widen in surprise and confusion the moment he had recognized his father intended to use him as bait in a trap.

For the first time in years, he felt a hotness in his eyes and a weakness in his limbs. Einar spotted the change, and drew closer. "What is it?"

"What have I done? What have I become?" He looked Einar in the eyes, and his young friend frowned in confusion. "I used Gunnar to bait a trap that has snared him instead. I've let Hakon linger in the hands of a monster when I could have saved him. I've deceived my wife, my friends. For what? Victory over my enemies? Glory? What?"

His voice rose and he did not care. Those nearby paused to stare at him, but he was not seeing them, only noting their presence. His thoughts were filled with his sons. "Not even my father would have done this, and he could be cruel."

"Ulfrik, you could not have known the Franks were on the march."

"Don't you see it? These dead men were slain for no better purpose than to deal a clever blow to my enemy."

"And so it is for all jarls," Einar raised his own voice, though tamed it as he realized his disrespect. "This is no different from all the other battles we've fought."

"No! I sent them out unsupported."

"We are the support!"

Einar's shout stopped the others at work, and they faced him with curious looks. Ulfrik too was snapped from his self-pity, and he blinked a few moments to gather his thoughts.

"I do not deserve what I have," Ulfrik said, far more quietly. He turned away from the others and began to walk slowly away. Einar followed.

"That is nonsense. You've more than earned your renown; Hrolf respects you above all others save Gunther One-Eye. That says much."

"Yes, and while earning that respect I have shamed myself before my family. Look at what I have wrought for my sons. I did not give Hakon to Throst, but I've left him there longer than needed. What excuse do I have? What if Throst maims him in the days I allowed Hakon to remain captive? I should be fed to dogs, Einar. If dogs would find my bones worth gnawing."

"Gods," Einar muttered his curse as he pulled Ulfrik to a halt. "Konal is with him and responsible for Hakon now. You have turned your enemies' wiles back upon them. It will make a song for skalds to praise you for ages."

Ulfrik laughed without mirth. "That is the problem. I thought the same, and I traded both my sons to make it so. I have driven my wife to near madness and lied to all of you about my intentions. I am mad for glory, Einar, blinded with it and destroyed by it. Do you know I left Toki on the Faereyjar all these years without any thought of what it did to him, just so I could say I possessed those lands? Even if I never intended to visit them again? How could I have done that to my greatest friend and such a noble warrior? He deserved better of me. And now he is lost as well."

Ulfrik stared at the horizon across the rolling plains of brown grass, and the stains of twilight in the east were chasing away the light. Stars already peered through the cheerless blue sky. Einar had no answer for him, and Ulfrik silently chuckled.

"I have much to make amends for," he continued. "I am sorry to have spilled out my bile in front of you. I am shamed once again. Men follow me because I win battles and give them gold and glory. But I've traded off too much of myself to do it. Now fate has shown me what it exchanged to make me the jarl of Ravndal, and it is a bitter price."

"Ulfrik, you talk as if you are defeated. That is your only shame to my mind. If you suffer so much for your son's fates, then by Odin's one eye do something about it rather than piss yourself with remorse. You want to win this battle, then fucking fight it."

Einar's face burned with intensity and his lip curled in a snarl. Ulfrik stood astonished and embarrassed, but he instantly recognized the truth. Einar grabbed his arm and shook him once as if to wake him from a dream, and he did feel as if he had slipped into a fog. He clasped his hand to Einar's arm and squeezed it.

"You are right. Completely right. You'll not hear my complaints again, nor will the men. My sons must come first. Gunnar might yet be saved, and all my imagined terrors need not come to be. I've wasted time. Let's finish the cairn for the dead and be on the march tonight."

Einar's face melted into a smile, and he gave a slow, solid nod. "I'll hurry the men."

He turned toward them, and as he left, Ulfrik called him back. "Thank you, Einar."

The huge man flashed a shy, boyish smile and then walked off to his task.

Ulfrik sighed heavily, not willing to forgive himself and still not comfortable looking too deeply into his heart. When the battles were done, there would be time to set right his mistakes. For now, Gunnar was his priority, and he prayed the gods that Hakon was now freed and on his way home.

37

Weak light suffused the morning sky, a pale and cold swath that framed the bare trees of the woods. Throst drew his cloak about himself as he waited for Astra to show. Her voice had been so thin when she whispered through the wall to rouse him, he still wondered if he had dreamed it. His breath puffed before him as he laughed at the thought of running out to meet a dream. Her voice had been small but urgent, filled with promise of something that grew more dire with each moment. Dream or no, he had to meet her on the hill with its lone oak as the voice had asked.

A crunch of dead leaves alerted him, and he leapt to the other side of the oak to find Astra climbing it in the gloom. Her hair was disheveled and her face smeared with dirt, making him realize that in past meetings she had paused to clean herself before seeking him. As much as the thought flattered him, her carelessness now spoke to her urgency and a spark of worry flickered in his chest.

"You are alone? No one saw you come?" she asked in a husky, low voice.

"You managed to only wake me and Dan, but I convinced him to return to sleep. You have news?"

"It's all a trap," she said, scrabbling the distance to tumble into his arms. "You are in danger."

He pushed her away and in the stain of dawn saw her eyes bright with fear. "What trap? Slow down and explain."

Drawing a breath, she smoothed her skirt and tried again in a steadier voice. "Lord Ulfrik sent Konal and his men to you on purpose, to free his son and kill you."

"What? You told me Konal was true, that he and Ulfrik fought and was banished. I found him camped at the border." Throst stopped, suddenly realizing how skillfully the deceit had been crafted. No one knew but Ulfrik and Konal; everyone else had been made to believe Konal's disgrace was genuine. Ulfrik knew Throst needed more men, particularly those with a grudge against him. He just set Konal out to be discovered, a means to ease any suspicions. A fire began to smolder in his guts and his teeth gnashed in anger.

"I was fooled," Astra explained, waving her hands palm out. "Everyone was fooled, even Gunnar and Runa."

"But why has Konal waited so long? And what has happened with Gunnar? I expected that he would be ready to follow you out of Ravndal."

"I don't know what delays Konal, but Gunnar is gone. He went with his uncle and thirty men to Rouen seeking aid from Hrolf the Strider."

Throst's brows raised at the news. Thirty men were little more than token guards, and Clovis might be willing to reward him for information that led to Gunnar's capture. Yet it was of little value if he could not slip Konal and his men. He hated to believe it, but his own warriors were little better than dogs and hardly a match for any of Konal's. He cursed himself for not seeing through the ruse, for not realizing these men were too good to be what they had seemed. While he had every confidence of victory in a one-on-one fight, Throst knew he could not defeat all of them.

"Listen to me," he said, grabbing Astra by the arm. "There is value in that bit of news, and if I can get it to Clovis in time he might be willing to pay for it. If he could capture Gunnar on the march that would make Hakon more valuable to him. But there is the issue of Konal. If he is delaying, it is because there is more to this trap than we know. What else have you learned?"

"Nothing more. It happened so fast, and I came here directly after Gunnar left."

"Does Gunnar suspect you, or anyone else for that matter?"

"Gunnar was strange when he left. I don't know for sure. Maybe he was afraid not having his father to hold his hand. But no one else knows my role."

Throst nodded, turned away to search the brightening sky. The situation had become far more desperate in the space of a few moments. Astra had probably spared his life. His best course was to fetch his mother and sister and fade away. But that would be a defeat. Defeat was not necessary, not when he still held a strong weapon in Hakon. Striking the thought from his mind, he began to mull other choices. Astra touched him as if to speak again, but he threw her arm off and hushed her. After several moments of consideration, he had settled upon his plan.

"Take word to my sister that she is to go with our mother to the caves where we hid before. I don't know if she will be able to find it on her own, maybe not, but they are not safe to go with me. After you do this, return to Ravndal."

"But what if I am discovered?" Astra grabbed his arm again, her fingernails digging into the flesh of his forearm. "I can't return until nightfall, or I will be discovered. I am amazed I slipped out so often without being caught. Anyway, if anyone marks my absence they might suspect me as your informer."

"Ulfrik will be looking for a man, not a girl. If you are discovered, lie to them about why you have left. Maybe you are fucking a farmer's son behind Gunnar's back. Is that so unlikely? You worry overmuch. Besides, I have one last blow to strike at Ulfrik. I want you to bring the third son to me, the strange child. Let Ulfrik lose all his family for the way he took my father from me. All three of his brats, wouldn't that be something!"

Astra reflected his smile, then frowned. "But what if the boy really is Konal's? Maybe he won't care."

"He's raising the brat, isn't he?" Throst pulled her arm away, but held her hand. "Anyway, our time here will be at an end. We turn over his children to Clovis for a good price and then the two of us will slip away to live a better life. Justice will have been done, and we will be richer for it."

Her smile widened and she hugged him in excitement. The soft warmth of her distracted Throst, and he wished he had more time to indulge his lust, but he had to act before Konal could.

"Go now to my sister," he said as he pulled back. "We will not meet again until all is done. Here, this is my cloak pin which I'll place under this rock. When you have Ulfrik's third son or you need to meet me, retrieve this pin and I will know to seek you in your mother's home village in the east. If the pin remains, I will wait nearby for you to show."

He slipped the pin under the rock and pressed it down with his boot. His cloak slipped from his shoulder, and he wrapped it into his hand. He might need it in the fight he expected upon his return to the hideout. Astra's eyes shimmered with tears and she kissed him gently. "I do not know how I will capture Aren on my own, or take him from Ravndal, but I will do all that I can."

"Do your best. If Clovis has all three sons, he would command Ulfrik's life and pay me well. But this youngest one seems less dear to either of them. Perhaps it would be better if you killed the brat outright. That Ulfrik suffer is more important than squeezing out the last bit of gold from Clovis."

Astra blinked and stared expressionless at him. Throst suppressed a smile, knowing his offhand request for murder hit her like a stone. He wondered at her loyalty, and enjoyed learning how far she could be pushed. For so long she had been as pliable but as unbreakable as a green sapling. Yet would she murder a child for his pleasure? It was an interesting question, and if so then what did it mean for his control over her? Would she even be interesting to him any longer, having so thoroughly dominated her?

"You could do that for me, couldn't you? You promised to be my agent in places where I could no longer go. Remember that terrible day I was torn from your side, barely a moment to say farewell. You told me those very words."

"I ..." Astra blinked again and her voice trailed off, though her wide eyes never left his.

"If you cannot kill him, then bring him to me. But do not return without achieving either outcome. Now, go. We waste time here, and I have to act before Konal and his men do."

hrost and Astra walked in silence until close to the hideout, and then she peeled away to warn his sister and mother. Throst watched her disappear into the trees with the grace of a doe, and he wondered if the girl really understood her talent. He regretted that he might be throwing her away too soon, but she could best serve him inside Ulfrik's hall. Should she be caught and the truth beaten out of her, then after this morning it would not matter anyway.

Dawn was yellow and cold, and brown leaves rolled across the dead grass. Silent footing was a precarious thing in autumn, and he would have liked more of it, but his revised plans did not require stealth. That was Astra's purview. He was going to enjoy handling Konal and his men in a way they would never expect.

Despite having no rooster to crow the arrival of the new day, men were already loitering in the yard before the hall. He was surprised, though he should not have been. Konal and his men were gathered together, with the pretense of collecting wood for the hearth, though too many hands made their task unconvincing. Throst noted how they strained to ignore him, only Konal successfully feigning he had no other thought but to kindle the morning fire. But all of them wore swords, giving away their clumsy performance.

"Good morning!" Throst called to them. "You are all gathered together. This is good. I've got news for you."

Konal flung the wedge of firewood back to the pile and turned, his hand reflexively reaching for his hilt. Throst never flinched as he approached, acting as if he did not see Konal barely gaining control of his killing reflex. Astra's news had come none too soon. Throst had but only an instant to make everything work in his favor.

"And where have you been?" Konal challenged him, his hand brushing past the hilt of his sword.

"Getting word from my contact in Ravndal, of course. It seems we've lost our chances at Gunnar."

Konal's men stood straighter, and Throst immediately guessed he had spoken the signal they had expected. His eyes did not leave Konal's, which seemed to glitter with a malevolence befitting his nightmarish scars. In the moment Konal reached for his sword, Dan exited the hall with Olaf behind him. Both men were unarmed but their sudden appearance gave Throst a lucky break.

"I want you to take Hakon to safety for me," he blurted out. The offer had the intended effect of stunning Konal and his men. He continued to surprise them, making their betrayal easier. "It's not safe here, not with Clovis knowing our hideout, and I'm about to deliver bad news to him. Hakon is our only play against Ulfrik for now. Konal, you and your men take him to the caves where we hid from Ulfrik. I will send all of my men with you, but Dan and Olaf will go with me to deliver news to Clovis."

Konal shared a bemused look with his crew, and stances relaxed. He had just offered them everything they wanted, except himself. "I want this done immediately, for Ulfrik may have had someone follow my contact. I can't have the two most powerful men in these lands seeking me at once. Now Konal, I know I promised we would get your son and revenge at one stroke."

"That you did, and I'm not ready to leave without both." Konal's hands flexed and veins stood out from his neck. He certainly relished his acting, Throst thought.

"I've a plan for that as well." He looked at Dan and Olaf, and between the two of them he had some wits and some brawn. They would have to do. "I will tell you in a moment, in private. But first, gather all the men and let's get ready to move."

Throst smiled amiably as Konal nodded, pretended to calm himself, and barked at his men to assemble as the others prepared. Thus far, his plans were coming together, but the remainder of it trusted to Astra warning his sister and for Dan and Olaf to follow him on faith alone.

The instant Konal turned away, Throst grabbed them both and tugged them close. His voice was a faint whisper. "Konal and his men are traitors. Get Hakon, forget the others."

He released them and the quick exchange seemed to pass unnoticed. To his surprise, neither Olaf nor Dan betrayed any surprise. They shared an expressionless glance, and Olaf melted away as Dan stepped up to Throst's side. He had expected confusion from him at least, but maybe they were even more astute than himself. He would consider it later, for now he had to get away with Hakon.

The others were still bleary with sleep and they trudged out to the cold morning with curses and belches, scratching lice-infested heads and stumbling into each other. Another night of stolen ale had rendered them useless, and it was no great loss to sacrifice these fools. Konal looked them over, then his eyes brightened.

"Where's Olaf?" he asked sharply.

"Gone to fetch Hakon and my family." Konal smiled and wrapped his cloak tighter into his hand. "I can tell from your face you don't trust him. Then let's both get Hakon and I can share my plan as we walk." He held his hands wide and saw Konal scan him for a weapon. He had only a small knife, nothing compared to Konal's sword. He wanted Konal to be completely confident in a fast kill.

"All right, let's go. Dan stays here."

"That's right, it won't be a secret if Dan comes with us."

The other farmhouse sheltered Hakon with his sister and mother, and the entrance was fortuitously out of sight around the corner. Hakon remained tethered to the columns inside, like the puppy he was. He had not been mistreated, except by Throst's mother who exorcised frustrations on him. In fact, over the weeks, Hakon and his sister were developing a friendship that only children seemed able to make.

Despite knowing Konal could whirl on him in an instant, Throst had no fear. His pulse had quickened, but that was all. He did not question the confidence, but welcomed it. This was going to work. Konal was going to strike the moment they rounded the corner. At the same time, his men would hack the others to ribbons. After all, Throst had neatly arranged them in the yard and then distracted them with travel preparations. Hakon would be awaiting freedom and only mousy Olaf stood in the way, a trifle to Konal. Throst had all but extended his head to be hacked off.

Neither spoke about the plan Throst had offered, and that should have been warning enough to Konal.

"I think you'll find my plan a bit confusing at first," Throst said as they approached the corner.

Then he swept his foot before Konal and shoved him over it. He tripped forward and, fast as a cat, Throst was on his back. He slapped his cloak over Konal's head like a bag and yanked it down. He had only just begun to struggle as Throst wound it tighter. Konal's free hand sought his short sword, the sax, used for close fighting. But Throst's left hand was as nimble as his right, and in one deft motion he snatched the blade out of the sheath.

"The rest of the plan should make sense to you now."

Throst rammed the blade into Konal's side and his scream was muffled by the heavy wool cloak. He drew the blade back for a second thrust, but Olaf stumbled out of the house dragging a kicking Hakon with him. Screams from behind told Throst that the slaughter had begun. Dan came running like a frightened moose.

Olaf stared wide eyed at him. "What do we do now? Your mother ..."

"They've gone to hiding," Throst stood up from Konal, who rolled over and moaned into a widening pool of blood. He had no time to finish the deed nor did he care for Konal's fate. "We're getting out of here now. Give me the boy."

One heavy slam with the pommel of Throst's sword and Hakon went limp. He shoved Hakon at Olaf, who slung the boy across his shoulder. They sprinted into the nearby woods to lose pursuers in the ever-shifting landscape of fallen leaves and woodland streams. Throst was laughing.

39

Astra ambled along the track leading to the northern gates of Ravndal. The sun was setting and the cold of nightfall matched the chill in her heart. Keeping to the cover of darkness no longer mattered and crossing the expanse of cleared fields demanded nothing of her in the light. Once on the track worn through the widest spaces between stumps, she only had to drag her feet with enough speed to reach the gates before nightfall.

Black forms of men patrolled the ramparts and she imagined their surprise at finding her outside their carefully guarded walls. The fools had let her come and go so often. Walls were only suited to halting stupid men blustering with their swords and spears. The small and unimportant burrowed under them, sneering at their bravado and mocking their vigilance. Knocking on their front gates would be worthy of laughter, if she could remember how laughter felt.

The shapes on the walls melded together, no doubt conferring on what threat lay before them. Finally the smile emerged on Astra's lips. They would never guess her threat, never consider she carried a blade taken from Throst. She would be mocked, ridiculed, cursed, and in the end she would be free.

Would she kill the boy? Could she? The sheathed knife at her hip clapped against her skin as she walked. She had the tool for murder. Did she have the heart? Even owning success, she left herself no means of escape. She had no intention of escape.

Throst had been her whole world, everything that furnished her life with meaning. Her father had been a tender man, but he spent his life fighting the Franks for Ulfrik. Her mother's people. Though her mother had gladly accepted her father's blood price from Ulfrik and remained to serve him, from that day she hated Ravndal and all Northmen. She loved her own daughter less for being half Norse. Even so her mother's death had plunged her into a drowning loneliness from which Throst had rescued her. For one year, he delighted her and loved her. He had dallied with other girls, but always returned to her. They would be married one day. Throst always dreamed of greatness and she believed in their future together.

Then Ulfrik ripped him away, just as he had discarded her father's life. She swore to follow Throst into the uncertain future, but he had asked her to remain behind to take his vengeance. Even in the chaos of his banishment, he had the wits to plan for the future. She admired that brilliance, was enthralled and mystified by it. Their parting kiss had afforded an expectation of joy, even when the future appeared so bleak. She had done all he had asked of her and more, all for the promise of living within Throst's dreams.

Ravndal drew closer now and the shapes on the wall resolved into men who watched her with arrows set to their bows. If they fired upon her, she did not care. What did it matter? Throst had commanded her to die, after all.

By the time she realized she could flee, she had already come within sight of Ravndal's walls. She had stumbled back in a daze, too stunned from his ultimatum to even consider what to do. Kidnap or kill Aren on her own, with no one left to help her.

And not return to Throst unless one or the other had been accomplished.

Death was what he had sent her to find.

Men hailed her at the gates, calling down from the wall in rough voices. Warning arrows were fired, thudding into the ground around her as she approached the gates. She did not flinch, but drifted forward to bang on the rough-hewn logs of the doors.

There was no place left for her in the world. If she did not belong to Throst, to whom did she belong? Ravndal was the home of the enemy, and she had never formed any connections to its people. The Franks would call her a traitor and sell her to slavery. Only Fate knew through what twisting path her future lay. She had merely to move forward and discover its end.

Protesting with loud curses, the gatekeepers lugged back the bars and opened the doors to allow her inside. Spears leveled at her body, so close that if she tripped she would be impaled three different ways.

"What are you doing beyond the gates?" one of the guards asked. "No one is to be outside."

"Take me to the hall," she said, her voice tired and flat. "I have news that cannot wait."

One of the guards seized her by the arm, his rough grip crushing her. He yanked her inside while the others swung the gates closed.

They marched her into Ravndal with spears at her back, and still her knife slapped her hip beneath her skirt.

Could she kill Aren? Did she have any choice before her own life ended?

40

"She came to the front gate and demanded to be let inside?" Runa lowered into her chair in the hall, eyes fixed on Snorri who stood beneath her.

"A bold girl, that one," he said. "She was spotted far before she arrived, no more sneaking for her. Claimed she had news that couldn't wait, but I had her locked up first. Just so you'd have time to decide what to do."

Runa collapsed in her chair, eyes fixed on nothing as she went through all the reasons Astra would return. She realized somehow Konal had either been overcome or not yet acted. Though she had always assumed Astra would return, Snorri had convinced Runa that she had no reason to show herself in Ravndal again. Now that Runa had been proved right, a tight fear gripped her.

"Did she give a reason why she was outside the walls?" Halla came forward with her question. It was past time for the evening meal but not late enough for sleep, and the hall had emptied of all but servants. Halla and her two daughters now lived in the main hall while Toki was gone. To Runa's chagrin, Halla acted a pleasant and grateful guest. She worried constantly for Toki, and Runa observed her caring for her two young daughters. She was not a bad mother to them, and Runa's nieces had shown themselves to be well mannered and intelligent. Of course, anyone could act such a part for a few days, she had told herself. Still, her nieces were winning her over and the youngest had the face of Runa's mother. Both had softened Runa's heart, even if only by a small fraction.

Halla's question hung like a bad odor and Snorri seemed unsure how to answer. The silence awakened Runa from her thoughts and she rescued Snorri from his quandary. "Whatever her reasons, she has broken Ulfrik's orders to remain within the walls. I will hear her excuses but they will make no difference."

She held Halla's cold eyes a moment. Was she aligned with Astra against her, Runa wondered. Aren had sensed it. Her innocent question, so sensible given the situation, hinted that she worried Astra would reveal their association. Could she truly know that, or was she criminalizing Halla for no reason other than dislike? Halla looked aside first, and Runa glanced at Aren sitting with a disturbing quiescence for a child his age. What did he see?

"Bring Astra to me," she said at last, shaking her head. She collapsed in her chair and stroked Aren's hair. He gave her the faintest of smiles, and she returned it. *Am I really counting on my child to tell me what to do*, she thought. *Am I so desperate*?

Snorri dispatched one of the few men left behind to fetch Astra. The palpable silence was long and uncomfortable, with both Halla and her daughters sitting to the side as if they wished to melt into the shadows. Runa considered sending the children out of the room, but she wanted both Aren present for his keen vision and Halla in attendance so she could read her face. So she patted Aren's arm and waited in tense quiet for the doors to again swing open with Astra held between two men.

They led her forward, but since her only crime, to their knowledge, had been leaving the walls, they allowed her to approach Runa without escort. Only Snorri, privy to her treachery, took a spear from the guard and pointed it at her. Runa was shocked at the change in the girl who had dazzled her son. Runa had never thought the girls a beauty, but whatever had happened to her had degraded what little charm she had possessed. Her face and clothing were smeared with mud and dirt. Uncovered hair hung in frizzy locks running over her shoulders, framing a face that had no light, no life, and no hope. Defeat hung about her as thick as the ragged wool cloak she wore off her shoulder. Thin hands hung at her sides, and one hand picked absently at her left thigh.

Runa recognized that motion and her stomach burned with fire.

"So, you have news?" Runa asked, arching her brow as if she could not care less. She contained her eagerness to learn of Hakon's fate and what tales she had to tell. She glanced at Halla, who remained fixed on Astra while she sheltered her daughters against her body as if protecting them from a hail storm.

Astra nodded and tears gathered in her eyes. She wiped at them with the back of her wrist, looking at the floor before her feet. Her voice was hoarse and thin. "I have been to Throst, and I have seen your son."

Halla gasped along with the few serving women and the guards. Only Runa and Snorri remained unmoved. Aren now stood beside his mother, and placed his small hand on her arm. The gesture was so reassuring, something Ulfrik would have done in times of trial.

"And is my son well?" She wanted to throttle the girl, but was willing to play her game to get her answers.

Another nod, and Astra wiped another tear again. "You would be proud of his bravery and his defiance. He is stronger than most men."

Runa allowed herself a small smile. Astra began weeping now, and she cupped a trembling hand over her mouth. Still, Runa noticed one hand lingered at her thigh. She stood, feeling her own blade strapped in nearly the same place beneath her skirt. Ulfrik had forbidden her to wear it in the hall, and hated her to wear it all. Yet with him gone and Halla living only one knife-length away from her throat, Runa carried it. She felt glad for it now.

"Why are you weeping, if you have gone to see my child's safety? You have gone to spy for me, to bring me glad news that my son is still alive and safe. Where are there tears in that? Now you can lead us to Throst and my son can be rescued."

Runa indulged in the pleasure of twisting this girl's anguish a little longer. She was a filthy creature, a traitor and a whore, and whatever respect she might have deserved she abandoned when she took up with Throst. So as Astra continued to weep, Runa merely smiled and stepped closer.

"You misunderstand me," she said through her tears. Runa paused as if surprised, gave a sly glance to Halla who quivered with her children held close. Astra continued. "I was not spying for you."

"Then what were you doing with Throst?"

Runa's smile vanished with the explosiveness of Astra's strike. A dull knife flashed in her hand and she lunged forward.

Halla and her girls shrieked and the serving women screamed in one voice. Even the guards stood leaden and unbelieving. Snorri thrust his spear, but age and injury had slowed him. The leaf blade caught her cloak and tore it from her shoulder.

The long knife felt good in Runa's hand, its balanced weight making it spring from its sheath. Expecting Astra to strike for her gut, she was unprepared for her to glide past her.

Aren stood with his eyes wide and mouth open.

Astra's blade flashed as she raised it to strike the child.

Then Runa and Astra were entangled on the floor. More screams erupted. Runa was facing the ceiling, looking up at smoke whorls amid the rafters. She had tackled Astra and her arms were as iron bands around the girl's neck and body. Despite her youth, she was outmatched by Runa's experience and strength. She kicked and screamed, her knife hand pinned to her side. She tried to bite Runa's arm, but only managed to leak warm spit over it. As fast as she had struck, she had been defeated.

Then dark shadows huddled around her and hands lifted Astra away. Snorri and the guards flung her to the floor, and one beat her with the butt of his spear. Runa sprung to her feet, recovered her knife, and sprang for Astra. In her youth, she would have eviscerated the bitch right on the floor of the hall. Her hands still itched with the desire for it. Halla and her daughters were still screaming. Runa's blade was poised over Astra's heaving chest.

"You are moments from feeling this iron pierce your heart," she hissed. "Be still or I will be tempted to blood this knife of mine."

She thrashed, heedless of the threats, though the two guards held her down. Snorri untangled his spear and struck her head with the butt. It slowed her, but she continued to fight. "You think you scare me?"

Runa stood and smiled. "I don't care whether or not I do. There was a time I would've cut out your tongue for your treachery. But you have information I need. We'll see how brave you are when I take a hot poker to your pretty face."

Realization of Runa's threat stilled her better than any physical blow. Runa ordered her restrained and locked up, which Snorri promised to oversee personally. Astra collapsed like a child's doll as the guards seized her. Snorri picked up the blade and offered it to Runa. "Have it melted down. I don't want to see that thing again."

She turned now to Aren, and to her surprise her boy was composed and pleasantly excited. He fell into her arms, something he never did, and looked up at her with intense admiration. She smiled at him, relieved that the violence had not disturbed him. Halla and her girls were different, all three jumbled into a trembling and sobbing clump.

About to offer them a soothing word, the doors burst open and yet another guard rushed inside. "My lady," the guard stopped in confusion at the scene before him, but started anew. "My lady, Konal's men have returned. They're at the gates and Konal's body is on a litter. What should we do? They claim you know their true allegiance."

The guard framed his statement more as a question. The fire returned to her belly. If Konal was on a litter and Hakon not with them ...

"By all the gods, open the gates and let them in. Take them here. Go!"

Snorri became pale and looked at Runa. They both in turn looked at Astra, but she hung between her captors as if she were a corpse.

"Don't let him be dead," she said to herself. "Not him nor my son."

41

Separated from the others, stripped of their mail coats and weapons, Gunnar and Toki sat in a small room within Clovis's castle. Toki had scoffed at it, calling it a pile of rocks surrounded by a rotten wood fence and fetid water. "The stone looks so solid, but it will topple faster than you think," he had told him as they waited in the empty room. "We once took down a real castle in half a day, and it burned too."

Gunnar could not imagine stone burning, but the floor was of dark, grooved wood and the rafters above were likewise wood beams supporting a wood roof stained black with age. With little else to do in captivity, he studied the stone walls and the flaky mortar holding them together. How men piled rocks so high amazed him. The room was on the second floor and towers stood higher still. The sole feature of their room besides the locked door was a small window cut into the wall too high offer any view other than sky. Light streamed from the morning sun and bounced off the walls to fill the space with a straw-colored light. It would have been cozy had they even been provided a blanket, but they had only their cloaks for warmth. Rock walls, Gunnar had found, were cold. He had shivered all night, and even as desperately exhausted as he was, sleep had eluded him.

"Do you think my father has discovered we are here?" His uncle, sitting enfolded within his stained cloak against the interior wall, shrugged.

"We've been kept aside for a reason," he said. "I can only imagine it's for ransom. But this Clovis, the way he howled when he saw you ..."

Gunnar stopped picking at the loose mortar. Clovis had prodded him like a fattened calf ready for slaughter, and his delight at Gunnar's capture had been shameless. Clovis was the nightmare stalking Gunnar's dreams, the madman bent on taking his hand in revenge for his own son's maiming. Both his parents had drummed this threat into Gunnar's head. He had nearly passed out when he learned their Frankish captors were reinforcements dispatched from Paris to reinforce Clovis's losses. They delivered him into the jaws of the wolf.

"Don't worry for it," Toki said, realizing the fears he had conjured. "Clovis will have to kill me before I allow him to touch you."

Gunnar smiled and crossed the room to sit by his uncle. Clovis could do what he wanted, and Gunnar knew no one could prevent him in his own castle. The only mystery was why he hadn't already taken his revenge. Maybe be waited to bargain, promising to leave Gunnar's hand attached if Ulfrik surrendered to his demands. He could only hope his father would listen, and not sacrifice his hand. It hurt him to wonder if his father might balk at the price Clovis would set.

The interior wall was warmer than the other two that faced the outside. They sat against it in long silence, until Toki chose to speak again.

"No matter what happens, it is Fate at work. The Norns weave a man's life, and he can do nothing to change it. We are here because we must be, and we will leave when the Norns pull that strand. I have few regrets, Gunnar. My life has been good—like croplands, giving me all I need, sometimes failing, other times overflowing. If I had to mark one regret, it has been that I stayed in the North too long. I belong with my family, you and your brothers, my sister, your father. I

219

belong where the battles are fought. Even imprisoned in this room, I am with you and the fight is not yet done. I feel good."

He reached a hand from beneath his cloak and squeezed Gunnar's arm. Unsure how to answer, Gunnar placed his other hand atop his uncle's and returned the gesture.

Then sounds of a door opening in the adjacent room and thumps on the floorboards. Both Gunnar and Toki turned to the door, and Gunnar peered through the spaces between the heavy slats. He could see only shadows, but the Frankish voices of Clovis and his guests were clear. Rattling metal and creaking leather obscured their voices, but Toki urged Gunnar to translate. He raised a hand for silence, then pressed his ear to the door, holding his breath to listen for every detail.

The first voice was of the leader who had captured them. His royal baritone filled the room, and even through the door commanded respect. "You're badgering is both unsuited to you and tiring to me, Clovis. Please stop. King Odo has answered your call with me. Understood? When I speak, it is with the king's authority."

The shadowy forms stilled in the wake of the rebuke, but Clovis did not hesitate for long. "I am not defying the king's authority. Are you questioning my loyalty?"

"Never," was the long-suffering reply. "But I am questioning your judgment. I know you want the boy. So do I, and I have captured him on the field of battle. He is my hostage, to use however I wish. I may just have his head mounted on my standard and end your peevishness today."

Gunnar pulled back from the door, and Toki hissed at him for a translation. He provided a smattering of the talk, but quickly pressed his ear back to the door. The voices had drawn closer in that moment.

"I will pay you whatever you think Ulfrik will, more if I must. And there'll be no trickery from me, unlike that Northman snake."

"Oh you will? You cannot pay what I ask, because you do not possess the lands I want. Lands you have ceded to the Northmen and have failed to reclaim. Lands that should be awarded to one capable of holding them."

The door shook as hands grabbed the locking bars and both Gunnar and Toki fell away. Spear points would enter first, and neither wanted to lose an eye to carelessness. Yet the door remained closed, and Clovis's voice was bright with anger.

"Those lands have been held by my family for generations, and I am the rightful ruler. King's authority or not, you've not the power nor right to take the land from me."

"Well, I'd be taking it from Ulfrik, wouldn't I?"

The door opened and the expected rush of spear blades pushed Gunnar and Toki into the room. The man who had captured them was dressed in fine clothes, a contrast to the mail and leather he had worn in the field. He flashed a hawkish smile as his two spearmen continued to drive into the room. Clovis followed close at his heels, his face red and shining with sweat, his jumpy posture like a man who had just stood after falling from a horse.

"My God, Clovis, not even a piss pot? Do you want your floor-boards to stink of Northman for the next decade?" Their captor frowned and snapped at the two guards to stop prodding. Gunnar tried to bat away a spear, but the blade flashed close to his hand and he recoiled. Toki, however, snagged a spear in his grip and tugged it, just to warn the Frank before releasing the weapon. The two stared at each other, and Toki's lips curled in a smile.

"Tell your protector to calm himself," said their captor. "He'll get through this alive if he behaves."

"He wants you to stop fighting," Gunnar translated. "He says you'll stay alive longer if you do."

Toki sneered at the Franks. "Says the wolf to the hare. But I'll go along. He's here to decide our ransoms, no doubt."

"I am Theodoric, and now, little man, you know what name to use for your song. I am here by the direct order of King Odo of West Frankia, and I bring three score of cavalry troops and three dozen footmen in my personal guard. You've seen what they can do. Counting the men under Clovis's banner, we are strong enough to wipe the stain of the Northmen from this land. More accurately, to trample it into the dirt. I will plant my banner in your father's heart, and I will have your mother shared with all my men. My spears will sag with the heads of your friends and kinsmen. Your homes will be smoke and ash, and nothing will remain to prove your filthy people ever polluted my domain with your repulsive countenance. And you will not be singing, little Gunnar Ulfrikson, not one note, for your body will be ground up and fed to pigs. Translate that for your friend."

Gunnar stared at his captor, Theodoric, and scowled. He turned to Toki, who waited for the translation. "He says he's going to defeat us."

"The Franks love to boast, and to hear themselves talk. Is that all he said?"

"He really dislikes our people." Toki snorted in laughter, and Gunnar joined him. The desperation of this situation, the complete hopelessness of it, left him no choices other than laughter or total collapse. He would not dishonor himself before going to Valhalla.

"Ah, bravado if the face of danger," Theodoric said. Clovis began to huff as if about to explode, but Theodoric commanded silence with a raised hand and thoughtful smile of his own. "Such is the way of your people. Believe me, I understand you pagan barbarians better than you think. Behind that brave face, you are as frightened as the child you are."

Theodoric's men had kept their spears leveled, and he had stood between them. Now, he stepped forward to Gunnar and placed a gentle hand on his shoulder. "I know what you are worth to your father. Clovis has explained it to me. Your friend? What is he to you? A kinsman?"

Suddenly Gunnar no longer felt bold, and his stomach tightened with dread. He blinked at Theodoric, whose smile contorted his face so that his high nose further resembled a bird of prey.

"The two of you look so similar, and so unlike others of your kind. Of course you are kinsmen." Theodoric patted Gunnar's shoulder. "Your expression tells me all I need. Now, I will send messengers to your father. Wouldn't he be more inclined to reason if he understood that not only his son but another of his kin were held here? His name?"

Gunnar swallowed, glanced at Toki who stared back without expression. The spear points hovered before them and Clovis seemed to lose patience with every heartbeat, wringing his hands and grinding his teeth. "His name is Toki, my uncle."

"Of course," Theodoric stepped back and clasped his hands behind himself. "I love neither death nor ruin, and wish it upon no man. The horrors I have foretold are avoidable. All your father need do is cede his lands to me. He can keep his gold, his men, his pride."

"An outrage," Clovis exclaimed, exploding forward. He grabbed at Theodoric's shoulder, but stopped short. Theodoric held still, flicking his eyes toward Clovis as if nothing more than a shadow had disturbed him. The tense moment passed, as Clovis stood down, snarling at Gunnar as he faded toward the door. Theodoric continued.

"Help me convince your father. Spare your people the shame of defeat and death."

"Shame and defeat are all you offer. Death in battle is glory." Gunnar turned up his chin, and repeated the words in Norse, so his uncle would understand. Theodoric smiled thoughtfully.

"Just like all of your ilk. If you will not leave, I will dig you all out by the roots. I wonder how glorious your women and children will feel when my horsemen catch them in flight?" He smiled at Gunnar before he turned for the door. "Your help was not expected, and I was a fool to try. But God has seen my attempt to do right, and that is all I required."

Theodoric exited before his two men followed. Clovis lingered and glared at both Gunnar and Toki, then he seized Gunnar's right arm. "As brash as your father, and just as stupid. I have a son, you know. He's without a hand thanks to your father. I'll see he's repaid in kind before you leave this place. Depend upon it."

He thrust Gunnar's hand away and stormed from the room. The bolts dropped back into place and both he and Toki stared after the door for long moments in silence. At last Toki settled to the floor and spoke. "Your father will pay whatever is demanded. Don't worry."

Gunnar nodded, but turned to face the wall, placing one hand on the damp cold rock. He wondered if his father really would, or if he even could, surrender everything for two lives. The doubt clawed at his heart, and he closed his eyes and touched his head to the wall.

42

Ulfrik's weary procession across the cleared fields to the weather-blackened gates of Ravndal seemed to last all day. To the north, the hanging tree clawed the morning sky and the shadow of a corpse dangled from a muscular bough. He scowled at the corpse, cursing the fool who had sparked this strange fire that consumed his life. Gudmund, Throst's father, must be laughing even as he wanders lost in the icy fog of Nifleheim. It made Ulfrik wish he could hang the bastard a second time, for all the suffering his drunken rage had caused him.

The gates opened after Ulfrik answered the challenges. Both he and Einar were pleased at the vigilance of the men left behind, recalling a time when careless watchmen would allow any snake to pass for the right coin. Had it only been a few weeks, a month ago? Ulfrik shook his head as he led his troops in somber quiet through the gates. Time had become something longer and more painful than anything before Hakon had been kidnapped. Time had become an elusive enemy, always retreating out of reach yet never losing the battlefield. How much time did he have now that Gunnar was in Clovis's grip?

The flat and cold day fit the hunched and defeated gait of the men. No battles had been fought, but brothers had been buried. No defeat but no victory, and no glory nor any shame had been earned. They shambled home like men dazzled by lightning that had struck too close. They assembled in the main square, and Ulfrik released them with his thanks. Within moments of return, groups of his warriors formed and floated away to their barracks or families. He would gather them again in the coming days, but not before he saw Hakon.

"Where is everyone?" Einar asked as he waited with Ulfrik for the last of the men to disperse. "Our women are too busy for us?"

"Konal should have returned with Hakon, probably last night. They must all be in the hall, recovering from the celebration." Ulfrik smiled thinly as he imagined his family worn out from a tearful reunion.

"Then let's not waste any time," Einar said, then paused as he realized their arrival brought ill news.

Ulfrik faced the main hall and sighed. "This is one of the hardest moments of my life. All of this is my fault, and I deserve their scorn."

Einar cocked his head and his eyes flashed with warning. "No more of that, Lord Ulfrik. You are the jarl and no one should hear you speak of defeat."

Ulfrik laughed despite the fear welling inside him. Not long ago, Einar was a boy looking to him for direction but now he stood a head taller and admonished him on points of leadership. Even short-lived laughter gave him fortitude to deliver his news, and the two went directly to the hall. No one stood guard outside, and Einar shook his head as he opened the door. "Must have been quite a celebration."

Inside the hall, Ulfrik found nothing resembling celebration.

The hearth had collapsed to glowing embers throwing a feeble heat. Windows remained shuttered and the smoke hole cover had not be properly drawn, throwing the hall into a gauzy haze. Darkness pressed on the outlines of people hunched at tables or curled up on the floor. At first he thought they had all been killed, so lifeless were their postures, but a figure stirred from the high table.

Runa stood up from the shadows of her chair. Others lifted their heads, squinting into frame of light cast from the door. Now Ulfrik caught the scent of blood mixed with the pungent smoke of the smoldering hearth. He surged into the room, scanning for Hakon.

"By all the gods, what has happened here?" He met tired and uncertain eyes, none willing to hold his for long. Halla stood, then her children beside her. Her face and hair were starkly pale in the darkness, and her expression panicked. One hand hovered at her chest, and when she did not see her husband she covered her mouth.

"Where is Gunnar?" Runa swept down from the high table, her voice taut with control that threatened to break. As if to accent the disastrous news, Snorri had appeared and fully opened the smoke hole cover to blast the room with white light.

Ulfrik shook his head, and held Runa's eyes. It stopped her dead, and both hands went to her mouth.

"And Toki?" Halla rushed forward to grab Ulfrik's arm. He gave her the same solemn shake of his head.

"Both have been captured. Most of the others are dead."

Runa collapsed and a commotion of servants and hirdmen gathered to her. Halla began to sob, asking how it happened even as Ulfrik pulled free of her to tend his wife. Bera was beside her, fanning her face with her hand as Runa stared ahead with unfocused eyes. Others crowded her, a servant offering a cup of water that she did not acknowledge. The feeling of helplessness was so overwhelming, and the confusion of what had occurred while he was gone so complete, Ulfrik stood like a man made of stone.

"What is happening?" he mumbled to himself. "Where is Hakon?"

Then he saw the familiar faces of Konal's men, and then Konal himself. He was laid out on a table, and his eyes were empty as he stared at him. Ulfrik's guts turned to watery ice, for if Konal was dead, then so was Hakon.

Then the lifeless eyes blinked, and Konal began to stir.

He left Runa, surrounded by her servants and friends. Halla chased after him, demanding to know what had happened to Toki. He ignored her and came to Konal's side. Snorri met him and placed a trembling hand on his shoulder. His voice was low and hoarse. "He only returned last night. Ornolf did what he could for the wound, but it's butcher's work."

Konal tried to raise himself, but Snorri pressed him down. A wool blanket covered him, and as he struggled it fell away to reveal his naked torso. Ulfrik peeled it back and saw the ragged gash in Konal's side. It was angry red and thick cord held it shut, Ornolf's handiwork. Ulfrik knew the agony of those stitches. Each stitch required a hole to be poked through the flesh with an awl before feeding the thread through it. Men went blind from such pain, usually passing out before it was done.

"My burns were worse than this." He tried to smile and rub his face, but instead he grimaced and dropped his hand to the table. "But I'll be pissing blood for while."

"I am glad you survived, but what happened?"

"We have the same question for you, lad?" Snorri's tired eyes fixed on him. He sighed and turned to check Runa. She was standing now with Bera and Einar's aid. Halla's children had come to her side and begun crying. This was going to be horrible to tell, and more horrible to hear. At last he searched for Aren, and not seeing him with Runa thought him asleep in their room. Only when he turned back to Konal did he see Aren's eyes barely reaching over the table to stare at him. He held Konal's hand.

"Give me your tale while Runa recovers," Ulfrik said. "And we will set everything in the clear."

Konal struggled with his story, and his men filled in where he stumbled. Ulfrik winced at how Konal had been beaten and Hakon carried off. "He was still in good spirits, and treated better than I would have thought," Konal said. By now Runa had stabilized and came to Ulfrik's side to hear the tale a second time. "Throst will take him to Clovis, that is my guess. He is destroyed now, only one or two men left to him. He shelters his mother and sister, but we hardly saw them. He feared what his men might do to them, I think. I am sorry I failed you, Lord Ulfrik."

"Never say it." Konal reached out for him and Ulfrik grabbed his arm, clasping both hands to it. "I know only too well how it is to meet with the unexpected. We could not have guessed Astra knew our plans."

Though he smiled and smoothed over the words, he had to suppress a shiver of dread. No one but Konal and he had known of their ploy, and only a few had been told of it after Astra had left. She had either guessed herself, or someone informed her. "Astra fled with Throst, I assume?"

"She returned to kill Aren and failed." Runa's voice was powerful yet emotionless, but Ulfrik still jumped with surprise.

"And she was killed in the attempt, I trust?" Runa shook her head and told him the remainder of the tale. By the end, Ulfrik was seated upon a bench and rubbing his face.

"This is like grabbing an adder by its tail," he said. "But at least you had the wisdom to let her live. I need answers from her."

"She's not talking," Halla offered, still standing while everyone else sat. "I don't think you will learn much from her."

"Do you think I will be merciful because she is a woman? Not for her crimes. I'll have her fingers cut off one by one until she tells me all I want to know, and there's plenty more of her to work on if she lasts through that."

"And then you will hang her?" Halla asked.

"Until her body rots off the tree." Ulfrik frowned at her, confused, and she waved away his confusion.

"She deserves death, especially if she led my husband into a trap. That is why I asked. What happened to Toki? Please, I cannot wait any longer."

Ulfrik stared at the floor, unwilling to meet anyone's gaze. He felt Runa staring at him and at last he met her eyes. Anger, sadness, confusion, and a raft of other emotions clouded her. It was as if she were another woman, so haggard and contorted was her expression. He drew a deep breath and related what they had discovered, leaving no detail out. "At last we followed their trail to Clovis's castle, and my worst fears had been confirmed. Along with Gunnar and Toki, they must have captured a dozen or so of Toki's men. I did not dare open contact with the Franks. We were tired and disheartened, and not prepared for battle with such a large force. We would be destroyed in open battle. So I returned."

"And left my husband a prisoner of your enemy?" Halla's voice was shrill as she glared at Ulfrik. Yet hard eyes turned on her unseemly outburst, and she schooled her tone. "How will you get him released? How soon?"

Ulfrik sighed again, looking instead to Runa who continued to watch him as if he were a stranger. "Clovis will demand a tremendous ransom, and I will pay all he asks. My one fear ..." He hesitated, wondering if sharing his concerns would only worsen matters, but he had already started and expectant faces awaited him. "My one fear is he will demand my land, which I cannot give, not without leave from Jarl Hrolf the Strider. I don't foresee him ceding any land to the Franks without a battle."

"That is nonsense," Halla said, forgetting herself once more. "Are you not the jarl here? You can do what you wish with your land, leave it if you will."

"I've sworn an oath," Ulfrik said, putting as much finality to it as he could muster in his weary condition. "Hrolf has awarded me the land and all in it, but I pay tribute to him. I've sworn to hold this land against his enemies. No matter the cost."

The bitter words sunk the room into gloomy silence. No one doubted Clovis and the Franks would demand land over gold. For his part, Ulfrik could already hear Hrolf's saddened but stern refusal to step back from the border. He imagined the request to Hrolf, could see his predatory eyes flash first with anger, then sympathy, and then the coldness of a king's decision. *I am sorry for your son*, he imagined him saying, *but a hundred men do not trade their honor and their homes for one man, no matter who he is.*

After a long silence, Ulfrik asked for a meal to be prepared for himself and his men. He would rest, if his troubled thoughts would allow him sleep, and then question Astra later in the day. Halla, tears overflowing, took her children from the hall. Others broke off into groups, leaving Ulfrik seated in the middle of his hall. Runa sat across from him. She shifted to sit beside Ulfrik, placed her arm around him and buried her face in his shoulder. She began to sob quietly, and he could do no more than hold her and let her spill her sorrow.

Faces turned away to allow them some privacy, only Snorri regarded him from across the room. Ulfrik returned his stare, and the two shared the same unspoken fear. Ransom or not, would Clovis enact his revenge on Gunnar and take his hand? Looking aside, Ulfrik mumbled a prayer to the gods and fought back his own stinging tears.

43

Snorri and Einar accompanied Ulfrik to the shack which imprisoned Astra. As they arrived at the small building squatting between the south and west barrack houses, Ulfrik mused that Gudmund had been held there before his hanging. It was a foolish connection, as he had nowhere else to hold a prisoner, but still something about it made him shiver. He wondered if the ghost of that cruel man was Astra's informant. He would learn soon enough.

While he had not rested, the guard outside the shack apparently had an easier time of it. Einar growled as he realized the man sat buried into his cloak, head tucked to his chest and spear balanced between his legs as he snoozed. Once they arrived before him, their shadows falling across his face, Ulfrik heard the man's snoring. Einar cursed him, snatched the spear from his lap and slammed the shaft into the man's gut.

He tumbled from the chair with a cry as Einar raised the shaft overhead with both hands. "Wake up, you've got visitors," he shouted, then slammed the spear shaft across the prone figure's head. The guard fell back with both hands outstretched, screaming for help.

"Enough," Ulfrik snapped. "We're all tired." To the guard lying on his back he snapped his fingers. "Get up and open the door. I want to see the bitch."

Taking a moment to recover, rubbing his head where a lump already started to form, he scrabbled to his feet. Einar continued to glare at the man, who recoiled beneath him. The door was barred with three bolts, which slid easily from the outside but from within made forcing the door impossible. The shed had no windows, and inside the only light came from beneath the door. In summer it stewed men in the humidity and in winter it froze them. Ulfrik had built it to be a sturdy, punishing cell.

The bolts thudded open and the guard pushed the heavy wooden door into the room. Light framed Astra directly against the wall opposite the entrance.

She was dead. A dagger pierced her throat and remained protruding from the base of her neck. Bright blood soaked her chest and lap. Her eyes were glassy and wide with shock, staring into the places only the dead could see.

The four men stood in silent shock, but the muscles in Einar's jaw were already twitching. His voice was a low threat. "How did this happen, you dog? You slept through this fucking butchery?"

The guard stammered and fell away, both hands raised in protest. Ulfrik regained himself and anger erupted from the depth of his guts. One arm struck out viper-quick, an iron grip seizing the guard by his neck. He slammed his other hand onto the guard's chest and threw him against the wall of the shack. Einar lowered the guard's own spear to his chest.

"I've had all I can take of stupid men causing me misery," Ulfrik said through gritted teeth. He glared into the guard's terror-widened eyes, trying to remember this man's name. It took a moment, but once recalled he twisted it into a threat. "Listen to me, Ingjald. Tell me what you've done and seen since you've been here. The truth, no matter how bad it makes you look, or you'll be searching for your teeth all over Frankia."

"I never heard anything or saw anyone," he said, stuttering. His breath smelled of beer and fish, and his eyes were bloodshot. "I swear it before the gods."

Snorri shook his head in disgust and limped inside the guard shack. Einar jabbed Ingjald with the tip of the spear, making him hiss with pain.

"And how long were you asleep?" Ulfrik tightened his grip, glancing past Ingjald at Snorri leaning over the corpse. "Did you ever leave your post?"

Ingjald's eyes fell away and Ulfrik had his answers, still he shook the guard until he spoke the words. "I met friends who returned with you. I was gone no longer than a man needs to share one drink with friends. It was not time at all."

Releasing him with disgust, Ulfrik would have to prove Ingjald's excuses. For all he knew, the murder could have been his handiwork. Einar never let his spear off Ingjald's chest. His face had deepened to an intense red as he yelled at his guard. "And your friends sent you back with more drink, no doubt. You never checked on your prisoner? Nothing made you suspect?"

Ulfrik did not remain for the interrogation, knowing full well Ingjald was useless. Inside the cramped shack, he stood beside Snorri and studied the bloodied heap slumped against the wall. Black flies danced in her blood and the heavy scent of death was thick. The knife jutting from her neck was commonplace. She did not seem to have struggled, which told him she was mostly likely killed by her informant.

"Einar," he called over his shoulder. "I need an accounting and inspection of every man, now. Keep Ingjald under guard until we prove his story."

Snorri prodded Astra's corpse with his foot. "Whoever did this should have bloody hands," he said. "Look at the blood spray on the floor. Someone has to be marked. Also, the smear here looks like the hem of a cloak dragged through the blood."

Ulfrik nodded agreement, searched for footprints or anything to indicate who had silenced Astra and finding nothing. Her eyes stared ahead, eternally frozen in shock at her final betrayal. *You got all you deserved*, he thought, *but I don't deserve your silence.*

Stepping back into the bracing, fresh air, Einar was already ordering men and having Ingjald bound. The hapless guard stared at his feet in quiet shame. Ulfrik knew he was a simple but well-liked man. His heart told him Ingjald had been honest, and that the real enemy had exploited his inattention. At the worst, his punishment would be a public shaming with every person of Ravndal pelting him with garbage and other refuse, while all his companions kicked him. He would be sore but hopefully chastened. The real traitor, whenever he was found, would be brutalized before dying in misery.

Assembling and inspecting the men consumed the morning, and revealed nothing. The worst blood stain revealed was from a nick to a hand that bled overmuch. The man even had witnesses to the accident. Eventually bloody rags were uncovered in a trash heap against the southern wall. It only proved someone had cleaned up. No one had entered or left Ravndal, meaning the person who wanted Astra silenced was still inside. He ordered no man to leave without his direct order, and to do so would equal an admission of guilt punishable by death.

By evening he had retreated to his hall, his mood fouled and his anger raw. Yet when he saw Runa and she smiled—a thin and ghostly smile, quick to vanish—Ulfrik renewed his heart. The remorse that had overwhelmed him at discovering Gunnar's defeat returned, and Runa's smile galvanized him to make amends. He put aside his foul mood and sat with her, taking her hand into his.

"I'm glad she died betrayed," Runa said, her voice a whisper. "I only wish we got more out of her. I needed her to prove ..."

As her voice trailed off, Ulfrik felt a tension flow out of his chest. Of course she was about to name Halla as the culprit. She had been away long enough, though witnesses claimed she had taken her children to the hall where Toki had left his possessions. Right now, he could not brook the ugly fight that would erupt if Runa accused her in public. It would only obscure the real search.

He squeezed her hand. "You are better than I deserve. Thank you for not speaking your mind on that count."

They sat together in silence, ate a meal prepared by Einar's wife and served at twilight. Men came to the hall in thoughtful silence, and Ulfrik recognized they all suspected one another of treachery. It was a horrible evening, though to his surprise Konal attempted to lighten the mood with foolish riddles he barely choked out in his weakened condition. At last, he had strength for no more and the hall again became a sullen gathering of suspicious people.

As the day ended and men returned to their own beds, Ulfrik sat groggy and tired overlooking the smoky gloom. Men presented themselves to him, swore loyalty and promised to uncover the culprit. Ulfrik thanked each man, but knew in the coming days there would be a dozen accusations and a dozen bloody fights over misunderstandings. Inevitably someone would be killed. All the while Ulfrik had to train his mind on the real issue of freeing both his sons and Toki from Clovis and Throst. He rubbed his face and closed his eyes.

"Ulfrik," a thin voice addressed him. He looked up and Halla and her children were before him. Runa had already taken Aren to bed, and Halla must have waited for her opportunity to approach. "I wanted to apologize for earlier. I am just frightened for Toki."

He smiled at her and nodded. "No need, we all share your worry. But he is a tough man, and he will hold his own. Do not fear for him. I will not rest until he is free and returned to your hearth. You have my word upon it."

She inclined her head, then gathered her children to her. "I prefer to stay in the bed you provided to Toki and me. It's better, I think. I feel nearer to him that way."

"As you wish. A good night to you, Halla." He winked at her children, who clung to her like frightened rabbits.

Returning his well wishes, she turned to leave.

It was an errant glimpse, a chance sweep of his gaze, but it made his hands chill. The murky light obscured it, maybe he even imagined it. Of course he only imagined it. It could not be what he had assumed it was.

As she had turned, her skirt spun and spread around her legs. The back of her skirt hem was darkened with heavy black stains as if dipped into a thick fluid. Though his eyes had seen blood stain and splatter a thousand times over, he had to have been mistaken. Surely she had dragged her skirt unknowingly through something. Not blood.

She left and he remained sitting straight at the high table. Suddenly he no longer felt groggy, but intensely awake. In the morning, he would have to satisfy himself that it had only been mud on Halla's skirt.

44

Throst waited in a crowded stone room that smelled of wood smoke and sweat. Rotten straw scattered on the floorboards added a hint of grass to the odors. The only things smelling worse than the room were Dan, Olaf, and himself. His head itched constantly and he realized he hadn't bathed since Ulfrik ejected him from Ravndal. Crates and barrels, mostly empty, competed for space with the rough table where he and the others sat. A broken pair of tongs were propped against the wooden interior wall, laced with cobwebs. The three men tried to appear relaxed in the square of light cast through a single window, though Throst judged his companions poor actors.

"This is taking too long," Olaf said, rubbing both his shoulders as if cold.

"You have to be somewhere?" Throst asked, and Olaf turned away with a frown.

"You shouldn't have surrendered Hakon without taking our ransom first," Olaf said. "It was a stupid thing to do."

"Weren't stupid," Dan said, his voice deepening with threat. "Do you forget the arrows and spears pointed at us? What was to be done?"

"Not coming here in the first place would've been better." Olaf continued to rub his shoulders and faced the light slanting in from the window. "More likely we'll be dancing from the end of a rope by day's end."

"I'll pull your legs if you promise to shut up now," Throst quipped. "You were not bound to follow me, but here you sit. That promise of silver was too much for you to resist after all. Maybe we're not going to be paid anything, and maybe Clovis will bury us in gold. But we've been too useful just to kill us out of hand. How could we have known he already captured Gunnar? That was a nice piece of luck for him, but made our news worthless. Still, delivering it showed him our value. It was not a poor choice to come."

"That's right. Shut up, Olaf." Dan's pronouncement drew a sneer from Olaf, but Throst chuckled.

Clovis had held them overlong, and had not even offered a drink. They had retained their weapons, and therefore could not be considered prisoners. Still their treatment did not bode well for the future. Throst would not admit the defeat Olaf was always prepared to embrace. Coming to Clovis was indeed a risky proposition, but Throst now lived in a world brimming with ridiculous risks. There was no choice that would not end with a blade through his guts, so he chose this path. At the least, he had the possibility of a reward.

Footfalls and murmured voices at the door preceded its opening. Framed in the entrance was regal Clovis, his clean and bright face full of wicked delight. Throst swallowed hard, but forced a smile.

"Pardon my delay, but your arrival surprised me." Clovis inclined his head slightly. "Hakon is now with his family, and it was actually a touching reunion given their circumstances."

Clovis did not enter the room, and figures backed him up. Throst did not enjoy the sense of entrapment. He stood carefully, wanting to show respect but not willing to be looked down upon.

"It was my pleasure to deliver Hakon to you, as well as news of Gunnar's vulnerability."

"Yes, Gunnar is the prize that makes keeping his runt brother worthwhile. Ulfrik is ruined now, unless I misjudge him."

"He stakes much pride on his sons," Throst said, daring to step closer. Clovis's eyes flickered with anger and his lip curled, so Throst halted. "He will pay whatever you ask of him, I am sure."

The men beyond the door stirred and at last Throst glimpsed a gangly young man hovering behind Clovis. The stump of his right arm was clutched against his belly, identifying him as Clovis's son. He was a sadder, more defeated version of his father, like something left submerged so long that its color had drained away. Clovis caught Throst's glance and he smiled, stepping aside to reveal his son and three more guards as well.

"You see my son's hand, how it has ruined him? Gunnar will return to his father just the same, ransom or no. That is the price for what he did to my family. How can he lead without a sword hand?"

Throst did not follow the logic, but Clovis's son sagged lower each time his father mentioned him. He would pour through the floor in a moment, and Throst pitied him. Yet, Clovis's battles with Ulfrik were no longer his concern. Unless Astra either killed or kidnapped his third son, their battles were done. He merely wanted his reward and a chance to flee with his small band.

"You will have justice for such a pitiless crime," he said, and his words drew frowns like he had fouled the air. Moving past his error, he pressed Clovis. "Now, there is the matter of the ransom price."

Letting the words linger, he watched as Clovis shared glances with his son and men. Then he spread his hands wide. "For such fine service, I grant you the very highest reward I can give. I will spare your miserable life."

"Are you joking with me?" Throst's vision flashed white with anger and he stepped forward into spears that rushed at him. He swatted one aside, though two more stuck into his ribs and halted him. "You promised a fucking reward. Now you throw me out with nothing more than your thanks?"

Clovis's face turned red and rather than anger he burst out laughing. The guards held their faces stern a moment, then joined him. Only the son did not share their laughter. "Then you'd rather I take back my offer?" he asked. "It is no matter to me. Your head will be a fine gift to Ulfrik. It will be my token of sincerity when I bargain with him."

The spear points in his ribs pressed harder and broke through the cloth of his shirt. The hotness of his anger turned to chill fear, and he stepped off the spear points with raised hands. "No, of course I will accept your offer. Forgive my outburst. I had high hopes."

"A little too high for such a small man," Clovis said, wiping a tear from his eye. "Though your boldness does entertain me and you've proved yourself to be a resourceful little rat. Since you've got nowhere to turn, and I have use for your talent, you may stay on. Not with the regular men, not for a while. But you'd be a freeman, and have a warm hearth with ready food. In time, you might become a regular in my army. How's that for a generous offer?"

Throst imagined Clovis lying on the floor, both hands on his throat and blood bubbling through his fingers. He imagined stomping his face until nothing but red mush clung to his foot. He imagined this whole fucking stone prison crumbling into a mound of flaming ruins. "We would be overjoyed at your generosity."

Both Olaf and Dan exhaled behind him as Throst inclined his head. Clovis again laughed. "Not those two lumps of shit. They've no place here."

His eyes flicked up to meet Clovis. The arrogant bastard still smirked but his eyes flashed with deadly seriousness. Something cracked in Throst's heart, and at that moment he would rather die than bend one more time to this man's will.

"Then I go with them. You cannot have me without them. They are loyal men, and deserve better than to send them out alone."

Clovis stared at him, long and hard. His tongue probed his cheek as he considered, then he shrugged. "As you wish. You all go."

Throst's gaze did not flinch. Clovis straightened at the challenge and the muscles in his jaw began to work. Throst felt his own palm itch for his weapon, even with spear points a thumb's distance from his torso. He cared not at all for his own life, not if it meant he had to live with a boot on his neck.

"Wait." The son spoke at last. "Father, we need his talent for spying. He has access to Ulfrik's hall, and we shouldn't let that get away. Keep his men; it's no burden to us. Take their weapons until they've proved their loyalty."

"Ulfrik is already defeated," Clovis said, not unlocking his eyes from Throst's. "I don't need to know what's happing in that dung heap."

"Still, until the deals are settled isn't it better to have such tools available if we need them?"

The silence stretched until it grew uncomfortable, and at last Clovis capitulated. "My son has a good deal of wisdom. If you relinquish your weapons to me, and swear an oath of service, then you may remain for a while. All three of you."

Without waiting for his companions' responses, Throst bowed his head. "We will agree to that."

Clovis grunted and waved back his spearmen. They relieved Throst and the others of their weapons while Clovis and his son observed. He met the son's stare, who surprisingly did not turn away. Throst let a weak smile lighten his face and tipped his head. *My thanks to you*, he thought. *I will spare your life when I tear this whole place to the ground and piss on your father's corpse.*

45

In the dawn of the next morning, Ulfrik awakened from a shapeless nightmare to Runa's hands shaking him. Her words oozed like sap through his sleep haze, but at the instant of comprehension he bolted upright.

"Messengers from Clovis have arrived. They're held outside the hall right now. Get up." Her smooth, cold hands pressed against his numb flesh as she hauled him to his feet. She began piling clothes next to him, while Aren held a wooden bowl of water for him to splash his face. After several moments of fumbling, Runa roughly combed his hair and Aren fetched him a cloak pin of polished silver to complete his transformation into a jarl.

"How many have come?" he asked as he ran his hand through his beard, tugging on the knots.

"There are four, one messenger and three guards. They have surrendered their weapons before entering the gates. Snorri and Einar are all over them." Runa pushed him toward the door, and Aren swung it open for him. He smiled at his son as he shuffled past, but Aren remained as stale as ever.

Taking his seat in the hall, Runa joined him. Snorri stood just inside the hall door and when Ulfrik motioned he opened the doors and spoke to the men beyond. A pale yellow light streamed down from the smoke hole and through the eastern windows. No one but a few servants remained in the hall, but that changed in moments. Snorri held open the main doors for hirdmen to file inside, taking up positions on the long walls of the hall. Next, Einar's giant frame filled the door, and finally the messengers were herded inside by the last of his own hirdmen.

They wore their hair in the Frankish style, straight and blunt-cut across their brows. They wore impractically bright clothing, fresh blue shirts with yellow pants. Royal colors, Ulfrik knew, but colors that proclaimed them to any enemy within a dozen miles. Mud stains splattered their legs from their journey, but otherwise they made a rich showing.

The lead man stopped before Ulfrik. Einar flanked them and pointed at the ground, demanding they kneel. They appeared shocked, but Einar's face reddened and snarled. The Franks quailed and took to their knees before Ulfrik. He left them kneeling until he noted their discomfort, then bade them to rise.

"You've got a message for me?" Ulfrik asked in Norse, trusting one or all of them to understand. The leader nodded and dusted off his pants with barely concealed disgust.

"I am sent on behalf of Baron Theodoric and Clovis. Your two sons, brother Toki, and twelve other men under your protection are hostages to my lords."

"Get on with it," Ulfrik demanded. "I know their names already."

"As you say, Jarl Ulfrik. My lords have commanded me to deliver you this message. For each man, excluding your two sons, the price is set at ten pounds of silver. To aid your understanding, that is one hundred thirty pounds of silver."

Gasps circled around the room but Ulfrik marshaled his feelings, showing no sign other than irritation at the assumption he could not add. "For your understanding, I can count that high."

The messenger pursed his lip and shrugged, continuing the demand. "For your two sons, silver alone is not enough, so it must be land. You are to evacuate this fort and turn it over to Baron

Theodoric. You and all your people will be allowed free passage to your master in Rouen."

Runa glanced at him, her face taut with worry that the ransom would be too much for him. The land could never be surrendered unless Hrolf the Strider allowed it. That was a plain fact to everyone listening. Ulfrik nodded to her, knowing he had to delay while he considered a way out of the problem.

"Your lords demand a terrible sum from me. They seek to destroy my wealth and deprive me of my land. They ask me to die."

The messenger shrugged once more, as if he agreed, but said nothing. Ulfrik leaned forward.

"To raise so much silver and arrange for all their other demands, I will need time. I will also need surety that all of these men and my sons are still alive. Your word is simply not good enough, so do not offer it to me. I am insulted they would send you four in their stead, for I am sending you back this morning with my reply. I must see all of the hostages and be satisfied of their welfare. Then, I will discuss with them the terms of their ransoms."

Opening his mouth as if to protest, Ulfrik waved his hand. Einar helped emphasize it by stepping forward. The messenger dropped his gaze.

"You will be fed this morning and provisioned for your return trip. You have my answer to your lords. I will meet with them in two days, enough time for you to deliver my reply and to prepare."

A flurry of activity followed as Ulfrik stood and dismissed the Franks. He retired to the back of the hall, while he waited for Einar to lead the Franks out and prepare them to leave. Runa stood close at his side, whispering harshly. "What are they doing, sending messengers? Do you think the boys are all right? What happened to Throst? I beg the gods that he did not hurt Hakon before ransoming him."

Ulfrik folded his arms and frowned. Runa's questions bounced around the periphery of his thoughts. She continued her worried chatter, and he slipped a comforting arm around her which did nothing to slow her. Snorri joined them, and Einar returned. Even Konal, barely able to move, had struggled to draw closer but surrendered to a bench farther away. They all look expectantly at him.

"I'll not surrender our homes. Hrolf would never allow it, not without good cause."

"They're our family," Runa blurted out. "Our children are not good cause?"

"Not for Hrolf," Ulfrik said, and both Snorri and Einar nodded in solemn agreement. "The silver I can pay, but the land I cannot. There is but one choice now. I must get inside Clovis's fortress myself and free our men."

Einar snorted at the idea. "And after that we shall slip inside Paris and take it as well."

"It's true, lad. Getting in might not be tricky, but getting out is." Snorri limped to his side and dropped a hand on his shoulder. "You'll be trapped."

"We'll walk out the front gate," Ulfrik said. "I'm not planning to fight my way out. Once inside, I get a hostage of my own. Clovis himself would be a prize, though I'd be sorely tempted to kill him instead."

"It sounds like a plan made to go wrong," Snorri contended.

"And do you foresee Hrolf pulling in his borders? I am the jarl of Ravndal, but Hrolf is jarl over all. If I gave up this land, even if it is mine to surrender, he would outlaw me without a thought. All these years of service to him would matter not at all and we would have to find a new land. Is there a place where there are no kings? Who would have me, an oath-breaker? For I've sworn an oath to hold this border in Hrolf's name and if it costs me my sons ..."

The words died and he slumped forward, placing his head in his hands. The room was quiet enough to hear rats scurrying in the corners of the walls. His oath to Hrolf was an iron band around both of his arms and as impossible to break. When he looked up again, Runa was staring at him expressionless. His words must have wounded her, but surely she had to understand their truth. He shook his head, and she turned away with closed eyes.

"If only we could get to grips with Clovis," Konal said, his voice strained with the pain of his wounds. "We would destroy him."

"You forget all those horsemen," Einar said. "This Baron Theodoric's strength will embolden the Franks."

A depressed silence settled upon them again. Finally, Aren tugged at Ulfrik's shirt sleeve. He looked down at his son, his face serious and eyes strangely glittering. Ulfrik thought he hurt for the suffering of his brothers, and he stroked his head as he held the boy close. Aren pulled back, and Ulfrik looked at him in confusion. He did not want comfort, but to speak.

"What is it?" he asked.

"Why can't Hrolf help us fight them? Doesn't he protect you like you protect us?"

Ulfrik's first thought was that he had protected no one, but he saw the men sit up straighter at the suggestion.

"Gunnar and Hakon would be killed if we attacked," Konal explained. "That is why hostages are difficult to handle."

But Ulfrik was searching Aren's face. The boy had all the innocent hope and simplicity of youth, unencumbered with adult concerns. Konal continued to lecture, and the others bowed their heads and nodded with somber agreement. Runa hid her face in a trembling hand.

And Ulfrik began to see his way out. Aren stared at him, and his eyes widened when he saw Ulfrik's confidence blooming.

"Aren is right. Hrolf will aid us and we will defeat Clovis and save all of our men. My sons included."

Konal stopped chattering, every head snapped toward him. Ulfrik could not help but smile.

"Does it involve taking King Odo hostage?" Einar said, folding his arms.

"Not at all. In fact, I will give Clovis everything he wants, then destroy him."

46

Ulfrik camped his army on the wide fields outside of Clovis's fortress. He left no one but the elderly and children behind Ravndal's walls. Nearly three hundred warriors arrayed themselves in an arc just beyond bow range of the wooden palisades surrounding Clovis's stone castle. Ulfrik's banner of black elk antlers on a green field fluttered from a pole erected before his tent. Rows of white tents billowed all around, filled with fighting men and craftsmen as well as all their families. It was as if a new village of cloth had spouted overnight in the dead grass of the fields.

The morning air bit hard with autumn cold, and the late dawn warned of the onset of winter. Ulfrik stood beneath his banner, hand shading his eyes as he strained to see the activity from Clovis's stronghold. Nothing appeared to stir.

"I will go with you," Runa said, emerging from the tent behind him. "Aren will stay with Konal and Bera."

"It's not a woman's place to attend the parley of men." He did not take his eyes from the distance, nor did he put any great stock in his words. They came unbidden through his preoccupied mind.

"Then I won't parley, but slice that bastard Clovis from crotch to throat and pull out his heart."

Smiling, he faced Runa. She wore fresh clothes of green and brown, with a full skirt and overdress of white. The curly ringlets of her hair splashed freely over her shoulders and accented her wild individualism. She remained the only married woman to eschew a hair cover. "No pants? Fighting in a skirt is a guarantee of defeat."

She did not acknowledge the taunt, but set her chin at the horizon. "What if he will not grant the delay you need?"

"Then he is a fool, for he would not get the land he desires. He doesn't want to kill our sons; it would cost him all his advantage." He neglected to state Clovis would rather maim them, not wanting to alarm Runa even though she knew that threat as well as he. She nodded silently at his assessment, leaving the two of them absorbed in their shared worries for their children.

In time, Einar approached with his picked men. Halla followed them, and the defiant tilt of her head warned that she would not be denied. Ulfrik's guts churned, for it was an ill thing to have so many women present at a parley. Twelve other men were imprisoned and many had wives or lovers who could make an equal claim to join them. A dozen weepy-eyed women were the last thing he needed at his back, even if they were all as murderously capable as Runa.

"She can't join us," Runa said flatly, and with that simple statement annulled their truce.

"You've no right. My husband is a hostage for your foolish quarrels with the Franks. I demand to attend."

"You demand?" Runa's voice rose and Ulfrik stepped between them.

"Both of you be silent. Stop acting as children. Halla may join, but both of you are to remain silent. Do you understand?" He glared at them, Halla smiling in triumph and Runa with arms folded in grudging acceptance.

Snorri limped up to the group, leaning on a spear and scanning them. "What a sad bunch this is. You couldn't scare a blind grandmother, never mind the lords of Frankia. Save your hate for Clovis and his scum, and maybe you'll do us all some good."

Chastened by Snorri's criticism, Ulfrik twisted his neck and loosed his shoulders before ordering the group to move out. Einar had already ordered the warriors into blocks of spearmen who would be ready to charge at any sign of danger. Ulfrik and his group of a dozen bodyguards passed through them in silence and made for the black walls of Clovis's fortress.

Its gate opened and a group emerged. Men lined the ramparts above it, bows readily visible but too distant to be a threat. Clovis's standard of a white swan on a black square unfurled above the group as Ulfrik waited.

The two groups met and only the wind rushing over dead grass made any sound. Clovis stood at the center, resplendent in his scoured mail. At his right stood a man who could only be Theodoric, such was his refined and clear-lined features. A white scare was all that marred his regal face. Clovis's son was at his left, and he appeared pasty white and ill. He clutched his ruined stump to his side, and looked nothing like the vibrant man he had met in battle last summer. Ulfrik made sure to let his eyes linger over the son.

A line of a dozen men formed behind these three, and Ulfrik did not see his sons among them. He schooled his expression, keeping any emotion from it even as his anger festered. He folded his arms and waited for Clovis to open the negotiations.

"You have traveled this far just to scowl at me?" Clovis asked. "Have you brought the ransom with you? I could send your sons home with you this very day. You seem to have already abandoned Ravndal for me."

"The men behind me will march through the ashes of your pitiful hall if you cannot prove all my men are unharmed. Were your messengers too stupid to deliver such a simple warning to you?"

Clovis shared a smile with Theodoric, and both turned to the line behind them. "I have your proof."

For a brief moment, Ulfrik's stomach ached with fear that the head of one of his sons would be produced. Instead, the line parted and revealed Toki standing with arms and legs tied with enough slack to walk. Theodoric waved him forward and two men shoved him ahead in response. Toki snarled at them, but turned a smile to Ulfrik.

"Where've you been? A little long in getting here." His eyes slid past Ulfrik to both Runa and Halla behind him. He winked at them, and continued. "So you're thinking about getting me out of this mess?"

"Maybe not you, but your crew. You look tired, but well. Didn't you even fight these dog-shit Franks?"

He shrugged, and was about to reply when Clovis struck him on the shoulder and yelled. "Enough, tell them about his sons and your men. Be quick."

"These cocksucking Franks have not harmed any of us," Toki said, emphasizing his words with a sneer at Clovis. "Gunnar is unhurt, and Hakon is thin and weak but that was Throst's doing. He's held in another room from Gunnar and me, so we only met once. We're on the top floor while Hakon is below somewhere. He cried for joy when he saw us, even in this state. I've not seen my men or know where they're held. Clovis promises they're alive, but that's all I know."

Ulfrik nodded, paying careful attention to the directions Toki provided right past the Frank's understanding. His Danish accent probably impeded their understanding, and so they missed that he was providing details of how to rescue them.

Snatching Toki back by his arm, Clovis shoved him into the care of guards who then escorted him to the back of the line. He looked one time over his shoulder, and called Halla's name before the men cuffed him to silence.

"So now you have your assurances," Clovis said.

Ulfrik noted how he continually resisted glancing at his own son. Gunnar remained intact for now, but that constant pull of Clovis's eyes to the stump of his son's hand warned that he could think of little more than inflicting the same fate on Gunnar. The son was worse than the women Ulfrik had taken to the parley. He wilted like a cut flower out of water, and his arm tremored. Sweat beaded on his head, and the fear emanating from him shamed all the Franks. The only reason for his presence had to be as an unspoken threat against Gunnar. For now, if Ulfrik understood correctly, Theodoric held the ransom for Gunnar, Toki, and the crew, while Clovis held only Hakon. So Gunnar was safe from Clovis while Theodoric held him hostage. Ulfrik counted that a small blessing.

"So I have been satisfied, and I will pay your ransoms."

Clovis drew breath for a rebuttal, but then realization struck. Both he and Theodoric paused in amazed silence. Theodoric was the first to rouse himself, speaking in poor Norse.

"A wise decision, Jarl Ulfrik. So much blood has been spilled already, and you cannot stand against us any longer. Your people will love you for your wisdom."

"My people will be homeless and poor, and I will be broken and shamed. No one will celebrate that." Theodoric shrugged in agreement. "The silver you demand of me is far greater than what I possess."

"Don't claim poverty now," Clovis interrupted. "You and your vermin have overturned every church and home from the coast to Chartes. You stood at Hrolf's side when Bishop Anscharic delivered wagon-loads of silver to ransom Paris. By all counts you are a wealthy jarl."

"You have imagined a fatter prize than I really am, poor Clovis. But the amount is not beyond my means. Hrolf is generous and, though it galls me, I shall beg a loan from him. He is a man of tremendous honor and would never fail me in my need. Now I ask if you are a patient man or a fool? Such sums of wealth are not raised overnight, and delivering it requires care against bandits. I need two weeks to raise the funds and prepare it for you."

Folding his arms and turning his head aside, Ulfrik anticipated flat denial. Instead, Theodoric answered. "You have one week, no more."

"That is half the time I need!" Ulfrik held his head, exaggerating his dismay. A week was all he required for his plans. "You cannot demand this of me."

"It is more than I would allow," Clovis shouted, glaring at Theodoric. "If you are late, I will hang one of your men for every day overdue. I will start with your dear brother. And if all your crew are dead I will move on to your sons. I will cut off a limb for each day you make me wait until both your children are no more than stumps."

Ulfrik waited for Theodoric to countermand Clovis, and a chill silence spread as the Frankish lord stared at him. At last, understanding a response was expected, he shrugged. "It is a fine plan. Do not waste time with your mouth hanging open, Ulfrik. One week from today we begin killing. When your men are no more, I will come to collect your head."

Stepping closer, a full head taller than Theodoric, he glowered down on him then whispered in a deep, rough voice, "Piss on you, Frank."

47

R una's head throbbed as she sat on a blanket stretched over the grass inside her tent. Yellow light glowed along the billowing panels, a circle of brilliant white above her head where the sun shined through the clouds. Aren assisted Ulfrik with the baldric of his sword, fastening it behind him as Ulfrik pulled his chain coat straight. His helmet had tumbled out of a sack and the empty eye guards seemed to stare up from the grass at Runa. She shuddered, not wanting to think of severed heads. He reached down and placed it on Aren's head while he fussed with his final preparations.

Unlike her other sons, Aren did not laugh or appreciate his father's humor. The levity was out of place, and strange for Ulfrik at such a crucial time. He had come back from the scene of Gunnar's defeat a different man, and it frightened her. Life was adrift in a raging sea and she needed him to be constant, not to change. Not even if it was good change. She needed one thing to stay the same, one thing she could trust and predict. Her heart had been through too much; fear and anger and worry had ravaged her. A day without shock or surprise would be a prize beyond measure.

The helmet hung lopsided on Aren's head, and he pulled it off with difficulty to hand it up to his father. He took it under his arm, shouldered a bag of gold he would present to Hrolf, and let out a long sigh.

"A week is more than enough," he said again. He had said it so often since the parley that Runa now realized a week was barely sufficient. He fit his helmet over his head and mumbled. "As long as everything goes right, it will be enough."

Runa laughed, choked it back when he frowned at her. Of course nothing would go right. Here was another plan of her husband's, fraught with danger and hinged upon circumstances he could not control, but certain to be song-worthy if victorious. At least this much had not changed in him. He could always be counted upon to take the most dangerous road.

"Snorri will advise you and Konal will remain behind as well. Don't let him strain his wounds."

"He'll be waiting like the rest of us. No strain in that."

"No," Ulfrik said, dropping the bag. "Remember what we discussed. Ensure the men are vigilant; that they practice and demonstrate their strength for the Franks. Do everything short of drawing them into a fight. Snorri will know what to do."

"What if Hrolf refuses to come to your aid?" She stood now, her eyes fixed on his. He put up a hand to protest, caught himself, and took her hand instead. His skin was warm and rough as he folded both hands over it.

"He will come. A lord who would not help his bondsman in such a time is no lord at all. Hrolf is a great man, or I would not serve him."

"And what if he cannot help? Then what will happen?"

They stared at each other, and he grinned as if he knew something she did not. His confidence usually was not misplaced, but Runa believed recently the gods took less interest in Ulfrik's success. He squeezed her hand.

"I will return within the week, do not fear. When I do, Clovis and Theodoric will grab the trap I set with both hands, but not before returning our children."

He drew her close, kissed her head, and stepped back. His back was straight and his step filled with energy. He believed in victory; it showed in his every motion. Such confidence had won him many battles, so why would this be any different?

"This is for our sons," she said, her voice small. She reviled its timidity, and her doubt seemed foolish in the light of Ulfrik's certainty.

"Always for our sons," he agreed. "I know what you are thinking, that this plan was made for glory more than anything else. There is that, but it is the surest way to trap our foes while extracting our sons from danger. I believe it, and you must as well." He smiled and added, "For our sons."

He kissed her again, ruffled Aren's hair, and stepped outside the tent where Einar waited with a small group of bodyguards and horses. They were all kitted for war in mail and fresh-painted shields rimmed with iron. They each carried two spears and two swords, and their fierce expressions made Runa wonder if the ten of them planned to storm Clovis's fortress on their own. Runa's hand felt for the hilt of her own long knife hidden beneath her skirts, finding the smooth pommel and touching it like a talisman against evil.

Snorri nodded at her, as if to tell her all would be well. She smiled and watched Ulfrik set out with his men. He departed without ceremony, as one man leading a group on a routine patrol. She watched him cut across the camp and then through the fields, until finally a dip in the land swallowed them from view. Her hand continued to run over the pommel of her hidden weapon, and she whispered to herself as she returned to the tent, "Gods grant you speed and victory, husband. Bring our children home."

48

By midmorning of the following day, Ulfrik and his band were intercepted by Hrolf's scouts and led to his hall. Unlike other visits to Hrolf in his seat of power, he was now keenly aware of the openness of it. No walls encircled his long houses or mead hall. Workers and children crisscrossed the lanes and tracks, oblivious to danger. A lone sheep sauntered across their path. Guards and hirdmen clustered in doorways or at the corners of houses, rolling dice and laughing. No cares here. No worried silence and no suspicious glances. Pleasant curls of smoke lifted over the gentle hum of life in this idyllic community.

Ulfrik frowned, glancing at Einar who walked at his side. If he had noticed the same carelessness, he gave no sign of it.

"Such a happy place," Ulfrik said. "Here you could forget the Franks are ever ready to ram a spear through a man's gut and burn his home to ash."

Their escorts smiled nervously, but Einar nodded. "We've lived too long on the border. I don't even remember a life like this."

They wended along a rutted path up the hill to where Hrolf had built his mead hall. Only here did a sense of vigilance form about its gray, rain-stained walls. Guards at the doors were stern, spears held straight and shields close to their bodies. The massive structure could hold more than hundred men. The double doors were carved with coiling serpents, fighting warriors of legend, though little else either on the exterior or interior bore any decoration. Hrolf favored size over beauty, strength over form. Everything about his hall, from the vaulting roof to its wide floors and massive tables, spoke to that taste.

They surrendered their weapons at the doors and were allowed inside. For a moment, Ulfrik's eyes saw only a burnt orange haze until they adjusted to the low light from lamps and the open smoke hole. One of the scouts went before them, announcing their arrival to the few who lingered in the hall.

"I expected you sooner." The voice boomed across the hall, but rather than Hrolf's it was the rough tones of Gunther One-Eye. He sat at the high table, not in Hrolf's chair but in the seat beside it.

"And I did not expect to return until spring." Ulfrik closed the distance to Gunther, and his old friend rose to greet him. Einar and the others of his group loosely fell in behind. The two men clasped arms and slapped each other's backs. Despite his age, Gunther's grip was firm and warm, and while his single eye was nestled behind the crevasses of age, it twinkled with intelligence and curiosity.

"The Franks are troubling you." Gunther did not ask Ulfrik, but told him. Ulfrik bowed his head in acknowledgment and Gunther grunted. "You've traveled in haste and with a heavy burden, but still let it not be said you could find no comfort in the Strider's hall. All of you, sit where you will and enjoy ale and food with me."

Gunther rounded his table and joined with Ulfrik and his men. From the dark corners of the hall, slave girls jumped to Gunther's commands, gathering horns and mugs for drink.

"We found the cairn and battlefield," Gunther explained as he settled onto the bench beside Ulfrik. The other men in the hall drew closer to listen, so that despite the vastness of the hall everyone clumped at tables in the center. "Followed the tracks and saw the hoof prints. Only the Franks are fool enough to ride horses to battle."

"Yet you sent no one to me? You must've realized the size of the Frankish force." Ulfrik immediately regretted the ungrateful tone of his question, and calmed himself. "Combined with Clovis, they are formidable enemies."

Gunther winced, flashing his yellow teeth. "If you needed help, you would've sent for it. Would I shame you by sending aid without your asking for it?"

The arrival of drinks saved the conversation from its unpleasant turn. Accepting a horn brimming with foamy ale, he raised it to Gunther. "Thank you for your hospitality, my friend. All glory to your name."

They drank as one and emptied their mugs for more. Gunther gave a gusty laugh as he dropped his horn on the table. "The finest anywhere. Makes what we brewed in the north taste like goat piss. Except that mead you used to brew. That was a rare treasure."

Cheese and dried fish were served to them next, and conversation turned to lighter topics. Pressing his needs so early was a crude and foolish move, and he had to play a better guest. He had time yet to lay plans and make requests. So he enjoyed the salty fish and bitter ale, kept his conversation to surface detail of recent news, and let the meeting flow naturally to his story.

At last he had detailed all of Throst's treachery, the capture of his sons, and the arrival of Theodoric. Attention remained fixed on him, and the flow of food and ale ceased as men forgot themselves. Gunther frowned angrily throughout, and at each mention of Clovis or Throst his fist clenched. When it was finished, he sat back and refreshed his mouth with the last drink from his horn.

"It is more dire than I had even considered," Gunther said at last. "King Odo has involved himself, even if only indirectly. We thought he had stopped looking west."

"No king stops looking for land, especially if he believes it to be his by right," Ulfrik said. "You hardly come to the border anymore, but if you did you would see the work I do in keeping the Franks off your backs. They pick at every loose thread, hoping to unravel the whole cloth. They think they may have found it this time. And maybe they have. Both of my sons are their hostages."

The gloomy silence prevailed as men looked into their mugs and Gunther shook his head. "What have they asked for ransom?"

"My fortune and my land, all that I possess."

Gunther raised his brow, but said nothing. Einar finally lost patience and asked the questions on everyone's mind.

"Will we be able to speak to Jarl Hrolf? Clovis has only given us seven days and two are spent already."

"He is gone to England for the winter, took three hundred men, all his family, and my son. Only my own men and a small number of Hrolf's remain behind. We cannot abandon our position."

He turned saddened eyes to Ulfrik, and placed a heavy hand on his forearm. Ulfrik pulled it back.

"You have not even heard my request, and you are already telling me what you cannot do." His heart raced and his breath grew hot in anger, yet he paused long enough to gird his emotion. "Will you at least hear me?"

Gunther closed his eye and nodded, twisting on the bench to face Ulfrik. "I merely wanted you to know the situation here. Please, speak to me as Hrolf's second and I will grant all that is within my power. You know I want to aid you."

The tone of his voice and his imploring eyes expressed more to Ulfrik than any speech. Without a doubt, he had sworn publicly to hold and defend Hrolf's land in his absence. Gunther was a shrewd man, and if he suspected Ulfrik had a plan to defeat the Franks, particularly King Odo's men, then he would want to share in that glory. He needed Ulfrik to provide a way to maintain his oath and still be able to assist. Ulfrik's beating heart calmed, and he gave the faintest smile as he rose to address Gunther. He did not need to persuade his old friend, only the men around him.

"Thank you for the opportunity. Hear what I ask, and judge whether it is within your power to help me. I think you will find aiding me is a better defense of your homes than staying put." Gunther smiled, and gestured for Ulfrik to continue. He clasped his arm behind his back and began to pace. "The Franks believe they have me in a perfect trap, that I would not sacrifice my own to defy them. They also know without help, I do not have enough men to face down Clovis and Theodoric."

"They do not know you are here?" Gunther asked.

"They believe I am here for a loan from Hrolf, so that I may pay the silver demanded of me. Were I to return with men at my back, my sons and all the others would die before we could reach Clovis's walls."

"So are you truly here for silver?" Gunther's frown filled with shadow from the light above. Some men looked at each other in disappointment or disgust. One even left the table.

"Hardly, in fact, I have prepared a gift of gold to you so no one may claim I am a poor guest." He paused and glared at those who frowned at him. "I am here for men. I am here to bring the fury of the north onto these warm-weather worms. I am here because not only will my sons and warriors be saved, but Clovis will be destroyed in one blow. With the fighting strength of your hall to help, the largest Frankish stronghold between us and Paris will be ripped open. Land and slaves will raise our treasure piles and the glory of our deed will be sung in every hall until Ragnarok."

He let his words echo in the hall, and even Einar, who had discussed the plan until exhausted, leaned forward to hear more. Gunther's eye shined with mischief, but he still had a role to play. "And this will be done without Clovis's executing your hostages?"

"He will release them before he ever sees your blades."

A murmur rippled through the hall and Gunther smiled. "Now that's a plan worth hearing. Go on."

"I will grant him all he asks. The silver is his to take, and I will give it down to my last bit of treasure. And my hall and fortress shall be his as well. My people will be waiting outside its walls, prepared to leave and never return." Ulfrik paused, relishing the drama and the wide eyes waiting for his reveal. He licked his lips before continuing.

"But inside my fortress, stuffed into every building and room, are hidden the fighting men of Hrolf the Strider and Gunther One-Eye. When Ravndal's gates close behind Clovis, the killing will begin. The gates will reopen and my men and yours will rend the Frankish army like old sailcloth. Theodoric's horsemen will be useful only as targets for your bowmen. His footmen will die in confusion. Then, when they are shattered, we turn to Clovis's home and demolish it."

The gathered men roared in delight, banging the tables and stomping the ground. Ulfrik swaggered about the table, smiling at Einar and Gunther as he gathered in the praise for his plan. Gunther, however, still had his oath and he began shouting for his men to quiet. At last, he restored order then folded his arms as he challenged Ulfrik.

"A cunning plan, certainly worthy of a song, but I fear you have wasted time coming here. My oath to Hrolf has bound me to the defense of his hall and lands, and to abandon it is to leave it open for attack."

The eager crowd was chastened at Gunther's reminder and the excited hum stilled. Ulfrik expected this, and had already determined a counter. "And to let me crumble is to encourage an attack on this very hall. I have gambled all on coming here, and there is no time left. To return now without your aid is to see my sons killed and my hall destroyed. Do not fear I will betray my own oath. I will die before a Frankish army slips across my borders. But they will. Then who will you summon to your aid? You must send messengers now; call back all you can to the defense of these lands. In one week I will be dead and my lands in the hands of the Franks.

"Unless you have the wisdom to understand Hrolf's true command. For I doubt he ever intended to allow the borders to crumble while you sit idle. In all our years, he has always sent aid to the borders and that is why your homes are not surrounded by walls and your people prosper. No Frank gets this far because you fight them farther afield. What has changed now?"

Many grumbled agreement, and Ulfrik was confident he had won the day. Gunther smiled, but then his expression grew serious.

"All very strong arguments. I must consult with the rest of my felag, and hear their thoughts. I will have your answer tomorrow."

"Tomorrow is too late," Ulfrik said, genuine surprise reaching into his voice. He had expected a quicker agreement from Gunther. "Gathering your men and moving them unseen into Ravndal will take time. Just the travel alone ..."

"Tomorrow morning," Gunther said with finality. "I am moved by your need, but you must understand mine. Hrolf left no room to misunderstand his intent. Your plan is a great temptation, but it cannot be undertaken lightly. Rest today, feast tonight, speak no more of this to me. You will have your answer in the morning, and if I may aid you then I will put all speed to that task."

A hush overtook all the men, and Gunther excused himself with no further ceremony. Ulfrik stared at Einar, who returned a harsh stare of his own. He thought of Runa's fears, then slowly sat on a bench and rubbed his mouth. He had no choice but to wait until tomorrow. When the sun rose he would be at Gunther's bedside to hear the decision.

49

R una waited, surrounded by hirdmen, Snorri at her side and Konal using a spear to support himself. Both could no longer restrain her, and had resigned themselves to following her. The hirdmen accompanying them were hard-bitten warriors of long service. She knew them all by name, as well as their wives or lovers and their children as well. They had insisted on escorting her out to the field where Clovis had met with Ulfrik. Ensconced in such care and strength, she should not fear, yet her hands were ice and her heart fluttered.

The sixth day was ending without word from Ulfrik. She had counted the time: two days to Hrolf, two days to return, and the rest of the time to prepare his trap. Even if he returned this night, would any time remain for his plan? If not, what happened to her children? Whether Ravndal stood or fell, or whether she surrendered every scrap of treasure to Clovis mattered not at all. Land and gold could be won again, but her family could never be replaced.

"They are coming," said one of the hirdmen, pointing at the group of shadows emerging from the distant gates. Runa swallowed. What had he summoned her to discuss if not the ransom due?

"You don't need to speak to him," Snorri whispered at her side. "We've got until tomorrow."

Runa waved him back without looking. He had repeated the same thing since receiving Clovis's messenger, and she no longer wished to hear it. Had he not been like a father, she would have been tempted to strike him.

Clovis arrived with his attendants, though Theodoric did not accompany him. The swaggering gait of the man irked her. She imagined kicking him square in the crotch and watching that smugness turn to agony. His hands fussed with his cloak, and jeweled rings glittered in the pink light of the evening. He scanned them, and not finding Ulfrik, his eyes did not know where to land. She stepped forward.

"Here, do you not recognize me?"

"I thought you a servant," he said. Runa's hirdmen growled and threatened, but she held up a hand to them.

"I am Runa the Bloody, and I lead while Ulfrik is gone."

Tipping his head to the side, he blinked several times before laughing. "Such a fearsome name, yet I've not heard it before. You are Ulfrik's wife?"

"I am that too. Now did you call this meeting to gawk at me or were you planning to surrender and spare me the trouble of teaching you how I earned my name?"

His mouth opened in genuine surprise and he had no words. Runa had long been known as the Bloody for the violence she saved for her enemies. She was glad Halla had been persuaded to remain with her children, as hearing that old title would make her even less tractable than she had been since Toki's capture. Runa gave a thin smile, her hand feeling for the blade hidden beneath her skirt. *Let me show you how different I am from the women you know*, she thought. *It'd be your last lesson.*

"Well, I summoned Ulfrik and he has not come. Do I take it to mean he is still away?"

"You are more clever than I ever expected," she said.

The jibe took a moment to penetrate Clovis's understanding. His face darkened and his bemused smile turned to a snarl. "Such a light spirit. I wonder if you will be laughing tomorrow when your husband fails to show."

Her cold hands trembled and she folded them under her arms to hide it. Annoying Clovis might not be a good idea, but provided mild relief for her urge to kill him. "He will return with your ransom. Now why did you summon me?"

"Because Theodoric and I are impatient with this delay. A week was more than generous, and tomorrow marks the end of it. If our demands cannot be satisfied by dawn tomorrow, your kin will die."

"We have through tomorrow," Runa said.

"Until tomorrow," Clovis said, his sneer widening. "It seems you barbarians are not smart enough to count as high as seven days."

"Trickery," Runa snapped. "You cannot change the day. It is breaking your word."

"Your failure to mark time is not my concern. And those men behind you look eager to strike. Remember your children. If I don't return, you will find their heads atop my walls."

Runa whirled on the men behind her, who had lowered spears or had their hands upon their swords. Even Snorri and Konal seemed ready to strike. "We're here to talk. Put up your weapons and don't risk my family's lives."

Clovis stroked his beard as if considering what to do. He regarded Runa with slitted eyes. "It seems I will not have my ransom. I should have expected it. Let me tell you what I am planning, Runa. By tomorrow morning, if there is no sign of your husband or my ransom, I will not kill Toki."

A rush of breath came from Runa, not even realizing she had been holding it.

"I will kill Hakon instead."

"You dare not."

"I do. I am tired of your arrogance, of the games you play, of every-thing about you. Your son is a brat, and if you won't pay for his life then I will dispose of him. The others are Theodoric's hostages, but don't expect him to be any more patient than me. In fact, he has wearied of this faster than I had expected. He's of a mind to kill all the hostages at once and destroy you now."

"He's bluffing," Snorri whispered from behind. "Their advantage isn't that big. If the hostages are dead, then we will pin them inside and all their horses won't matter."

"What are you whispering about?" Clovis demanded. "Do you have no answer for me?"

"Tomorrow you will have all you ask, whether Ulfrik has returned or not."

Snorri gasped, then rasped in her ear. "Lass, you can't do that. It's not our land to give."

She nearly bowled him over as she rounded to leave Clovis. Konal grabbed her arm, and their eyes met. Her glare withered him, and he let her go. No more games, no more tricks. If Ulfrik failed, then she was not surrendering her children to death. Let him live in shame, let him pay, but not her sons.

"Tomorrow at dawn," Clovis called after her.

The hirdmen fell in behind, and she closed her ears to their murmurs of protest. These games were finished.

50

In the predawn light, Throst and his two companions entered the square tower where Clovis imprisoned the hostages. No one minded them, as all but a scattering of watchmen on the palisades still slumbered. The Franks had proved to be indolent people who looked to their slaves whenever real work needed to be done. The fortress was asleep, and would not awaken until the roosters forced them to accept a new day had arrived. They entered the empty ground floor and cautiously moved to the wooden stairs leading up.

"This is a fool's business," Olaf whispered. "If we're going, then let's be gone. This is the wrong fucking way."

"Shut up, Olaf," Dan grumbled and pushed him forward.

Throst glared at both of them, paused before setting foot on the creaking steps, then started up. In one hand he carried an ax which had been looted from the Danes, more than likely Ulfrik's people. In his other, he clutched a sheath sword of Frankish make. Both had been given to him for sharpening by one stupid brute who had not understood Clovis had forbidden them weapons. If it was not a sign of the gods' favor, Throst did not know what else would be.

The darkness was unbroken but for the candle Dan carried. They moved through a murky circle of light that barely revealed their feet, and Throst caught his foot on more than one step as they climbed. On the second floor two men slept on pallets covered in straw. One had his back turned while another lay on his side facing them. Neither stirred and both snored like thunder. They guarded a barred door where Hakon was kept.

Throst was tempted to say farewell to the boy. In truth, he was not a bad child, and had he been another man's son, Throst could have liked him. Still, he was a tool that had no more use. Today, unless Ulfrik produced his ransom, poor Hakon would die and no one at all would have benefited from all his suffering.

Continuing to the third floor, they paused and Throst gave a silent look to both his men. Dan nodded in understanding and handed the candle to Olaf. The light began to quake, and Throst smirked at Olaf's fearful quake. He shot Throst a frown and looked away. Using hand gestures, Throst pantomimed strangling a man with both hands. Dan mimicked him with a wicked smile. Throst stepped down and let Dan go first. Though he had an ax and sword, a silent death was necessary for their eventual escape. Besides, blood would run through the floorboards and alert the guards below.

Unfortunately, the guard on this level had already awakened. He sat at the edge of his makeshift bed, hair a tangle with bits of straw still clinging to it. He rested on his knees, and stared at them as if he hadn't yet awakened. Throst feared the guard would shout a warning, but Dan struck fast. His ponderous weight thudded heavily across the floorboards, loud enough to Throst's ears to awaken everyone between here and Paris. Yet Dan's thick hands seized the Frank's throat, and the two fell back on his bed.

The swaying light of Olaf's candle flashed across the struggle. The Frank began kicking, and Throst grabbed his legs to still him. A desperate choking sound was all the Frank managed, and ceased long before Dan released him. After a few more moments, Throst tapped Dan's shoulder.

"Don't pop off his head," he whispered. "I think you can drop him. He's bluer than a dolphin."

Olaf hissed for silence, and the three froze. Olaf shielded his candle and all three watched the dark hole of the stairs down. Relieved it was nothing more than snoring, they returned to their task.

"Let's get gone." Olaf's voice cracked as he tried to keep it low. Throst ignored him, picked up his ax and sword, then faced the bolted door where Gunnar and Toki were imprisoned.

"Just a few more things to do, and we're finished." Throst drew the sword and placed the sheath by the dead guard. With both weapons in hand, he gestured for Dan to unbolt the door.

The heavy bolts lifted out of the brackets, and Dan gripped one like a hammer ready to strike. Olaf, lofting his candle high with one hand, pulled the door open.

At first Throst saw nothing in the darkness but the faintest rectangle of gray predawn light high to the left. Olaf's candle feebly lit the entrance and nothing but rotten straw showed. A terrible smell of sweat and urine spilled out of the room. Impatient, he nodded Olaf forward with the candle, which he hesitated to do until prodded with the point of Throst's sword.

The circle of light crawled across two sets of booted feet peeking from beneath a single wool blanket. Throst recognized Gunnar and assumed the other man was Toki. Both slept soundly, and Throst let out a relieved laugh. He had expected a rush from the shadows.

"Good morning," he said as he pricked at their feet with his sword. "Time to get up and face the most important day of your life."

Gunnar recoiled from the blade, his eyes wild and disoriented. Toki, startled by the commotion, reacted with more alertness. He too backed up, but he had already gathered the blanket into his hand to serve as a net if he needed it. Throst stepped back from both of them.

"We're not Franks; so keep your voices down if you don't want to summon every man in this tower."

Toki was on his feet and Gunnar regained himself. Throst had Dan to flank him and Olaf to block the exit. His two weapons flashed candlelight, and Toki's eyes flickered to them.

"And you don't seem much like friends, either. Who are you?"

"You would not recognize me, but your nephew should. Olaf, bring that candle closer."

Throst smiled as Gunnar studied him. He enjoyed the rapid transition of expressions, from confusion, to curiosity, then to recognition and finally rage.

"Throst, you fucking bastard!" Gunnar leapt forward but Toki barred him with an outstretched arm, his eyes never leaving the gleaming point of the sword facing them.

"Voices, please. Only the guard on this floor is dead but the others are quite alive. The sun will rise soon, and so will they, if you don't awaken them now."

"What is this all about?" Toki asked, pulling Gunnar closer to his side. "If you're here to kill us, then you won't get the quiet you demand."

"Killing either of you was never my intent, at least not directly."

"Then what about Hakon?" Gunnar hissed, and again Toki laid his arm across his chest.

"Your father hanged my father then tossed my family into the wild. That should be all the explanation you need, but let me be clearer. My father was a stupid drunk, worthless to everyone. Your father knew it and I'm sure he was glad to be rid of him. Honestly, so was I. But it's not for anyone to take what is mine and no one treats me like your father did. No one."

Throst checked his own growing rage and cleared his throat. "I had a chance to build something great, or at least I thought I did, and a chance to make your father pay. I've done that part, I would think. But now everything is different. My plans are all failures. I've gotten nothing for my efforts, but for these two friends with me this morning. Clovis stole my only hostage, your dear brother, and has stripped me of my honor. He has me shoveling horse shit. Do you know how much one horse can shit in a day, never mind the dozens that Theodoric has stabled here?"

Gunnar and Toki stared at him as if he were mad. Perhaps he was, and he did not care. He was telling them the truth and it felt good. No one treats a freeman like a slave, and makes a skilled warrior a stable boy.

"Your hardship touches me," Toki said. "It's too bad that deceit and treachery don't pay more coin."

"I agree, for I should be a rich man by now. I should've grabbed Ulfrik's first offer and ran, but there was more for the taking. I just couldn't get it. Now Clovis will have all the fun. Or at least he thinks he will."

Throst let their confusion bloom in the pause, then he lowered the sword to the floor, keeping his ax at the ready. Toki and Gunnar stared blankly at the weapon as he backed away from it. Dan stood poised to bash them with the heavy wooden bolt if they attacked. Both edged to the door, and Olaf was tugging at the back of Throst's shirt. "Hurry, dawn is coming."

"I've no means to get back at Clovis other than to ruin his plans. Take this sword and find your way out, or earn yourself a good death. As long as Clovis can't profit from you, I'm happy. Now I've got to go. Your brother is held on the floor below us, and the rest of your men somewhere below this tower. I've never seen that place."

"By Freya's tits, man, shut up. I'm leaving," Olaf pulled back, but Dan caught him before he could go.

"How are you getting out?" Gunnar asked.

"This ax, darkness, and a rope is all I need." Throst winked at him. "But I'm not leaving it behind for you."

Gunnar stepped forward to retrieve the sword, he pointed it at Throst and hissed as loudly as he dared. "This bit of help won't save your hide. When I find you next, you will die."

"You won't find me, not unless I want you to, little boy."

Olaf glided down the stairs, followed by Throst and Dan covering the rear. Neither bothered to check if the others followed. At the exit of the tower, Olaf extinguished the candle and they flitted into the shadows between buildings. Throst glanced at the tower behind them, wondering how Gunnar would fare. He shook his head. That whole adventure was over now. He had to settle a few more things before moving on.

"Dan, the coil of rope." Throst held out his hand. "I'll take a running leap at the wall, and once Olaf and I are on the other side we should be able to anchor this rope well enough for you to climb. But you've got to be quick."

Throst hefted the ax, ran for the wall and jumped. The ax head bit into the wood just short of the top, and he let out a stifled shout of success. Working quickly, he pulled up and straddled the wall, then dropped the rope down to his men. As he waited for Olaf to grip it, he surveyed Clovis's fortress, noting a few orange lights wink into life.

"I hope Gunnar drives that sword into your smirking face, Clovis," he said to himself. "I only wish I could stay to see it."

51

Gunnar ranged the sword in the gloom before him. Throst may have left a weapon, but he left no light, and they could not afford to wait for dawn. A dozen misshapen plans crowded his thoughts, and none made any sense. He had prayed often enough for a rescue, but never planned to have to conduct it himself. Shame fought with fear as he stepped onto the barest outline of the stairs leading down. Toki had his hand upon his shoulder, having declared Gunnar's eyes better than his own. He wanted to remind Toki that youth did not grant the ability to see in the dark.

The stair creaked, and once he found the rhythm of the steps, he guided them to the floor below. Now what? The layout of this floor was the same as the one above: a living area for guards and a cell with a bolt across the wooden door. He could guess a path through the room by the faint light that filtered down from a single window. The snores of the guards were the only other clues. The killing had to be swift and confident, or the alarm would destroy the tenuous plans Gunnar managed to hold together in his excited mind.

Toki still gripped his shoulder, and his fingers were like iron nails digging into his flesh. In his other hand he held the wooden door bolt. It was the best weapon they had until they could find another. He tugged Gunnar toward the beds in the dark. The blue-gray outlines of breathing lumps under covers were the targets, though he could not tell legs from heads. If he stabbed a foot, their surprise would be nullified.

Raising his blade, he stopped short as Toki yanked his shoulder. He could hardly see his uncle in the dark, but his head shake was clear. Gunnar's heart thundered such that he feared it could wake the guards. One of them turned on his side, and his snoring ceased. Gunnar worried the man may have awakened, yet Toki had him remain still. At last he released Gunnar's shoulder and began to move carefully toward their victims. Toki's raised bolt was outlined in white light above his head.

Gunnar focused on what appeared to be a man's head, lining up his sword with it as he drew nearer.

Then his hip caught a table, and the sound of it dragging sounded like thunder.

A jug toppled and crashed with a splash on the wooden floor.

The head turned, and for a moment Gunnar did not understand a face was looking directly at him. It seemed an eternity that the sleepy, confused eyes shined out in the darkness.

Another rose up, and Toki's door bolt slammed down across the head with a wet crack. The body slumped with a groan.

A third man stirred, mumbling Frankish nonsense.

Another strike from Toki's bolt landed across his chest. He gasped but his breath vacated from his lungs, and Toki smashed him again. This time his face caught the blow and he snapped back onto his bed and lay still.

Gunnar's man was already rising, finally comprehending. Gunnar lunged and the sword caught the side of his face.

The scream was ghastly, and the man thrashed in agony as blood splashed between his fingers and over the blanket. Toki swung from the side, as if striking at a ball, connecting with the man's head and sending him crashing out of bed. He whimpered, and Gunnar wasted no time in plunging his blade into the dark mass beneath him. He did not see where he had struck, but it was deep and he felt the man's pulse thrumming in the blade, weakening until it stopped.

They froze, awaiting the alarm they expected. A noise from Hakon's cell drew both their eyes. The door shook, probably as Hakon tried to peek beneath it.

Toki and Gunnar stared at each other across the darkness. At last, when it seemed there would be no alarm. Gunnar withdrew his blade from the corpse at his feet. The body shifted, but the man was dead. Hot blood leaked beneath Gunnar's feet, and he skipped back from it.

Nothing moved. Gunnar held his breath. He refused to look toward the stairs leading down, as if to peek at it would summon more guards. Toki stared at him, the whites of his eyes bright in the gloom. No one came, and soon Gunnar let his breath out and Toki relaxed.

"There must be weapons here and upstairs." Toki began rummaging in the dark, shoving bodies aside like sacks of grain.

Gunnar wiped his sword off on a blanket, feeling a queasiness he had not anticipated. He had just killed a sleeping man. Even if he had been an enemy and only death could decide their fates, it still stank of murder. He had trained for war and glory, not gutting a man in his sleep. That had been the crime for which Throst's father had hanged. He shuddered at the thought, reminding himself of the circumstances.

Toki pulled up a sword with a purr of satisfaction. "This'll do fine. And a knife, too. Hey, what are you doing? Grab another weapon and let's move."

If his uncle's words did not galvanize him, the crowing of roosters did. Their crowing was like the calls of demons from the mist realms of death. Gunnar could think of no better comparison, for they had no hope of escaping in daylight. Toki paused, then strode to the bolted door and lifted it off without hesitation.

Hakon stumbled out, crashing into Toki's arms. He began to sob, clinging to his uncle with both arms. Toki stroked his head, but gently plied him off.

"You are well? You can walk? Take this knife and use it if you must."

Hakon nodded, wiped his nose with the back of his arm, and when Gunnar approached he began to cry again.

"It will soon be over," Gunnar offered. "We've only got to rescue the others before we escape."

"Do you trust Throst to have told us the truth of their where-abouts?" Toki asked, and now he started down the stairs first. The darkness was no longer so deep that he needed young eyes to aid his own. Gunnar glanced at the corpses, all but one still appearing as if they were only asleep in their beds.

"I don't know," Gunnar said, turning from the grisly scene and tugging Hakon along with one hand. "If he wants to get back at Clovis, he'd tell us the truth."

"And if he wanted us to get lost and die fighting, setting us against the Franks so that both of his enemies kill each other? He might be misdirecting us."

They reached the bottom floor, where nothing but supply barrels and crates were piled against one wall, and other detritus was stacked under the wooden stairs. A single trapdoor was set into the floor opposite the exit. A rooster crowed again.

Toki stared at him, a hard and fierce cast to his eyes. At first Gunnar considered Throst's words, but as Toki's silence swelled he began to understand. The realization staggered him.

"You don't want to look for the others?"

No answer, just a sharp and cold expression.

"They are your men. You must protect them. Toki, you can't be thinking of leaving them?"

"Fifteen of us are not going to sneak out of here in the morning light, and we won't find enough weapons for everyone before we're caught."

"They don't need weapons," Gunnar said, his voice rising from the careful tone of a moment earlier. "They need a chance to fight. Even if it's to die, they die as men."

"We've no time to waste. If we go now, we can hide and steal a

277

chance to escape before Clovis locks down his gates. If we search, even if my men are under our feet, we will be caught."

"I want to go," Hakon whined. "I want to see Ma and Da again. Please, Gunnar."

All that he had imagined of how men conducted themselves in war vanished. The noble battle, the glorious sacrifice, the proud battle scars, all of it was horseshit. Sworn men were cast aside so that a privileged few might live. Though they were bound to serve their lord in any circumstance, their lord only served them when it was convenient. Such cowardice, and from his own uncle, a man who he had idealized all his life. He could not be part of it.

"I am in charge. We look for the men." Gunnar stood straighter, and glared at Toki. He shot back his own withering gaze.

"Gods, I have a family to get back to," Toki said. "Think of your brother."

"Think of the men you swore to protect. Think of the oath you gave my father."

Toki's face turned grape-dark and his nostrils flared. Gunnar did not back down, even as Toki's hands flexed as if to strike him. At last, he growled in a low voice, "I am thinking of the oath I gave your father. Now, we waste time. Come with me or I will drag you out by the three whiskers on your chin."

Blinking in shock, Gunnar watched Toki gather Hakon to his side and pull open the door to the outside. He did not know what to do. The trapdoor pressed on the back of his head, as if he could hear the voices of men imprisoned beyond it. Yet there were not such voices, and Toki was already pulling Hakon out the door into the thin light of morning. He had to make a choice.

He followed. His stomach sank, his heart cracked, and he meekly obeyed his uncle. He was right about the odds of escape; fewer people stood a far better chance. There was no more true choice in this than there had been in killing guards while they slept. This was truly war, all shit through and through.

Fresh, bracing morning air was a welcomed taste after the stink of the tower. Toki and Hakon were already sprinting for nearby buildings where the darkness was deepest. A white stain in the clear skies warned of daylight. They had to gain the gates before anyone discovered their absence and then await an opportunity to slip away. It was desperate and inarticulate, but was the only plan Gunnar could keep in his head.

The plan shattered with a shout.

Emerging from the darkness between the buildings, directly in their path, appeared a group of Franks.

The world spun into icy confusion, slow and unreal, replete with terror and fear. There were six men, four of them armored guards and two in bright clothing. Toki and Hakon seemed to stand motionless before them, and the Franks mirrored their reaction. But the shout came again, from high in the tower they had left, a weary voice called out in Frankish, "Alarm!"

Toki's sword flashed and the lead guard collapsed with his hand at his neck and blood pouring across his chest. The two unarmored men drew long knives that caught the yellow light of the rising sun. Gunnar recognized them now as Clovis and Theodoric.

He raced to join Toki's side, the three other guards lowering spears and fanning out around them. Clovis had backed away, shouting to his men, "Take them in the legs. I want them alive."

"Kill the bastards," countered Theodoric, who stepped forward with his knife raised at Hakon. "They're worth nothing."

The conflicting orders created hesitation and an opening for Gunnar. He leapt into it with a roar. Theodoric, his regal face now a disfigured mass of angry wrinkles and bared teeth, lunged at Hakon who waved his knife like a child. Gunnar intercepted the strike with his sword, knocking the knife up and then turning the stroke down at Theodoric's trunk.

Striking true, without anything more than fine cloth for protection, Gunnar's blade sliced open Theodoric's belly. It was a keen edge on a well-crafted weapon, and Theodoric's stomach opened and expelled his guts like a shattered barrel of eels. The stink of entrails filled Gunnar's nose and Theodoric crumpled with nothing but a whimper. The amazing strike left Gunnar flat-footed, and he only had time to hear Hakon scream when a spear swept him off his feet.

The sky above was a cheerful blue, a stark contrast to the roiling madness unfolding beneath it. He tried to snap up, heard Hakon screech again, then the spear shaft slammed into his face. The world swam, and he was struck again, hard across the crown of his head. Another strike pummeled him flat, and more blows rained down on him until he could only ball up under the pain. His vision was a scrambled mess of blurry motion and his ears rang with a high-pitched wail. He thought he saw Toki stagger and fall.

Then pain bloomed over his head, his eyes filled with white, then nothing more than cold blackness.

52

Gunnar awakened to darkness and the smell of burning charcoal. Cold wetness crawled down his back and flowed down his chest. Raising his head, he realized he had been doused with water, only to have another bucket sloshed into his face.

"Awake now? It's no good if you're asleep for this."

Gunnar shook the water out of his hair, and realized his hands were trussed in front of him as he attempted to wipe his face. He blew the sour water out of his mouth, and blinked open his eyes. Everything was a blur and his ears still rang with a distant squeal. A shape stood before him, a man with hands on his hips. He was inside a stone room, gloom pervaded everything and was relieved only by the orange glow of a brazier filled with hot embers. Another fuzzy shape turned a metal rod in it, holding it with a thick leather glove.

"Where is my brother?" Gunnar asked, his voice cracking and weak.

"Alive, for now," the man standing before him answered. Gunnar squinted at him, and recognized Clovis. "We'll see if your father pays ransom today. Maybe little Hakon will remain alive after all."

"He's just a boy. Don't hurt him." Gunnar could think of nothing better to say. His plea drew derisive laughter from Clovis and a few others who remained out of sight. Gunnar sat up straighter, but realized he had been tied to a wooden support post.

"A noble brother to the end," Clovis said. "I would worry less for him right now. Do you know what you did?"

"I killed that turd who captured me, just like I promised I would."

"You did, and I thank you for it. For now at least, I will command his men and you have become my hostage." He stepped closer into Gunnar's fuzzy vision, then knelt down to bring his face level to Gunnar sitting on the floor. "I say God is good to me, little man. He has answered my prayers at last."

The crazed gleam in Clovis's eyes turned Gunnar's stomach to icy water. His breath was hot and foul upon his face, he leaned in so close. Gunnar tugged on his bindings, but had no slack. A wicked grin crawled across Clovis's features, and filled Gunnar with revulsion. With nothing left, he scrapped together what spit remained in his cotton-dry mouth and shot it into Clovis's face.

He recoiled in disgust, wiping the spit from himself, then stood. "I'm going to break that spirit of yours. You'll regret that flash of defiance."

"I regret nothing," Gunnar said, his heart beating so fast he hardly had breath to speak. "You are a coward and a fool. My father will have your head before the day is done."

"Strong words, but your father has disappeared. Did you not know?" Clovis turned his back to accept something from another man standing out of the edge of light. "Did Throst not tell this when he let you out? Don't look surprised. Toki explained how you escaped. I should've expected treachery from one of your kind."

He whirled, but faced another to his left. "It was your stupid idea to take him into service. If I had not listened to you, none of this would've happened."

Gunnar realized Clovis's son was present. His father's ire pushed his head down between his shoulders, and his craven posture disgusted Gunnar. Such a weak-willed man had no use to anyone. The lost of his sword hand was of little consequence to one so timid.

The thought froze him. An anvil was laid out beside the brazier.

Clovis now bore a large ax in his hand. Gunnar felt his right hand tingle in dread.

As if reading his thoughts, two men grabbed both of his arms while another began to unbind him. He began to struggle, but was weak and dizzy. The dread welled up in him, mixing with the nausea caused from the blows to his head. Watery vomit ejected onto the stone floor with a splash. The men holding him cursed but Clovis laughed.

"Where's the bravery now." His voice dropped as he commanded his men. "Hold him still and put his arm on the anvil. Have the brand ready."

"You can't do this. This is madness. My father will kill you."

"Your father deserves this. He deserves to have his eldest son made into less than a man. He deserves to look at you and see nothing but weakness, a man with no ability to fight or lead. A cripple."

"No!" Gunnar was swept off his feet as men grabbed his legs. His hands were unbound, though his right hand remained tied. One of the men yanked on the rope and wrestled Gunnar's forearm over the anvil. "That was done in battle. This is wrong. Stop!"

"Get a good look," Clovis said to his son. "I do this in your name, to take the revenge you will never take on your own."

Gunnar bucked against the crowd of men restraining him, but their weight held him down. His feet had no leverage being held off the floor, and his left arm was pinioned. He watched Clovis position the ax over his forearm, saw his lusty smile. His son watched dispassionately, cradling the stump of his arm against his body. The brand was lifted out of the brazier, glowing white with heat as smoke rolled off its tip.

"I will kill you," Gunnar stammered between clenched teeth. "I will dance in your guts."

No one acknowledged him. Clovis laid the cold edge of the ax across the middle of his forearm. The keen blade stung as it drew a line of blood. Gunnar held his breath. At any moment, his father would burst into the room and cut the heads off all his enemies in one swoop. The Franks would die, and Gunnar would join his father in safety. They would laugh together in the hall at sunset, joking of the frailty of their enemies.

The ax crashed down and clanged against the anvil. He lurched back, suddenly freed from his binding.

He saw the stump.

Just behind his wrist, a clean, slanted cut had severed his hand. Bone jutted from the flesh and blood pumped in bright scarlet jets. He felt nothing. It wasn't even his stump. The arm was someone else's. But how had he come free, and whose arm was it?

The confusion vanished when the searing iron brand rolled along the stump of his arm. One man used tongs to yank flaps of skin over the bone and another burned it shut. A lightning bolt of pain surged up his arm, overpowering him so that he screamed with all the might of his body. He thrashed and flexed in agony while the men worked on his stump.

"This is more aid than you deserve." Clovis had retrieved Gunnar's hand, and held it up to him. "I'll send this back to your mother. If I don't have my ransoms today, I'll send along Hakon's head as well."

The pain consumed him and though he heard the words, he did not understand. He comprehended only fire and fear, and smelled the sweet tang of his own burnt flesh. He coiled and twisted, but was immobilized as the men continued to bind his stump.

They doused him with water to keep him awake, but in the end he could withstand no more. The last thing he saw before succumbing to blessed darkness was the sorry eyes of Clovis's son studying him as he collapsed.

53

The wagon of silver rolled behind Ulfrik as he approached his camp. Draft horses plodded through the soft ground and the wagon's weight caused it to sink, necessitating frequent stops. It was one final aggravation amid many Ulfrik had endured all week. People had run to him, each one crowing different versions of the events during his absence. In one, the Franks had decided to shorten the time and killed all the hostages. In another, Toki, Gunnar, and Hakon were seen escaping from Clovis's fortress in the early dawn. He was inclined to believe it, as many repeated similar versions of three figures seen fleeing. Yet they had not arrived in camp, and no one had an explanation as to why. Soon, Ulfrik stopped listening and smiled blithely at the various tales.

Runa met him at the edge of the camp. Aren held her hand, clinging to her leg. In her other hand, she held a shield and had belted a sword to her waist. Her face wore no expression, though he could feel the pulse of her fury stretching across the grass to him. A dozen men crowded behind her and Snorri and Konal both leaned on spears and bowed their heads. A slight smile came to his lips, knowing how thoroughly defeated those men must feel when dealing with Runa's anger. Ulfrik searched for the other women, but found neither Halla nor Bera come to greet them. Likely Runa had frightened them off as well.

"He's going to kill Hakon first," Runa shouted to him as he closed the distance. Einar, who had led the wagon of silver packed in boxes and sacks, slowed the horses behind him. "Today. The ransom was due at dawn."

"Dawn tomorrow," Ulfrik corrected. He had counted the days carefully, had pleaded with Gunther One-Eye to hurry, and knew he had barely made time. He had been seven days in constant motion, bringing everything together while the sun shined so that his plans would succeed. He could not have been wrong about the day, but Runa stood shaking her head.

"He gave me a warning yesterday. If you hadn't sent a messenger, I'd have already been gone to fetch the ransom myself." Runa let go of Aren, who watched them thoughtfully as Runa met him. They did not embrace, but only offered a curt nod and smile to each other. "You are late, and I was ready to bargain for more time."

He pointed at the shield. "Planning on joining a battle?"

"Whatever must be done," she said. "I am getting older but I will still fight for my children."

"So what happened at dawn?" Ulfrik started past her, greeting Snorri and Konal then the other men. He squinted past the rows of tents to the black shape of Clovis's fortress hiding in the sunlight.

"Nothing, but a horn was sounded. Some of our scouts claim men escaped over the wall, though they did not dare to get closer with the sun rising. Maybe it was Toki and the boys." Runa's voice was disbelieving, and she glided past the idea without allowing more speculation. "Whatever happened, it has delayed Clovis and that frightens me. He was eager for you to break your word, and I expected him at dawn with Hakon's head."

The image was made more gruesome for the dispassionate delivery. He faced her, brow raised, but she merely frowned into the morning light like he had done. The anger was in her, as well as hate, fear, and hopelessness, but she buried it. Ulfrik had known his wife's tempers better than she did, and after so many years to see her acting out of stride with what he expected frightened him worse than any battle. With only this last piece of the plan to carry out, he hoped she would return to her old self when all was done.

"Staring at me won't get our sons out alive," she said. "Is it true that Gunther One-Eye has agreed to your plan?"

"It is, though it took longer to get him to act on it. There was trouble with an oath he had given to Hrolf." Ulfrik thought back to the tumultuous argument they had on the morning when Gunther refused his offer. After a night of feasting and toasting each other like best friends, the next morning he claimed his oath did not allow him to leave the land. They nearly drew swords on each other. Yet Ulfrik soon realized Gunther had not been enticed enough. A mercenary consideration, yet once understood, Gunther became more tractable. It was awful business, and a stain on their friendship, but the oath had been real enough as well as the danger. Had the situation been reversed, he might have done the same.

"But don't worry about Gunther. He's warm and fed in our hall, if not crowded." He smiled, thinking of all the work to smuggle men into Ravndal without Clovis's own spies catching them. "You should see it. There are swords and spears in every room of every building."

Runa's smile was faint. "A proud achievement worth nothing if our children are headless for it. You took your fucking leisure, didn't you?"

The flare of anger in her eyes riled him, but the sudden show of her old fury was welcomed. At least he understood this woman. "Leisure? Do you know what it's like to sneak an army overland and then station them in hiding? There's more than men, but supplies also. I had to dig up the silver, and keep that secret lest bandits try for it. Gods, woman, it's just me, Einar, and a few others doing all of this. We made the best time we could."

"Well, take the silver forward to Clovis. Let's see how well he keeps his word." The fire went out and Runa stepped back into her reserved stance.

Ulfrik arrayed his men and the cart of silver in the center of the field and flew his standard to alert Clovis. He gathered enough men

287

with him to discourage Frankish aggression. The remainder of his force shaped into fighting blocks in front of the camp. Runa accompanied him, and at last Halla dared to insert herself. Aren was left in Konal's care, for his wounds still prevented him from doing much more than holding a child's hand. Ulfrik sounded a horn and waited to the edge of his patience for a sign of activity. At last, a group of mounted men led a column of footmen out of the wooden gates.

"That took long enough," Einar muttered, standing beside Ulfrik beneath the banner.

"It's like they weren't expecting us," Ulfrik said. "Seems like they're taking every man out to visit us. I'm flattered."

He was nothing but impatient and irritated. As the column snaked across the fields of brown grass, disappearing into dips and rising again into sight, he strained to see if any of his own accompanied the Franks. He saw no familiar faces but for Clovis and his handless son. The sight of the boy sent a cold trickle down his back.

Clovis dismounted and swaggered forward, his eyes alighting on the wagon behind Ulfrik. Ten men accompanied him, and Ulfrik gathered ten of his own to meet them.

"You're late," Ulfrik said, folding his arms and squaring his shoulders. His eyes flicked over the Franks, and he noticed Theodoric was missing from their company. "I expected you at dawn."

"Dawn," Clovis repeated the word, sharing a glance with his son and a few others. "We were delayed."

"And I thought you were drooling for the ransom like the dog you are. What were you doing all morning? Fucking your horses?"

"More of that northern bravado." Ulfrik didn't understand the Frankish word, but took it for the intended insult. "Still you dragged your cart through the mud to deliver tribute."

"Ransom," Ulfrik corrected. "The silver is all there. Cost me dear. Now my sons had better be safe."

Clovis's smile brightened the morning shadows crowding his face. "Your sons are quite active. In fact, they were the cause of the delay. Your dear friend Throst Shield-Biter let them out of their cells and provided weapons."

"What? Throst is no friend to me or mine."

"In the end he hated me more than you. Your sons never had a chance, and your brother Toki is old and slow. Completely out of fighting condition. We herded them back into their cells, but they served Throst's purposes well enough."

"And they're unharmed?" Ulfrik squinted at Clovis, and his smile twisted into a sneer.

"Your eldest son enjoyed a bit of luck. He cut out Theodoric's bowels before we subdued him. Quite a mess of guts to clean up."

Pride and dread clashed within Ulfrik, and he dared not look away from Clovis. Killing the man who had captured him was justice, but he had still been overcome.

"With Theodoric dead, I am in command of all his forces." Clovis swept a hand across the men behind him. "At least until word from Paris arrives. Theodoric's brother may assume ultimate control, but I suppose you don't care about that."

"Make your point, or I'll rip out your tongue and spare the world you blather."

"I've claimed Theodoric's hostages as my own. There were a few disputes over their ownership, but I am persuasive. Your son has committed a crime, directly against our beloved King Odo."

"You dare not harm my son," Ulfrik growled.

"And by holy law, it is said that a man must be punished in accordance with his crime."

"I'll dance in your guts." Ulfrik's hand went to his sword, but scores of Franks reached for theirs and gave him pause.

"I've heard that threat quite recently. In fact, as I administered your son's punishment."

He raised his hand and one of his men produced a box. Ulfrik felt himself dizzy, already knowing its contents. He did not want to look as the dark wood cover was lifted back to reveal the gray and bloody mass inside.

"His sword hand, Ulfrik. Just like the one you took from my son. But unlike you, I did it right. I had the wound cauterized and a salve applied. The cut was clean, and he will survive. His crime has been punished. Some would say too lightly."

Ulfrik did not realize he had lunged forward until the arms restraining him yanked back. Men on both sides of the field reached for their weapons and prepared to fight. Einar was hissing in his ear. "Get a hold of yourself. We're not ready for battle. Don't set us on that path."

Clovis laughed, dumping the hand out of the box. It flopped onto the dead grass with a thump. No body part had ever looked so foreign, so cruelly disgusting as that hand. He wished it had been his own. He would have traded both of his hands and his feet to replace Gunnar's loss. Einar finally contained Ulfrik's struggles, and slowly released him. Another man wisely threw his cloak over the dismembered hand.

"Back away from the cart of silver," Clovis barked. "We will need a day to reconcile it, and then we will come for Ravndal. Until that time, your sons and the others remain my prisoners. Any violence from you, and they will all die. Would you rather that be your son's head beneath the cloak?"

"When this is over, I will come for you," Ulfrik said, stabbing his finger at him. "You will eat both of your hands before I cut out your black heart. I promise."

"Be ready to turn over Ravndal tomorrow," he said with no indication he had heard Ulfrik's threat. "I will release all the hostages once my men are inside and yours are marching away."

Ulfrik pointed at Clovis's son, a dark shadow behind his father. "And you, so sad you lost your cock-fondling hand. No one will find all the pieces when I'm done carving you up. You're a corpse I should've made last summer and I won't repeat that mistake."

Einar pulled Ulfrik away, and the Franks stood in confused silence, as if unsure they had won a victory or sealed their defeat.

54

The gates of Ravndal all stood open and every resident from hirdmen to craftsmen, women and children to the elderly, milled outside the walls. Carts lined up in a rough column, piled with a lifetime of valuables. Herds of livestock were prodded into groups, dogs barking at stray sheep. The afternoon sun floated between dark clouds that shrouded the scene in periodic darkness. Despite the massive gathering, they made little noise and only muted conversation. Pensive faces were not keen to meet another's gaze, and the ground received careful scrutiny from the folk of Ravndal.

Ulfrik spoke as little as necessary since his meeting with Clovis. Everyone understood their part; all were ready to spring a trap that would destroy their hated enemies. His words were best left in his head, for he only had loathing and anger to offer. He blamed himself for Gunnar's fate. He had placed him in harm's way, then failed to save him in time. The sight of that bloodless hand, frozen into a fist when it had been hacked from Gunnar's limb, was burnt into his memory. He would never forget, nor forgive himself.

Runa's reaction had been mute shock, but the tears followed in the deep night when she curled into herself while lying beside Ulfrik. She had recoiled from his touch as if he were an open flame. He could not fault her, and half expected her to demand a divorce once all was finished. Where he had excelled as a warrior, he failed as a husband and father. She had at least the clarity to burn Gunnar's hand, placing a gold coin into the palm before dropping it into the flame. Ulfrik did not understand the tradition, but it seemed the right thing to do, and Runa had offered no explanation. Like him, she said nothing beyond the barest need.

"Clovis is coming with all his men," Einar said as he approached Ulfrik. He and the hirdmen waited at the rear of the column, prepared to turn back into the fight when Gunther sprung his trap. "They should be coming into sight soon."

Nodding, he rubbed his face and turned toward the open gates. "Feels wrong to have them open while Clovis approaches, but it's what he expects. Is Gunther prepared?"

"Prepared and frothing mad. The close quarters have not agreed with our mighty guest." Einar smiled, but it faded when Ulfrik did not return it.

"Do you think I offered enough to the gods?" At dawn Ulfrik had killed and burned his best rams and threw a tenth of all his remaining wealth into a local lake as sacrifice for luck in the day's battle. "Will they hear me?"

"I'm taller than you, but not so tall that I can see into Asgard. How can I know what pleases the gods? But you've always said they favor a daring plan, and what could be more daring than this? It's clever work."

"Clever," Ulfrik repeated. Being clever had led him to this disaster. He should have ordered Throst's death and let Clovis suffer through the winter, and his sons would be free and Gunnar's hand still attached to his arm. Clever was no longer a compliment, but a curse.

"Lad, you can't show the men that face or your battle is over before it starts." Snorri hobbled up to him, dressed in mail and carrying a shield.

"You're not fighting today."

"I've obeyed you all my days, but not today. This is a fight for home and honor as well as glory." Snorri glared at Einar. "And I'm not letting my big-headed son steal all of that fun. Besides, I'm not planning to die in my bed."

"You're not fighting today," Ulfrik repeated, and pushed Snorri's shoulder. As expected, he stumbled back and nearly collapsed under his bad leg. "You'll die before you land a blow."

"You're welcome to stop me, but I expect you'll have your hands full when the fighting starts." Snorri regained himself, and attempted to stride away but only succeeded in something short of a drunken stagger. Ulfrik shook his head, knowing he could not deny his old friend a good death.

Einar stared after his father. "He fears the bed more than the blade these days."

"A great warrior should draw his last breath lying atop corpses in a battlefield, not beneath a bedsheet. I just need his guidance a little longer. My sons must still learn the old ways from him."

The mention of his sons drew both to silence, and soon the first appearance of Clovis's outriders captured everyone's attention. Ulfrik joined with Runa, the families of the captured men, and Halla with her children. They studied the approach with silent awe, most of the common people having never witnessed the splendor of a full Frankish army on the march. Ulfrik disdained their love of bright colors and shining mail. All battles ended in bloody mud, with both victor and vanquished leaving their dead for the ravens. The Franks dressed as if attending a festival. Yet their ordered ranks and brilliant colors drew whispered concerns from those who did not understand the vulnerability of the men beneath that armor.

At the side of the column rode Theodoric's cavalry beneath an unfamiliar banner of blue and white. Those were King Odo's colors, but a shape of some beast was outlined over it, too far still for Ulfrik to determine what is represented. No matter. He would see that banner soon enough lying in the dirt, trapped under a dead standard bearer. Not one of those splendid champions would survive the day.

"Clovis has bought us many to kill." Ulfrik spoke loud enough for those nearby to hear, but not so loud as to arouse the notice of the approaching enemy. "Remember the advantage we have at our backs."

A grumble of agreement circulated through the crowd, though mothers and worried fathers gathered their children to the carts as if the sight of the Franks alone was enough to endanger them.

At last, Clovis mounted the steep slopes to where Ulfrik waited. His men formed into tight blocks, and for an instant Ulfrik worried he might lead a charge. Even Runa, standing silently beside him, put her hand to her chest in fear. But the Franks remained steady and did not draw weapons. The horsemen did not dismount, but instead formed two groups on either flank of the main body. Clovis rode at the front, a lone figure on a horse that he doubtlessly acquired at Theodoric's death. He dismounted with careless ease, and gathered his bodyguard before making the final approach uphill.

"Let him come to us," Ulfrik said. Runa touched his shoulder and then pointed.

"There, Gunnar and Hakon."

They followed behind Clovis's guards, with a few spearmen to herd them along. The twelve men remaining from Toki's crew shambled in a ragged, dark clump. Before them, both Hakon and Toki walked hand in hand.

The sight of Gunnar stung. He slung his left arm around Toki's neck for support, and he clutched his butchered right arm into the shadow of his body. He looked just like Clovis's son, limp and defeated.

"I'm going to carve that bastard from crotch to crown," he said under his breath. Runa's hand on his shoulder tightened, the force of it penetrating the mail and leather armor he wore.

"I'll join you in that," she said. "But he is alive. They're both alive."

Clovis mounted the final distance to stand a spear's length from Ulfrik. He smiled like a child given the gift of a toy sword at a Yuletide feast. Barely acknowledging Ulfrik or his assembled men, he swept his eyes lustily across the black palisades of Ravndal and settled on the open gates.

"You weighed the silver and were satisfied?" Ulfrik asked.

"Two pounds short, but I will not argue. No two scales are ever the same. You've kept your word." Still absorbing the enormity of his achievement, Clovis never met Ulfrik's eye as he surveyed Ravndal. Though Gunther and his men were all concealed within, a niggling fear persisted that Clovis knew it was a trap. Yet his words were breathless and seemingly sincere. "I had expected a fight from you to the last. A bid to wrest your sons away and still keep your land."

"You've got spears at their backs. How stupid must I be to attempt something like that."

At last Clovis's eyes flickered to his. "You've never been smart, just lucky. Even that pig-witted Throst ran you in circles. Anyway, aren't you Northmen all eager to sell your lives for nothing more than a moment of glory? You disappoint me, Ulfrik."

"I did what you asked. If you'd like to be delighted, come closer and I'll ram my sword through your smirking face. I can relieve your disappointment."

"Always bold threats from you. Well, you are finished. I will keep my word. Your sons and your men are all accounted for. Once inside, I will send them out to you."

"You'll not get inside until you release them."

"And I'm certain you'll all stand down and let us pass once your hostages are safe. Do you think I am a fool?"

"I think you're about to be delighted. If you won't release my sons, then I'll have your spearmen filled with arrows and cut your fucking head off your shoulders."

"Your sons will die."

"Your men don't even know which end of the spear does the cutting. I'll take my chances."

"Silence!" Runa shouted, stepping between Ulfrik and Clovis. "We have agreed to surrender Ravndal in exchange for our sons and my brother. There is no Ravndal without their return, yet you will not trust the word of a man who has obeyed your every condition."

Clovis raised a brow at Runa, the intercession of a woman in man's world a foreign idea. Still, he inclined his head, taking a decidedly polite tone with Runa. "I would sooner trust a starving wolf to remain at bay after my campfire died than trust your husband to not turn on me once he had his way."

Runa glanced at Ulfrik, and her eyes were bright with ferocity. That brief look informed him she had decided upon something and would not be swayed, so he folded his arms and listened.

"It is true we could do as you fear," she continued. "More, we cannot convince you of our sincerity in the time we have today."

"A point I earnestly agree upon," Clovis said.

"Then here is my answer to your doubts. Release my sons and the others as agreed. We will turn over Ravndal to you. But as a measure of our good faith, you will take me as a hostage in their place. If my husband moves against you, then I'll offer you my throat without hesitation."

Ulfrik leapt to her side, grabbed her back by the shoulder. "Are you mad? He will keep you long after we are gone. You've nothing but his worthless promise to ensure you are released."

"That is an acceptable arrangement," Clovis said, addressing Runa now as if she owned the decision. "I give you my word, no woman would come to harm under my care. I am not a beast like your kind."

"My wife will not be your possession," Ulfrik shouted.

Runa took his hand into her own, pressed it to her lips, then guided it down to her side. She stepped in to whisper gently, "I am a woman, and pose no threat to him. Let him learn otherwise."

She pushed his hand against her skirt, pressing the back of it into the hard sheath of the long knife strapped to her leg. His eyes widened with realization, and she looked into them with solemn resolve. She planned to use Clovis's expectations against him. Women did not fight, did not hide weapons in their skirts, and could never best a man in arms. Yet she had not earned the title of the Bloody by weaving at her loom all day.

"This is a dangerous game, wife."

"No more than the games you have played. Besides, I've a thirst for this fool's blood."

Ulfrik fought back a smile, and frowned instead. He let Runa go as if abandoning her forever. "Only for my sons. Send them forward and you take my wife. Release her to me after my people are gone from your sight."

"A fair agreement," Clovis said, hands on his hips. He waved at his men and ordered the hostages freed. "Your wife will be under my personal protection. You have my word she will be at my side at all times."

Runa gave Ulfrik a knowing glance. He looked past her to Clovis. "Ensure that she is."

55

Runa had dwelt so long in a twilight of despair that she had numbed to the listlessness shrouding her. Now as Clovis gently guided her by the arm to his side, tender as a lover, her heart beat with purpose and drive. Death and vengeance rode on her shoulders, twin demons that lifted away her despair and filled her with strength. Her palm itched to grasp the long knife at her hip. Drawing it would bring release like nothing else.

Death to her enemies. Freedom for herself. Vengeance for Gunnar.

"A strange thing to be returning home while all your people leave," Clovis mused in his fractured Norse, scanning the slow column trundling downslope and around the wall. Runa watched as they departed, faces turning back hopefully to the walls. She feared their expectant looks would give away the ruse. Of course, what seemed plain to her did not raise any concern among the Franks. They had broken their formations, dismounted their horses, and clapped each other on their backs in congratulations. All appeared relieved to not have drawn their weapons.

Runa did not answer Clovis's inane observation. Up close he seemed far less grand than he had in her imagination. For all the fierce battles, the streams of dead and wounded made by his hand, he was not much to behold. He was soft, smelled foul, and smiled more than a leader should. Maybe he was proud of his victory, but to Runa's mind he acted a fool. How had such a man defied her husband for so long?

Her palm continued to itch. He would not defy her.

Two young men trotted up to Clovis, spoke in bubbling, scrambled Frankish she only half understood. Clovis nodded and dismissed them, both snatching a glance at Runa before skittering away. The whole army acted like boys, with their effusive laughter and silly fascination with her. Dozens had come to gawk at the prized wife of their enemy. She even caught Clovis stealing a peek at her, and had she not expected to kill him shortly she would have worried for his intentions.

"My men say Ravndal is truly empty." Clovis's eyebrow cocked as he spoke.

"You needed men to tell you that? The homeless departing before your eyes are not proof enough?"

His laugh was fake, the kind made to please a child who had spoken a simple riddle. "We are still at war, my lady. Better to be certain no surprises lay ahead."

Runa swallowed. By all the gods, how had the Franks failed to uncover Gunther's army? She searched for the two lads who had given him the report, found them leaning into a group of other young men. They were all laughter and boasts, standing tall among their peers while the others pandered to their vanity. None of them wore beards and their jawlines were soft. Her pulse settled, realizing Clovis had sent children to do men's work.

He plucked at her shoulder, indicating she should follow. The two guards assigned to her allowed her to pass before them, one hatchet-faced man stealing a lustful glance at her chest as she did. He crowded her, forcing Runa to keep pace with Clovis or otherwise bump into him. She would stick him right after dealing with Clovis.

Ravndal's gates hung open and groups of men flanked the doors to await Clovis's entrance. He joined with his son, placing his arm around him as the two walked to the gates. He blathered in Frankish, but Runa guessed from the sweeping gestures he was promising Ravndal to his boy. That soggy, defeated child would never make a leader even with both hands.

Glancing a final time at her back, she saw Ulfrik and her sons watching from a distance. She had been allowed no time to greet her children. While her heart broke at the sight of Gunnar, he at least seemed only partly aware of the world around him. Hakon had hurt more, being led off before he could reach her. She had heard him wailing when the guards took her, and she could not bear to look back. She consoled herself knowing soon they would be rejoined.

"Do the honor of escorting me into Ravndal," Clovis said, stepping forward with arm held out.

She stared at it, thought of slicing his arm into a match for his son's, but chose to have a grip on his sword arm once the trap was sprung. She inclined her head, and laced her arm into his.

Her mouth became tacky and her neck pulsed. They passed beneath the gate, and she scanned the black boards of the tracks leading into the town. No one leaned on fences, no chickens wandered in the roads, no hearth smoke curled above thatched roofs. The silence was perfect, yet an army was packed into the buildings. Ulfrik had warned her they were along the walls and in the main hall. They would recapture the gates and split the Franks for an easy fight. "Get away and hide," Ulfrik had warned her. "Don't try to carry the battle. And leave a piece of Clovis for me."

The Franks were strolling inside, and Runa wondered how much longer before Gunther emerged. Clovis prattled in his hideous language, laughing and pointing as if weather-worn buildings in need of new thatch were a vision rarely beheld. She rested her right hand across her lap, slipping into the folds of her skirt. Grasping the long knife would be awkward, but she was poised for a lightning draw.

"Take me to the hall," Clovis said. "Your people make such a fuss of them, and I've never been inside one before."

Runa smiled. "You can see it from here."

"Not quite as big as I expected."

Horns blared and mad howls burst from all around. The Franks halted like frightened cats, backs arched and eyes wide. Northmen appeared from the periphery, spilling out of buildings, crashing through fences, and busting open gates. Men tumbled out of hay stacks piled on abandoned carts, no doubt left behind for this purpose. She even spotted a short man fumbling out of a barrel. Everywhere a roar went up, and the Franks were leaden in shock.

Men gained the palisades and arrows began to stream down. Screams followed and it galvanized the Franks.

Clovis was as shocked as any, maybe worse. He clutched her arm as his head cocked sided-to-side like a chicken searching for a fox, only there were hundreds of foxes and his beady eyes couldn't fix on any one.

Her blade was in hand, drawn with the precision imbued of daily practice. The bright iron flashed, as long as a man's forearm, and its point quivered with the desire for flesh.

Runa twisted Clovis's arm forward, jerking him toward her blade with a grunt.

"Die, you pig," she hissed into his ear as she thrust the blade up at the soft flesh of his armpit.

Only she did not connect.

She slammed to the hard wood boards of the path. Her teeth clamped on her tongue and coppery blood squirted in her mouth. Clovis's son loomed over her, his stump arm flailing uselessly, but his left arm cocked back with a sword flashing in the sun. He was blathering in Frankish and he glanced back at his father for a moment.

Her long knife shot up, driving under the links of mail into the base of his belly. A pink loop of entrails slid out with a cascade of blood, but he slashed down nonetheless. Had she not shifted to strike, the sword would have cleaved her head. Instead the blade shaved away a lock of her hair. He collapsed atop her with a gurgling hiss, his stump arm batting at her has he died. She was pinned beneath him, hot lifeblood washing over her legs.

Struggling to free herself, suddenly the body lifted aside. Clovis had flipped his son over, his face chalky and taut with shock. He screamed as his son's corpse flopped to the side like a gutted fish.

Runa flipped away. Many years had passed since she had last fought in a battle, and she had forgotten the hellish roar of it. All around blades and shields clanged together and screams and curses traded between combatants. In his eagerness to claim Ravndal, Clovis had outpaced the range of his men to aid him. The two guards watching her were now entangled with a pair of yellow-haired men in black furs who were chopping at them like trying to fell a tree. Only his son had been close enough, and had traded his life for his father's. Runa now had to escape while Clovis was numb.

She got to her feet, staggered a few steps, then something heavy collided with her head. She sprawled forward, her knife falling away as she plowed into the ground.

Warm, rough hands grabbed her shoulders and flipped her over. She looked up into Clovis's red, hate-filled face framed against the blue of the sky.

"You killed my son, you fucking bitch!"

He picked up his helmet, which Runa realized he had thrown to knock her down. He slammed it across her face and she felt a bone in her cheek crumple. Her vision turned white. When it returned, he had his sword drawn.

"I'll feed your heart to the dogs, you whore!"

The point of his blade rested on her chest and Clovis's frown deepened.

She closed her eyes and braced for death.

56

Ulfrik yanked his sword from the belly of a Frank, blood slushing out of the cut as the man crumbled, and he raised his shield to deflect a spear thrust. All around him men writhed in grass that had been churned to bloody mud in the space of moments. He glided under the spear thrust, a foolish strike that left the attacker exposed, and stabbed into the Frank's leg. He staggered and Ulfrik shoved him over with his shield, sprawling him into the twirling chaos of combat. He flopped down, and Ulfrik paid him no further mind. A man on the ground was as good as dead.

Horses screamed and reared, catching Ulfrik's attention. Over the jostling heads of the combatants he saw the Frankish horses shot by his archers. The death of such useful animals was a great loss, but he did not want the Franks to remount and turn the battle, which had strongly favored Ulfrik from the opening blows. His instructions had been clear: kill the riders first and their horses second. The dying horses indicated the dismounted cavalry had already been destroyed.

"A fine day for killing," Einar shouted at him across the din. The giant man had gore up to his elbows and his hands firmly wrapped on the haft of his war ax. His smile shined out from a blood-smeared face.

"Finest day in years," Ulfrik said. The two stood inside a pocket of calm. Men struggled in pairs and groups, tight as lovers in a dance. A tidemark of corpses, all in bright Frankish colors, walled them off from the melee.

"Gunther One-Eye's men closed the gates." Einar pointed with his ax, a string of blood hanging from its head.

"I need to find Runa, and I don't trust Gunther's men to know who she is."

"Should be the only woman inside." Einar stared at Ulfrik, and his face softened after a moment. "But I guess that might be a problem, too."

Grunting, Ulfrik searched for a path through the fight. "We've won the battle out here. Inside is where we finish it. Lend me your ax."

Einar handed it over, the wood handle slick with blood.

"Fall back to Toki and my sons. They are out of harm's way, but trouble still might've found them. Watch for your family, too, especially Snorri. Now go while I reopen the gates."

He dashed through the combat, shield out and Einar's ax in hand. Where enemies tangled with him, he bashed them aside with the shield or clumsily struck with the ax. The chaos of battle swallowed them as he pushed forward to his own palisades. The dark walls seemed higher from this side of the embankments, but he had overseen their construction himself. They were higher than a man, but undefended they could be scaled. Flipping his shield to his back, he took a running leap with ax held overhead.

Launching up the wall, he slammed the long-hafted ax over the top of the palisade. His feet caught the rough wood and he pulled himself up the length of the haft until he reached the top. With a shout of success, he flipped over the wall and dangled on the opposite side. He dropped down into the shadows, pulling over his shield and unsheathing his sword.

People ran between buildings, shouting echoed down the alleys, and the clamor of battle filled the streets. He could not decide who was winning this fight, but he rushed along the edges of the wall toward the gates. As he progressed, he gathered two other of Gunther's men. "Are we winning?" he asked over the roar of battle.

"Can't tell. The Franks scattered all over. Count the bodies for yourself." The man who replied had a gash on his brow that bled like a high mountain stream, turning half his face red. His companion was far better; the blood on his face was another's.

The three arrived at the gates, a pleasing heap of Frankish corpses laced with arrows piled before it. "Open these gates," Ulfrik ordered. "The battle outside is done, so let my men in to finish here."

"Right you are," said the bleeding man, his eye blinking in the stream of blood.

Satisfied the gates would be opened, he turned toward the main street. The boards were littered with corpses, broken weapons, and arrow shafts. The battle had moved into the side lanes and alleys, the buildings and halls of Ravndal. Shrieks and dying curses were amplified inside the buildings, but for a scattered few men, the main road seemed abandoned. He could not decide where Runa would have gone in the confusion, but it would have to be with Clovis. He considered his hall, but doubted they made it before Gunther sprang his trap.

He had lost too much already and his family had paid a heavy toll. He would not allow them to suffer another moment. Runa could hold her own, up to a point, and then she would be at the mercy of whoever found her. He had to be the first one to her. Not the enemy.

57

R una squealed when instead of the expected sword thrust into her heart, an iron-gripped hand hauled her off the ground. She opened her eye, her left one watery and fuzzy from where Clovis had struck her. She still felt the sword jabbing at her kidney as Clovis guided her before him.

"You are more useful alive for now. This battle is lost and I need a hostage," he said. "But I swear before God that my hounds will eat your heart one day."

He shoved her toward the hall. All around lay the detritus of a sharp and awful battle: broken swords and spent arrows, puddles of blood covered with shattered shields. Bodies both Norse and Frankish sprawled in the shadows and corners where desperate combats had been waged and lost. Weapons still clanged in the distance, but the fight seemed to have burnt out like a flash fire. Through her gauzy vision, she saw a giant man hulking at the entrance to the hall. A wolfskin flowed over his shoulders, bulking him out like a monster and making the thick sword in his hand seem no more than a splinter. It was Gunther One-Eye.

"Do you know who this is?" Clovis demanded of Gunther, jabbing her with his sword for emphasis. Runa jerked to the side with a yelp, but he reined her in.

"Runa the Bloody," Gunther answered, his voice low and careful. He raised his sword at Clovis. "And you best let her go if you expect any mercy."

"Mercy! From you lying scum? My trust died today with all my good men. I pray God has seen fit to grant me better luck outside of these walls."

Gunther shrugged and lowered his sword. "Your God does not see you today. Too many clouds in the sky."

Runa heard rough voices laughing to the sides and behind. Her face throbbed and her vision had narrowed from the swelling on her left cheek. Gunther looked past her and smiled.

"Clovis! Let go of my wife."

She nearly collapsed at the sound of Ulfrik's voice. She wanted to cry, scream, or jump. Instead, the sword at her side dug deeper as Clovis whirled around with her shielding him.

Ulfrik stood carrying a blood-smeared shield and glittering sword in hand. The faceguard of his helmet concealed his eyes, but the shock in his expression was plain. She wondered how bad the injury to her face had been. Would she be disfigured like Konal? The odd thought made her cringe with shame, but it had come unbidden to her mind. All that mattered was the safety of her children, and no price was too heavy for it.

"What have you done to her?"

"Less than what she deserved. She killed my son."

"That was a favor, and you know it."

Clovis did not answer, but she felt his hand tighten on her arm. He twisted the point of his sword over her kidney but she resolved to give no sign of pain.

"So you have defeated me today," Clovis said, his voice affecting a jaunty tone as if shattering his army had been no more a setback than losing a favorite pair of boots. "Bravo to you, Ulfrik. You baited your trap well, but left me a way out with your beautiful wife. You can have her back once I am safely away."

307

"No more hostages. I tire of this game. Release my wife. You and I will fight and settle like men."

Clovis laughed loud in Runa's ear, though she felt the tremble in his grip. She began to plot escape, realizing Ulfrik must be waiting for her to give him an opening. The sword at her side dug deeper and Clovis pulled her closer, but it was an awkward position and the length of the blade could be used against him. She only had to deflect it and stay close to him where he could not use a sword. The others would overpower him.

"Fight you? We have fought enough, and while I hold your wife, there is no need for it."

"This is my last offer. A fair fight to the death. I'll get you a shield."

"Piss on your shield! I've seen all your tricks and I'm through with them. Let me go then I'll set your wife free. "

Ulfrik frowned, then carefully placed his sword and shield next to his feet. He unhooked a throwing ax at his hip. "You've not seen this trick."

The plan flashed through Runa's mind. She yanked violently back and to the side. The blade point dragged across her flesh like a hot brand.

Ulfrik lined up his throw as if he had all day to make it. She closed her eyes but heard Clovis's intake of breath, then felt him jerk her back toward his sword.

She opened her eyes.

The ax flew.

A swoosh of air passed her head and a wet crack followed. Hot blood splattered the side of her face, and Clovis stumbled back. She did not turn around, but pushed forward from his dead grasp, content to hear him thud to the dirt. She rushed into Ulfrik's arms.

"No more hostages," he said as he pulled her close. "And no more tricks. The Franks are defeated. Our family will be together again, here in our home."

A wry comment formed then died in her throat. Was the madness finally over? No more fear and worry, no more dreams of dead children. She wanted to laugh but instead buried her face in his shoulder and sobbed.

58

---

hrost turned Astra's comb over in his hand. The day was late,
the wind cold, and the lone oak tree on the hill had shed its last
leaf. It was the dawn of winter and he had to secure a haven
now that Ulfrik had defeated the Franks. *What a lucky bastard*, he thought
and shoved the comb back into his pack. From the top of this hill he could
see Ravndal's smudgy outline. He had been staring at it for days, telling
Olaf and Dan that he was hunting without much luck. Only his mother
knew the lie, and she had enough sense not to try him. His reasons for
staring at Ravndal were unclear even to himself. It squatted atop its
perch, hearths chugging smoke into the sky, its black walls defying all
enemies. He imagined it collapsing into fire, but it never did. It endured.

The comb had been a promise of a meeting. Someone had left it
after he had gone the prior day, carefully laid out on a rock. To
deepen his interest, a small wedge of silver rested atop it. Another
promise. Whereas Olaf would sensibly tell him silver can't fill a belly,
wealth of any sort would see him a long way toward finding passage
to safety away from here. So he waited all afternoon, circling the area
and biding his time until boredom threatened to overwhelm him.

Then he spotted the figure in the distance. A woman shrouded in a heavy green cloak. She picked her way carefully, but with an artlessness that made Throst wonder how she navigated the unfamiliar paths. He thought of going downhill to spare the woman, but reconsidered. He did not know her or her purpose, and maybe this was all part of Ulfrik's final trick. So he watched the woman stumble up the hill.

He leaned against the tree, feigning nonchalance but keeping a hand on the hilt of his sword. He had filched it from the battlefield outside Ravndal, along with mail coats, helmets, bows, and Frankish surcoats. Those would be handy for crossing Frankish territory. They had even found a horse that had escaped the battle.

"Throst," she said, panting from her effort. "You found the comb, I see. It has been no easy thing to meet you here, but I am glad Fate has put us together at last."

"What's your game, woman? You're too old to warm my bed, if you came all this way for it."

The woman's expression was lost in the shadow of the cowl, but she drew up straighter, a pale white hand touching her chest. He noted the clean nails, fine-boned fingers, and smooth skin. Blue veins stood out, but otherwise these were the hands of a woman who made others work for her. A wooden cross of the Christians hung from a plain cord around her neck.

"I hope I haven't risked so much for a fool. Astra had nothing but praise for you."

"For all a dead girl's praise means to me. Thanks for her comb and the bit of silver, got me interested in meeting you. Want to tell me who you are?"

The pale hand slid up to the edge of her cowl and she pulled it back. "We have never met directly, though your lover may have spoken of me."

She revealed a pretty face marred only by a snub nose. Her hair was nearly white, and might have been beautiful in her youth though now its luster had exhausted.

"My name is Halla Hardasdottir."

He shrugged. "She did not speak much of you. Other things were more important. We had work to do and little time for it."

"Of course. I have had much work myself."

"Hard to believe, with those precious hands of yours."

Halla's eyes flashed, and it was as if she saw right through his bluster to the heart of his failure. "Hands are all anyone talks about these days. Did you know Ulfrik's son lost his hand before he was ransomed?"

"I'd heard something like that."

"Did you? You hear what goes on inside Ravndal since Astra died?"

He stiffened at the confirmation of her death. He had sent her on a suicidal task, but hardly expected her to die in the attempt. The thrill of a woman sacrificing her life for his whim was only a fleeting spark that failed to ignite anything better in him. Considering how everything had turned out, he regretted the decision. Such blind loyalty was irreplaceable, and he sorely needed followers now.

"Time is short," she said. "I assume you found the comb and the silver bit I had delivered to your meeting place?"

"I did, and guessed Astra's informer wanted to meet. I was curious how you were going to get here without being caught. Astra had a talent for it, but you plainly don't."

"The chaos of these last few days has allowed me to move at will, but that will soon end. My husband is still recovering from his captivity. I understand you set him free. That's what cost Gunnar his hand, and nearly cost my husband his life."

"So that's who you are? No wonder Astra knew so much. You're the wife of Ulfrik's brother." He put a hand on his head and laughed. "No wonder she wouldn't tell me where she got her news. I'd have come up with something better than snatching children if I thought I could get at Ulfrik's brother."

"He's Runa's brother," she said, eyes drawing to slits. "Now listen to me, Throst Shield-Biter." She twisted his name as if it were a joke, another mark against her. "I've come with an offer that you would do well to accept."

"Unless you're offering a ship across the sea, I'm not interested."

"Do you know how Astra died?"

"Bleeding."

"Yes, but by Runa's hand. Astra tried to kill her son, no doubt on your foolish orders. Well, they don't call her Runa the Bloody for no reason. She chopped her head off right in the hall, hacked her body till it was mince. I saw it myself, and I'll never forget it." Halla covered her face as if witnessing the horrible scene again. "It was a horrifying death."

"Death by the sword is hardly anything else."

"Don't you want revenge on the woman who did this to your lover?"

"I want revenge on all of the people shitting in that den of bastard dog-fuckers. Ulfrik killed my father, threw me out, humiliated me. Ruined my life."

"Yes," Halla's sympathetic urgency even frightened Throst. He recoiled from her as she leaned closer. "And his wife did the same to me. Now I've got to live out my days under her heel. Imagine all you've endured until now only for the span of years. All the while you've got to bow and scrape before Ulfrik. You've got to care for his children and smile in his presence, listen to his bragging and watch him revel in what he stole from your family. Everyone around you speaks of him as if he were a god. Oh, and he'll remind you every day that your father and mother were his enemies and their deaths were just. That's my life, Throst Shield-Biter, and I want to change it."

"Best of luck with that, then. I'm none too interested in your problems."

"We have a common interest." She stepped back, cooed the words as if to seduce him though all Throst felt was revulsion. "I want Runa dead and you want to hurt Ulfrik."

"I have hurt him. Now I just want to be away."

"Did you?" She cocked her head, one eye wider than the other. "Your name is already forgotten. Hakon is safe and doing well. All anyone worries about is Gunnar, and who dealt him that blow? It was not Throst Shield-Biter." Again she mocked the name. "You're just a bit of unfinished business, a rodent to stamp out once the bigger things are in order. Before the winter is done, all of your schemes would have left no mark on Ulfrik. You'll be forgotten, and as well you should. At best you were a nuisance. Was that your grand revenge? To annoy Ulfrik? Astra threw her life away just to spoil his wife's evening meal?"

"Your words are a bit sharp." Throst laughed off the shame, but every word was a hot brand on his soul. What in the name of all the gods had he achieved? What lesson had he taught Ulfrik? The white-haired bitch was right, and he hated her for it.

"Your plans held promise, but Fate was unkind to you." She placed a light hand on his shoulder, and feigned sympathy that could not fool a child. "Now is the time to leave a mark that will last forever. Take from him something that can never be replaced. Strike down his wife, that whoring, murderous bitch. Claim the true revenge that has eluded you. Make him grind his teeth at the thought of your name."

Throst swallowed. "An attractive idea, but I prefer a simpler target to his wife. That's why I went after the children in the first place."

"I'll make it easy for you, and offer payment. You can't be too rich, or a silver bit wouldn't have kept you waiting for me today."

He nodded. "True."

"Kill Runa. The time and the place are prepared. I'll get you access inside the walls."

"You're a powerful woman to arrange all that." Throst folded his arms and glanced past her toward Ravndal. "You're going to do this under their noses?"

"No one pays me any mind, but for Runa who has falsely blamed me for so many things that no one listens to her. My husband is like a brother to Ulfrik, and my husband tells me everything I want to know."

"Why not just piss off from this place if you've got gold to spend? Seems a fair bit easier than treachery."

Her head lowered and the crazed response Throst had expected emerged only as a thoughtful pause. She rubbed her face before answering. "She killed my mother, cut out her tongue. Took her a year to die from the wound, and all that time Runa whored around with Konal and scorned me. Wouldn't attend my mother's funeral, or even recognize her death. The day she left for Frankia was the greatest day of my life. But now Toki has vowed to serve Ulfrik again. He sees glory and riches here. I can't deny him, nor convince him to leave. But that doesn't mean I intend to live with that witch. The only good for coming south is the chance to avenge my parents, my mother in particular."

The wind filled the silence between them. Throst considered her reasons understandable if not practical. He wouldn't dissuade her, especially if she planned to bring chaos to Ulfrik's home. Besides, it wasn't his concern.

"What's the payment for taking your revenge?"

"So you'll do it?"

"Payment, enough for me and for my men. They'll have to help."

Halla's smile widened like a child discovering all the toys in the hall were hers. "Good gold for all of you. Rings and chains, a golden cross carried from the north. It will be enough for you all to barter a safe passage to anywhere you desire."

"Sounds like a pittance." It sounded like a hundred times more than he possessed, but he looked again at Halla's clean fingers and guessed more was available.

"This is your revenge, too. How much should I pay for something you'd do anyway?" She glared at him, but he did not flinch. She shook her head. "I've got three pounds of my own gold. Any more and I'd be stealing from my husband, which I can't do. Take that offer or not."

"I've a mind to take you and get a bigger reward for exposing your plot."

Her face paled and hand touched her neck, then just as fast she recovered. "And who'd believe you? Only Runa and that's not saying much. Besides, haven't we been partners all along? Astra was just our go-between."

Throst shrugged and laughed. "I wasn't serious about that. The price is fair. Tell me how to put Runa in the ground, and how you'll

315

pay me, then you better get gone before twilight. Don't want your treachery discovered before all the fun starts."

Halla giggled, the disconcerting titter of a person touched with madness. She stepped closer, as if her plan might be overheard. "Killing her will never be easier."

59

Ulfrik sat beside Gunnar's bed, hand resting on his son's leg. He realized Gunnar was awake from his shifting beneath the covers, but did not disturb him with words. He just waited for Gunnar to decide if he wanted to talk. He had not parted with many words since returning home. Looking at the arm hooked over the blankets and furs and lying across his chest, Ulfrik understood his reticence. He could not help imagining if they ignored the wound, then his hand would grow back. Yet the clean bandages changed during the morning were already spotted brown at the stump. No magic would restore him. No hero, however beloved of the gods, regrew a lost limb. It was one boon the gods never chose to grant a man.

Outside the low murmur of voices vibrated through the walls into the dark. Only a candle offered fitful light, glistening in the sweat on Gunnar's forehead. Noticing this, Ulfrik dipped a cloth into a bowl of water, wrung it out and dabbed Gunnar's head. He turned to the side in protest.

"If you are hot, remove these skins." Ulfrik began to pull back one and Gunnar clamped it down with his stump. "All right, then. How is the pain? Do you want more ale?"

He shook his head, the rustling of his pillow the only sound.

Victory lacked the sweetness Ulfrik had anticipated. His son lay crippled in his bed, sullen and unspeaking. He had lost more men than he had hoped, and Ravndal had taken more damage than expected. All cost him a good share of gold to make right. Gunther One-Eye had claimed Clovis's land as price for his aid, and was now out raiding the countryside for whatever he could carry away. But worse than any of these losses was the silence of his son.

The door creaked open. The light and sound it allowed into the room drew Ulfrik from his dark thoughts. Hakon's shape hovered in the door, and Aren was behind him. A yellow block of light framed them hesitating, but Ulfrik waved them closer.

"Your brother is awake. See if you can cheer him better than me."

Hakon stepped into the candlelight, coming to Ulfrik's side. He smiled and patted Hakon's shoulder. Though he had grown thin in captivity, the ordeal seemed to have left no other mark upon him. Perhaps it was his youth that gave him resilience, or the damage was not yet made visible. Ulfrik was grateful for Hakon simply returning to his old life as if he had only been gone with friends.

"How is your hand?" he asked Gunnar. When he did not answer, he pushed on him as if to awaken him. "Uncle Toki says you will learn to fight with your left hand. He says it can be an advantage."

The silence stretched uncomfortably, and Gunnar faced the opposite wall. Hakon's big eyes fixed on Ulfrik's and he shrugged. Hakon lowered his head and stepped back from the bed. Aren waddled up to the edge, gripping something in his small hand. He stretched on his tiptoes to place a flat rock next to Gunnar's side. "For you," he said. "Found it at the creek."

Aren stepped down, not waiting to see if Gunnar recognized the gift, which he did not. Ulfrik, however, thought it curious and picked up the rock. It was flat and smooth from being in the water. It was a blue-gray rock with a vein of white through its heart. He smiled and placed it back where Aren had left it.

"Why this rock for Gunnar?"

"Because it is special and hard, like Gunnar."

The reason struck Ulfrik as too profound to be from a child, but Aren was unlike any child of his own age. Even Gunnar turned to glance at the rock, but then flipped back over. Neither Hakon nor Aren seemed to know what to do next, so Ulfrik gestured for them to leave. "Your brother is tired now. Go tell your mother I will join her in a moment."

The door shut behind them, the yellow light and clear sound shut out from Gunnar's world of silence. Ulfrik sighed and waited, but Gunnar did not move.

"Fate has woven a black thread into your life," Ulfrik said, folding his hands around his knee and staring into the darkness. "But it does not mean the whole cloth will be black. You are a man now, son, and my pride for you is fierce. Toki told me you insisted on rescuing the others. He also told me that he was a coward, and your bravery shamed him. I am no judge of what was the right choice at that moment, but to stand with your crew and hold their lives as valuable as your own will never be wrong. You are a leader, not because you are my son, but because you are in your heart."

Gunnar remained facing the opposite wall in silence. Ulfrik watched the shadows from the candle dance across the lump of his body, then continued.

"I had tried to protect you from the ugliness of the world. Such is my arrogance that I believed Fate would not touch you' on my command. For that I made you suffer, and I am sorry. And my scheming from glory led you to this black thread. Had I chosen to be more practical and less bold, perhaps you would not have lost your hand."

"It's not your fault." Gunnar's voice was weak and quiet. He still remained facing away. "The Franks surprised us all."

Ulfrik nodded. "I can't help but feel responsibility. If I had only returned from Gunther faster ..."

"It's not your fault. Don't say it anymore."

Glad to have his son speaking again but loath to sour his mood with the topic, he sat in chastened silence. Soon Gunnar flipped to his back, and the streaks of tears on his cheeks glittered in the candle-light. He stared up for a long moment before speaking.

"I will never stand in a shieldwall, never gather any glory to my name."

"You will stand in front of the shieldwall. You will point your sword at foemen and they will quail before you. None would even dare charge."

Gunnar snorted. "Don't joke with me, Father."

"I have seen it done, and I don't joke. A shield will be lashed to your right arm, and your left arm will become stronger than before. You have the heart of a bear and the fangs of a wolf. You will learn to lead and fight and make widows by the score. You will not falter and die like Clovis's son. Men will swear their oaths to you because you will bring them glory."

Closing his eyes, Gunnar turned his head aside. Ulfrik swallowed, fearing his own voice might crack, but he believed all he had said. Though the figure in the bed was of a man, he was still Ulfrik's little boy and he would never abandon him to failure.

"When this wound is healed you will believe all I've said. You will taste success and desire more."

"What if I fail? If I can't learn to fight with my left hand?"

"You can learn, and you will succeed. I will not let you fail. I will hold you up until you can stand again, and when that day comes I will be behind you as proud as any man can be. You must believe me."

Gunnar met his eyes through the gloom, and Ulfrik read all the conflicting fear, hope, despair, and desire shimmering in them. He knew Gunnar's path would be hard and fraught with dozens of holes to trip him on the way. He did not need to show Gunnar that now, only just set his foot on the path.

"I want to believe."

"Then do. In the end you must believe something, and why not believe in success?"

Gunnar smiled and Ulfrik patted his shoulder. They sat in a more pleasant silence, and soon Ulfrik decided he had accomplished all he had set out to do for Gunnar today. He stood and stretched, then paused at the door before leaving.

"Everyone needs to have their spirits raised, so I've announced a feast with games and plenty of drink to be held within two days. We must celebrate the destruction of Clovis and the Franks, before King Odo sends more to harass us. Rest up so you may join us. It will do everyone good to see you out of bed, particularly your mother. At least consider it for her."

Gunnar nodded, and Ulfrik closed the door behind him. He worried a feast and games would stretch their stores for winter, but something had to be done to make victory feel less like defeat.

60

Throst had found the north gate of Ravndal unbarred, just as Halla had promised. He gently widened it only enough to slide his body through the crack. He had to hold his bow in one hand and quiver in the other to pass. Sounds of celebration carried high over the black walls, so far that even Dan and Olaf had commented on it when they left him at the edge of the woods. "Don't stay for a drink," Olaf had quipped. "We're going to have to run faster than last time."

Only now Throst had a horse. The Franks raised obedient beasts that could fly like ravens over the ground even under his unskilled direction. He left the piebald tethered to a rock within sprinting distance of the walls. The celebration consumed the attention of every person in Ravndal. After all, there were no enemies remaining in the land worth watching. He had ridden to the walls without a care, passing the wreckage of battle and stopping to examine overlooked bits of potential value. Nothing of worth turned up, but then he had already picked the best days ago.

Inside he clung to the walls. The scent of roasting meat filled the air, where only days ago it had been the scent of the burned dead. Ravndal bore the scars of its recent battle. Fences were destroyed, barrels shattered, and walls breached. Animal pens were mended but doors still sat crooked in their frames, having been battered down and not properly rehung. Rust stains dappled the wall of a home as Throst sneaked past it. He noted a bloody handprint that had slid down to the dirt. The cheering and laughing celebration in the distance was a stark contrast to the vestiges of death.

A ladder hung against the wall, right where Halla had said she would have it placed. While other ladders could get him onto the parapets, this one was obscured from view in the central square where the contests were taking place, and where Runa and all Throst's other targets would be gathered. Checking for people and finding none, he swept up the ladder with bow and quiver slung across his back.

He crouched on the parapet, a slim board barely suitable for standing and never for fighting. Guards could observe the surrounding fields and fire bows, but would never have the footing to do battle. He crawled slowly on hands and feet, both for stability and concealment. His heart beat heavily and he dared not to look down at the celebration for fear of being caught. The thought was stupid, he knew, but yet he believed a look was equal to a shout.

Progress went slowly, until he found a vantage point revealing most of the square. Every motion had to be swift and faultless from this point. He placed his bow and quiver carefully aside, took a rope he had lengthened with sheets tied to the end, and fished it over the side of the wall before securing it. He dug out the bowstring from his pouch, first finding the gold chain Halla had offered as a good faith payment. Once he had strung the bow, working with quiet intensity as the milky light of day lit him for the world to see, he drew an arrow from the quiver. Each arrowhead had been blackened in fire and rubbed with soot for good measure. A stray glint of light would make him a target for every bow in Ravndal.

Laying the arrow across the staff, touching it to the string, he scanned the square. People milled in throngs: men and women, children and the old, dogs and chickens, all pilled together in a press of overzealous celebration. The greatest concentration of people were at the rows of wooden kegs where women kept ale flowing for anyone who had an empty mug. No one he sought would be there, and so he ranged wider. He caught a man and woman humping behind a pig pen, snorted at the sight, and eventually settled on the ax throwing competition.

Ulfrik and all of his kin were clustered at the sideline as a fat man in a scraggly wolf pelt lined up his two-handed ax on the target. He let it fly and it spun with tremendous force but poor accuracy to chop into the target painted on a thick section of tree. He held out both hands as if he did not own them and the crowd laughed or cheered at his good humor. Runa and Ulfrik both stood clearly before anyone else, their children gathered close. He paused at the horrid bruise and swelling on the left side of Runa's face. He smiled and continued to scan. Hakon looked especially hale since Throst had seen him last. Gunnar, however, seemed barely aware of the celebration. Runa stood with his arm entwined in hers, never a more motherly scene had Throst ever witnessed.

Had he taken enough arrows, he could kill all of Ulfrik's family and a fair number of his friends, so tight was the clutch of targets. He raised the bow and leveled it.

Runa's swollen face hung on the end of the arrowhead. He swiveled farther left, past Gunnar, Hakon, and Aren, over Einar and his family, past the scar-faced Konal—who surprised him for being alive—and settled on Halla.

She stood stiff, hands clutched to her chest, and recoiled at every jostle as if a pile of crockery had crashed unexpectedly behind her. Her two children clung to her skirts and Toki shouted with the crowd while spilling ale from his drinking horn, all seemingly oblivious to Halla's distress.

He waited as Toki and Ulfrik began to shout to each other. Soon the crowd was encouraging Toki and he came forward to pick up an ax to the applause of the crowd. Ulfrik came forward, held up Toki's arm and proclaimed something to the crowd.

Throst lined up his shot.

Halla had used him. She had played his weaknesses with skill, manipulating him into feeling small and stupid. Once she had left, he realized how easily he had been played. But she had done something far worse. She had lied about Astra.

Throst had seen Astra's corpse hung from the walls of Ravndal, apparently to send a warning message. The body had not been hacked to bits, nor had she been beheaded. From the distance he had viewed the body, the black blood stains on her dress made it seem she had been stabbed or had her neck slashed. If Halla had witnessed all she claimed, there could be nothing to hang from the walls, and if she had lied it could only be an attempted diversion from her guilt. Who else had a reason to stifle Astra? Runa would have wanted to question rather than kill her, and thereby uncover Halla's treachery.

He flicked his eyes up, glancing across the roofs of Ravndal to the dark silhouette of the hanging tree atop its rocky hill. His father's corpse still dangled there.

"No one takes from me," he said low in his throat. "I will teach you that lesson, bitch. Piss on your gold. Both you and Ulfrik will remember this."

Toki was lining up his shot. All eyes were down range on the target. He let the ax fly.

Throst released his arrow.

The shaft took Toki in the side of the neck. He clamped his hand over it like swatting a bug. Throst had already loosed another shaft, and it lanced into his ear.

Toki collapsed even as the crowd cheered his expert throw.

Looping the bow over his shoulder, he did not stay to watch the reaction. He left Astra's comb and an arrow on the parapet. He grabbed his rope, scaled halfway down the walls and jumped the final distance, then dashed for his horse. He was already galloping for the trees when he heard cheers turn to screams.

He threw his head back and laughed. No one takes from Throst Shield-Biter without twice the payback.

61

Ulfrik heard a woman screaming as if she were dying. In the swell of people, it was a distant but shrill note over the roar of celebration. Still, he did not want to turn away from Toki's expert throw. The ax spun with grace and plunked into the wooden target a finger's breadth from the center mark. Cheers went up, and the foolish who had bet against Toki groaned. Runa leapt with excitement and even Snorri, himself a former ax-throwing champion, sucked his breath at the incredible throw.

He turned to congratulate Toki, but did not see him. The screaming grew more insistent and began to compete with the cheering.

"That was amazing," Runa said, grabbing Ulfrik's arm. "When did he learn to throw like that?"

"I don't know." Ulfrik's reply had fallen to a whisper. Runa continued to speak, but the words were muddled. He was pulling out of her grip, coming into a scene that made no sense.

He saw a body on the ground and a woman huddling over it. The woman was the source of screaming, but two children jumped about her and joined in the wailing. The prone body was soaked with blood.

"Toki?" he whispered, then charged through the gathering crowd. He pulled a man away and looked down on someone he barely recognized.

"My husband! Help him!" The woman, Halla, was cradling the body as if she were afraid to break it. Her girls clutched her skirts and screamed. Every inch of Halla's dress was drenched with blood, even the ends of her platinum hair were stained red.

Ulfrik rushed to her side, brusher her away as she screamed. Urgent voices filled the air, screams began to spread like fire, and shadow engulfed Ulfrik as he touched his hand to the hot blood flowing over the face of the man at his feet.

An arrow had entered Toki's neck beneath his right ear, shattered, and burst through his throat. Blood had pumped from the ragged wound in a stream that ebbed down his chest. More horrifying was the arrow shaft protruding from his skull just above the same ear. It had poked out beneath his left eye which had rolled back and filled with blood. The right eye stared up, lusterless and empty.

Ulfrik pressed his fingers to the base of Toki's neck, but he felt nothing. Halla was screeching, trying to rip Ulfrik off Toki and press his wounds closed. The blood on her hands was so thick she seemed to be wearing gloves of red satin. "It wasn't supposed to be you. Not you! No!"

Grabbing Toki's hand and placing it on the hilt of his sword, Ulfrik dared no words. A pain more powerful than anything he had ever felt welled up in him, and it would explode from his open mouth and damn him to a senseless wreck. He stared at the man who had been as a blood brother to him. How many battles had they fought together? How much had they dared and dreamed? Now two arrows jutted from his head, and a life of glory and adventure had ended with the throw of an ax and a fall into the dirt.

Runa began screaming, trying to reach her brother, as if he could be saved. Ulfrik continued to stare at him, a red lump of a man he had called his kin. Now Gunnar and Hakon joined the outcry and it seemed as if every person in the circle of the world were standing around Toki's corpse and wailing.

A strong hand grabbed him up, tearing him from his silent and horrible fixation. It was Einar.

"The shots had to have come from the north wall." He was pointing at it with his ax. "I've got men headed to it now, and more to search the houses. Do you think it was one of Clovis's?"

The question struck Ulfrik odd. He stared at Einar, not really knowing who he was of what he was saying. "Toki is dead. What does it matter?"

Einar's mouth fell open, then he clamped it shut and turned away, shouting orders and shoving men out of his path. Snorri stood in his wake, his face now more ancient and worn than ever. He stared blankly at Ulfrik, his thin hair lifting in the cold breeze.

Then women were shrieking from behind. He whirled and Halla was on top of Runa, her bloody hands throttling her.

"Fucking whore! It was supposed to be you. You were supposed to die. Why Toki? I'll kill you myself, you bitch!"

Ulfrik seized Halla's arm, but she was possessed by the strength of madness and remained latched to Runa's throat. She did not struggle, as if accepting death. Halla leaned down to bite her face, and only then did she react with a lame kick.

With a grunt he dragged her off, only for her to spring back with a mad howl. Runa crawled away holding her neck and gasping. Halla landed on her legs and clawed at Runa even as she kicked at her face. Ulfrik lifted her off and threw her aside, sending her careening into Konal.

"Hold her down," Ulfrik ordered and Konal grabbed her along with another man. Ulfrik knelt to Runa's side, Gunnar following. Coughing, she waved them both off as she struggled to her feet. Bloody hand prints smeared her clothes and face.

People were scrambling in confusion. Halla's girls sat in the dirt and cried. Hakon joined them in it while Aren silently observed Konal restraining Halla. Toki stared at the sky in a massive pool of blood.

Eyeballs throbbing, blood roaring in his ears, Ulfrik stalked up to Halla. "Runa was supposed to die? What have you done, woman?"

Her thrashing only slowed. She looked up at him with crazed eyes. "Fuck yourself."

His fist balled and he was ready to strike when he heard Einar calling. He turned back across the confusion, saw him standing on the wall and read the defeat in his posture. Another man was coiling a rope that had been hung from the wall while Einar lifted a lone arrow for Ulfrik to see, then he pointed out across the fields. The killer had escaped, or that was Ulfrik's assumption.

Halla sobbed behind him, and it all began to form in his mind: Astra's as-yet unrevealed informant and her murder under guard; the brown stains on Halla's cloak; even Aren's insistence that Halla was evil. Now this. He turned slowly, first looked at Aren who studied Halla with a hint of smug arrogance, then faced Halla who writhed in grief while Konal restrained her collapsed to the ground.

"Why did he have to die?" she asked through her tears.

Ulfrik stood before her, then turned away.

He still did not understand what had happened, but he was certain Toki had died for the convoluted treacheries of his wife.

And Ulfrik had lost half of his soul for it as well.

62

Ulfrik faced Toki's burial mound, a pile of black earth still wet from the melted snow. Snorri leaned on his staff at his left, and Einar stood with folded hands at his right. They all kept a thoughtful silence. The mound still looked a like a scar in the earth, but he knew soon grass would crawl up the slopes and cover it. The fresh earth scent was sharp, carried on the first springtime breezes. He had not come to the mound all winter, and now before he traveled to Hrolf the Strider and Gunther One-Eye he felt it was time.

The loss still hurt.

"He will be waiting for us in Valhalla with all the other heroes," Snorri said, his voice a tired whisper.

Ulfrik nodded.

"We will sing songs about him until that happy day," Einar said, his voice loud in the morning quiet.

Ulfrik nodded.

Even now he could not speak Toki's name, much less praise his memory. Many nights he wanted to cry, to mourn the loss of a dear friend and brother, but instead he sat at the edge of his bed in confusion, eyes dry but heart as dead as stone. He had so many regrets, apologies, excuses, and rage left unexpressed, yet nothing could find its way out of him.

A magpie hopped along the top of the mound, pecking at the dirt for a while, then flitting off. Ulfrik mused life was like that, all pecking in the dirt in search of something and then gone without a trace.

They stood longer, Snorri shifting his weight and massaging his leg. He stole glances at Ulfrik, and finally prompted him. "You've got a stretch of road to travel, lad. Maybe we should be getting you ready for it."

"Everything is prepared," Einar said, and Ulfrik saw from the corner of his eye Snorri glaring at him.

"You're right," Ulfrik said, continuing to stare at the mound. "I don't know why I wanted to come here today. Nothing special about it."

"No wrong in it, lad. I expect you'll come here many more times."

"I want to raise a stone to mark his life." Ulfrik clasped both hands behind his neck. "It ended too soon, without the glory due him."

Einar grunted agreement and Snorri nodded. "Fate is a strange thing, and can't be changed. Such was Toki's weave, short but filled with the glory of ten men's lives."

"Throst cut his life short, and when I find him I will cut the bloody eagle into his back and send him to Nifleheim."

"Halla never admitted it was Throst," Einar said.

"She didn't need to. Gunnar said that comb belonged to Astra." Ulfrik dropped his hands to his side and let out a long breath. "Throst left it with an arrow, a coward's way to admit he was Toki's killer. A gutless murderer, like his father."

The three men fell silent again. Halla's madness had turned all her words to curses, and since the day of Toki's death she alternated between raving and weeping. All Ulfrik had pried from her was that Runa should have died instead of Toki.

For her part, Runa had borne Halla's madness with surprising patience. Halla stopped caring for her children, not even recognizing them, and Runa adopted the girls once she realized they would get no love from their mother. Eventually Halla had grabbed a knife to attack Runa, and so ended her time in Ravndal. In a rare peaceful contact with the Franks, Ulfrik negotiated to have Frankish nuns care for Halla. She had been gone for a month, and finally healing had a chance in his home.

"All right, let's go," Ulfrik said, and the three men turned from the grave. Ulfrik looked south where Clovis's fortress hung in ruins. Unable to fill the place with their own men, Gunther and Ulfrik's people tore down the stronghold and burned it to ash. Ulfrik wondered how such a complete and total victory felt so miserable.

"Do you think Gunther One-Eye has stolen all the glory for himself by now?" Einar asked as they walked toward Ravndal. "I mean, he has Hrolf's ear and can tell the story however he likes. It wouldn't be fair to you."

"Gunther can take all the glory he wants," Ulfrik said. "I've had my fill of it, besides, without his men I couldn't have done what I did."

"But the plan was yours, and it was one for the songs."

"I'm done with creating lyrics for the skalds. All the tricks and feints, living my life behind a shield of lies, look what it earned me."

"Victory over your enemies, the pride of your people, and domination of the border," Snorri said, and Einar agreed.

"And the price was the death of my brother, the hand of my son, and the love of my wife. I've no heart for such victories again."

Moody silence enveloped them as their feet swished through the grass on the return to Ravndal. After a few more strides, Einar broke the quiet.

"Then what do you want?"

Ulfrik stopped and looked Einar in the eye. "I want back all I've lost, but more than anything I want revenge. And I swear to you that I will have it."

AUTHOR'S NOTE

In 892, Frankia experienced a famine that encouraged many of the Norse invaders to seek fortunes elsewhere. Many of them decided to relocate to England during this period. The famine offered a brief respite to the beleaguered Franks, though ultimately the famine would prove to be inconsequential to the ongoing presence of the Northmen. They remained a problem, especially along the Seine River.

The king of the Western Franks, Odo, had been chosen as a replacement for Charles the Fat who had famously thrown away victory over the Northmen at Paris in 886. Odo proved to be a capable leader who dealt a hard blow to the Northmen in 888. Though this victory slowed the expansion of Viking power, it did not ultimately change the trajectory of their advance. Odo soon found himself embroiled in his own political concerns and unable to focus on eradicating the menace of the Northmen. The Franks found themselves on the defensive again, giving the Vikings a chance to consolidate.

The Northmen themselves did not have any single leader organizing their adventures. In fact, the Vikings in Eastern Frankia enjoyed many positive victories against the Franks under King Arnulf during the years immediately following the reign of Charles the Fat.

However, in 891, they were decisively defeated in Lorraine and progress halted. Farther south in Brittany, the Northmen were organizing under numerous banners and pushing their own agendas. Their lack of organization made them ineffective as a group but also difficult to stop.

This is the background that Ulfrik finds himself against at the start of this tale. Many Northman leaders were holding onto their own parcels of territory and their own spoils. The Franks were distracted and fighting among themselves. Enterprising Northmen could exploit that weakness, while others more intent on blunt military force only succeeded in giving the Franks a common enemy to fight. Hrolf the Strider's history during this time is still not clearly understood. However, we do know that he enjoyed excellent relations with the people of Rouen and that he operated out of that area. By keeping himself along the Seine and in the graces of a powerful city, he was in a good position to challenge Paris. He never specifically carried out any more attacks on Paris, not after his "victory in defeat" in 886, but he would have remained a visible threat to the Western Franks.

Ulfrik himself now commands that border with the Franks. Clovis, his allies, and his fortress are all fiction, though doubtlessly the Franks held strong-points in strategic locations. Whether Hrolf can exploit the opening Ulfrik has created remains to be seen. The establishment of Normandy as a part of Frankia is still nearly two decades away. A lot of adventure is yet to be had, and many fortunes stand to be made or lost, or both.

If you have enjoyed this book and would like to show your support for my writing, consider leaving a review where you purchased this book or on Goodreads. I need help from readers like you to get the word out about my books. So if you have a moment, please share your thoughts about this book with other readers. I appreciate it!

Printed in Great Britain
by Amazon

79154443R00193